THE BEARPIT

Brian Freemantle

<u>C</u>

CENTURY
LONDON SYDNEY AUCKLAND JOHANNESBURG

Copyright © Brian Freemantle 1988

First published in Great Britain in 1988 by
Century Hutchinson Ltd
Brookmount House, 62–65 Chandos Place
London WC2N 4NW

Century Hutchinson South Africa (Pty) Ltd
PO Box 337, Bergvlei, 2012 South Africa

Century Hutchinson Australia Pty Ltd
89–91 Albion Street, Surry Hills, NSW 2010, Australia

Century Hutchinson New Zealand Ltd
PO Box 41–086, Glenfield, Auckland 10
New Zealand

ISBN 0 7126 1964 X

Phototypeset by Input Typesetting Ltd, London SW19 8DR

Printed in Great Britain by
Mackays of Chatham

*For Sally and John, with
great affection.*

I must say that change is going on not without difficulties. And the main obstacle is mentality, the mentality which has taken shape over the years should be changed. The new is waging battle against the old, sometimes in pointed form.

Soviet leader Mikhail Gorbachov,
at a press conference for Indian
journalists, November 1986.

Let dogs delight to bark and bite,
For God hath made them so;
Let bears and lions growl and fight,
For 'tis their nature too.

'Against Quarrelling': Isaac Watts

Prologue

The ambush was brilliantly conceived, although not by Soviet military intelligence who imagined they were initiating it after so much detailed planning. Six troop companies had been divided at either end of the mist-obscured pass through the Hazarajat mountains for the exit of the *mujahideen* weapons convoy. In addition there were four squads of *spetsnaz* commandos which the Glavnoye Razvedyvatelnoye Upravleniye or GRU had time to ferry in from Moscow, because the entry from Pakistan into Afghanistan of the heavily guarded mule train had been tracked for nearly two weeks. There had been time, too, to transfer from Kabul to Shindad two squadrons of MIG–22s and establish fuel dumps on the outskirts of Shah Juy for the helicopter gunships.

A later Moscow inquiry determined the *mujahideen* timed their attack by the actual emergence from the defile for which the Russians were waiting. As the guerillas came out, already firing, the assault upon the Shah Juy dump began at the rear, with captured Soviet rocket launchers which scored direct hits. They destroyed all the carefully stored fuel – immobilizing the helicopters after their first sorties – and wrecked four machines parked in readiness for the Russian attack that was never to be mounted. The gushing plume of black smoke was visible from the entrance to the pass but its warning came too late for the tightly grouped soldiers who were already under simultaneous attack from *mujahideen* massed unseen and unsuspected in the crags and gulleys all around and others who, equally unsuspected, turned back from the mule train to re-emerge from the entrance and pincer the Russian forces trapped between in withering fire. A panicked attempt at air support from the gunships which survived the Shah Juy sabotage actually increased the Soviet casualties. The *mujahideen* both front and rear had the protection of the rocks but the close-together soldiers and *spetsnaz* were fully exposed in the middle and so close to the Afghan guerillas that rockets and tracer fire hit Russian troops instead. In further panic the MIGs dropped napalm, which resulted in the most extensive casualties of all.

The Russians lost five hundred and fifty men, eight helicopter gunships and two hundred tons of fuel. Which Moscow did not regard as the most serious damage. Both Afghan groups were accompanied by television crews from America's CBS infiltrated across the border from Pakistan. The Soviet rout and humiliation was given worldwide coverage, with verbal reports relayed directly back to Russia through London's BBC and the Munich-based Voice of America transmissions.

The entire GRU *rezidentura* in Kabul was replaced and jail sentences imposed upon everyone withdrawn to Moscow, in two cases for periods of ten years. And from the Politburo came specific instructions that in future the military should place greater reliance upon the Komitet Gosudarstvennoy Bezopasnosti or KGB, rather than its own disgraced intelligence service.

In Moscow it was an edict to be seized upon by one KGB officer to attempt a very personal ambush. The man's name was Victor Ivanovich Kazin.

1

Victor Kazin had been stunned after the interview with the KGB chairman in Dzerzhinsky Square, initially unable properly to think. Even before he had been unsettled, hardly able to believe that the Gorbachov changes would reach into the KGB. The rest of Soviet society and life maybe – what the hell did they matter! – but not actually into the Committee for State Security. They were sacrosanct, beyond any interference: an elite society within a society whose recognized and acknowledged position was – or should have been – uninterfered and unquestioned. Always had been: always should be. Didn't they – but more importantly, didn't Gorbachov – realize that without the KGB and its controls and its surveillance and its loyalty to the leadership there wouldn't *be* a Union of Socialist Soviet Republics! A Politburo, even! All the others had. No matter what the outside upheavals, the KGB had until this aberration remained untouchable. The chairmen had been shuffled and purged, certainly: that was understandable. Expectable. Yagoda and Yezhov under Stalin. Beria, under Krushchev. But nothing more than that; nothing more than changes at the absolute top where changes had cosmetically to be made. Who would have imagined – ever conceived – provincial KGB officers actually being brought to trial and openly criticized in newspapers for minor infractions of laws that did not apply to them anyway!

And now this, the most shattering of all. Not just a humiliating diminution of his authority. But for it to be *him!* It was beyond surprise: beyond belief. It was as if someone had found out – that there were long-ago records – but Kazin knew that couldn't be because one of his first actions upon being appointed initially sole head of the KGB's First Chief Directorate had been to check the archives to guarantee there were no such

9

reports that might one day be resurrected and used against him. Despite which Kazin thought it impossible for Vasili Malik's appointment to now share the rôle of joint controller of the Chief Directorate to be a coincidence. Malik, of all people! The man he hated and despised more than he'd ever hated and despised anyone: someone he would do anything to destroy.

And he would destroy the man, Kazin vowed. Malik had stolen from him once. Robbed him of something more precious than he had ever known, before or since. The bastard would not steal anything from him again: certainly not the First Chief Directorate, the control of which had been Kazin's ambition from the moment of joining the Soviet intelligence service in the distant days of Stalin's reign, before it was even known as the KGB.

Alone in his expansive office in the Chief Directorate headquarters overlooking Moscow's peripheral road, Kazin actually sniggered to himself, the earlier burning, impotent fury diminishing. Malik had been forever and permanently safe from the longed-for vengeance within the KGB's Second Chief Directorate, too independently powerful. It was the very fact of the man being untouchable that led Kazin to target the son, determined to hurt by proxy if that were the only way. But it wasn't now: not any longer. Now he would be able to destroy them both, father and son.

He would have to be careful, though. At the moment Kazin objectively accepted his was the weaker position, someone suspect because of initial and admittedly mistaken opposition to Gorbachov, a stance he'd taken because he had been sure the Kremlin establishment would neuter the man. He'd had no alternative anyway: he was provably on record as declaring for Brezhnev and then Andropov. And by so doing branding himself an Old Order traditionalist.

So it was essential to get his survival priorities right. Which meant first proving himself to Gorbachov and his new broom acolytes, with some spectacular intelligence coup. Kazin smiled to himself again. The American operation could not have matured at a more fortuitous time.

The appointments buzzer sounded on his desk and Kazin responded at once, the dossier already open before him.

Vladislav Andreevich Belov was the director of the department within the First Chief Directorate responsible for espionage within the United States and Canada. He was a stick-dry, unemotional man who had linked himself to Kazin's support of the old, out-of-date regimes and now, too late, accepted the mistake. The American proposal would provide the essential recovery, he knew: the uncertainty was presenting it through Kazin. The appointment of a new man to share overall control of the Directorate had to indicate that Kazin was in decline. It was too late now to switch the operation to the supervision of Vasili Malik, who was anyway someone with whom so far he had had no contact. Belov felt trapped; trapped and helpless.

'We are finally ready!' greeted Kazin. He was a small, fleshy man who perspired easily. He was sweating now, partially from an habitual nervousness which kept his leg pumping unseen beneath the desk, partially from the anticipation of how he could use the other man's idea to his own benefit.

'Almost,' said Belov guardedly.

'How long have we had John Willick as a CIA source?' asked Kazin.

'Five years.'

'Burned out?'

'It was getting close,' said Belov. 'He's being transferred. We don't know yet to what department.'

'Suspicion?'

Why did Kazin need to query what was already in the report in front of him? Belov said: 'He doesn't think so. There is some personality clash with a new department head.'

'Sacrificial then?'

'That was the intention, from the beginning,' reminded Belov.

'Who is the conduit to be to the CIA?'

'Kapalet,' said Belov. 'He's been operating out of our

embassy in Paris. We're sure Washington is convinced he's genuine.'

Kazin nodded, coming to the most important person in a deception that had taken years to evolve. 'And Levin is ready?' he demanded.

'We've simulated every imaginable possibility,' assured Belov. 'He's never failed.' Yevgennie Pavlovich Levin was going to be a Hero of the Soviet Union but never acknowledged as such, Belov thought. He supposed the award could be given *in absentia*.

'The CIA will be thrown into turmoil,' said Kazin distantly. 'Absolute and utter turmoil.' And I will be protected and saved from whatever changes are being considered, he thought.

'Turmoil is not the intended purpose of the operation at all,' said Belov in further reminder.

Belatedly Kazin realized the other man's need. 'It has been brilliantly conceived,' he said in delayed praise. 'Absolutely brilliant.'

'Thank you, Comrade First Deputy,' said Belov. Who else would ever learn it was his idea, he wondered. The answer was quick in coming.

Kazin gazed directly across the desk and said: 'I intend taking full control of this operation.'

The whore's ass was going to steal the credit! Belov, who was adept at remaining dry-footed in the political swamp of Moscow, betrayed no facial reaction. He said: 'I understand.'

'You will be acknowledged the architect,' promised Kazin.

Liar, thought Belov. He said: 'You are very generous, Comrade First Deputy.'

Kazin realized allies were going to be important in the coming months. He said: 'You have my personal assurance on that.'

There was a legend, Belov remembered, that Stalin had been fond of assuring his victims of personal support just before sending them before the firing squads in Lubyanka. He said: 'Shall I issue the orders?'

'No!' refused Kazin, almost too quickly. More slowly he added: 'I will decide the timing.'

Whore's ass, thought Belov again.

Alone once more in his office, Kazin stared unseeingly down at his desk, continuing in his determined order. The son first, he decided. That had always been the intention: why he'd manipulated the brat into the Directorate he governed, enjoying the thought of Malik's helplessness. The man had been politically astute in not trying to interfere over the Afghan posting of his son, although isolated as he had been in another Chief Directorate there would have been little he could have done anyway. But Malik had not been able to hold back after the slaughter of the military following the GRU fiasco. That's when the opportunity had come.

Kazin focused upon the memorandum to which Malik had identifiably assigned his name, one of the man's first actions upon his transfer. Not obviously self-destructive, acknowledged Kazin. Nor could it be construed to be nepotistic. It just had to be made to seem that way. And it would be. Gorbachov might be causing tidal waves within the KGB but Victor Ivanovich Kazin didn't intend being washed away by them. It was others who were going to be engulfed.

So far the scarcity of sex hadn't made the sheep look any more attractive but Yuri Vasilivich Malik wondered, in private amusement because there were so few other sorts of joke in a place like Afghanistan, just how long it would take for them to seem beautiful. There were only two unattached women – a secretary and a translator – with both of whom Yuri was sleeping and with both of whom he was bored. The wife of the Third Secretary was clearly available and he was sure the wife of the Third Secretary was also interested.

But so far Yuri had held back, unwilling to take any careless risks with his first embassy appointment. He only wanted to be fucked in the literal sense of the word. He already considered himself fucked every other way.

Yuri, a slight but compact man, fair-haired and blue-eyed and permanently diet-careful against becoming heavy, which he knew he could easily do, was unable to forgive his father's refusal to intervene to prevent his posting to this stinking sewer of a place. Talk of inseparable divisions between Chief Directorates was so much bullshit: just like the lecture about the necessity of avoiding political infighting within the organization was so much bullshit. Yuri was . . . was what? Surprised wasn't strong enough. Bewildered was better: bewildered because his father had never before refused him, in anything he had asked. Until now, when he'd made the most important request of all.

One realization brought another: that from now on Yuri Vasilivich Malik was the only person likely to help Yuri Vasilivich Malik.

Even his Kabul sex life was linked to that philosophy.

Both the secretary and the translator sensed his indifference and both tried with the desperation of single women in an environment of attached men to keep him in their beds, willing to share him unprotestingly and to innovate any sort of sexual experimentation he cared to suggest.

Yuri suggested a lot. And not all of it sexual. Yuri was circumspect, never appearing obviously to question but simply to listen sympathetically as they pillow-gossiped their day-to-day activities. It gave him access to the innermost secrets of the Kabul embassy; secrets, he was sure, unknown even to the official KGB security officer who was supposed to be informed of everything.

'There's a lot of Eyes-Only traffic being directed to the *rezident* from Moscow,' disclosed the secretary, whose name was Ilena and who worked exclusively for the Kabul KGB controller, Georgi Petrovich Solov.

'What about?' said Yuri, the casualness successfully concealing his immediate interest.

They had just finished one of his favourite ways of making love and she still lay with her mouth wetly against his thigh. She said: 'I've not seen it all: it looks as if a major operation is being planned.'

'A lot of extra work for you, then?' he lured.

'I could find out more,' she offered at once, anxious to please him in everything.

'It's inevitable I shall be involved, eventually,' Yuri encouraged. 'You wouldn't be doing anything wrong in letting me know early.'

2

Vasili Dmitrevich Malik was a huge man, barrel-chested, bulge-bellied and well over six feet, maybe as tall as six and a half feet. And the disfigurement appeared strangely to accord him even greater height, from how he held himself because of it. The injury occurred during the Stalingrad siege, long before General Zhukov's relief forces had encircled von Paulus' attackers. No one had ever been able to establish how it had happened – certainly not Malik, who'd mercifully been rendered immediately unconscious – but the consensus was a shrapnel ricochet from an incoming Soviet shell. It would have had to have been a very large and very sharp piece of metal. Malik's left arm had been instantly severed high at the shoulder, which had further been crushed by the impact. It was still only October, 1942 – almost three months before the lifting of the Nazi assault – but even by then only the most basic medical treatment had been possible. The doctors had been able to save his life by sealing the obvious wound, although they'd had little anaesthetic left either, but there were no facilities in the holed and cratered makeshift field hospital to rebuild the shattered shoulder. It had set pressed high, almost in a hump. Malik had completely adjusted to the loss of his arm, not needing any assistance after the first six months, but the right side of his body remained lower than the left and as he had grown older he had developed the tendency to walk with something resembling a limp. In the last five years it had been necessary to have his right shoe reinforced, to compensate for the constant pressure.

What other – and different – types of pressure was he going to encounter because of the transfer of Chief Directorates, Malik wondered. A lot, he guessed: some that were impossible, at this early stage, even to antici- pate. It was inevitable that Victor Kazin, a man he had once considered his closest friend, would regard the split directorship as a reduction of his authority. Logically it had to be so despite the insistence of KGB chairman Victor Chebrikov at the appointment interview that it was merely a provisional division of the largest and most important Chief Directorate within the organization. How long had it been, since his last proper encounter with Kazin? It would have to be almost forty years, he supposed: the three of them at the Gertsena apartment, Olga sobbing emptily and he and Kazin holding back when each had wanted physically to tear at the other: kill each other. Certainly that's what he'd wanted to do. Kazin would have won if it had come to that, Malik conceded, because he'd hardly healed by then. He remembered realizing that at the time but he'd still wanted to try because the hatred was so strong. So what about now? Was there any hate left? No, Malik decided at once. It was all too long ago; too distant. There was no hatred, no disappointment, no urge to cause hurt. He'd actually found it possible to love again, Malik remembered; love again completely. He wondered if he would have difficulty in recognizing the other man.

And he was going to have to recognize him. Recognize him and work with him. An experiment, the KGB chairman had called the decision to divide the Directorate control: an experiment from which greater efficiency was expected. If only the chairman had known what real sort of experiment he was creating!

Malik sighed, staring around the still-new office, momentarily unwilling to confront the necessary decision. It had been naive expecting the approach to come from Kazin; preposterous, even if he had just been the newcomer into the other man's domain. And he was anything but that. His had to be the offer, not the other way around.

Kazin's agreement to Malik's request for a meeting took three days, which Malik considered pointedly too long, almost childishly petulant; he, not Kazin, had been the victim, after all! Kazin's memorandum stipulated the encounter should be in his office – making Malik go to him – rather than somewhere neutral like the Dzer-zhinsky Square headquarters. Passingly Malik thought of suggesting an alternative but just as quickly dismissed the idea: it would have been matching petulance with petulance. He did not want any longer to fight.

Kazin's office was at the front of the Directorate head-quarters and obviously better established than that of Malik. The furnishings were predominantly Scandina-vian, all light wood except for a conference area to one side where there were dark leather chairs and a couch and a long, chair-bordered table around which at least a dozen people could have assembled. Kazin's desk, which was quite bare, even the blotter unmarked, was directly in front of floor-to-ceiling windows overlooking the traffic-clogged ring road. There was complete double glazing, creating a disorienting effect of scurrying vehicles devoid of noise, television picture with the sound turned down.

Malik hesitated immediately inside the door, unsure now that they were at last face to face how to proceed. Malik's immediate impression was of Kazin's weight. When they were friends the man had been stocky, but Malik had never imagined his becoming this fat. Kazin seemed bloated, like an inflated carnival figure. Malik knew he would not have recognized the other man if the encounter had been unexpected.

From the far side of the room, seated behind his desk, Kazin examined Malik. The hair, which Kazin remem-bered to be deeply black, was absolutely white now but still thick, and Malik wore it surprisingly long, almost an affectation. And the stance was peculiar. After the return from Stalingrad and that one confrontation there had not been many meetings – not with Malik, at least – so Kazin's strongest memory was of the man before his injury: certainly there was no recollection of him like this, oddly sloped and lopsided. Old; until this moment he'd never thought of Malik as being old.

'Victor Ivanovich,' greeted Malik, not moving.

'Vasili Dmitrevich,' responded Kazin. He did not rise from his high-backed seat.

They remained motionless, each looking expressionlessly at the other. It was Malik who moved, limping uninvited further into the room. There was a stiff-backed seat near the desk but Malik ignored it, making much of bringing one of the leather chairs from the conference area and lowering himself heavily into it.

'I did not seek the transfer,' announced Malik at once. Kazin said nothing.

'And there's no feeling left, about what happened before.'

Why was the lying bastard even bothering! Kazin said: 'Comrade Chairman Chebrikov explained the idea to me: an experimental division from which a permanent decision could be made.'

He'd made concessions enough, Malik decided. By rights Kazin should be the supplicant, not him. Malik said: 'So there has to be a working arrangement, difficult though it might be.'

You can't begin to imagine the difficulties I am going to create, thought Kazin. Stiffly he said: 'Comrade Chairman Chebrikov defined the responsibilities, too.' And allocated you Afghanistan, Kazin thought: he could not have devised the trap better himself. The division of the First Chief Directorate between them was not going to be the demotion that everyone would regard it as being: it was going to be the opportunity for which he'd dreamed, all these years. His chance: the chance he was not going to miss.

'Olga's dead,' said Malik, in another abrupt announcement.

'I know,' said Kazin. Like I know the very day and the very year and the very cemetery plot in which she is buried: the plot I have discreetly visited so often and from which I have so often cleared the wind-flustered leaves and so often tidied the stones and where I have held so many one-sided conversations. One-sided conversations where 'why' had been the most frequently uttered word, the most frequently uttered question.

'It's too long ago for anything to be left between us,' persisted Malik. Was it important, to make such an effort? If Kazin were going to have conceded any sort of

19

response – the proper sort of response – it would have come by now.

'I don't understand,' protested Kazin, who did but who was enjoying the other man's efforts to rebuild bridges across divides too wide ever to be crossed again.

Malik sighed determinedly. He said: 'Whatever happened, happened. It's past. Gone . . .' He hesitated and said: 'Olga and I were very happy, afterwards. She loved me. I loved her.'

Fool! thought Kazin. He wanted to speak: was desperate to hurt the other man as he knew the words would hurt him, but Kazin held back because the words weren't any longer enough. With a difficulty he thought he managed to keep from Malik, Kazin said: 'Yes. It all happened a very long time ago.'

'I did not seek this.'

'You already made that clear.'

'I'm prepared to try: not to forget – we neither of us could ever forget – but to try.' Malik felt once more that he was prostrating himself too much.

'So am I,' said Kazin, a remark for his own benefit. 'I am prepared to try.' Starting with the meeting which is directly to follow this, he thought.

Deciding upon a test he felt necessary, Malik said: 'Did you know that my son served in this Chief Directorate?'

'No,' said Kazin immediately.

The man was lying, Malik knew at once. He'd already checked the posting records and identified Kazin's signature on the authorization for Yuri to be sent to Kabul. Malik was glad he had not interfered when Yuri had asked him to block the assignment.

Malik stood, towering over the other man in his unusually apportioned height. He regretted the movement at once, recognizing it to be physically intimidating, which it was not intended to be. He said: 'I hope we will be able to work successfully together,' already resigned to the fact that they would not.

Kazin said: 'I hope it will be successful, too,' and knew it would be, although differently from how Malik imagined.

*
20

KGB activities in Afghanistan are the responsibility of the Eighth Department of the First Chief Directorate, whose head was Igor Fedorovich Agayans. He was a gauntly featured, almost ungainly bachelor whose flop of prematurely grey hair appeared permanently to curtain his forehead. It came forward as he entered Kazin's rooms and he thrust up to clear his vision, smiling in apparent apology. Because regulations were specific Kazin had already received copies of the organization's monitoring doctors reporting the medical evidence – the increasingly spreading psoriasis and sleeplessness needing ever stronger barbiturates – and Agayans' uncertain demeanour supported their assessment of nervous stress. Which had been the diagnosis returned upon himself, Kazin remembered in abrupt irritation. The doctors were bloody fools. He made a conscious effort to quieten his pumping leg and took his nibbled finger from his mouth. Nervous, possibly; but not stressed. He didn't need any soothing balms or multi-coloured tablets. He said: 'The memorandum from Comrade First Deputy Malik demanded that efforts should be made to locate *mujahideen* cells for possible punishment.'

'I would have welcomed clearer indication of precisely the sort of punishment required,' said Agayans.

'An operation of the utmost severity,' said Kazin.

'That was not stipulated in the original memorandum,' argued Agayans.

'This is an authorized demand for retribution,' insisted the obese man.

Agayans hesitated momentarily and Kazin thought the division head was going to argue further that the order should come from Malik, who was now the controller of that part of Asia. Instead Agayans took a dossier from his briefcase, offering it across the desk, and said simply: 'I propose gas attacks on selected villages proven to support the *mujahideen*. Well-poisoning, in addition, along all the major and recognized supply and infiltration routes.'

Agayans had a clerk-like mentality, his life ruled by regulations and documentation, and he'd assembled his

21

proposal with a single-sheet precis uppermost, encompassing the most important of the listed suggestions. Kazin's eyes fixed upon just one part of the summary: he had never expected the man positively to refer to Vasili Malik and his Kabul memorandum by name in the file that lay before him. Curbing his excitement he said: 'What is the casualty estimation?'

'I am putting the figure provisionally at between seven to eight thousand,' said the twitching man. 'I have already ordered the *rezidentura* in Kabul to identify target villages for the maximum impact.'

'Initiate it,' instructed Kazin. There would be a supreme irony in establishing himself in the eyes of the Gorbachov regime not as the traditionalist he was suspected of being but as someone embracing the new principles when he very publicly cancelled what amounted practically to genocide.

'What about Comrade First Deputy Malik?'

'I will be responsible for Comrade First Deputy Malik,' said Kazin. There was something almost orgasmic in openly uttering the private promise.

3

Yuri Malik stood at the window of his cramped quarters in the guarded and prison-like Soviet compound in Kabul, looking out over the Afghanistan capital. The sun was almost down, reddening the sky against the foothills of the faraway mountains and from two separate mosques the *muezzin* prayer calls to the Muslim devout jarred slightly out of unison, priests in competition with each other for the salvation of the faithful. Priests or mullahs? It didn't matter. Whatever, they were cheerleading a lot of press-ups for nothing: this place was beyond redemption. Beyond anything. Where's my salvation, Comrade God? If he'd believed it would work he would have prayed himself, Malik thought: even done the press-ups. Are you listening, Comrade God? Malik wished someone were. Yuri still could not lose his astonishment at his father's attitude: always before the man had been omnipotent, the purveyor of miracles. OK, so maybe when he was attached to an entirely different Chief Directorate there was a barely acceptable explanation for his refusal, but that did not apply any longer. The damned man was actually joint chairman of the very Chief Directorate controlling this stinking country. So why hadn't there been any intervention, the sort of intervention he'd pleaded for that last night, during that stiff and resentful final dinner? Nepotism had been another of his father's arguments: said it was an accusation he could not risk, at that time. Rubbish, like every other excuse. The Soviet Union existed and ran on nepotism, family helping family, friends helping friends! Always had done: always would do. There had to be another reason, a proper reason. So far it didn't make sense; nothing made sense.

It was dark outside now, smoke from the fires cooking the inevitable lamb roping up whitely against the sky,

23

but Yuri was not looking any more out into Kabul but at his own reflection, mirrored in the blackened window. Not even his appearance made sense! The tan from the Afghan sun accentuated the fairness of his hair and although it was not as positive as a mirror he knew it heightened the blueness of his eyes as well. Actually Western, not Slavic! And more incongruous – ridiculous, considering the posting – positively unlike the other Asian-skinned and Asian-featured and Asian-speaking operatives at the embassy. He looked – and felt – as conspicuous as a VD warning tattooed on a tart's navel.

And to be inconspicuous, a never-seen, never-heard man, had been the repeated lesson at those training centres at Gofkovskoye Shosse and Metrostroevskaya Street and Turnaninski Pereulok. And insisted upon again in those mock-up American and Continental cities specially built at Kuchino where he had been trained to think and behave and live like a Westerner. To *be* the Westerner he had become.

All wasted: four years of dawn to dusk study – of top-grade passes in every test and examination – utterly and completely wasted. But Yuri's concern was not in the KGB's loss. His concern was as his own, personal potential loss.

Yuri had liked – come to need and expect – the cosseted life of the son of someone secure within the Soviet hierarchy. He'd never known anything but an apartment in Kutuzovsky Prospekt and the dacha in the Lenin Hills and the cars that had always been the surefire aphrodisiac with the girls. He'd enjoyed the concessionary allowances and the freely available foreign imports and never having to wait or to queue for anything; and then to be told it was not available. Nothing ever had been unavailable to him.

So it was unthinkable for it not to continue. But eventually properly awarded and allowed, for himself, not obtained through his father. Which was why he had responded so immediately to the KGB recruitment approach at college – and until his enrolment kept that approach secret from his father, striving then for the independence he would so willingly have surrendered now, to be spared Afghanistan. He'd never doubted his ultimate promotion to the Dzerzhinsky Square headquarters, with all its benefits. Nor underestimated that irrespective of his ability – and Yuri had never been unsure of his own ability – there would be political pitfalls it was necessary to avoid.

Which was why Afghanistan was so dangerous. Moscow was trapped in a no-win situation and so, correspondingly, was every Russian posted here. Georgi Solov, the *rezident*, and all the others in the KGB *rezidentura* were mad, pissing over their boots in their vodka celebrations and infantile boasts of success after the Moscow edict entrusting them with greater responsibility. Yesterday the GRU, tomorrow the KGB. Then there wouldn't be any luxury flats or weekend villas or chauffeured cars: if it were anything like the Hararajat disaster it could be instead a cell in Lefortovo or Butyrki.

Yuri supposed he could write to the old man. But to say what? Something his father already knew? And had already refused to do anything about, despite the danger argument being patiently set out and actually agreed! He wouldn't beg, Yuri determined. Not like he'd begged at that farewell dinner, demeaning himself like some pant-wetting schoolboy and to be humiliated again as he had been then. Yuri actually flushed, hot with embarrassment at the memory. Never again, he thought. Ever.

What then?

Continue jockeying Ilena and the translator, he supposed, although more for what was in their heads than beneath their skirts. Maybe explore beneath the bedcovers with the eager wife of the cultural attaché and that of the Third Secretary, as well and for the same reason. If he were going to establish a personal, protective intelligence system the wisdom of extending it as widely as possible overrode the hazards of outraged husbands who seemed to be limp-pricked anyway. Anything else? Nothing that he could think of. He wished there were. It didn't seem enough.

The embassy mess was in the basement, the ceiling-level windows taped against bomb blasts and with defensive sandbags beyond after the repeated guerilla mortar attacks. The air conditioning was broken, as it always was, and the stale air was thick with tobacco smoke and body odour. There was the obligatory portrait of Gorbachov on the inner wall, as far away as possible from any attack damage, and posters of Black Sea holiday resorts and of Red Square during the May Day parade of two years before, showing the pass-by of SS–22 missiles.

Solov was holding court at his accustomed table, close to the serving hatch, with the other three senior officers in the *rezidentura* – Gusev, Bunin and Anishenko – in obedient attendance. They all had their jackets off and their collars loosened, because of the heat, but they were all sweating, adding to the smell of the room. Yuri, who was still considered junior from the newness of his posting, did not intend to join them but as he went to the hatch Solov thrust a chair away from the table with his foot and said: 'Sit down.'

It was more an order than an invitation and Yuri guessed the men were drunk: because of his father's changed position within the KGB the attitude had for the past few weeks been more cautious. Yuri sat but brought his own beer to the table, shaking his head against their offer to share the diminishing bottle of vodka. Another stupid celebration to imagined triumphs to come, he decided.

'The GRU *rezidentura* is being scaled down,' announced Solov. 'They're only replacing with ten embassy officers, not fifteen like before. Less than half the field agents, too.'

The controller spoke proudly, as if he were personally responsible for the continued demotion. Taunting, Yuri said: 'It's a recognized algebraic equation: one KGB man equals two GRU.'

'Bloody right,' slurred Gusev. 'Right every time.'

Fool, thought Yuri. The alcohol heightened Gusev's blood pressure, so that he appeared almost cosmetically made up. Yuri said: 'When are they arriving?'

'Beginning tomorrow,' said Anishenko.

'Officer in charge is named Nikandrov, Anatoli Nikandrov,' further disclosed Solov. 'Being transferred from Vienna.'

Poor bastard, thought Yuri: coming from Austria to Afghanistan would be like arriving from another planet. The amount of information his superior officers appeared to possess could only mean that during the withdrawal of the military intelligence personnel the KGB had managed to get a tie-line into the restricted GRU telex and cable channels normally precluded to them. He wondered how long it would take for the GRU to discover and remove it. Not too long, he guessed: they were stupid, each of these men sitting and sweating and smelling around him, to boast so openly. He said: 'They will be cautious after what happened.'

'Just as long as they don't get in our way,' said Bunin.

'We'll walk all over them!' goaded Yuri.

'Bloody right,' said Gusev, his mind jammed on replay.

'Prove to everyone why we've been given the responsibility!' said Yuri, cheerleading like the *muezzin* in the mosques outside.

'Prove it like no one will believe!' endorsed Solov.

Yuri hesitated, curiously, unsure if the remark were anything more than braggadocio buoyed up on a sea of alcohol. He'd been idly amusing himself, prodding their stupid reaction. More intently now, Yuri said: 'Hararajat showed the *mujahideen* aren't to be underestimated: it's important not to forget that.'

'It's important for the *mujahideen* to be shown that the KGB is not to be underestimated, either. Or forget it,' said Solov, and Bunin laughed.

Eyes-Only traffic, remembered Yuri. He said: 'I have things to do here in the compound. But I would consider it an honour to buy you another bottle of vodka: this one is exhausted.'

'And we would consider it a pleasure to accept,' sniggered Anishenko.

Russian tradition dictated that Yuri, although a departing host, should accept the initial toast.

'Socialism!' proposed Solov.

'Socialism,' echoed everyone, including Yuri, who said it dutifully. The vodka was cheap and harsh to his throat: Russian style, each man emptied his glass in one gulp.

Yuri made to rise but Solov waved him down, refilling the glasses. 'To the Cheka,' toasted the *rezident*, calling the KGB by the name by which it has traditionally been known from the time of Feliks Dzerzhinsky's inception, and by which they still privately referred to themselves, boasting their membership of a special club.

'The Cheka,' intoned everyone around the table.

Yuri used the internal telephone in the main lobby of the compound and Ilena answered after the second ring, as if she had been expecting the call.

'I wanted it to be you,' she said.

'I'm lonely,' said Yuri. And inquisitive, he thought.

'So am I.'

'The Bolshoi, the State Circus or just a quiet dinner at the Aragvi?' said Yuri. The Aragvi, on the Ulitza Gor'kovo, served the best Georgian food in Moscow. It had been one of Yuri's favourite restaurants, with a table always available because of whose son he was.

She giggled, responding to the irony, and said: 'Why don't we eat in, just to be different for once?'

'Maybe some lamb?'

'And I've got lamb! What a coincidence!'

What were the Muslems going to do when they'd eaten all the sheep in the world, wondered Yuri. Camel maybe? He said: 'Looks like lamb for a change then.'

'What about afterwards?' said the woman coquettishly.

'We can talk about this and that,' said Yuri, another remark for his own benefit. The woman misunderstood, of course, and laughed.

Victor Kazin savoured the intrigue he was initiating and was sure of winning. He felt like one of the jugglers at the State Circus, keeping more and more coloured balls in the air until it was difficult to see how many there were aloft at any one time. No, he corrected, at once. Not a juggler. Not a clever enough analogy. A chess player. Grand master class, all the pieces set out, a classic

28

game already formulated in his mind and Malik without any defence. Agayans, he decided, was definitely a pawn. Fittingly the first move then. The Directorate security man, Major Panchenko, had soon to be introduced defensively into the game. A rook perhaps. What about the brat of a son? Another pawn. And Yevgennie Levin? A knight, maybe: possibly a king, eventually. Certainly the piece to be moved next.

Kazin snorted contemptuously at Vladislav Belov's recommendation that the operation be delayed because Levin's daughter was here in Moscow undergoing medical treatment. It had been one of Stalin's most basic principles that people performed better under the pressure of retribution if they failed. Old styles – old practices – were still the best.

He signed the authorization, because it was essential this operation was one with which he should be provably linked, and marked it for immediate transmission to America.

The Central Intelligence Agency weren't just going to be thrown into turmoil, reflected Kazin, remembering further his conversation with Belov. They were going to be wrecked.

4

Moscow's signal, activating the mission for which most of his operational life had been spent in preparation, bewildered Yevgennie Levin. Galina had always been part of it and was prepared but the children, Natalia and Petr, were always going to be confused, unknowing. Which the planning had allowed for with the positive agreement that they would remain together, as a family, never divided. So the signal coming when Natalia was in Moscow was nonsense!

Levin's was a cell-like room, a small box within a bigger box at the United Nations headquarters, but his seniority at least gave him a view of the East River. A linked line of barges, flat in the water, made a disjointed, arthritic line downstream in the direction of the unseen Statue of Liberty and the sea beyond, pushed officiously by a fat-bellied tug that seemed inadequate for the job. What about his adequacy for the job towards which he was now being prematurely pushed? At the self-question the nervousness positively vibrated through him, making the supposed recall cable shake in his hand. Despite all the training he didn't really *know* what was to come: they had only been able to guess and to suggest and now the moment was here – the moment he had grown increasingly frightened would actually arrive – it all seemed utterly insufficient. Enough uncertainties then, without the inexplicable complication of Natalia trapped in Moscow. It could only be a mistake, an oversight. But there was no way he could query it, get it resolved before he had to move, because to everyone at the UN mission his defection had to appear genuine. Just as the need for absolute security dictated it had to appear that way to almost everyone in Dzerzhinsky Square, as well. So he was trapped, like Natalia, before he even began. Why! agonized Levin. Why! Why! Why!

He squeezed his eyes tightly shut against the river view, striving for control before he confronted the *rezident*, which protocol decreed he do immediately. He contacted Vadim Dolya on the internal telephone and as he expected the *rezident* agreed to see him within thirty minutes; although the cable was designated for his attention only, Levin knew a copy would have been sent separately to the controller, who would therefore have been waiting for the approach. Levin replaced one receiver and looked at the other, the outside line, wanting to speak to Galina but never forgetting the standard, insisted-upon procedure always was to act in the belief that open Soviet connections in the United Nations were monitored by the FBI. Which after all would have been a sensible precaution for America's counter-intelligence service to take. Russians attached to the UN had the status of international civil servants, were not governed by the radius-to-city limitations imposed upon other Soviet installations within the United States and so it was regarded – and used – by the KGB and GRU as the most important intelligence base anywhere in the world.

Levin left his cramped office to make his way to the more spacious quarters of the UN's mineral resources unit, where his official designation as economic affairs officer had enabled him during his tenure to advise Dzerzhinsky Square of every major – and some not so major – natural mineral deposit in Western and Third World countries. He made the pretence of looking at the incoming mail and the diary of that day's events, relieved there were no committee meetings demanding his presence, and left for the appointment with Dolya still with time to spare. Always being on time was a trait of Levin's, which sometimes surprised people who did not know him well because he was a shambling, untidy man, stray-haired and baggily suited; not someone who would immediately appear a stickler for appointments. But then Yevgennie Levin's entire training had been to appear different from the person he was. And forever had to remain.

Dolya's attachment – and cover – was to the UN's

peace and security studies section, but they did not meet there because the precautions against eavesdropping extended beyond telephone lines to include the offices they occupied. Instead they talked as most of the other delegations talked when they sought conversations they did not want overheard, pacing head-bent the wide, art-donated and decorated corridors of the skyscraper building.

'Back to Moscow, then?' said Dolya, at once. In contrast to Levin, the *rezident* was a fussily neat, bespectacled man given to studying his reflection in passing mirrors, constantly to ensure everything about himself was properly in place.

'Earlier than I expected,' said Levin. It was essential — safer — always to be as honest as possible. So much to remember!

'The normal tour is two years,' pointed out Dolya.

'I have only been here eighteen months,' said Levin.

'No indication of any posting beyond Moscow?'

If there had been it would have breached security to have disclosed it to Dolya, which the man knew, and Levin was surprised at the question. He wondered what would happen to the man after the defection: he was a required victim. Levin said: 'None at all.'

'You'll be missed,' said Dolya.

Levin guessed there was truth as well as politeness in the platitude. His posting within the minerals section had provided Moscow with an enormous amount of information from which the government ministries had been able to make economic calculations and assessments extending at least three years into the future, particularly involving their own oil and natural gas deposits. Matching platitude with platitude Levin said: 'I shall miss being here.' Then he added: 'The recall stipulates two weeks.'

'I will inform the secretariat: see that all the necessary paperwork is completed,' assured Dolya. On apparent impulse he added: 'And maybe a farewell party. Nothing too large: just a few friends. Galina would be included, of course.'

'That would be kind,' said Levin. There was the vaguest stir of guilt at cheating the other man.

'Has Galina enjoyed it here?'

'Very much.'

'And the children?'

'It's been a different experience.' Natalia! he thought. Why did there have to be this stupidity with Natalia!

'Perhaps whatever you do next will be as worthwhile,' said Dolya.

'I hope so,' said Levin, with more feeling than the other man would ever know.

'Is there anything else I can do apart from the bureaucratic formalities?' offered Dolya generously.

'Nothing,' said Levin. Poor bastard, he thought.

'You'll be taking back as much electrical stuff as possible?' anticipated Dolya, because every returning Russian did. 'I'll tell dispatch so they can arrange shipment. Don't forget to buy an electrical converter: it's surprising how many people do.'

'I'll remember,' undertook Levin. Why should he feel the hypocrite he did? He was making a greater sacrifice for Russia than Dolya ever would.

'Don't just buy the article itself,' urged the *rezident*, enjoying the role of expert. 'Get spares, as well, for when it goes wrong.'

They had walked the complete circle of the building, arriving back where they started, and Levin knew the other man expected the conversation to end: take-home spoils were always the conclusion of such encounters. He said: 'There is something. I would like to take Galina out, sometimes, during the last few evenings.' Despite their supposed status in the United Nations, the Soviet Union did not regard its nationals as unfettered international diplomats. They were bussed daily to and from the securely guarded compound at Riverdale, in the South Bronx, and their whereabouts at all times logged in movement books both there and throughout the UN building, so permission for any change from normal had to be granted.

The KGB *rezident* looked up sharply from his head-bent stance against any directional microphone intercept or visual lipreading and said: 'Take her out!'

Levin felt a jump of unease. 'A restaurant. The theatre, maybe. . .' He smiled, inviting the other man's understanding after the lecture on the superiority of American consumer goods. 'Whatever or wherever the next posting, I doubt it will be anything like New York.'

'It could be London? Paris?' suggested Dolya.

'Still not the same.' Please don't let the imbecile become suspicious, not at this moment! Another contingency for which no allowance had been made.

Dolya smiled, an expression as abrupt as his looking up from the protective conversation. 'You're right,' he agreed. 'Nothing is quite like New York.'

'You approve it?'

'Of course.'

'Two or three nights, that's all.'

'Advise me in advance.'

Levin wondered how deeply the local KGB chief would later personally regret this particular acquiescence: he sincerely hoped it would not be too bad for the man. He said: 'Of course. Every time.'

'Travel safely, Yevgennie Pavlovich.'

Of everything that had happened on this uncertain day, the unexpected invocation of one of the oldest Russian proverbs came close to causing Levin's open collapse. He swallowed against the sensation, feigning a cough so that he could raise a hand to his mouth to cover his distress from the other man. 'To return to be your companion again, Vadim Alekseevich,' he said, completing the rote-like ritual. He listened intently to the sound of his own voice, surprised at its evenness.

The recall notice gave Levin the excuse to leave ahead of the normal, mass departure of the other Soviet officials. He felt safe telephoning ahead, to warn Galina he would be early: she was too well prepared to respond wrongly over the open line but Levin was confident she would understand something was happening because he rarely departed from normality when he was working within the confines of the United Nations.

34

She was still cautious when he entered the compound apartment, following his lead, which he offered quickly, not wanting her to give any blurted sort of reaction too soon to be discerned by those who daily transcribed the monitors he knew to be installed in their apartment. Very early in the posting Levin had found three listening devices in the most obvious places – the telephone receiver, the light socket and inside the actual keyhole of the door separating the living room from the main bedroom – before abandoning the search as a useless exercise, because he knew they were the ones he was expected to find and that there would be others more cleverly concealed. Quickly, to guide her, he said: 'I thought we might go out tonight. Dinner, I mean.'

Galina, who was as heavy as her husband, bulge-hipped and droop-busted, but unlike Levin worked harder to disguise it, always dressing carefully in voluminous, folding dresses and smocks, was instantly alert, aware of two departures from the norm within the space of an hour. 'A mission party?' she probed tentatively.

'Just the two of us.'

Galina knew from Levin's monitoring search that there was no visual surveillance. Confident therefore that the gesture was safe she nodded, knowingly, raising her voice in apparant anticipation. 'That would be wonderful.'

'Petr will be all right by himself,' Levin insisted, in further guidance to her that their son was not to accompany them.

Galina became sober-faced in more complete aware-ness, but for the benefit of the listening devices she main-tained the necessary charade. 'Yes,' she said. 'He'll be quite all right.'

Levin decided upon the Café Europa on 54th Street, not talking within earshot of the cab driver on the way and politely asking when they arrived for their table to be changed, to ensure greater privacy. Galina had been involved from the beginning – that had been one of Levin's insistences – so there was no necessity for detailed explanations. He still watched her intently as he spoke, alert for her reaction to match his earlier bewilderment.

'This morning?' she demanded, not able to believe it either.

'Waiting for me when I arrived.' He was glad of the waiter's interruption for drinks orders although it delayed the inevitable question by only a few seconds.

'How long?'

'A fortnight.'

Galina looked at him doubtfully, as if she had misheard. Then, flatly, she said: 'Natalia is not due back from Moscow for another month.'

'Do you think I need reminding of that!'

'So it's got to be a mistake.'

'Which I can't do anything to rectify.'

'You must query it!'

'How can I!'

'How can you not!'

'I can't go back!' protested Levin. 'I'd wreck years of preparation. The punishment would be their using the association with the FBI as the very evidence to send me to a *gulag*. Maybe worse. I'm helpless: we're both helpless.'

The woman waited until the drinks were put before them and the waiter withdrew and then she said, quiet-voiced: 'My darling Yevgennie Pavlovich. From the beginning, all those years ago in Moscow, I agreed to be in this with you. I agreed to defect with you and to live for the rest of my life in whatever unreal sort of existence I would be called upon to endure just to be with you. Because I love you. I'll always love you. But I love our son and daughter just as much; maybe more, in some ways, because they'll need greater protection than you do. Because they don't *know:* they'll never be able to know. You're properly trained . . . a professional. For them it was always going to be a monumental upheaval, changing their lives, just like that . . .' Galina stopped, snapping her fingers. She took up again: 'I was prepared for that monumental upheaval: to help them and to explain as much as I could to them and maybe in time

– a very long time – to make them understand you weren't the traitor to your country they would believe you to be . . .' She stopped, swallowing heavily from her drink, needing it. 'I only ever made one condition. That we were never split. I will not do it . . . cannot do it, with Natalia still in Russia. Neither of us can.'

'I'll get her out,' blurted Levin. 'Not at once, of course. That won't be possible. But in time. In time they'll let her out . . .'

Galina shook her head sadly. 'We can't be certain of that, my darling. We can't take that risk.'

'Can we take the other risk!'

'Not without Natalia,' insisted the woman adamantly, refusing to answer the question. 'I won't go without Natalia.'

'Things are different, under Gorbachov!'

'Stop it, Yevgennie Pavlovich!' said the woman sadly.

'You've got to choose.'

'Don't ask me.'

'I'll make a meeting, with the Americans . . .'

' . . .What can they do?' interrupted Galina objectively.

'I can't go without you.'

'I can't go without the children. Both of them.'

'I don't know what to do!' said Levin, who did but did not want to confront the decision.

'You really can't go back, can you?' accepted Galina.

'No,' he said shortly.

'Why did it have to happen like this!'

'I don't know.'

The waiter arrived to take their order from a menu at which neither of them had looked.

'What do you want?' asked Levin.

'Nothing,' she said, 'I'm not hungry.'

'We'd better eat something,' he said. 'For appearance sake.'

'Appearance sake!' erupted Galina bitterly. 'Always for appearance sake! Will there ever be a time when we can do something other than for appearance sake!'

'I hope so,' said Levin doubtfully. 'One day.' He'd

never imagined it was going to be as bad as this. And it hadn't even started yet.

Major Lev Konstantinovich Panchenko, the deputy security commander for the First Chief Directorate, stumped heavy-booted into Kazin's office, a recruiting poster image of a militarily trained officer, shaven-headed, polished-face, starch-stiff. The salute was like the movement of machinery: he stood ramrod straight, eyes pitched just above Kazin's head.

'At ease,' said Kazin.

There was a barely perceptible relaxation from the other man.

'Comrade Major,' opened Kazin, almost conversationally. 'You have been attached to this Directorate security division for ten years?'

'Yes, Comrade First Deputy.'

'It is a vocation you enjoy?'

'Yes, Comrade First Deputy.'

'One in which you see a continuing future?'

'Yes, Comrade First Deputy.'

'Comrade Major Panchenko, for the past five of those ten years you accepted money from Jews seeking exit visas to Israel: bribes for linking them with the responsible officials at the Dutch embassy from which they can obtain finance necessary to purchase those exits,' announced Kazin. 'Through a KGB deputy in Tbilisi you import once a fortnight prime Georgian fruit and meat, for black market sale on a street stall in Moscow . . .' The knee-pumping man stopped, apparently to consult some notes. ' . . . The KGB deputy's name is Afansasiev,' Kazin recited. 'The market is in Grebnoy Alley, every Wednesday. You have also, on occasions, exchanged money in the foreign currency bars at the Rossiya and Intourist hotels . . .'

Panchenko remained statued, gaze fixed over Kazin's head.

'Well?' demanded Kazin.

'Nothing to say,' replied Panchenko, tight-lipped.

'Under the corruption legislation introduced by

38

Comrade General Secretary Gorbachov you are liable to fifteen years' imprisonment.'

Panchenko still did not speak.

'But I do not intend to initiate proceedings,' disclosed Kazin. 'I intend to promote you to replace the comrade colonel commanding this security division . . .' Again Kazin paused. Then he added: 'Who tried to switch the entire investigation on to you, when he himself came under suspicion. You really should not have trusted him as a business associate. Not to be relied on. Not, like I am, a man to be relied on. Never forget the need for loyalty, will you?'

'Never, Comrade First Deputy,' assured the man immediately.

'You'll remove all the evidence from records once you get your appointment, of course,' predicted Kazin. 'Never forget, either, that I have a complete file, will you?'

'No, Comrade First Deputy.'

'That from now on you are absolutely dependent upon me?'

'No, Comrade First Deputy.'

The old ways, the good old ways, thought Kazin.

In Kabul, Yuri Malik moved away from Ilena, not wanting the irritating distraction of sex, listening incredulously as she recounted the details of the cable traffic that had passed between the Afghan capital and Moscow.

When she finished Yuri said distantly: 'Maybe there really is a Comrade God.' And without the need for press-ups, he thought.

'I don't understand,' she said, confused by his reaction.

'Neither do I,' admitted Yuri. But he would, he determined: very soon he would.

5

Levin was not completely sure he had persuaded Galina; wouldn't know whether or not she would actually come with him until the very act of defection – almost literally the cutting of the umbilical cord – but knew he had to act quickly before the already existing and heavy doubts hardened to outweigh the fragile arguments with which he'd worked to convince her. He walked apparently unhurriedly – but inwardly churning – through the upper corridor in the United Nations building, anxious to complete the established contact procedure and begin it all. The library – housing the hundreds of reports and pamphlets poured out by the UN but never, he suspected, read by anyone except their authors – was surprisingly full, at least a dozen people browsing among the partitioned gangways. But not, fortunately, cluttering the section devoted to his own subject, worldwide mineral deposits. Nervously impatient though he was, Levin proceeded with the proper professional caution, forcing himself to browse like the others through an American assessment of oil-bearing shale deposits, a necessary explanation for his presence there if he were challenged by a suspicious security officer of his own Soviet delegation. It was a full fifteen minutes before he made the move, with seeming casualness, picking up a Soviet account for what appeared to be comparison with some statistic from one of the other books and then replacing it. But not upright, as it had been: on its spine, the emergency, meeting-at-once request. Rigidly maintaining the professionalism, he did not immediately hurry away from the section, making protective time pass by staring down at type which blurred before his eyes and making meaningless notations on a pocket pad before finally putting the other two publications back in their designated places in the racks, but both properly upright this time. Would it be an hour, like they'd always promised? He hoped so. He was desperate for the impression at least that some action – some movement – was being started.

Despite the stomach-tensed, perpetual apprehension, Levin found a small amusement in the fact that Vadim Dolya had provided the way undetectably for him to make a meeting with the FBI. He'd already checked the other man's commitments for the day, to ensure his presence in the peace studies office, and Dolya smiled up when Levin entered.

'A favour,' announced Levin.

'What?'

'You were right about the electrical goods: I think Galina is going to be an actual drain upon Moscow's central grid system!'

Dolya continued smiling at the weak attempt at humour. 'A shopping list?'

'Almost a computer print-out: irons, toasters, microwaves, curling tongs . . . there seems to be nothing she hasn't thought of.'

'Is there anything to keep you here today?' asked Dolya, who knew anyway that Levin's diary was clear because it was his primary function to know at all times the activities of the KGB operatives for whom he was responsible.

'No,' said Levin.

'Take as long as you want,' offered Dolya generously. 'And Yevgennie Pavlovich?'

'What?'

'Buy Japanese imports: they're much more reliable than the American products.'

'I'll remember that,' said Levin uncomfortably.

Levin walked purposefully from the United Nations building, veering right through the forecourt and by so doing going close to the Soviet-presented peace status of the figure wielding a hammer over a broadsword. In the early days of his appointment its inscription – 'Let us beat swords into ploughshares' – had amused Levin with its insincerity, but not any longer. He wondered how

41

difficult it would be for him to be amused, ever again. He managed to catch the lights on UN Plaza and continued on down 44th Street, going a full block until he reached Second Avenue upon which he had already isolated a number of electrical stores and shops. He made no effort to establish any surveillance, either hoped-for (so fervently hoped-for) American or hoped-against Russian. The spine-downwards alert dictated that the FBI place him under observation from his moment of departure from the UN building and only make an approach – at their chosen time and location – when they were absolutely certain he was not being followed by his own people. No approach after an hour meant he was being monitored by the Russians and that any American meeting had to be abandoned, to await a later effort signalled by another misplaced book. At the thought of there being no encounter Levin felt perspiration prick out upon his back and form into rivulets. Galina would not be able to withstand any delay: he knew she wouldn't. He was unsure if he could endure much delay himself. Near 45th Street he bought an electrical travelling iron and a small, electrically operated coffee-bean grinder, unwilling to burden himself with things that were too heavy because he didn't intend transporting them anywhere anyway. To give his protectors as much help as possible identifying any pursuit Levin went further westwards on 45th, turning to complete the square on Park and skirting the overpowering PanAm building to regain 42nd Street. At the corner with Lexington, near the Grand Central Station complex and its rash of beer-crate and orange-box shoeshine vendors, he felt a presence to his right. A voice said: 'The Hyatt bar. Not the garden.'

Levin showed no reaction, nor did he attempt to locate the person who gave the instruction, going instead immediately to his left into the waterfall-dominated foyer of the hotel built over the station. As he ascended the escalator to the mid-floor level Levin acknowledged the wisdom of the choice: it was huge and open plan, a human anthill of a place where the FBI could undetect-

42

ably position as many watchers as they wanted without their becoming the focus of any attention. He turned away from the registration area and went up the next set of steps to the higher level but shook his head against the captain's smiled invitation to be seated in the frond and flower bedecked garden area overhanging the street, going instead to the squared bar and carefully positioning himself with seats available either side. He paid at once and in cash for his whisky, not charging it to an accumulating tab; it was automatic not to involve himself in hindering delays in case he had to move with abrupt urgency.

Levin didn't react to the person settling to his left. The voice said: 'Quite some place', and Levin smiled sideways, nodding agreement to the most casual of casual conversations, knowing his control wanted it to seem a chance encounter to enable the protectors arranged unseen around them to make the final, positive check for any Russian surveillance.

'Very impressive,' agreed Levin.

'I guess they recycle the water.' David Proctor was a compact, hard-bodied man who constantly removed and then replaced his heavy horn-rimmed spectacles, as if he were ashamed of the physical frailty which made it necessary to wear them. The man had been appointed Levin's control immediately upon the Russian's first approach to the FBI: the circumstances had prevented their becoming anything like friends but from the odd remark Levin knew the American jogged most weekdays and worked out in a gymnasium on Saturdays and Sundays.

'I guess they do,' agreed Levin.

'You put the frighteners into us, Yevgennie,' said Proctor.

Levin had not been conscious of the clearance being signalled to the other man by someone in the foyer and was glad; it proved they were professional and that he was well protected. He said: 'I'm frightened myself.'

'What's the problem?'

'I'm being recalled.'

43

With the mixer straw Proctor eased the lemon peel from his martini and idly squeezed it back into the drink. 'Didn't expect that,' he admitted.

'Neither did I,' said Levin, waiting.

'This could be good, Yevgennie. Very good.'

Levin's response to the predictable suggestion that he continue spying from Moscow was immediate. 'No,' he refused.

'Why not?'

'A dozen reasons why not,' said Levin, as forcefully as their surroundings would allow. 'Working with you here, as I have done for the past year, is altogether different from working for you back in Moscow. And I wouldn't anyway be working for you, would I? It would mean a transfer to the CIA: extending the knowledge of my identity to another agency and increasing the risk of detection. But that's not my biggest fear: my biggest fear is that the recall at this time, ahead of when we both expected it, means there's already some suspicion.'

Trained as he was, Proctor was still unable to prevent the instinctive look beyond them into the vast foyer. He removed, polished and then replaced the spectacles and said: 'You got any reason for thinking that?'

'The early recall, like I said. That's always the most obvious indication. And I haven't been assigned anything but routine for at least the past three months. You know that.'

'Frozen out?' said Proctor, more to himself than to the other man.

'That's what I think.'

'When are you supposed to go back?'

'Two weeks.'

'That's quick, too,' said the man, in growing acceptance.

'Too quick. I'm frightened, David. I need help.'

'Don't worry,' placated the American. 'It'll be all right.'

'You any idea how the KGB treat people they believe to be traitors? Remember Penkovsky, who told your CIA about the Cuban missiles so that Kennedy could confront Krushchev? They fed him alive – slowly – into a furnace!

We're shown a warning film at training schools. He melts!'

'Easy, Yevgennie. Easy.'

'I want to come across,' insisted Levin. 'There's a lot I could offer. Structure at the UN. Training. Some of the agent set-up throughout the United States . . .'

Again the American gave a startled reaction. 'You got that sort of detail . . . names . . . places . . . !'

'Some.'

'You never told me.'

'My insurance, David: my very necessary insurance.'

The barman approached inquiringly and both nodded agreement to fresh drinks. They paid separately, as strangers would have done.

Proctor said: 'Your wife and kids, too?'

Levin did not immediately respond, gazing down into his glass. Then he said: 'Natalia is still in Moscow: I told you about the operation on her eyes. She's not due back for a month.'

Proctor paused. Then he said: 'That's a bitch.'

'I think I've persuaded Galina but I'm not sure: she still might refuse.'

'No chance of getting the girl back sooner?'

'What reason would there be now? It's logical for her to remain in Russia until we return: to start trying to get her back here would set off every alarm bell in Moscow.'

'I'm sorry, Yevgennie. Really sorry.'

'I'm hoping they'll let her out, eventually. I know it wouldn't be for a long time. But eventually,' said Levin.

Proctor hesitated again. Finally he said 'Sure' in a voice from which he didn't try to keep the doubt.

'How quickly can you get me out?' demanded Levin.

'A day or two. Three at the outside.'

'How?'

'We'll use the book displacement, like before. But the American edition. Check every afternoon: it'll mean we'll be ready, that night.'

'Where?'

'How freely can you move?'

45

'Dolya has agreed to my taking Galina out in the evenings,' said Levin. 'It shouldn't be difficult.'

'You know the Plaza Hotel?'

'Yes.'

'There are two entrances, one directly from Central Park South, with the main doors fronting on to Fifth Avenue,' set out Proctor. 'When you get the signal enter from the park, as if you're going to Trader Vic's or the Oak Room. I'll pick you up in the lobby: we'll go straight around and exit by the main door. We'll have cars waiting: the parking area is convenient. How's that sound?'

'Almost too simple.'

'The simple way is always the best way.'

'What time?'

'It's got to seem like a dinner outing, right? Let's say seven: but we'll build in contingency time. Don't want to screw up over something as innocent as a traffic block, crossing town.'

'How long?'

'Thirty minutes,' said the American. 'I'll definitely be there at seven – earlier, in fact – and I'll wait until seven thirty. If you're not there by then I'll know there's a problem.'

'It wouldn't automatically mean I've been stopped.'

'I realize that,' said Proctor. 'If you've got to cry off for any reason, just let yourself be seen around the UN the following day: we'll be watching. And waiting in exactly the same way, that night. And the following night, if necessary.'

'It'll work, won't it?' said Levin in sudden urgency.

'We'll make it work,' assured Proctor. 'Everything's going to be all right, Yevgennie. Believe me.'

'I want to,' said Levin. Then he said: 'Petr is sixteen.'

'Yes?' said the American curiously.

'You'll make everything possible for him, won't you? High school, college. Things like that? I've earned it, after all.'

'It'll all be taken care of,' promised Proctor in further

46

reassurance. 'There'll be a safe house. New identities. Money.'

'I'll cooperate,' said Levin, making a promise of his own.

'I know you will.'

'And Natalia?'

'What about her?'

'Will you – your people – try to help me there, too? Through the State Department, maybe?'

'We'll do what we can: I'll personally ask Washington for advice, to work out the best way.'

'Just three days?' queried Levin, as if he found it difficult to believe.

'At the outside.'

'Thank you, David. For everything. You're a good friend.'

'There won't be any problems.'

'It's difficult to imagine that right now,' said Levin. 'All I can think of right now is that I've made a terrible mistake.'

On the other side of the World, Yuri Vasilivich Malik was also reflecting upon mistakes, trying to assess their potential – and personal – danger. At his inferior, first-posting level it would be a mistake to interfere in what he knew was being planned but of which he was officially supposed to know nothing. Yet the retribution operation that Ilena had disclosed to him was madness. And could only result in the sort of disaster that had so very recently engulfed the GRU; maybe even a worse disaster. By which, therefore, he could be destroyed. So either way he lost. The decision, then, had to be one of degrees, between the greater and the lesser.

One of his instructors at the Metrostroevskaya Street training school – into the idiosyncracies of the American language and its slang – had been a pale-skinned, pale-haired American trapped by his homosexuality into passing over US defence secrets from Silicon Valley who'd chosen defection when his FBI arrest became inevitable. Yuri had particularly liked the expression encompassing indecision: either shit or get off the pot. He'd never expected it to become personally applicable.

It took only three hours for Yuri to complete the confirmatory round journey to the military section of Kabul airport – aware it might also provide some minimal protection against any later punishment of Ilena, if there were an inquiry into his source – and return to the embassy by noon. He bypassed his own cramped, junior office in the *rezidentura* – and Ilena's separate accommodation, because he did not want to frighten her – to make his way directly to the comparatively expansive quarters of Georgi Petrovich Solov.

'Yes?' inquired the duty clerk.

'I have to see the Comrade Rezident,' said Yuri. He added: 'Upon a matter of the utmost urgency and importance.'

6

Protocol within the KGB is more strictly regimented and observed than it ever was in the court of the Tsars and the Kabul controller considered himself in an impossible position having the son of someone now a First Deputy dumped upon him. More so because there had been no instruction – not even discreet guidance – from Moscow how to treat the man, which there should have been. It left him exposed. Forced into creating his own guidelines, Georgi Solov had so far proceeded with caution, even supported by the courage imbued by vodka. A native of Askhabad, just across the border in Turkmeniya – where his parents had actually been practising Muslims – the narrow-faced, burnt-skinned Solov was fluent in three local dialects as well as Farsi, looked more Afghan than southern Russian and rightly considered himself a natural choice to head the *rezidentura*. Assigning this man, with his fair-haired, open-faced Western complexion, collar-and-tie-and-suit appearance (which he made no effort to modify) and complete lack of any language qualifications, made as much sense as delegating him to the moon. Probably less; on the moon he could have mingled more easily with the American astronauts. Without question it was an appointment about which to be suspicious. And careful. But at the same time not allowing the slightest indication of subservience, which might equally be an error. With that in mind, Solov actually thought of refusing the demand for an unscheduled meeting, insisting the man return for a later appointment. But there was the high-priority retribution business, so Solov decided a delay was an unnecessary reminder of his seniority. But with some regret.

Solov didn't offer a chair and tried to open forcefully, intending the younger man to be intimidated by his appearing irritated. He said: 'I certainly hope this is something of the utmost urgency and importance!'

'I have just returned from the airport,' announced Yuri, unimpressed. 'Seen barrels and containers of gas and poison being unloaded from transporters.' Two things were important: frightening the pompous fool and hinting he knew everything, which he almost did.

Impressions – uncertainties – swirled through Solov's mind like sand in a storm. It was strictly forbidden for a junior KGB officer to go in or out of the *rezidentura* without stating his destination and reason in the logbook. Which Yuri Malik well knew. Yet the man was standing there almost proudly declaring a breach of regulations. Unworried by any thought of being disciplined then: an important consideration. At once there came to Solov another and maybe more important awareness. The Eyes-Only Moscow traffic had been strictly limited to himself and maybe five other people, although he supposed wider gossip was inevitable once the shipments started to arrive by air. But had the man known in advance, through some other channel? Could the damned man's posting – the retribution proposal itself – be some sort of test, of loyalty or ability? Proceed cautiously, Solov thought; very cautiously. Trying for the protective barrier of the operating procedure within the intelligence section of the embassy, Solov said: 'You made no entry of your movements this morning.'

'If this operation goes ahead – if people are poisoned and gassed – you will end up in a *gulag* serving a sentence that will make the GRU imprisonment seem like a holiday,' said Yuri. The outrage at the insubordination would come now if it were going to come at all.

Solov's mental sandstorm raged on. Contemptuously dismissive of regulations now, not even bothering to respond. So the man was completely unworried. Not just unworried: sure enough of himself to threaten a superior officer with imprisonment. Unthinkable. Solov said: 'How did you come into possession of classified information?' The stilted formality weakened the demand and he recognized it.

So did Yuri, who thought the ploy of keeping him standing was juvenile. Further psychologically to pressure the other man, he pulled an available chair close to Solov's desk and sat on it, leaning forward in an attitude of urgency. He said: 'The GRU catastrophe was not the *mujahideen* ambush, the number of men and the amount of equipment we lost. It was the fact that the disaster – the apparent stupidity – was witnessed and broadcast in the West. The *mujahideen* know the value of such exposure. It will be impossible to disguise or hide the extent of the slaughter being planned: hundreds, thousands, will die. And they'll smuggle cameras in again to record it and the Soviet Union will be pilloried again. But worse this time. Not just shown losing a battle. Shown like some sort of barbaric savages, killing women and children . . .'

Solov was visibly sweating, subservient though he'd determined not to be. He said: 'They are the orders, from Moscow.'

'From whom?'

'Comrade Director Agayans.'

It was not a name Yuri knew but there was no reason why he should. Confident he controlled the meeting now, he said: 'Initiated by Moscow?'

Solov isolated the danger in the question. 'Oh yes,' he said hurriedly. 'Definitely from Moscow.'

Yuri decided it was necessary to frighten the other man further. Knowing the answer already, he said: 'But there has been some liaison?'

'Communication, yes,' agreed Solov reluctantly.

'So the inquiry will have evidence of your involvement, from your signed messages?'

'What inquiry?'

'Don't you think there'll be one?' demanded Yuri, going back to answering a question with a question. 'Can't you honestly conceive this being anything but a debacle, resulting in a worse inquiry than last time? And punishment worse than last time?'

'It's a possibility,' Solov conceded. He'd abdicated almost completely, just wanting the conversation to continue, to hear what the other man had to say: to learn what the escape could be.

But Yuri was not prepared to abandon the pressure quite so soon. He said: 'You didn't query the order?'

Solov blinked at him. 'One does not query Moscow. Not a Comrade Director.'

'Never!'

'Moscow is the authority: that is where the policy is determined and made.'

Yuri sat across the desk, studying the other man curiously as one might look at an exhibit in a laboratory. Was this a typical senior officer of the country's intelligence organization: a conditioned animal unquestioningly and unprotestingly obeying, like Pavlov's dogs? He said: 'This must be protested. Stopped.'

'How?'

A dullness seemed to settle over Solov. Exactly like a conditioned dog, Yuri thought. One reflection directly followed another, but less critically: there was *some* explanation for Solov's apparently docile helplessness. The enshrined regulations, as restrictive as the straps on an experimental animal, strictly dictated a pyramid order of communication: a field office could never exchange messages with an authority higher than the department, division or section director controlling that field office. In this case someone named Agayans. Who had initiated the operation. And was unlikely to accept any challenge to it, at this late stage. Or ever, if Solov's belief in the infallibility of Moscow orders were correct. Certainly it precluded the use of the normal cable channels because they were automatically routed to the Director's secretariat, with no allowance whatsoever for variance. He said: 'The *rezidentura* ships to Moscow in the diplomatic pouch?'

'Yes.'

'Every night?'

'Yes.'

Yuri sighed, hesitating. Precisely the sort of action his father had urged him to avoid, during those final, mutually irritated days – *'don't invoke our relationship . . .*

regard it as something to make life more difficult than easier ... think politically ... ' The last part of the injunction stayed with Yuri. Politically was exactly how he was thinking: politically and beyond his father's fragile eyrie. Time to shit or get off the pot. He said: 'I would like to include something in tonight's shipment.'

'A personal package?'

Yuri no longer felt contempt for the man. If there were an emotion it was pity. He said: 'Something addressed to my father ...' He paused again, deciding to offer the man a way out. He added: 'Will you require it to be left unsealed, to be read?'

'No!' said Solov. The rejection burst out in his eagerness to dissociate himself from any more unknown and unimagined dangers. 'Our part of the pouch has to be completed by five,' advised Solov, helpfully. He'd debated enough; he wanted the meeting over, to think.

Yuri offered no explanation for what was a memorandum, not a letter. He presented it with absolutely correct formality, at the same time embarrassed that the phrasing were as if the person to whom he was communicating were *not* his father. *Don't invoke our relationship*, he thought. Yuri's arguments were so well formulated that it did not take him long and he was back at Solov's office – again avoiding Ilena's cubicle – with an hour to spare.

Solov accepted the sealed envelope and hurried it into the larger leather package in which other parcels and letters were already secured against unauthorized interception during the journey to Moscow. The interruption had allowed the *rezident* to recover some of his composure and he was anxious, too, to recover something of what he considered was the proper superior-to-subordinate relationship with the other man. He said: 'There'd better be the right sort of reaction to this.'

There was.

Because of Vasili Malik's rank it was delivered within minutes of its arrival in Moscow, ahead of all the other pouch contents, and because of the source – and obvious sender – Malik opened it at once, initially believing in worried irritation that his son was improperly using a diplomatic communication channel. Which, technically, he was. But that was the briefest of Malik's thoughts, just as quickly dismissed as irrelevant. The assessments and implications of what was apparently being planned in Afghanistan – a country for which he was supposed to be responsible – crowded in upon him, appalling him. There was initial and instinctive fury, which he subdued, not wanting his reasoning clouded by emotion. And there was a lot to reason out, beyond the immediate crisis.

Malik personally issued and signed the cabled instructions to the Kabul *rezidentura* to abandon the gassing and poisoning and insisted that the *rezident*, Georgi Solov, acknowledge each section of the abandonment instructions to ensure that it was completely understood but more importantly to guarantee that no detail was overlooked. Still determined to be absolutely sure, Malik contacted – personally again – the Ministry of Defence and insisted upon duplicate orders being sent to the army, air force and *spetsnaz* units and acknowledged in the same manner as he demanded from the KGB personnel in Kabul.

The preliminary planning – air transporting the gas and poison, for instance – made it inevitable that the GRU were already aware of most, if not all of the planning. Malik accepted that their knowledge would become complete by his involving the military in the cancellation plans and that the back-biting gossip would begin within days. Just as he accepted that despite the supposed compartmenting within the KGB, details would spread throughout Dzerzhinsky Square. Which he welcomed, wanting as wide a circulation and awareness as possible that it had been his name upon the abort orders and no one else who made the calls to the Ministry of Defence.

Because even while he worked upon the cancellation, Malik was thinking beyond. This had not been a mistake, an aberration. This had been an attempted entrapment, something intended to destroy him within the first tentatively exploring weeks of his appointment.

The truth had to be investigated by official inquiry.

And such inquiries – certainly the sort of official inquiry Malik envisaged, damning indictments against the perpetrators, resounding praise for himself – needed documentary proof. Which had to be seized before there was any opportunity of it being destroyed or altered.

It was late afternoon before Malik was satisfied everything in Afghanistan was safely closed down. At once he issued a fresh set of instructions, the most urgent to the cipher room that all cable traffic between Moscow and Kabul for the preceding two months be sealed and delivered to him at once. He remembered his own memorandum well enough, of course. He recalled it from records and reread it carefully. Satisfied completely with its propriety, Malik put it to one side of his desk, ready to form part of the file he intended to create when the cables arrived.

What about witnesses? Yuri, he decided: the resounding praise deserved to be spread and nepotism wasn't a charge here. And Agayans, of course: the most significant cog in the entire machination. Vital not to miscalculate here by one iota. Certainly necessary to avoid any personal interrogation, to appear as if he were interfering or prejudging: it had to be the inquiry which returned a verdict, not him. Wrong, equally, not to make some sort of investigatory move into what could – without Yuri's intercession – have been an inconceivable catastrophe. Malik smiled to himself, at the ease of the resolve. It *was* an investigation. And on the prima-facie evidence there was sufficient for Agayans to be put under detention.

Vasili Dmitrevich Malik reached once more for the telephone that had been used so much that day. And made his only – but disastrous – mistake.

The security sections of all KGB directorates are run upon military guidelines – uniforms are invariably worn, for instance – with military requirements. One of those requirements is monthly attendance at a firearms installation to ensure that a necessary standard of marksmanship is maintained. The installation is established at Gofkovskoye Shosse and it was here that Malik located the newly promoted head of his directorate's internal discipline, Colonel Lev Konstantinovich Panchenko.

In his own office, which was just one hundred yards from that in which Malik had minutes before completed his conversation, Victor Kazin went physically cold, actually shivering, at Panchenko's immediate warning on the private, untraceable telephone.

'I'm to arrest Agayans,' reported the colonel. 'Something to do with Afghanistan.'

Kazin swallowed against the sensation of paralysis, driving himself to think. 'Do it,' he said, hoarse-voiced. 'But do it the way I've already ordered you to do it.'

'I need more time!'

'Do it!'

Georgi Solov still did not completely understand – in fact, he understood very little – but he was fairly sure that what could have created some personal difficulties for him had been avoided. He smiled across the desk in the Kabul *rezidentura* and said: 'Everything cancelled.'

'Of course,' said Yuri curtly. He guessed Solov wanted to make it appear a joint intervention.

'And you're to return at once?' smiled Solov, gesturing to the message that lay between them.

'That's what it says,' agreed Yuri. He didn't try to keep the impatience from his voice: he couldn't think now why he'd earlier felt pity for the dance-to-any-tune idiot.

'Seems as if we were right to intervene,' attempted Solov, directly.

'I was, wasn't I?' corrected Yuri. If there were to be credit given, Solov literally had to be weak in the head to imagine it would be shared.

7

He could not lose the numbness, the actual sensation of shivering coldness. It was far worse than the nervous, habitual shaking to which Kazin was now so accustomed that he was scarcely any longer aware of it. How had it happened! How had such an intricate but perfect scenario collapsed? How had Malik discovered it, to the apparent degree of issuing arrest orders, arrest orders that should have been in *his* name, not that of the very man it had all been designed to destroy: the very man who should have been arrested, destined for a *gulag*. Or worse!

Who'd talked: defected to Malik's camp, so soon? Agayans? An internal spy in the cipher section? A leak from the Kabul *rezidentura* to which the man's son was attached? Panchenko, he thought abruptly. He'd ordered Panchenko to go ahead as planned. Was that the mistake! Had he himself stupidly stumbled into a Malik-designed trap? Or . . . ? Kazin tried to halt the unanswerable demands flooding into his mind, someone desperate to close the watertight doors of a sinking vessel against the destructive inrush of water. Good word, destructive: appropriate. That's what he risked being, destroyed, if he continued sitting there, letting the panic engulf him. Stop! Had to stop to think properly: analyse as best he could what might have happened. Then work it out. Dispassionately. No fear. No panic. Not more than it was possible to avoid, at least. Then plan. Blindly perhaps, in the immediate moment. But still try to plan. Minimize the potential dangers. If only . . . Kazin got the doors finally closed, actually panting like someone relieved after expending a great effort. Analyse was another good word, just as appropriate. One question – one consideration – at a time. Agayans first, then.

Agayans was a traditionalist, one of the old school acolytes, stretched to the absolute extreme of his ability, who ensured safety by unquestioning obedience. But there were those medical warnings of the man's increasing uncertainty. Might Agayans not have worried at the orders from one joint Chief Deputy to initiate retribution proposals upon a memorandum issued by the other? And seen safety in approaching Malik? Kazin's coldness spread further through him, at a further recollection; hadn't Agayans actually queried whether Malik should be included in the supposed Afghanistan planning? Quickly – to Kazin's sighed relief – came the contradiction, the strongest and most convincing argument *against* it being Agayans. Malik would not have ordered the arrest of his prime witness; rather he'd be embalming Agayans in featherdown, ensuring every comfort and protection.

The cipher room? Again unlikely to the point of impossibility. There were rotating shifts so no one single man would have encoded all the messages to Kabul and so been able to evolve a complete picture of what was intended. And even if one man had handled everything, there would have been no reason for protest. Or – more important still – have any reason to link Malik with it.

Kabul *had* to be the most likely source. From that cosseted, spoiled bastard of a son. But yet again that was impossible: any message from Kabul would invariably have been routed through Agayans. Who could then have intercepted it?

So how? And how much? Useless conjecture: he wanted positives and all he could speculate were negatives. Positives then. Protect himself. Against the unknown and the unseen but protect himself as much as he felt possible. Definite links with Agayans had to be the most dangerous and he'd already planned here: planned, he reflected bitterly, to prove his complete uninvolvement in a politically absurd proposal which should – but couldn't any longer – have entrapped Malik into appearing to be the architect.

The most direct link was the memorandum in which Agayans had set out the proposal and to which Kazin had been careful only to give unprovable verbal acceptance. He took it now from his safe, with no need to read it again. Across it he scrawled 'Unacceptable. Unequivocable rejection' and added the date to coincide with that of the day Agayans had written and annotated it. Also from the safe he extracted a backlog of documentation for his secretariat's attention and dispersal, carefully sorting through until he reached the appropriate and matching date, inserting the Agayans document into the place it would have properly occupied if his supposed refusal had occurred on the day he received it. Just as carefully he placed the whole pile in the Out tray, for the following morning's collection. Kazin pulled his appointment diary towards him, studying the two entries. Both read: 'Review of position in Afghanistan. No further action.'

What would the entries in Agayans' diary read? The floodwaters began to seep in again as Kazin realized there would be no opportunity for him to seize and have undetectably changed whatever notes or documentation Agayans might have left, which had always been the intention. A fresh numbness began to move through the plump, sweat-dampened man and then the telephone sounded.

'There's been an unforeseen incident,' reported Panchenko, using the coded phrase that had been agreed between them.

Relief – slight but still relief – moved through Kazin. He said: 'Thank you for telling me,' and replaced the receiver. There still remained too many uncertainties, too many unknown dangers.

The first two days there had been anxiety, a will-there-won't-there-be tenseness, but the designated book had been properly upright in its rack in the United Nations library. On the following day Yevgennie Levin's attitude changed to one of expectation because Proctor, who had never let him down, had after all promised three days at the outside. And this was the third day. The boring, unread census document was there, like before; still upright, still undisturbed, still unread.

Levin's eyes clouded in frustration, and careless of being seen he closed them tight against the emotion. All the preparation had been against difficulties arising on his side, not that of the Americans. So what had happened? What had gone wrong?

8

'Dead!'

'Yes.'

'How?' There was a report, as stiffly formal as the colonel standing before him, but Malik wanted more, much more. He wanted *everything*.

'I responded immediately to your telephone instructions,' recited Panchenko, monotone. 'But it was evening, as you know. It entailed going to the Comrade Director's home . . .'

Malik sighed, curbing the impatience. It was as if the man were reading from the inadequate report he had already submitted. Malik said: 'How did you know Agayans would be at home?'

'I did not,' said Panchenko. 'I learned by telephoning the duty registration clerk here that Agayans had already left. The garage said the journey was logged to his home, on Gogolevskiy Boulevard . . .'

Unimpeachable police work, acknowledged Malik. He said: 'Was any indication given that you were coming?'

Panchenko allowed himself a frown. 'Telephoning ahead, you mean?'

'Yes.' His broken shoulder ached, like it often did, always an unnecessary intrusion. He resisted massaging it.

'There was no prior contact,' insisted Pancheno stiffly.

Malik wondered if the man slept in an attitude of permanent attention. He said: 'How many men were assembled?'

'A squad. Four men besides myself,' said the security chief.

'Were the four with you at Gofkovskoye Shosse?'

'I telephoned the department here, instructing they should be assembled.'

'So you returned here to pick them up?'

'No. We arranged a meeting point at Verdandskovo.'

'So there was no possibility of Agayans being aware of any security men gathering outside his home?'

'None whatsoever,' assured Panchenko. He thought the other man's disability made him appear ominous and threatening.

'Continue.'

'The Comrade Director answered the door himself. He was a bachelor, as I have said in the report. He lived alone.'

'The door opened at once?'

'Yes.'

Malik inferred the colonel's impatience at being taken entirely through an episode he believed already properly accounted for. Further to irritate the impatience, Malik said: 'You haven't set out in the report what his attitude was at being confronted by you.'

Panchenko hesitated, then said: 'Surprise.'

'Surprise would have been obvious,' said Malik. 'What about fear?'

'Not until after we entered the apartment.'

'Before which there was some conversation?'

'Yes.'

'Who spoke first?'

Again there was a pause, as if for recall. Panchenko said: 'We practically spoke together. The Comrade Director asked what we were there for as I announced I had orders for his arrest.'

'What was Agayans' reply to that?'

'He asked for what offence. I told him I did not know.'

Malik isolated Panchenko's mistake and decided to wait to use it to undermine the stiff-backed attitude later. Hurrying on to prevent Panchenko realizing it, Malik said: 'What then?'

'He asked upon whose authority – I said yours,' recounted the security chief. 'He said he had done nothing wrong and asked if he could get dressed: that's how he got to the bedroom.'

'Dressed?' queried Malik.

'When we got to the apartment Agayans was in bed,' reminded Panchenko. 'It's in the report.'

'What time was this?'

'Approximately nine.'

'He was wearing nightclothes at nine o'clock at night?'

'And a robe.'

'At once,' prompted Malik.

'I do not understand,' complained Panchenko.

'You told me earlier that when you knocked the door was opened *at once* by Agayans,' said Malik. 'If he had been in bed – and before answering the door had to put on a robe – there should have been a delay.'

'I . . .' started Panchenko and stopped. Then he resumed: 'It appeared to me that the door opened at once: I agree now there would have been some slight delay.'

'So that part of your report is wrong?'

'Yes,' conceded the colonel tightly.

'You agreed to his getting dressed?'

'Although he was under arrest upon your orders I did not think I should detain a Comrade Director in his nightclothes.'

'You said Agayans showed fear, after his initial surprise,' prompted Malik. 'So far I don't get any impression of fear. It seems almost a normal conversation.'

'The request to get dressed was made very subserviently,' insisted Panchenko. 'It was anything but a normal conversation.'

'Tell me about going into the bedroom.'

Panchenko swallowed and said: 'He walked directly from the main room into the bedroom. With my squad I remained in the living area. After a while it occurred to me that Agayans was taking a long time to get ready. I hurried into the bedroom. He was on the far side with the bed between us. The gun was already against his head. The moment I entered, he fired.'

Malik intentionally let the silence build up between them, all the time staring fixedly at the colonel. Panchenko remained rigidly to attention: Malik supposed the man would have learned to remain immobile like that on a hundred parade grounds. He said: 'Does the main living room lead directly into the bedroom?'

'No,' conceded Panchenko.

'You said he walked directly from the main room into the bedroom,' reminded Malik.

'I meant to convey there was no further conversation between us,' said Panchenko. 'There is a corridor leading to the kitchen, bathroom and bedroom.'

'So without any further conversation between you, Igor Fedorovich Agayans walked from the living room, down the corridor and into his bedroom?' Malik was not sure but there appeared to be a sheen of perspiration upon the other man's forehead. Raising his voice to make the demand, he said: 'The corridor is straight, from the main living area? With the bedroom at its far end?'

'No,' admitted Panchenko, in further desperate concession. 'The corridor bends, halfway along.'

'So you did not know if Agayans had gone directly into the bedroom?'

'There was only the bathroom or kitchen, as alternatives.'

'When you assembled your men on Verdandskovo you went at once to Gogolevskiy Boulevard?'

'Yes.' In his caution Panchenko's stance broke, the man's head going slightly to one side in his effort to anticipate a new direction.

'Without any outside reconnaissance of the block? Obtaining plans, even?' Like I did, Malik thought.

'There was no outside reconnaissance,' conceded the security man.

'There might have been a fire escape from the unseen bathroom into which Agayans could easily have gone!' said Malik. 'A fire escape down which he could have fled. Is it normal for you, as an arresting officer, to allow a detainee to go out of sight?'

'No,' said Panchenko, tightly again.

'Desperate enough, he could have returned instead to shoot all of you rather than shooting himself, couldn't he?'

'I walked with him to the beginning of the corridor,' blurted Panchenko.

'That isn't in your report,' challenged Malik at once. 'You said: "I – and my squad – remained in the living room".'

'I . . . we . . . did. I went with him to the commencement of the corridor: he went from there by himself.'

'Why walk to the beginning of the corridor and then stop?' demanded Malik. He shifted, trying to alleviate the shoulder ache.

'He said he wanted privacy to get dressed.'

'A detainee giving an order to the arresting head of security of the First Chief Directorate!' said Malik, allowing the incredulity.

'A mistake,' admitted Panchenko, collapsing further.

'Twice you've told me there was no further conversation after Agayans asked to dress,' reminded Malik. 'That was a lie, wasn't it?'

'It was not a lie,' tried Panchenko desperately. Sweat was visibly leaking from the man now.

'But you said nothing about the request for privacy.'

'It did not seem important.'

'Not important!' exclaimed Malik, incredulous again. 'It allowed the most vital witness in an ongoing inquiry to kill himself! They were probably the most important words he spoke!'

'Probably,' mumbled Panchenko, his voice difficult to hear.

'Isn't it regulations, having once taken a person into custody, that that person shall remain at all times under observation, until placed in a cell?' persisted Malik relentlessly.

'At that precise moment I did not consider I had taken Comrade Director Agayans into custody,' avoided Panchenko, attempting to rally. 'I was not formally in possession of any specific charge.'

'Don't be pedantic,' rejected Malik impatiently.

'That is the wording of the regulation,' said Panchenko, achieving a small victory.

Choosing his words carefully, Malik said: 'Having

been dismissed by an arrested man, what did you then do? Remain at the corridor mouth? Or return to your squad?'

Panchenko's face burned. 'Returned to my squad.'

'Was there any conversation between you?'

'There was some discussion about how the passengers would be split between two cars,' remembered Panchenko. 'I said I would accompany the Comrade Director, with the driver and one back-up man and the other car should provide escort.' Panchenko appeared to relax slightly, feet touching safer ground.

'How long did that discussion take?'

'Ten minutes,' replied Panchenko at once.

'Approximately ten? Or exactly ten?'

'Exactly ten.'

'How do you know it was ten minutes exactly?'

'As I walked from the head of the corridor I checked my watch. It was automatic to look again the moment I became concerned about Agayans.'

'You went to the bedroom without saying anything to the rest of the squad?'

Panchenko's throat was moving. 'I think I may have told them to stay where they were.'

'How did you go to the bedroom?' picked up Malik. 'Did you walk? Or did you run?'

'I walked quickly.'

'You were wearing uniform?'

'Of course,' said Panchenko, almost truculently.

'The regulation boots are comparatively heavy. Do you think Agayans might have heard you?'

'I have no way of telling.'

'You didn't shout?'

'No.'

'Having respected the man's wish for privacy, you didn't call a warning that you were coming into his bedroom?'

'No.'

'Was the door closed or open?'

'Ajar.'

'Did you knock?'

66

'No.'

'Or shout, finally?'

'No.'

'What did you do?'

'Pushed straight in.'

'Privacy was completely unimportant now?'

'I was alarmed. With good reason.'

'Very good reason,' sneered Malik. 'So what did you see, in the bedroom that you finally entered?'

'Agayans was on the far side of the room. The bed was between us. He had the gun to his head. As I went into the room he pulled the trigger.'

Malik sighed once more. He said: 'How was he dressed? Still in his nightclothes? Or had he changed?'

'Still in his nightclothes.'

'So for ten minutes he had stood in his nightclothes holding a gun to his head. Why do you think it took him ten minutes to pull the trigger?'

Panchenko shrugged. 'Indecision, perhaps: he was choosing whether or not to kill himself.'

'There was a moment, as you entered, before he pulled the trigger?'

'Seconds.'

'Did you say anything, in those seconds?'

'I shouted.'

'At last!' mocked Malik. 'What did you shout?'

'I think "Stop". Maybe it was "Don't do it".'

'You weren't frightened he might turn the gun on you?'

'It was against his head. It was obvious what he intended to do.'

'But you couldn't get to him?'

'Not in time,' said Panchenko. 'The impact of the shot threw him against the wall, near the bedhead. His body overturned a side table. He fell half on and half off the bed.'

'You checked he was dead?'

'That wasn't necessary. A lot of his head was gone. The squad came running. I told them to call an ambulance.'

'Not a doctor?'

'It was obviously too late for a doctor.'

'What about the civilian militia?'

'I am empowered to investigate and handle crimes affecting KGB personnel,' said Panchenko, quoting regulations again.

'In those first few moments in the apartment you told him the arrest was upon my orders?' backtracked Malik.

'Yes.'

'And all he said was that he wanted to change?' persisted Malik. 'No protests? Not something like "This is a mistake"?'

'No.'

Abruptly, trying further to off-balance the man, Malik demanded: 'No insistence upon making a telephone call to see what it was all about?'

Panchenko blinked. 'None at all.'

It hadn't worked, Malik realized. Still hoping, he said: 'What about names?'

'Names?'

The chance was getting away. Malik said: 'To what names did Agayans refer?'

'I have told you everything about the conversation between Agayans and myself,' insisted Panchenko. 'There was no reference to anyone by name.'

'No further reference to me?'

'No.'

'Or to anyone else?'

'No one.'

He had not unsettled the other man as he imagined, thought Malik, disappointed. He needed time to analyse everything that had emerged. What more could there be from Panchenko? Malik said: 'Do you consider from this meeting that your report was satisfactory?'

'I did not understand the importance of several things.'

'The arrest of a KGB division director! The suicide of a KGB division director! And you did not understand the importance of several things!' The idea came as Malik spoke and he decided it was a good one.

'I apologize with the utmost regret,' said Panchenko.

Malik guessed that had been the most difficult concession of all for Panchenko to make. He picked up

68

the report and tossed it contemptuously across the desk towards the security man and said: 'I am rejecting this as totally unsatisfactory. And recording that rejection upon your file. I want another account covering all the facts that have emerged during this meeting. Within two hours.'

There was no longer redness in that burnished face. The colour now was an unnatural, white fury. Possibly worthwhile, Malik thought. Furious, the man might include in the revised file something that had not come out under questioning, which was the suddenly occurred reason for making him write it again. To maintain the anger, Malik said as dismissively as possible: 'You may go now.'

It was actually the superficiality of Panchenko's written account that had prompted Malik to conduct a personal interview without imagining so much would be disclosed. But what exactly *had* been disclosed? Malik demanded of himself objectively. Facts? Or merely impressions, formed from inconsistencies. It was inconsistent for a trained investigator – a strict observer of rules of procedure – to have begun so properly in establishing Agayans' whereabouts and assembling his squad and then not bothering to time his arrival at the man's apartment: and then to be so adamant about the length of time Agayans was alone in the bedroom. Which brought him to the biggest inconsistency of all. It was inconceivable for Panchenko to have allowed Agayans go to his bedroom unaccompanied: here Malik thought the explanation unacceptable to the extent of being a downright lie. And why had the man denied knowing the reason for the arrest? Malik distinctly remembered mentioning Afghanistan when he telephoned Gofkovskoye Shosse because he'd immediately considered it a mistake, ahead of the formulation of any specific charge. And what about Panchenko's demeanour? At the start the man's attitude had been one of arrogance, practically contempt. Unthinkable from someone so newly promoted, appearing before a joint First Chief Deputy. And then the change. From arrogance to sweated uncertainty. Uncertainty about

69

what? The realization that his behaviour was wrong? Irritation at having his expertise questioned and so easily shown up to be wanting? Or apprehension, at something more? What was it that could be more? Too many questions lacking too many answers. So what was there? Only impressions that he was in danger of imagining to be facts: unsubstantiated, unpresentable, unprovable facts.

Abruptly Malik recalled the inquiry that had occurred to him during the interview, and reached just as abruptly for the internal telephone. It took less than an hour to get the information from Personnel Records and Malik sat gazing down at the print-out, sure at last of a fact. And even surer that it had significance. Lev Konstantinovich Panchenko had been promoted to colonel and to head the internal security division upon the instigation and personally endorsed recommendation of Victor Ivanovich Kazin.

The link, decided Malik. Not proof of anything but enough to support the suspicion about Kazin that had arisen and stayed with him from that first encounter. Certainly enough to subject whatever revised report he received from Panchenko to an examination even more rigorous than that which it – and its author – had already undergone. But possibly not an isolated examination. There had been a four-man squad. How much would their individual recollections differ from that of the man who had commanded them? Maybe not at all. But then again, maybe a lot. It was certainly worth conducting individual interviews. Would there be enough time before the inquiry? He regretted now demanding a hearing so quickly.

Yevgennie Levin was suffused with an unnatural feeling: a sensation verging on the supernatural. He felt as if he were suspended over his own body, like some outside commentator judging himself perform and act and observe the rituals of his normal day. Maybe it was the effect of his mind – or whatever the responsible organ – flooding his body with adrenaline, hyping him through the final moments: keeping him alert. It was absolutely essential he remain totally alert. It had been from the moment he went into the United Nations library to see at once the signal for which he had waited so anxiously, telling him it was tonight. He'd watched himself go through the ritual of a committee meeting (the last ever!) and make his contribution to the Minute records (never read!) and supported a recommendation for a conservation proposal for the rain forests of Brazil (meaningless!) and sought Solov's approval for the outing that night with Galina and Petr (approved!) and still he watched himself, unable after so long actually to believe it was happening. Judgement so far? Acting entirely as he should have been, unobtrusively, properly, making all the necessary and proper moves.

Levin's control wavered the moment he arrived back at the apartment, with Natalia's shyly smiling photograph on a table and another on the mantelpiece, and felt Galina's concentration burning into him when he announced to her and Petr that they were dining out.

'Great!' responded Petr in English, immediately enthusiastic.

Petr was a fervent American television watcher and was wearing American jeans and a sweatshirt proclaiming UCLA, which occurred to Levin – why did such small things intrude, at a time like this? – to be 3,000 miles out of place. Like he and Galina and Petr were 3,000 miles out of place: more, to be geographically accurate.

'Where?' asked Galina. She asked the question with dulled expectation.

'The Plaza,' announced Levin.

Galina said nothing. Petr said: 'Neat!'

Petr wore his American suit – the one he'd bought at Bloomingdale's – and Levin changed, too: a new suit for a new life. Galina remained in the clothes she was already wearing. They got a cab immediately and the crosstown traffic was unaccountably light, with no holdups or gridlocks. Levin, unthinking and anxious to make conversation, said: 'Easy tonight, isn't it?' and at once Galina said: 'No, it isn't easy at all.'

It was two minutes before seven when Levin guided his wife and son through the narrow side doors off Central Park South but Proctor was already there, waiting by the promised jewellery display directly beyond the central elevator bank.

Three other people – one a woman and none of whom Levin had seen at any previous meeting – moved protectively and at the same time as the American came forward. Proctor didn't smile. He said: 'OK?'

'I think so,' said Levin.

'Ma'am,' greeted Proctor politely.

Galina did not respond.

'Hi, Petr,' tried Proctor.

The boy looked curiously between his parents and the strangers but didn't speak either.

'We'd better go,' said Proctor.

'Dadda, what is this?' asked the boy at last.

'You must come,' said Levin.

All but Galina started off.

'Please!' Levin implored her, stopping.

'I want to know what's happening,' insisted Petr weakly.

'I can't,' protested Galina, unmoving.

'Don't abandon me! Not now!' said Levin, imploring more.

Petr began to back away, frightened. One of the escorts reached out towards him and Galina said, too loud: 'Don't you touch him! Don't you dare touch him!'

The man stopped the gesture and Proctor said: 'This isn't the way, Yevgennie. You know this isn't the way.'

'Galina!' begged Levin.

There were isolated looks from people in the crowded foyer.

'There's no going back, not now,' said Proctor.

'Going back where?' demanded Petr, halfway between belligerence and bewilderment.

'We should go now,' said Proctor, alert to the woman's weakening.

Levin was conscious of it too. He said: 'I promise I'll get her out.'

'Who?' intruded Petr.

The boy was ignored again.

'Ready, Yevgennie?' asked Proctor.

'Yes,' said the Russian with a sigh of finality.

The group started to move in a slow, inviting way and after a moment's hesitation Galina started to walk with them, head bent in an effort to hide the sobbing. The unidentified woman immediately went to her, both comforting and concealing. Petr was in the middle, his head in constant movement, eyes bulged. They rounded the Palm Court lobby café to go through the swing doors instead of the central, revolving exit. Two of a fleet of three or maybe four window-blackened limousines pulled immediately away from the far pavement to come against their kerb and Levin felt a push, urging him into the back. Proctor got in to his left and Galina was helped in to his right. Petr was ushered into the front, alongside the driver, with one of the escorts protectively against the door, arm outstretched.

The cavalcade immediately took off across town, eastwards. Petr said: 'Please tell me what is happening!'

'We're going to live in America,' said Levin simply.

There was a moment of silence and then the boy tried to turn in the front seat, arms flailing. 'Defector!' he shouted. 'Traitor!'

The man beside him easily but carefully encompassed the boy in the already outstretched arm. He said: 'Easy does it, kid. Easy does it.'

'I brought a photograph,' announced Galina, brokenvoiced. 'I brought a photograph of Natalia.' Now that it no longer mattered, she wept uncontrollably.

It was to take five days of frantic but unsuccessful searching through New York by a United Nations *rezidentura* frightened of recrimination before the defection of Yevgennie Pavlovich Levin was reluctantly admitted to Moscow.

9

Determined against any provable association with Panchenko, whom internal, record-keeping security would have had to vet before admission to his office, Kazin decreed their contact be made outside the Directorate building. And insisted, too, that for such a meeting Panchenko wear civilian clothes. There was too much braid and colour in the uniform: too much chance of being remembered by someone. Kazin had not considered the circumstances of *where* and *why* it might be remembered. Desperately he was trying to be as protectively careful as he could. In everything. He still knew so little!

Kazin selected the Marx Prospekt because normally it was busily congested, wanting his to be one car unnoticed among so many. Ironically, adding to his frustration, there was not much traffic because the evening rush was unaccountably light. He drove slowly and in the ordinary lane, tonight keeping away from the restricted central path reserved for government officials. Usually Kazin enjoyed the privilege, disregarding speed limits or traffic signals, always confident of the permanently placed militia stopping any traffic to ensure his unhindered progress.

He slowed further approaching the Lenina metro station, isolating the waiting Panchenko well before he reached him. The man's military bearing was obvious without the identifying uniform. He was wearing a grey suit and carrying a dark-coloured topcoat, maybe grey again or blue, and appeared discomfited, as if he were without any clothes at all, shifting from one foot to the other and gazing around, embarrassed. Or perhaps, corrected Kazin immediately, it had nothing at all to do with his unaccustomed dress. Perhaps the man was simply frightened, as Kazin was.

Panchenko saw him while the car was still some yards

away. Kazin pulled against the kerb without the need positively to stop, just brake sufficiently for Panchenko to open the door and get in: the door was still not fully closed when Kazin moved off again.

'I thought this was best,' said Kazin. It was difficult to remain apparently calm: the questions and demands churned in Kazin's mind. To avoid unsettling the other man it was vitally important not to sound as desperate as he was. Certainly important for Panchenko never to suspect that Kazin might be trying to distance himself by this unrecorded – but more important, absolutely deniable – meeting.

'Yes,' accepted Panchenko shortly. He took a handkerchief from his jacket pocket, using the movement of wiping his nose to cover clearing his forehead, and Kazin knew the security man was sweating.

'There were no problems at the metro?' Kazin did not really know what he meant by the question: he was simply holding back, refusing to hurry. He was perspiring too, and glad he could grip the wheel so that the unsteadiness did not show in his hands.

'There are big problems,' announced Panchenko.

This was how the conversation had to begin and to continue, with Panchenko and not himself showing the anxiety. Kazin said: 'Tell me. Everything.'

'Humiliated,' complained Panchenko, almost petulantly. 'The fucker humiliated me.'

Kazin pulled off the Marx Prospekt on to Kalinina to gain a quieter thoroughfare where he would not have to concentrate so much upon the traffic about him. This was not how he expected the account to come from the other man, but the outburst was important. It was precisely the way the security chief had to feel about Vasili Dmitrevich Malik. Kazin said: 'I need everything from the very beginning: everything in its proper sequence.'

After compiling two official reports with the hostile interview in between, a chronological recall was easy for Panchenko. Kazin turned off Kalinina to an even lesser used road, putting the Kremlin monolith actually behind them. More questions crowded in upon those he already wanted to ask but he rigidly maintained the private control, saying nothing, knowing it would be wrong to break the narrative. This fury the man had to release, as a safety valve: he could be stoked again if hatred were necessary for anything further.

'See!' demanded Panchenko. 'Humiliated! Like I said, the fucker humiliated me!'

'Oh, he did,' agreed Kazin, jabbing the exposed nerve. 'He most certainly did: you've an enemy there, Lev Konstantinovich. A very bad enemy.'

'And he's got an enemy in me,' said Panchenko, with exaggerated, almost childlike bombast. 'He doesn't know how bad.'

Good, thought Kazin, recognizing the attitude; very good. He said: 'Tell me what really happened. Then we'll decide the problems.'

'I had no time to prepare: the time I needed to make plans,' began Panchenko, the defence as rehearsed as the earlier account. 'You said there would be time to set everything up carefully . . .'

'I know that,' encouraged Kazin reassuringly. 'There's no criticism.'

'I was bewildered by the call to Gofkovskoye Shosse. More so because it was Malik, not you. When you told me to kill him, as we'd planned, I discovered Agayans had left the building and that the car was logged to his apartment, on Gogolevskiy . . .'

'So that much of your account is completely accurate?' interrupted Kazin. It was vital to know what could be relied upon and defended and what could not.

'Yes,' confirmed Panchenko. 'The assembly of the squad, too. Although they were not the people I would have taken with me if I'd had the time properly to choose . . . we met at Verdandskovo: that's accurate, too. A major – Chernov – a corporal and two rankers. And Agayans did answer the door in his nightclothes.'

'Nine o'clock and he was in bed?' queried Kazin, remembering the doctors' reports of sleeplessness.

'There were a lot of pills on the side table in the

bedroom. He saw me looking and said the doctors had recommended he try to sleep earlier, using them. Complained it wasn't working.'

'Did you tell Malik this? Put it in either report?'

'Of course not!' said Panchenko irritably. 'The story of my being in the bedroom has got to be that I surprised him in the act of suicide, hasn't it!'

Who the hell did Panchenko think he was, addressing him like that! Kazin controlled any reaction. Wrong to focus upon the wrong person. Malik was the target: always had been. Why, agonized Kazin, had he done what he did that October day in Stalingrad! Why hadn't he let the bastard bleed to death! He'd thought Olga was sure by then, as sure as he had been of her. Kazin supposed he'd done it to prove just how much he loved her. Poor Olga: poor darling, confused, uncertain Olga. Sidestepping both his recollections and Panchenko's petulant anger, Kazin said: 'We've moved ahead.'

'And he appeared surprised, too,' continued Panchenko. 'Almost like he regarded it as some sort of joke. I couldn't understand until later. Then I remembered his slow reaction in the bedroom. And the pills. He'd already taken his tranquillizers . . .' Panchenko sniggered to himself and Kazin looked curiously across the car at the man. Panchenko went on: 'It *must* have been the tranquillizers. They were what made everything that much easier.'

'Something else only you and I know?' demanded Kazin. He was driving parallel with the river now, only vaguely aware of the direction in which they were travelling.

'Who else could be told!' demanded Panchenko, still showing irritation. 'I didn't know anything about pills at the beginning, of course. So I was apprehensive: I knew those initial moments were the greatest risk. When he might say something involving you . . .'

'And he didn't!' seized Kazin. It was the most important question of all, the cause of the fear lumping inside him like a weight, pulling him down.

'No,' confirmed Panchenko and just as Kazin was

about carelessly to release a sigh of relief he added: 'Not then.'

'Not then!'

'He started to talk so to cut him off I spoke over him. The official approach, about there being an order for his arrest. It deflected him because he asked what the offence was . . .' Panchenko hesitated and said: 'There's a difficulty here.'

'What?' demanded Kazin.

'When Malik reached me at Gofkovskoye he said it was about Afghanistan: that's how I was able to warn you. When Agayans asked about the offence, I had to say that I did not know. If I'd said Afghanistan he would definitely have used your name,' said the colonel.

'I appreciate the caution,' said Kazin. 'I don't see the problem.'

'I've had to say that in the report to Malik because the squad were witness to the entire conversation. And tell him the same during that damned interrogation,' said Panchenko. 'But Malik will surely remember he told me?'

Kazin turned over the Moskva bridge to double back upon himself on the far side of the river, considering the question. 'So what?' he demanded after several minutes. 'He told you in a telephone call, you told Agayans you didn't know. It would have been easy enough for you to have forgotten.'

'Would you have forgotten, in the same circumstances?'

'Certainly that alone isn't sufficient to cause any deeper investigation,' said Kazin, avoiding the question.

'Let's hope the other things aren't.'

'What other things?'

'When I got to the apartment I still hadn't worked out how I was going to be able to do it. Agayans being in his nightclothes made it easy, because it meant he would have to change. And it was he who suggested it. I've told Malik and put in the report that he showed fear and was subservient: but I don't think that was his attitude at all. I think it was the tranquillizers again. He couldn't think properly . . .'

'To our benefit, surely!' broke in Kazin again.

'I hope so,' said Panchenko. 'I hope, if they're questioned, that the others don't say he was drugged.'

Kazin supposed the other man's nitpicking doubts were understandable but he didn't regard that as a serious risk, any more than the man not having initially mentioned Afghanistan. *Initially*, recalled Kazin. Urgently he said: 'So he asked to get dressed?'

'I saw it as the opportunity – *exactly* – that I wanted. As he set out towards the corridor leading into the bedroom I went with him. But at the beginning of the corridor he stopped. And *that* was when he asked again what it was all about and I said Afghanistan. He came out of his lethargy at that. Said it was nonsense and that you could sort it out: that it could all be settled by a telephone call. He was angry. He turned back into the room – there was a telephone on a table near the entrance – and that's when I saw what was happening . . .'

'What!' demanded Kazin. He hadn't intended it but the question came out as a shout.

'That fucking major, Chernov! He'd started to follow,' recounted Panchenko. 'For a few seconds I didn't know what to do. Agayans was already going back into the room. I stopped him and told him to call from the bedroom: said there should be privacy. He nodded, seeming to agree. So he went on down the corridor and I stopped Chernov and walked back with him to the others. I didn't know what the hell to say! I improvised and set out the supposed travelling arrangements back to headquarters. Then I told them to stay where they were and wait for me and caught up as quickly as possible with Agayans. He hadn't started to change. He was by the side of the bed, confused. The telephone was on the same table as the pills. I stopped just inside the door: it was then that he told me what the pills were for. He said he'd better call you and he supposed you would be home. I was moving around the bed: he had his back to me, concentrating on the telephone. It seemed difficult for him: he turned, I think to ask me something. Maybe your home number. I don't know. That was when he saw the gun in my hand. He yelled out, like he was suddenly waking up. Which I guess he was . . .'

' . . . What did he yell?'

'No!' replied Panchenko. 'That's what he said. No! He came towards me, as if he were going to try to fight me and I shot him: it blew him back, over the table and on to the bed. The others were coming: running. I heard them. I was still leaning over him, pressing his hand around the gun when they came in. I don't think they saw what I did: I think the bed hid me.'

'Think!' demanded Kazin, isolating the uncertainty. 'You don't *know!*' Kazin drew the car against the side of the road, into the darkness of a park. Illogically he wondered which park it was and couldn't decide and irritably dismissed it as the intrusion it was. 'I've got to know *everything* about that moment. About his shouting and your firing and their coming into the room.'

Panchenko thought, annoyed, that this meeting was practically a repeat of the humiliating encounter with Malik. He said: 'Agayans had closed but not locked the door. I opened it quietly and I know he did not hear me come in. He was half turned away from me, oblivious to anything behind him. I didn't completely close it, just left it ajar: having got in without his hearing I didn't want to alert him by the slightest noise. When I saw him by the table I thought he appeared uncertain whether or not to take any more pills. It was at that moment he heard me move. As I started from the door area there was a sound – a floorboard, I don't know – and he turned and he saw me. He didn't seem alarmed, not at that actual moment . . .'

'The gun?' intervened Kazin. 'Weren't you holding the gun?'

Panchenko hesitated, not immediately responding. Then he said: 'That's the biggest problem.'

Kazin was twisted in his seat, looking directly across the vehicle at the other man. He saw Panchenko's head go forward, practically an admission of defeat.

'I had no time to prepare,' said the man, mounting a defence before an attack. 'I intended getting an untrace-

80

able weapon: something from the militia evidence store on Pushkinskaya. But when Malik called, I couldn't . . .'

'What did you use!'

'My own.'

'Your own! You were at a weapons training area! There had to be guns everywhere!'

'There aren't!' protested Panchenko in immediate rejection. 'The security at Gofkovskoye is absolute: everything checked and double-checked and recorded and attributed. Don't you think I saw the irony: was exasperated, surrounded with every sort of weapon and unable to use any of them, knowing a forensic examination would show up the source at once!'

Kazin was impatient with the explanation. He said: 'You put Agayans' hand around the butt, to get the fingerprints recorded. So where now is your gun, identifiably issued against your name?'

'I've got it back,' disclosed Panchenko. 'When they burst into the room I said I couldn't stop him shooting himself and that they were to call an ambulance. Having put the damned thing in the man's hand I took it out again, in front of them. Went through an absurd charade of putting a pencil in the muzzle to keep the prints intact and actually delivered it myself to our forensic section. Let them do their tests and got it back, yesterday: I'm responsible for security there, as well.'

'How?'

'Last night. Late. Used my own key.'

'What if they've checked the registration number?'

'They haven't,' insisted Panchenko. 'I opened the file drawer and read everything they'd done so far. There was just a ballistics test and the confirmation that the prints upon the butt were those of Agayans. At the moment, apart from Malik's intervention, this is still being treated as a suicide witnessed by me: not a crime that needs any deep investigation.'

'What's the explanation for the gun disappearing if Malik presses the investigation?'

'Not ours to provide,' said Panchenko easily. 'Forensic sign a receipt for exhibits: theirs is the responsibility for loss. And I shall be the person called in to investigate.' The man's head came up and Kazin revised his impression of defeat: now Panchenko's movement appeared almost triumphant.

'I think you're safe there,' conceded Kazin. 'Nothing could link it with you.'

'Us,' corrected Panchenko pointedly. 'Link it with us.'

Kazin had wondered how long it would be in coming. The anger fired through him but he gave no outward sign: now was most definitely not the time to confront the man and put him in his place with the reminder of his previous crimes. 'Us,' Kazin agreed. Then he said: 'What happened when the others came into the bedroom?'

'I'm *sure* the bed concealed what I was doing; it had to be the most natural thing in the world to be kneeling over the body of a prisoner who had just killed himself!' said Panchenko, with the renewed confidence of his explanation for retrieving the gun. 'And there was a lot of confusion, jostling, in the doorway.'

'What about Agayans' shout?'

For the first time Panchenko looked across the car and in the uncertain light Kazin was conscious of the man nodding his head in acknowledgement of another weakness being isolated. Panchenko said: 'I had to improvise again here, of course. Agayans wouldn't be shouting "No!" if he were killing himself.'

'But the rest of the squad would surely have heard it?'

'Unquestionably,' accepted Panchenko. 'But the corridor has an angled bend. And I'd pushed-to the bedroom door. I gambled on what they heard being blurred, indistinct. As they came in I said: "I shouted to him not to do it but I couldn't get to him in time." '

'And they accepted it was you?'

'There was no challenge,' replied Panchenko. 'The instinct of men trained militarily is to accept the explanation of a superior officer.'

'Which leaves the uncertainty of whether or not Chernov was aware of any conversation between you and Agayans at the beginning of the corridor,' reminded Kazin.

'I tried to allow for that, too,' said Panchenko. 'I let Malik extend the interrogation while I tried to work out how to cover Chernov hearing what was said. It was the best I could think of at the time: I said when he realized I was coming to the bedroom with him Agayans insisted on getting dressed in privacy.'

'And Malik accepted that?'

'No,' conceded Panchenko. 'He accused me of bad policing. But that's all it is: bad policing. Agayans and I talked softly. We've got to take the chance of Chernov realizing a conversation took place but not hearing Afghanistan being mentioned . . .' The hesitation was intentional. 'Or your name.'

Kazin understood the pause. Like he understood the security colonel using the plural 'we'. He let both go, like the earlier threat. He said: 'What have you done?'

'I had Chernov submit a report. Insisted it should be complete.'

'And?'

'He makes no reference at all to the corridor conversation. And attributes the shout in the bedroom to me.'

'The rest of the squad?'

'The same.'

Not bad, admitted Kazin. Far better, in fact, than he had expected from the earlier panicked telephone call from the man. Kazin said: 'Anything else that might be challenged?'

Panchenko considered the question and said: 'Malik kept making demands about timekeeping. I had to say I only went to Agayans' bedroom when I became concerned about the amount of time he had been in there. So I had to create a time gap greater than really occurred. I said it was ten minutes from the time Agayans left the room, before I went in: it wasn't more than a minute or two.'

Searching for the dangers, Kazin said: 'There's one thing missing. How did Malik discover what was going on in Afghanistan, to be able to stop it, as he did?'

'I don't know,' admitted Panchenko.

'Wasn't there any indication at all where his information came from?'

'Nothing.'

A brilliant intelligence officer, remembered Kazin: that had been the assessment of Malik when they had graduated together from the training academy while his had only been commended. He said: 'What about the son in Afghanistan, Yuri Vasilivich? Did Malik mention him?'

'Not once.'

Still too much he didn't know, thought Kazin irritably. He said: 'There's to be an inquiry, at Malik's demand.'

'I've already received a witness summons.'

Like I have, thought Kazin. He said: 'I want a tight rein kept on the others who formed the squad with you that night. They're to inform you if they are questioned: particularly if they're questioned by Malik.'

'It is regulations anyway that they do so.'

'Reinforce it,' insisted Kazin. 'The only danger is what Chernov might have overheard.'

'I don't see how I can avoid being accused of negligence by the inquiry,' said Panchenko.

Kazin sought for a reassuring response but couldn't think of one. So he said: 'No, neither do I.'

'It will not be good, so soon after promotion.'

'Better than accusations of other things,' said Kazin at last.

Panchenko met threat with threat. 'You'll support me? It's important I know you'll support me.'

With no alternative Kazin said: 'Of course I'll support you.'

'I'm glad,' continued Panchenko, maintaining the pressure, 'After all any problem for me will be a problem for you, won't it?'

'Yes,' conceded Kazin, mouth a tight line. 'It can't be otherwise.'

Kazin recognized that with Panchenko he had created a potentially difficult problem for himself. Kazin revised, too, his earlier impression of sweated uncertainty in the man. At times as they talked Kazin believed he'd detected in the colonel an almost overconfident belief – conceit even – that there was some sort of equal partnership between them. For the moment it was an impression for Panchenko to be allowed. But some way would have to be found of dispensing with the man. Kazin said: 'Maintain tonight's account and I do not foresee any difficulty for us. Reprimand, perhaps. But that's all.'

'I would rather not be reprimanded at all: not be summoned before an inquiry at all.'

Neither would I, thought Kazin. He felt a burn of frustration at the awareness that his already weak position was being further eroded while Malik's was strengthening. He'd tried to mount his attack too soon, without proper thought. To the colonel he said: 'Beware of Vasili Dmitrevich Malik. He's a bad enemy to have.'

'So am I,' said Panchenko, bombastic as before.

And as such you will always be taunted and goaded, thought Kazin. Determined upon every precaution, he said: 'Post everyone in that squad as far away from Moscow as possible. And as soon as it's practicable to do so.'

There had been no indication in the recall messages to Kabul exactly what Yuri was expected to do upon his return to Moscow: where he was to live, for instance. Uncertainly, he called his father from Sheremet'yevo airport and was surprised by the apparent eagerness with which the older man greeted him, ordering him at once to Kutuzovsky Prospekt.

In the taxi Yuri gazed out over the flat plain that spreads like a voluminous skirt before Moscow, conscious of how unfamiliar everything looked to him, although he had been away for less than a year. There was an occasional wooden house – sometimes two or three clustered together – but the view was predominantly of trees, birch and fir mostly. It hadn't occurred to him until now but there didn't seem to be any trees in Afghanistan. How long, he wondered, would this respite last?

His father responded at once when he sounded the

apartment bell. The old man said: 'I'm glad you're safely here, Yuri Vasilivich.'

Yuri's airport surprise returned. 'What is it?' he said.

The witnesses' list he had obtained that morning of people who had been summoned to appear before the inquiry removed any doubt from Malik's mind of Kazin's involvement. Malik said: 'I think an attempt has been made to bring me down . . . maybe bring both of us down.'

Yuri couldn't recognize the sensation he immediately experienced, a feeling he'd never known before. Was this what fear felt like?

10

Yevgennie Levin had naturally never been a prospective buyer but he had watched a lot of American television advertising praising the integrity of estate agents and imagined this had to resemble the real experience. Proctor cupped Galina's arm almost protectively in his hand to guide her to the chintz-decorated drawing room, heavy with a furniture style the Russian did not yet know to be New England, deferring to Levin when they came to something he described as a den, which had some books and a stocked bar and a TV set with the screen almost as large as he'd encountered in the few cinemas he had visited, but then going back to Galina for approval when they came to the kitchen. It was a huge laboratory of a place, a refrigerator/freezer larger than a grown man, with a soft-drink dispensing device in its front, a cooking hob separate from an oven controlled by a cockpit of knobs and a preparation area clustered with mixers and blenders and cutters and grinders, like mushrooms in a dawn field. There were seats for eight around a large, long table but Levin guessed another four could be accommodated with room sufficient to spread their arms. And a dining room, in addition. Again there was a lot of heavy furniture, this time including a serving sideboard and an open-fronted cupboard displaying glasses of every size. There was a downstairs lavatory and a further two upstairs, each separate from the two bathrooms, the larger of which was en suite to the main bedroom and included a jacuzzi fitment in the actual bath, with a slide-door shower and a bidet. There was a bidet in the second bathroom and Levin hoped Petr – who was regarding it curiously – would not ask him what it was for because he didn't know either. The master bedroom had a walk-in dressing area, with sliding-door closets extending along two walls and a four-poster bed complete with canopy.

At its foot was a manoeuvrable television and there were further television sets in each of the other three bedrooms, but there the beds were not canopied.

On the upstairs level Proctor let the obviously impressed Galina and Petr move away from them, taking Levin back into the master bedroom and pulling aside the heavy drapes of the bed. There was a red button, set in a white surround. The American said: 'It'll never be necessary because this is a CIA safe property and the protection here makes Fort Knox look like the gingerbread house. But it's a panic button. They're on every floor: I'll show you where . . .' As he talked Proctor went across to the mullioned windows, rapping the glass hard. 'Not just double glazed,' he said dismissively. 'This stuff is resistant up to the impact of an Armalite . . .' He turned away, smiling. 'Again, quite unnecessary. We want you to know how safe you are, Yevgennie.'

'It's reassuring,' said the Russian.

'The entire property is walled: you wouldn't have seen that last night when you came in, but I'll show you around later,' went on the FBI man. 'The wall is electronically sensored. In addition there are ground sensors: three separate arrangements, in fact. Absolutely undetectable: look just like blades of grass, believe me. There's also television and video monitoring: three separate guardhouses, manned twenty-four hours a day. The video is infra-red. Operates at night like it's noon on a summer's day.'

'Seems very safe,' said Levin, knowing it was expected.

'Nothing's been forgotten,' Proctor pressed on. 'There'll be ground guards, in addition to those in the watch houses. And household staff: a cook and a maid. Our people, of course: completely vetted.'

'It's going to be difficult to adjust,' said Levin.

Proctor went to speak and then stopped and Levin wondered if the man intended a remark about the difficulties of adjustment. Instead the American said: 'Here for reassurance, really. Just until you settle in.'

'Where are we?' demanded Levin.

Proctor hesitated, smiling, then said: 'That's not

important, Yevgennie. What's important is your recognizing how highly we regard you. How safe you are.'

So they didn't trust him. Levin supposed it was naive for him to have expected trust, this soon. He'd estimated four hours' driving and he'd watched the speedometer and knew they had obeyed the speed limit. They'd crossed the East River, not the Hudson: he was sure of that although the curtains had been drawn in the rear section of the car and the glass separating them from the driver had been smoked. Upstate New York? Or further?

'This isn't your permanent home, of course . . .' resumed Proctor.

' . . . A debriefing place,' interrupted Levin.

'Here for as long as it takes,' picked up the American. 'A tutor for Petr, until he's ready for enrolment at a school. Any help Galina wants: language lessons, things like that.'

'It seems very comprehensive,' said Levin.

'You're not the first,' reminded Proctor. 'We've had a lot of practice. When the debriefing's over there'll be another house. Wherever you choose. New identities. A pension to live on.'

Levin was uncertain whether to risk the question because there was a risk in being premature. Deciding it fitted naturally into the conversation, he said: 'Pensions are for people who retire.'

'What do you mean?' asked Proctor at once.

Careful, thought Levin. Intentionally vague, he said: 'I don't know: I've just never thought of stopping work. I could get a job, I suppose? I don't know what, but a job. Would that be possible once I'd completely assimilated?'

'I imagine so,' said Proctor, intentionally vague himself. 'I'd have to talk it through with people.'

Time to retreat, Levin recognized. He was the one who now smiled. He said: 'We're getting a little ahead of ourselves, aren't we. What about immediately?'

'Move about a bit,' said Proctor reassuringly. 'Get to know the place. We're meeting Billy Bowden in a while. He'll be taking you through things.'

'Debriefing?'

'He's a nice guy.' Proctor's spectacles came off and went immediately back on again, in his strange mannerism.

'What about us? You and I?'

'From time to time. I was your case officer, don't forget.'

'You made me a promise, David.'

'I haven't forgotten. I'll get on to the State Department.'

'I must have Natalia here with us,' insisted Levin.

'As far as we are concerned she can come tomorrow,' insisted Proctor. 'That's a decision for your people.'

'I don't think I could stand it without her. Certainly Galina couldn't.'

'I'll do everything I can,' promised Proctor. 'My word.' The American paused and then said: 'What about Petr? That was kind of a strange outburst last night.'

'I could hardly have prepared him for what was to happen, could I?'

'I guess he'll settle down,' agreed Proctor.

'I hope so,' said Levin sincerely. Not enough attention had been given to how Petr might react.

'Let's take in the grounds,' suggested Proctor.

Obediently Levin followed the other man from the house, gazing intently around the moment he was outside. The house was white clapboard, dominating a rise with lawns sweeping away on every side to what appeared to be a fringe of completely encircling trees. The treeline was so thick it was impossible to detect the electrified wall or the guard houses about which Proctor had spoken. Far away to the left – north, south, east or west? – began a ripple of thickly forested promontories but that's all there were, trees. No landmarks; carefully or more likely cleverly chosen, he accepted.

Proctor ignored the sweeping drive, heading off with head bent in concentration across the grass to the right of the main entrance. He stooped suddenly and said: 'There!'

Levin followed the outstretched hand and saw the sensor. It protruded about four inches from the ground, about a quarter of an inch wide and coloured green. It looked as if the outer covering were plastic. Positively identified it was clearly false but otherwise it merged perfectly into the long tufted grass.

'You can hear the worms fart on these things,' guaranteed Proctor. He began walking further towards the trees but a car appeared from where the driveway made a left-hand curve and the American stopped. He said: 'Billy's early.'

They cut diagonally back towards the house, arriving at the same time as the car. Levin saw that it was very dirty, the front and rear bumpers dented from careless parking: there was a further dent, long ignored and rusting, in the rear wing. The driver seemed to unfold from behind the wheel, a towering, heavy man.

'Hi, you guys,' he said.

'Billy Bowden,' identified Proctor.

'Good to see you, Yevgennie,' said Bowden, thrusting out a hair-matted hand: gingerish blond, like the hair that straggled almost to the collar of his checked shirt, open at the neck, without a tie. There was no jacket, either, and the left cuff of his washed-out jeans was caught up against the edge of his half-calf cowboy boots. The metal-strapped watch was very heavy and thick and calibrated, with a number of smaller dials and buttons, the timepiece of an outdoor man: or maybe someone who spent a lot of time underwater swimming.

Practised casual, like the car was practised neglect, Levin decided. He said: 'Hello.'

Bowden made an expansive gesture to include the house and the grounds and said: 'Great place, eh?'

'You've debriefed here before then?' said Levin. Bowden came back to him almost sharply.

'Got on fine with the guy, too,' confirmed Bowden. 'Just like you and I are going to get on fine.'

The friendship appeared genuine — genuine enough, anyway — but Levin knew it wasn't sincere, not even from Proctor with whom he'd dealt for so long. A defector from an intelligence organization was always considered a traitor by members of another intelligence organization.

Bowden confidently led the way back into the house, further showing he knew it well. Proctor allowed Levin to follow directly behind and the Russian got the impression that Bowden was the superior ranking officer. Levin had assumed his debriefer to be FBI but wondered fleetingly if Bowden were CIA. Unlikely, he thought; the Moscow legend had always been that the rivalry between the CIA and FBI matched that which existed between the KGB and the GRU. The Moscow account could always be wrong, of course. Bowden went directly to what had been described as the den, standing legs astride in front of the fireplace. It was laid with logs but unlighted. He said: 'Dave explained things to you?'

The FBI would have maintained a case file upon him and it was logical Bowden would know everything in it, Levin accepted. He said: 'Yes.'

Bowden grinned, as broadly as he appeared to do everything else. 'No positive ground rules, Yevgennie. We'll just kick things around. Chat.'

Levin considered the lie to be a stupid one. An interrogation had to be structured: it was basic tradecraft. If they were to talk one to one then everything was being recorded. He glanced idly around the room, wondering where the apparatus was concealed. He said: 'I'll take my guidance from you.'

'Everything at your speed,' insisted the man. 'You feel like stopping, we stop. OK?'

'OK,' said the Russian.

'You feel comfortable enough with English? Or would you prefer Russian?'

So Bowden was bilingual. Levin supposed that was logical, too, but he hadn't expected it. He said: 'English is fine.'

'You want to, you can change your mind any time,' offered the man.

'I'll remember.'

'And nothing today,' said Bowden. 'This is just getting to know each other.'

'I think I should get going,' said Proctor.

'Don't forget Natalia!' demanded Levin urgently.

'Trust me, Yevgennie,' said the man.

'We all know the importance of getting the girl across,' said Bowden.

The debriefer seemed to know everything, thought Levin. To Proctor he said: 'When will we meet again?'

Proctor looked briefly at the other American and then said: 'How about a month?'

'Too long,' said Levin at once.

'Nothing is going to happen quickly,' said Proctor, using his spectacles like worry beads. 'It's going to take a lot of negotiation.'

Levin nodded, accepting the fact. 'Not longer than a month, even if there's nothing positive.'

'Definitely a month,' guaranteed Proctor.

The man seemed embarrassed at the moment of departure, as if he were unsure how to break the contact. Abruptly he put out his hand and, surprised, Levin took it. It was something they had never done before: but every previous encounter had been clandestine when neither had wanted to appear aware of the other.

'Everything is going to work out fine, Yevgennie. Just fine,' said Proctor at the door, in familiar reassurance.

'He's right, you know,' said Bowden after the man had gone.

'I'm trying to think so,' said Levin.

'There's got to be one or two formalities,' announced Bowden.

'Formalities?'

'You know what the business is like, Yevgennie. Everyone claiming their little bit of turf . . . the technical people want in.'

'How?' asked Levin, guessing the answer.

'An independent check,' said the American. 'A polygraph.'

The lie detector: so they *didn't* trust him. Levin said: 'After all I've done!'

'Not my idea,' insisted Bowden. 'Don't you think I haven't told them it's a stupid waste of time?'

No, thought Levin. His reaction would be another test, he realized. He said: 'Don't worry about it. Of course I'll take a lie-detector test.'

They didn't eat that evening in the dining room, agreeing without any discussion to a shared discomfort at the surroundings: even the kitchen eating area seemed overwhelmingly lavish. The uneasiness was heightened by having people cook and wait upon them: twice Galina half rose, instinctively moving to clear away or fetch something, then hurriedly sat again. The second time she actually blushed. The food – steak for the main course – was good and there was wine but none of them ate or drank very much. There was hardly any conversation, either. Petr did not speak throughout, not until the very end of the meal.

Then he said: 'What about Natalia?'

'We're getting her out,' said Levin.

The exaggeration was obvious and the boy seized upon it. 'Getting her out? How? When?'

'It's being arranged.'

'Who by?'

'The Americans.'

'Rubbish!' rejected Petr. 'The Americans can't arrange that. And you know it.'

'Respect your father!' intruded Galina, thoughtless with the words.

Petr seized that, too. 'What's there to respect about him any more?'

'She'll be got out,' insisted Levin doggedly.

'When?' Petr repeated.

'As soon as possible.'

'You're pitiful!' spat out the boy.

'You'll understand, one day,' said Levin, flushing at the cliché.

'What do you imagine I am going to do?'

'There is going to be a tutor. School later, when you've completely adjusted,' said Levin.

'Adjusted?'

'Settled in.'

'You think I'm going to stay here!'

94

'Of course you are.'

'You're the defector, not me,' said Petr, leaning across the table, his face contorted by contempt. 'I'm Russian. And I'm going to stay Russian. Always.'

Having initiated it, Vasili Malik had been excluded from any of the inquiry planning, and its timing worked against what he'd hoped to achieve. The official reaction to the thwarted Kabul operation had been immediate outrage. Which resulted in the commission – headed by KGB chairman Victor Chebrikov himself – being empanelled in just over twenty-four hours and the sittings being convened within three days, not the weeks which Malik had expected. He did not, either, have any investigatory role in the presented evidence. Nor sufficient evidence – beyond suspicion – to demand in the time available that the interrogation of Panchenko be extended by other examiners to the rest of the arrest squad that had gone that night to Agayans' apartment with the security chief.

Victor Ivanovich Kazin was censured for lax and careless bureaucracy and Lev Konstantinovich Panchenko was officially criticized for lax and careless policing.

Malik, more convinced after than before the inquiry that he had been an intended victim of the Kabul operation, considered the outcome a travesty.

The further findings – effusive praise for himself, for interceding as he had, and an official commendation for Yuri, for his part in preventing a disaster – did nothing to balance Malik's dismayed fury. The major conclusion, absolute condemnation of the medically proven unstable (and clearly maverick) Igor Fedorovich Agayans, only worsened that fury.

'A commendation!' said Yuri, tasting the sound of the word in the car taking them from the inquiry direct to the dacha in the Lenin Hills, not to the Kutuzovsky apartment. The image of the dacha – and a Zil like that in which they were travelling – had been one of the younger man's first reactions standing back there, listening to the praise accorded to him. When there was no reply Yuri believed his father had failed to hear him so he said: 'I thought the verdicts were very good.'

'They were absurd!'

Yuri frowned sideways across the luxury limousine. 'You were officially praised!'

'They survived!' said Malik bitterly, gazing straight ahead as the vehicle climbed from the sprawl of the city. 'Escaped, both of them.' Malik stopped talking, deep inside himself. He said nothing for several moments and then faintly, almost in private conversation, said: 'Kazin was always good at avoiding responsibility for what he did.'

Yuri remained gazing curiously across the car. 'It sounds as if you've known him for a long time?'

Malik appeared to become aware of his son, answering the stare and smiling, without humour. 'Once my life depended upon him,' Malik said suddenly. He humped the misshapen shoulder and said: 'I would have died if he hadn't got me to the field hospital . . .'

' . . . You were in Stalingrad together?'

Malik's empty smile broadened. 'I was too heavy, too big, for him to carry. He found a bicycle, an abandoned German machine, and folded me over it. The front wheel was buckled and apparently I fell off twice. Actually broke a rib, apart from this. He was in a direct line of Nazi fire for a long time. As long as thirty minutes, I was told later. He was awarded a medal: Defender of the Nation.'

'So what . . . ?' started Yuri but his father shook his head, stopping him.

'The siege wasn't absolute at that stage,' remembered Malik, the recollections coming piecemeal. 'I could not be moved, of course: I had no value anyway. But he could . . . it wasn't the KGB then: then we were both in the Eastern division of Beria's NKGB. Kazin was flown out because Moscow thought Stalingrad was going to be overrun and Beria wanted to salvage as much of his intelligence personnel as he could.'

'I still don't understand . . .' tried Yuri again but once more his father stopped him.

Malik said: 'There was a time when I actually wished he hadn't bothered: that Kazin had let me die.'

Back at the First Chief Directorate headquarters the man about whom they were talking stood at the window of his office, gazing out over the bee-swarming weekend traffic, still hardly able to rationalize his escape. There was only one central thought in Kazin's mind: he'd got away with it! Censure, certainly, which was a further minus in his official file. But still an incredible escape, considering how badly against him it could have gone: all it would have needed was just one piece of incriminating documentary evidence from Agayans' secretariat – which there hadn't been – and now he would be in Lefortovo prison instead of back here in his own warm, protected quarters. Not the easy chess game he'd imagined it to be, accepted Kazin honestly. Nor a personal disaster, either. Today had been a setback, that's all: a setback from which he could recover. And *would* recover. He had a promise to fulfil. And not just to himself; to someone else, as well.

11

It was what the Russians call a gift day, a break in the late autumn weather already breathing winter's cold, the sun throbbing from a cloudless sky and the air heavy with heat. The protective shutters were closed, as they always were during the week, so it was cool inside and it stayed that way after they opened them to the brightness. The double glazing would help to keep it cold, Yuri guessed, just like it kept the country house warm in winter. The house was wood shingled over a timber frame, with an encircling verandah built high to allow for the winter snows, and the log store was raised on stilts, for the same reason. The main room was dominated by a wood-burning stove.

Yuri knew the use of all government guest houses was expected to be transient but realized that his father had been accorded the use of this place for as long as he could remember: even as a child, with his nurse, he had been brought here at weekends to play out among the trees or the stream that ran through the property. Yet never had his father made any attempt to impose his own personality upon the place; bothered to alter the government-decreed decor or the government-decreed furnishings. The wood stove, which smoked and made his eyes sting, and the huge flocked bedcover and the rustic drapes and the prints of brave soldiers marching out to fight in the Patriotic War remained as he recalled from those childhood days: as if, despite the length of time he'd been allowed its use, the old man didn't expect his occupation to be anything but transient either.

The only additions to the property appeared to be the photographs upon two side tables and a third upon the mantelpiece over the wood stove of a fair-haired, shyly smiling woman in a buttoned-to-the-neck-dress whom he had never known but had been told was his mother.

Perhaps the dacha would have been different, been a home instead of a temporary resting place, if she had not died giving birth to him. He wondered if he had inherited his fair hair from her.

Yuri helped his father carry their weekend provisions into the kitchen, original and basic like everything else. There was a cold pantry instead of a refrigerator and the cooker was wood fired and smoked only slightly less than the heating stove in the main room. It had to be fired summer as well as winter, because there was no hot-water system, so everything had to be heated upon it, just like the big-bellied boiler in the outhouse had to be stoked to provide water for the enamelled bath which was also in the outhouse and therefore unusable at those occasional freezing times of the winter when it was possible to come up from the city. He watched his father unpack, aware that only the bread and the milk were fresh. Everything else was in tins and once more he had the impression of being in transit, equipped with provisions that were easily transportable.

His father had halted the stop-start reminiscence long before they reached the dacha. Hoping to prompt him into beginning again, Yuri said, immediately after they had unpacked, 'I still don't understand why you consider the inquiry such a failure.'

'Let's walk,' suggested the other man.

Yuri did not find the suggestion out of place. Yuri thought it odd for someone so awkwardly affected by permanent injury to make walking his only concession to physical exercise. One of his frequent student recollections was trailing around Moscow at his father's heels, panting to keep up. The limp appeared to have worsened since their last such expedition and his father seemed to have developed a sagging stomach and become thicker around the hips, too. Yuri wondered if he would inherit a tendency to fat. Hopefully not, he thought: he lacked his father's height by several inches. Another legacy from his unknown mother? So much he didn't know: could never know.

As he followed his father across the verandah, he

thought that when he was awarded his own dacha – and who could doubt it would eventually be awarded, after the praise of today's enquiry? – he would do the opposite to his father and very much stamp his own personality upon it. He'd insist upon his own decoration and certainly dictate the fittings. Which would most definitely include a proper hot-water bathroom, not the ball-freezing torture of his father's outhouse.

They reached the bank of the stream meandering through the grounds. It appeared wider and deeper than last time and Yuri stared around, caught by the impression of remoteness. Trees encircled them on three sides and there was emptiness on the fourth, beyond the water, apart from a wooden cottage – or maybe it was a shed – far away in a fold of a hill, like an ornament on a shelf. There was no sign of life around it. Nearer, directly over the water, insects startled awake by the unexpected heat misted in surprised confusion and birds – swallows he thought, although he was not sure – dived and swooped, to feed on the unexpected feast. Probably eating better than he would, from the contents of the cans back in the house, Yuri thought. The older man sat awkwardly on the grass beside the stream, an abrupt, slumping movement that reminded Yuri of a large animal, a horse or a cow maybe, collapsing to rest. The irreverent reflection made him feel uncomfortable: he wondered why, now, he seemed so conscious of his father's deformity. He sat down too, waiting.

'I think Agayans' death is suspicious,' announced Malik abruptly.

'How suspicious?'

'Possibly that it wasn't suicide,' said Malik. His son's disbelief was obvious and Malik regretted beginning so dramatically: he wanted agreement, not doubt. More carefully he told of his interview with Panchenko and of learning the man's sponsorship by Kazin and why, because of the quickness with which the inquiry had been convened, he had not been able to extend the necessary interrogation to the rest of the seizure squad on the night of Agayans' death.

Throughout the explanation Yuri sat nodding, not needing to be convinced of the absurdity of what had been proposed in Kabul but finding difficulty with everything else. When his father stopped talking, Yuri said: 'You believe he was killed!'

'Such things have happened before.'

'In Stalin's day, maybe. Not now.'

'There are still a lot of people nostalgic for Stalin's days,' insisted Malik. 'The sort of people who don't want the type of changes being introduced now.'

No! rejected Yuri. Dzerzhinsky Square politics and infighting maybe, but not killing. This was real life, reality, not fiction. The reflection brought him up short. He leaned forward curiously towards his father and said: 'Would you? Kill, I mean?' and was surprised when there was not an immediate dismissal.

Instead Malik remained silent for several moments, carefully choosing his reply. Then he said: 'Not cold bloodedly: premeditatedly. But I think I could kill someone who tried to kill me.'

'That's not an answer to the question,' said the younger man, refusing his father the escape. 'What you're talking about is self-defence, against attack.'

Again there was a hesitation and then the man said: 'Isn't that what we *are* talking about: ourselves being under attack?'

Now it was Yuri's turn to remain silent. The second answer was better than the first but he still couldn't conceive that the paunchy, high-shouldered man idly plucking at grass tufts with his hand honestly meant what he was saying. It was like debating with a complete stranger. At once came the contradiction. It wasn't like that at all. Rather it was getting to know the man for the first time, if it weren't preposterous to imagine getting to know his father for the first time at the age of twenty-three. Preposterous or not, that was definitely his feeling. He said: 'What are you going to do?'

'Inquiries can be reopened,' suggested Malik.

'You're going to interrogate the rest of the squad?'

'To start with.'

'What else?'

'I haven't decided yet, not completely. Save things, certainly.'

'Save things?'

'I've made copies, of everything. Files, cipher records, Panchenko's report: even the diary entries.'

'Isn't that taking a risk?'

'It's the sort of risk you had to decide upon in Kabul . . . which I'm glad you did, incidentally.'

'Will it be difficult, to reopen the inquiry?'

'Impossible without some evidence directly contradictory to that already presented,' admitted Malik.

Yuri shifted from the position in which he was sitting, although his discomfort was not physical. The night of his arrival from Kabul his father had suggested that the scheming might involve him, as well. He said: 'What else can you do? Something positive, I mean?'

'Nothing, not unless I get the proper evidence,' conceded Malik.

It was all too uncertain, thought Yuri. And he didn't like uncertainty. Along with all the other formative-year images of his father, Yuri had always considered the man to be invulnerable. He did not like the sudden contradiction. Reminded by the reflection of Kabul, Yuri said: 'But you're in the superior position now?'

'Yes,' agreed Malik.

'I don't want to stay any longer in Afghanistan.'

Malik nodded reflectively. 'Yes,' he said. 'I can intercede now. In fact to do so would show up Kazin's weakness. I've got to capitalize upon that as much as I can.'

Yuri was about to speak again when the telephone shrilled, back in the house. He watched his father lope back in his odd, rocking gait, aware there was another explanation he was still lacking. It was a very quick call, the older man reappearing almost at once from the house to return, head sunk in thought against his chest, to where they had been sitting. He didn't sit again, so Yuri had to squint up against the sunlight.

'There even seems to be a vacancy for you,' Malik said. 'There's been a defection, in New York.'

'You didn't tell me what happened between you and Kazin,' reminded Yuri.

For several moments his father remained staring down at him and because of the brightness it was difficult for Yuri to see the expression on the man's face. Then Malik said: 'I know I didn't,' and turned back towards the dacha.

The supposed compartmenting failed to prevent the outcome of the inquiry becoming known throughout every department and Vladislav Belov approached the meeting with the censured Kazin even more reluctantly than he had on the previous occasion, when they'd finalized the American operation. Angry, too, at Kazin stupidly initiating the defection without any consultation. The whole scheme could have been ruined: might still be. In Dzerzhinsky Square there could be a whirlpool effect from being linked to a sinking man, and Kazin appeared inevitably to be sinking.

'The timing was premature,' Belov said, immediately critical.

'I didn't consider it to be,' said Kazin. He knew this was going to provide a better recovery than he'd already imagined: when it all meshed together, like cogs engaging a gear, it would erase completely the setback of the tribunal. Beneath the desk his leg pumped in its usual nervousness.

'The promise to Levin was always that they could go together, as a family.'

'Keeping the girl makes it look more genuine.'

'What if Levin hadn't crossed?'

'He didn't have a choice. There was the evidence of his association with the FBI and he knew it.'

Belov succeeded in keeping the incredulity from showing, but only just. Surely the mad fool would not have done that? Unless he *was* mad. He said: 'You mean she's some sort of hostage?'

'After the blandishments of the West, wasn't there a possibility of his defection being genuine?' asked Kazin, question for question.

'It wasn't necessary,' insisted Belov. He wondered if the other man believed the reflection he saw in his shaving mirror every morning.

'I thought it was,' said Kazin, in the voice of a superior indicating that the conversation was at an end. 'It's an academic discussion anyway. He *did* defect.'

Belov refused to be dismissed, seeing the weakness. He said: 'Isn't the greater risk of the defection *becoming* genuine because of our keeping the child? Of his trusting the Americans more than us?'

'He'd know that way there'd never be a chance of his seeing her again,' rejected Kazin. 'Holding the daughter ensures that Levin behaves exactly as we want him to. As it's been planned.'

'She's to be allowed to leave, then?' seized Belov.

'In time,' said Kazin. 'When the proper indications start to come from America. Which is what we're supposed to be discussing.'

'Activate Kapalet?'

'At once,' ordered Kazin. 'But just sufficient at this stage to start the panic: nothing more than a hint from which the Americans can discover for themselves that there's a Soviet spy within the CIA.'

'Could we in future discuss everything in advance?'

'I guarantee it,' said Kazin.

Liar, thought Belov. Or was madman more accurate?

12

The technician appeared modelled for the job, a neatly suited, neatly barbered, neatly precise man who set the polygraph apparatus upon the desk as if lines had been drawn to receive it, placed a file and notebook alongside with matching care and then arranged the chair with similar caution, actually sitting in it himself to measure its positioning and then, dissatisfied, shifting it further out of view of the paper drum to prevent Levin seeing the needle's wavering reaction to the questions.

Levin waited to see if Bowden would make any formal introductions but he didn't. Instead the American appeared fascinated by the preparations, as if he were seeing the set-up for the first time.

When the man straightened, indicating he was ready, Bowden smiled at Levin, gesturing palms-upwards apologetically. 'Waste of time,' he said. The clothes were the same as before, even the shirt, although it appeared freshly pressed.

Would he remember the training? worried Levin. It seemed such a long time ago. 'Whenever you're ready,' he said.

'You don't need me, Doc, do you?'

Levin thought the question was stupid, just as the first-day remark about there being no ground rules had been stupid. Was Bowden genuinely careless? Or was the man intentionally trying to manufacture such an inference to lure him into reacting over-confidently and by so doing become careless himself? It was a possible entrapment.

'No,' said the polygraph operator. 'It'll be better if we're alone.'

Levin's instruction had been that such sessions were always conducted one-to-one. To Bowden he said: 'Will you wait?'

'You're the job now, Yevgennie,' said the American, at the door. 'I'll just grab a cup of coffee.'

Levin realized they wanted an immediate assessment. He wished the training were clearer in his mind.

'Are you familiar with this?' asked the technician.

'No,' lied Levin.

'It might seem complicated but really it's not,' said the man. 'I want you to sit in the chair that I have arranged there. I shall fix attachments to your hand, chest and arm. Monitors. OK so far?'

Levin hesitated before replying, waiting to see if the man would explain the function of the attachments, but he didn't. Palm monitor to measure sweat level, chest band to register perceptible change in breathing pattern, blood-pressure belt around the arm, the Russian recalled, easily. He said: 'I understand.'

'I shall ask you some questions,' continued the operator. 'Here it's important that you remember there can only be yes or no answers. No discussion or explanation. Is that clear?'

He would be expected to query that, decided Levin. He said: 'Is that going to be possible? A straight yes or no can convey a misleading impression.'

'We try to phrase the questions so that doesn't happen,' said the technician. 'It works fine, believe me.'

If it worked fine, why was it possible to cheat the machine, thought Levin. Careful, he warned himself: he hadn't beaten it yet. He said: 'What else?'

'That's it,' assured the man. 'Simple, like I said. Ready to get started?'

'Whenever you like,' agreed Levin. He took his time removing his rumpled, sagging jacket and rolling up his sleeve, trying to bring everything back to mind. The initial questions were actually arranged to get lying replies: if they were answered honestly it indicated training to beat the machine. Essential to avoid that mistake then. A painful distraction was necessary, when the actual test was carried out. At Kuchino he'd put a pebble into his shoe and pressed down hard against it, but that wasn't possible here. Important that the pain didn't cause any perspiration or blood-rate increase. The inside of his mouth, he decided. He'd bite the inside of his mouth until the very moment he had to speak, hard enough to cause discomfort but not hard enough to draw blood. He would have to appear to forget about the yes or no replies, of course: that would be an anticipated mistake. Just like a certain perspiration and heart-rate increase would be expected, because it was a tension situation.

The technician's hands were very cold, attaching the straps. The blood-pressure band to the arm was last and as he secured it the man said: 'Just relax, OK? Nothing to worry about.'

'I'm OK,' announced Levin, I hope, he thought.

The fastidious man walked out of Levin's view and there was the scrape of a chair as he seated himself in front of his apparatus. There was a cough and the man said: 'Do you masturbate?'

Levin recognized the immediate trick question. 'No,' he said.

'Have you ever masturbated?'

'No.'

'Not when you were a kid, at school?'

'No.'

'Is your marriage to Galina happy?'

'Yes.'

'Have you ever had an extra-marital affair?'

'No.'

'Ever had a homosexual affair?'

'No.'

'Never been attracted, homosexually?'

'No.'

'Have you ever indulged in fellatio?'

'No.'

'Have you ever engaged in cunnilingus?'

'No.'

'You've become a traitor, to your country?'

For the first time Levin trapped a piece of his lower lip between his teeth, acknowledging that the technician was good. The testing sex ritual had practically been recited, as if the man were hurrying through the prelimi-

107

naries, and the last query had been posed in the same dull monotone. 'Yes,' he said.

'A willing traitor?'

Time to appear to make a mistake. He managed: 'I am unwilling about . . .' before the other man stopped him.

'Yes or no,' he insisted.

'No.'

'An unwilling traitor?'

'Yes.'

'Were you tricked into defecting?'

'No.'

'But you are unwilling?'

'Yes.' There would be a query in the notebook about the apparent ambiguity.

'Your name is Yevgennie Pavlovich Levin?'

'Yes.' He relaxed the pressure against his lower lip, but only slightly.

'You are forty-three years old?'

'Yes.'

'An officer of the Komitet Gosudarstvennoy Bezopasnosti attached to the Soviet mission at the United Nations?'

'Yes.'

'As an agent operating against the United States of America?'

'Yes.'

'Have you engaged in activities endangering the security of the United States of America?'

Before the sentence was completed the skin was pincered between Levin's teeth but the phrasing of the question made it easier than he expected. 'Yes,' he said.

'Do you regret engaging in activities endangering the security of the United States of America?'

Careful, thought Levin, biting slightly harder. He said: 'No.' There was a pause in the questioning and Levin knew there would be another notebook notation.

'Do you consider yourself a traitor?'

'Yes.'

'Do you imagine you will regret what you have done?'

Need for caution again. 'Yes,' he replied.

'Do you consider the United States of America a freer country than the Union of Soviet Socialist Republics?'

'Yes.'

'Have you become a traitor for money?'

It was necessary permanently to bite now. 'Yes,' Levin said.

'Is money the primary cause for your becoming a traitor?'

'No,' said Levin. The perpetual use of traitor was intentional, he recognized. It was not antagonizing him as it was intended.

'Do you consider you have become a traitor for reasons of ideology?'

'Yes.'

'Do you no longer regard yourself as a communist?'

Time for another lapse. 'I was never . . .'

'Yes or no.'

'No.'

'Do you intend completely to cooperate with people who will be interviewing you in the coming weeks and months?'

'Yes.'

'Cooperating with complete honesty?'

'Yes.' That had not been as difficult as he had feared.

'Have you provided members of the FBI with material concerning the KGB mission within the United Nations?'

'Yes.'

'Was all the information accurate?'

'Yes.'

'Do you have knowledge that you believe will be useful for the continued security of the United States of America?'

'Yes.'

'Do you know the identities of people domiciled in this country engaged in activities contrary to the security of the United States of America?'

'Yes.'

'Will you provide details of those identities, to your questioners?'

'Yes.'

'Do you regard yourself as an honest man?'

The question was as clever as the one that had followed the testing sex queries and it was the closest Levin came to faltering. 'No,' he said, alert for the reaction. It came exactly as he expected.

'You do not regard yourself as an honest man?'

'No.' He imagined he heard the sound of the pen, making the notebook entry.

'Yet you intend cooperating honestly with your debriefers?'

'Yes.' Levin reckoned at the moment the technician was more unsettled than he was but knew it would be dangerous to relax. Part of his lip was becoming numbed under the pressure and he nipped at the left side, needing the continued pain.

'Have you operated as a member of the KGB in parts of the world other than the United States of America?'

'Yes.'

'Were there to be requests from those other countries, would you cooperate with their counter-intelligence organizations in disclosing details of those operations?'

'No.' The pause for the notebook query was obvious this time.

'Do you find this test difficult?'

'Yes.'

'Did you expect to be subjected to it?'

'I did not . . .' started Levin, aware of the danger and needing the time.

'Yes or no.'

'No.'

'Would you be prepared to undergo further polygraph examination, if it were considered necessary?'

'Yes.' There was hardly a choice, but Levin wondered if it were a standard question or whether he had made a mistake. Wrong to become nervous, risking any increase in the sweat or heart rate.

'Do you believe in God?'

An intentional leapfrog, to disorient him, guessed Levin. He said: 'No.'

'In truth?'

'Yes.'

'Do you always tell the truth?'

Now it was the technician who was being very clever. 'No,' said Levin.

'Do the KGB use the United Nations as a spy base?'

'Yes.'

'Can you identify KGB personnel among the Soviet mission to the United Nations?'

Practically repetition of an earlier question. Checking the previous answers then. 'Yes,' Levin said.

'Are you aware of KGB personnel in places other than the United Nations?'

Time to throw the needle off course. 'I do not believe . . .'

'Yes or no.'

'No, but . . .'

'Yes or no.'

'No.' Come on! come on! thought Levin.

'Do you have knowledge of people working on behalf of the KGB in places other than the United Nations?'

'Yes!' The man had responded exactly as Levin had hoped.

'Can you identify them?'

'Yes. No.'

'One or the other.'

'Maybe.'

'Yes or no.'

'Maybe,' refused the Russian.

There was another pause which Levin imagined to be for a further notebook entry, but then the technician was by his side, sliding the palm monitor off his hand. So intense had been Levin's concentration that he had been unaware of the man's approach. The ease with which the palm pad came off indicted that he was sweating quite heavily: to an acceptable degree or too much? 'Well?' asked Levin, as the man removed the other two straps. It was the sort of question they would expect.

'We'll have to see,' avoided the man, noncommittal. 'Please wait here.'

He left the room awkwardly, carrying the drum and

the file and his notebook. An instant discussion with the waiting Bowden, guessed Levin. He rose from the chair, aware for the first time of the ache of tension in his back and legs. Sweating hands and tension sufficient to make him ache: would that have translated on to the recordings? Possibly, but he'd tried enough to throw the needles with his answers, so hopefully the two would correlate and be explainable: if he were given the chance to explain, that is. He stood at the window, gazing out over the trimmed and sensored grounds, the tension still gripping him, the perspiration increasing. This really was testing time: the moment when he either passed, to be accepted. Or failed to satisfy them. What happened then? There were accounts of some distrusted defectors being held and interrogated in solitary confinement for months on end. And he didn't have months. Everything was very carefully timed. The contradiction was immediate. If everything was so carefully timed, why had the signal come with Natalia still in the Soviet Union?

It was a full hour before anyone entered the room again, an hour for Levin's mood to plunge from fragile confidence to worry to fear. And then to go almost beyond simple fear into terror as his mind focused upon Galina and Petr. What would happen to them if he hadn't been clever enough? Imprisonment? Unlikely but possible, he supposed. Maybe repatriation, which would be as big a disaster because if they were once further split Levin couldn't see how they would ever be reunited. Maybe . . . The jostling fears stopped at a sound, and Levin turned to face Bowden. The American was serious-faced and the usual bonhomie, which Levin suspected was forced anyway, was missing.

'Well?' asked Levin again. There was the metallic taste of blood in his mouth and he realized he had mistakenly bitten through his lip somewhere. He'd have to be careful it didn't show.

'One or two inconsistencies, Yevgennie. Quite a bunch, in fact.'

In addition to a file of his own, Levin saw the American was carrying the technician's notebook and the paper upon which there was a criss-cross of different-coloured lines. The paper from the polygraph drum, Levin guessed. The reaction prepared, he said in apparent anger: 'It was a ridiculous test! I was assured the questions would be phrased for yes or no answers but they weren't. It was impossible!'

'Why don't we talk it through a little?'

It was important to maintain the indignation longer. Levin said: 'I was promised by Proctor to be treated properly. Considerately. Promised by you, too. It isn't happening. If you do not want me then I will go back to my own country!' He hoped he had not over-pitched the outrage.

'Slow down, Yevgennie. Slow down,' placated Bowden. 'Let's just talk it through, like I said. Sit down and take it easy.'

Levin walked further into the room with apparent reluctance, going not to the upright chair in which he had sat for the polygraph but to a low, easy chair to one side of the desk. Bowden eased his huge frame on to the chair in which the technician had sat, awkwardly too large for it.

'Inconsistencies,' opened Bowden. 'Maybe there are simple explanations.'

'What inconsistencies?' demanded Levin, feigning the anger.

Bowden bent over the notebook he arranged alongside the polygraph reading: the paper was numbered, for the queries to accord with the entries in the notebook, which was specially printed, numerically. He said: 'Found it strange that you should regard yourself as a traitor?'

He'd succeeded there, realized Levin, relieved. He said: 'I was being tested for honesty? To see if I could be trusted?'

'Just that,' agreed Bowden.

'So I told the *truth*,' insisted Levin. 'I *am* a traitor. To my country. And to you. Let's not pretend: wrap things up in other words, like coloured ribbon: call me a defector like it's an honourable description. You and Proctor and anyone else I might meet will pretend to be

113

friendly but you'll always despise me, for betraying my service . . .' He paused, trying to discern a reaction from the other man. He thought there was a slight flush to the man's face but he wasn't sure. He pressed on: 'So now you be honest with me! That's how you think of me, isn't it?'

There was a pause and then Bowden said: 'I guess something like that.'

He couldn't let the American get away. 'Not *something* like that: *exactly* like that. So to have answered no would not have been the right reply, would it?'

'Let's move on,' urged Bowden uneasily. 'You approached our people, in the beginning. Offering stuff. And approached us again, asking to come over, when you got the recall notice. So why did you say you were unwilling to come across? That doesn't make sense.'

'It makes every sense!' disputed Levin. 'I've abandoned a daughter, whom I love. That's why I am unwilling. If she had been here the answer would have been the opposite.'

Bowden nodded, making some sort of entry against the notebook log. He said: 'You've come over to our side now, Yevgennie. Decided to settle in America?'

'Yes.'

'So how come you don't regret spying against the United States? That's what you said. When you were asked . . .'

'I know what I was asked,' interrupted Levin, mentally ticking off the man's uncertainties, every one of which he had so far anticipated. 'I was being honest again. At the time I carried out those activities I was an officer of the KGB, properly performing my assigned functions. So why should I regret it? Again, I was trying to answer in complete honesty.'

Bowden made another entry. The American was bending over the records, not bothering – or not wanting – to look up at Levin. He jabbed several times at the query sheet with the tip of his pencil, and said: 'There's something here that we don't understand at all. Not at all . . .' He came up at last, appearing to seek some facial reaction from the Russian. 'You said you imagine you'll regret coming across.'

'But of course I will!' said Levin, as if he found the query surprising. 'I'll never stop being a Russian. Thinking like a Russian. Feeling like a Russian. I might have become disillusioned with it and what I was being called upon to do but there's always going to be a part of me uncertain if I made the right decision by coming across. And it's a regret that is going to be a very positive attitude until I get Natalia here, with us.'

'Disillusioned?' picked up Bowden. 'You say you've come across because you're disillusioned but you said on the polygraph that you've done it for money.'

'And then I made it clear that was not the primary cause,' came back Levin confidently. 'I had to answer yes – the honest answer – because that was the order in which the question was asked.'

Bowden sat nodding but Levin was unsure whether the gesture was in acceptance of the reply. The American said: 'There were some responses to questions about truth and honesty that just worry the hell out of me.'

'Let's get the sequence right,' insisted Levin. 'It was honesty first, then truth. I replied no when I was asked if I considered myself an honest man because it was the right reply. How can I consider myself honest when I have betrayed my country? Which is what I have done and will always carry, as a burden. But I do intend to cooperate honestly if there is a proper debriefing. And I was accurate when I replied to the question about truth. We are *trained* not to tell the truth, you and I: to lie, if the occasion or the need arises. But again I intend to tell the truth if we debrief.' Levin wondered if the perspiration would be visible against the back of his jacket, when he stood: trying to reduce the risk, he leaned forward slightly, to enable air to get between himself and the back of the chair.

'Why did you find the polygraph difficult?' Bowden snapped the question out sharply.

Remembering that the room was doubtless wired and that there would be a recording of his conversation with

115

the technician, Levin said: 'Before the test began, the operator asked me if I were familiar with the polygraph. I wasn't and said so. I did not like being strapped in as I was and I did not like the restriction of yes or no answers. It's too easy to convey a misleading impression by giving an absolutely accurate answer to a wrongly phrased question.'

Bowden's head was moving again but Levin was still unsure whether or not it was in acceptance of what he was saying. The American said: 'Why won't you cooperate with the counter-intelligence services of other countries?'

'I'm not setting myself up as a performing monkey,' said Levin at once. 'When I told Proctor I was being recalled he immediately suggested I *should* return to Moscow and act there for the CIA. Quite apart from the fact that it would not have been possible – because I believed I was being taken back for investigation – I refused. It would have meant switching to a different agency, spreading my identity: just like cooperating with other counter-intelligence would risk my being further exposed . . .' He hesitated. 'Russia – and the KGB – never forgive anyone who defects: you know that! There's always an attempt at retribution, as an example to others.' The ache now was beyond tension, settling into a draining fatigue not just from the pressure but from the effort of staying ahead of that pressure.

'You had a lot of difficulty at the end, about identifying KGB personnel?'

'The same difficulty as always: the phrasing of the questions and the insistence upon simple answers,' Levin fought back. 'The people I know at the United Nations *are* KGB personnel. Agents. Those I think I know outside are not *personnel*. I think they are suborned spies. I don't know how it is in your service, but in Russia we differentiate between agents and spies.'

'American, you mean!'

'That's what I think.'

'Think!' qualified Bowden.

He's taken the bait, thought Levin. He said: 'I do not

116

have a name. Just scraps: bits of operational detail. It may be impossible to trace backwards.'

'Operational detail!' seized Bowden. 'You mean you think there's a spy in the FBI?'

'No,' said Levin.

'Where then?'

'The CIA.'

Bowden remained hunched over the polygraph material for a long time, his head actually moving as he went over the tracings and the queries and now these responses. He looked up at last with the familiar smile in place. 'You know what I think, Yevgennie?'

'What?' asked Levin, the euphoria already beginning to move through him.

'I think you're too fucking honest for the stupid machine.'

'You mean you believe me?'

'Welcome to America,' said Bowden.

'Thank you,' said Levin. It would be natural to let the relief show and he did.

'There's one thing,' said Bowden.

'What?'

'You shouldn't have lied about masturbation,' smiled Bowden. 'Everybody jerks off. Everybody lies about it, too.'

Sergei Kapalet was a classic KGB emplacement within a Soviet legation in a Western capital. Holding the rank of colonel within the service, he was described upon the French diplomatic list as a driver at the Soviet Embassy in Paris. It was a position low enough to be ignored by French counter-intelligence yet one that gave him the excuse and the facility to drive at will around the city. Which he had done constantly since his posting eighteen months earlier, preparing for this small but essential part in the most destructive operation ever devised by the KGB against the CIA. His job was to insert a few pieces into the whole of a very complicated jigsaw. For him to have known all the details would have put at risk the entire operation if he were detected as an intelligence

117

operative, to avoid which was the purpose of the rehearsals. Kapalet drove and drove and drove again around the *arrondissements* of the city – amusing himself by going first around Le Kremlin area – until he was familiar with every avenue and boulevard. And during every journey he was alert for surveillance which would have warned him he was suspected by the French. It never happened. A superbly trained operative, Kapalet did not rely solely upon a car, but became an expert on the metro as well, journeying as far as Mairie des Lilas and Eglise de Pantin and Pont de Levallois Becon and memorizing all the transfer stations in between, again, all the time, trying to spot any pursuit. There wasn't any here, either.

He initiated the approach to the Americans during the third month of his posting, while officially on duty as the driver he was supposed to be at a reception at the West German embassy. The Americans were initially extremely cautious, which professionally he admired, so it was not until a further three months that he was accepted and given a case officer. The man was a black New Yorker whose name Kapalet knew, from KGB files, to be Wilson Drew even before the CIA man introduced himself. The American was given to three-piece suits, French wine and jazz, which made for convenient rendezvous. Together – although not obviously – they went to the Slow Club and the Caveau de la Montagne and Le Petit Journal.

The legend had been carefully prepared and rehearsed in Moscow. Kapalet's motivation was supposed to be entirely financial, to support a decadent Western lifestyle to which he had become addicted, and so as well as jazz clubs they went to the Crazy Horse Saloon and the Moulin Rouge and the Lido and La Coupole and New Jimmy's.

The information that Kapalet passed over was as carefully selected as everything else, guaranteed always to be absolutely accurate. And provably so. Over the months Kapalet disclosed Soviet finance to a peace movement protesting against US missile bases in Europe and denounced a minor official in the French foreign ministry

118

who was being run by the Paris *rezidentura* after being shown photographs of himself, naked apart from his socks, with two teenage prostitutes in a brothel off the Boulevard Saint Germain. The brothel was financed by the KGB as well, specifically to obtain incriminating material for blackmail purposes and Kapalet revealed that, too. Every disclosure was authorized by Vladislav Belov, in Moscow, each sacrifice considered justified for the success of the ultimate plan.

The contact procedure for the two to meet was for Kapalet to insert a bicycle For Sale notice in the window display of a small tobacconists' shop off the Rue Saint Giles, the venue having been decided between them at the previous encounter. That night it was to be at the Brasserie Flo, on the Cour des Petites Ecuries.

Kapalet was as cautious as ever, going by metro and arriving early but not entering the restaurant, instead positioning himself to see Drew arrive first to ensure the American was not being followed either, so risking discovery by association.

The CIA man had been equally careful in his choice of table, at the rear, near the unpopular noise of the kitchen entry and exit. It would provide a cover for their conversation.

Drew deferred to the Russian for the drinks. Kapalet ordered kir and a 1980 Hermitage la Chapelle and they both chose venison.

'Hope the information is as good as the wine,' said Drew. He was a big, heavily muscled man who had boxed heavyweight at college.

'I am not sure what it is,' said Kapalet. 'There's just been a transfer to the *rezidentura* here, from Washington.' Like everything else, that was true. Kapalet knew that the Americans monitored movements and would already be aware of it. The man's name was Shelenkov.

'What about him?'

'He drinks.' That was also true and the Americans would know that, as well.

'So what?'

'He was boasting in the mess, three nights ago. Said

he had your people by the balls. Those were his words: he likes to show off his Americanisms.'

Drew was eating slowly but concentrating upon the conversation, not the food. 'Had us by the balls?'

'That's what he said.'

'What's he mean by "us"? The Agency? Or America?'

'I thought you'd want to know that. So I manoeuvred the conversation. It's the Agency.'

Drew pushed his plate away, as if he were suddenly sickened. 'Son of a bitch!' he said.

'Well, is the information as good as the wine?' It was important always to try to drive up the price.

Drew ignored the question. 'Who? I need a name.'

'Come on!' said Kapalet. 'Do you imagine I was going to come straight out and ask him? Or that he would have told me, if I had?'

'Listen, Sergei. Listen good. You get this for me – get anything and everything you can for me – and you can name your own price. We'll keep you in Roederer Cristal for life. You understand me?'

'I understand,' said the Russian.

An hour later the first alert reached Langley that they had a spy within the CIA headquarters. Such information is automatically classified red priority, so the Director was awakened at his Georgetown home.

'Son of a bitch!' he said, unwittingly echoing his agent.

'What's the matter?' said his drowsy wife.

'For fuck's sake, shut up!' said the distressed man.

13

Vladislav Belov finally decided it was time to shift allegiance. Not openly of course. Rather to begin to move away from someone certainly in personal decline and arguably in mental decline, as well. Someone, therefore, through whom there was the risk of being carried down in the whirlpool he'd thought about before. Maybe the suck of dirty water going down a plughole was a better analogy. More had become common knowledge now, carefully distributed by the GRU, for Belov to know that Kazin's failure to respond quickly enough to the Afghanistan insanity had risked an unthinkable disaster. Just as the maniac had endangered years of careful planning by signalling Levin prematurely, while his child was still in Moscow. That had actually been the greatest insanity, knowingly creating a situation in which Levin might not have gone at all. So maniac was certainly the right word. And maniacs had to be avoided if they weren't removed altogether: it was unfortunate the inquiry had merely censured the man, rather than getting rid of him completely. Definitely the time to move away. And now, luckily, the opportunity had presented itself. He knew he'd have to be careful, as careful as he had been in formulating the proposal that was going to disrupt the CIA with festering suspicion, as British intelligence had been disrupted by the festering suspicions left over from the time of Burgess and Maclean, Philby and Blunt. But he was sure he could do it.

Personally interviewing Yuri Malik, rather than deputing a subordinate, showed just how careful. There would be no indication of favouritism, because of who his father was, nor any preference instructions sent ahead to New York. That would be too heavy footed. At the beginning, protective association in Dzerzhinsky Square began with nuance and suggestion. But Vasili Malik would recognize it, when his son reported back that he had been briefed by the division head himself. And Belov was confident that the very fact of his being head of the division to which Malik's son was going to be attached would automatically result in more contact between the joint Chief Deputy and himself. Having initiated the approach by conducting this meeting, the pace had in future to be dictated by Malik, a reciprocal invitation for him to respond. Which he would. But very carefully, very slowly, very safely. Belov had moved too quickly, far too quickly, coming out as a Kazin supporter in the past. He had no intention of making the same mistake twice.

'There is no way we can determine the supposed function that will be assigned you at the United Nations,' began Belov. 'That is the decision of the secretariat of the Secretary General. We have people in that secretariat, of course. So I will exert as much pressure as possible to ensure a position giving you the greatest opportunity to fulfil your proper role.'

'I understand, Comrade Director,' said Yuri.

Belov liked the other man. And decided he would have done so without the family connection. Certainly the appearance and demeanour were perfect for a New York posting. There was not a vestige of any Slavic colouring, no dumplings-and-black-bread heaviness. He was clear-eyed and clear-skinned and the fair hair was perfectly cropped to suggest the recent change from the sort of crew cut that seemed inevitable in American college graduation pictures. The man would be able to move around America, under the cover about to be explained to him, and never once appear different from anyone else beside him on the train or plane or street. The attitude was right, too: respectful but not cowed. Confident, like Americans were at his age. Belov said: 'There's been a defection from our United Nations *rezidentura*.'

'Yes,' said Yuri.

Belov waited but the younger man did not continue. 'Because of which some of our people will inevitably be identified.' Dolya, of course. And two others – Onukhov and Lubiako – whom it had been decided Levin was to

122

name to substantiate his defection. There would have to be some token punishment against Dolya, because the man would have been punished if the crossing were genuine, but Belov intended to be as lenient as possible. He picked up: 'The new head of station is Anatoli Stepanovich Granov. He has been attached to the New York mission for two years. He has already been advised what you are to do.'

'A special function?' queried Yuri. To which faction was this man attaching himself? His father's? Or Kazin's? Important to be ultra-cautious until he was sure of the answer. If his father were to be believed he was as much a target as the old man. Why, wondered Yuri, in recurring, intrusive irritation, wouldn't his father tell him what had happened between himself and Kazin? It appeared there would always be some connection between them.

'You are to be the courier,' declared Belov. Surely the most positive indication to the joint Chief Deputy which way he was declaring himself! To be courier was to occupy a position of great trust and responsibility.

'I would like that explained to me,' said Yuri curiously. In ancient Rome couriers of bad news were put to death.

'The FBI are aware how we use the United Nations,' expanded Belov. 'They'd be fools if they didn't. They spy on us as much as they can, electronically, and we are not prepared completely to trust the diplomatic pouch. Which is why we have a courier personally to ferry the most highly classified material. It was formerly the function of Granov, before his promotion to *rezident*.'

'Surely it's not possible for me to move in and out of America at will!' queried Yuri at once. 'I'd be detected after the first trip.'

'Of course you would,' agreed Belov. 'There is an apartment block on the corner of Second Avenue and 53rd Street. Flat 415 is rented permanently in the name of a publishing company which has provable head-quarters in Amsterdam. You will be provided with a bona fide British passport – an American document could be too easily checked – in which you will be described as a travel writer. Your legend name is William Bell. We issue four publications a year from the Amsterdam house and contributions under the name of William Bell will regularly appear, particularly from North America and from the Latin American countries you will visit: in your passport, of course, there are valid visas wherever necessary.'

It was superb tradecraft, thought Yuri admiringly.

'Naturally you must expect surveillance because you *are* Russian, attached to the United Nations,' continued Belov. 'Always take the greatest care to clear your path before undertaking any journey: this system has taken a long time to establish and must not be endangered.'

After the last few days in Moscow Yuri was determined to take the greatest care about everything. Politely he said: 'I will do nothing to endanger it.' Was that a promise he could keep, surrounded by so much uncertainty?

'As a supposed travel writer you've every reason to fly in and out of New York direct to Europe,' went on Belov. 'But use that routing sparingly. On a British passport you can cross into Canada without any record being made. And from there don't always travel West to East, to reach Europe. Asia is available, from Vancouver: it's protracted, I know, but it's secure.'

Yuri tried to remember how early trail-clearing and route variation had been instilled into him, at training school: certainly one of the first sessions. He said: 'And Latin America is to be used the same way?'

'The Caribbean, too,' said Belov. 'There are direct flights across the Atlantic from nearly all of the islands. But minimize the use of Colombia and Bolivia and Peru and Mexico. They're target countries for drug smuggling into America. So more attention is paid to people on incoming flights than from other parts of the region. Always travel light, if you've no alternative: no large luggage to bring yourself to any Customs attention.'

Or hammer and sickle motif on his tie or ear-flapped fur hats, thought Yuri. This really was very basic.

'At all times, during these return trips, you will be travelling on the William Bell passport,' said Belov.

'There must be no occasion whatsoever, no matter what the emergency or crisis, when you make contact with any Soviet embassy. We have, for instance, made extensive use in the past of the Soviet legation in Mexico City: so much so that the Americans maintain permanent surveillance upon it. We ignore it now, happy for them to waste their time and manpower. But I don't want you detected, making such a mistake.'

That he might have done so was even more unlikely than over-using Colombia or Bolivia on return trips, thought Yuri. He said: 'I would not consider using the same entry points into Europe, either. I would always employ transfer connections, between one country and another, before routing myself back here . . .' He saw Belov preparing to speak, but hurried on: 'And of course I would not always enter direct, through Moscow. There is always Leningrad, either by air or the ferry, from Finland.'

Belov nodded, smiling slightly, conscious of the other man's need to prove himself. Why not? Confidence was one of the most important requirements for an operator forced constantly to maintain a false identity in false – or alien – surroundings. He said: 'How do you regard this posting?'

'With great anticipation,' said Yuri honestly. He was about to add that it was precisely what he had been trained for but realized it might indicate some criticism of the briefing, so he stopped.

'There will be long periods when you are absolutely by yourself, without the support of any *rezidentura*,' warned Belov.

That had always been made obvious during his training. Yuri knew he would have no difficulty operating entirely alone. He said: 'How will my absences from New York be explained?'

'Without difficulty, if we succeed in the United Nations assignment we want.'

Which they did. Yuri's posting was into the public affairs division, from which representatives travelled freely and frequently around America, explaining to colleges and universities and contributing governmental bodies the value and necessity of the organization's existence. The travelling was not even restricted to America because the United Nations has separate establishments in Geneva and Vienna.

On the morning of his departure for New York, Yuri said to his father: 'I think I should know what it is between you and Kazin.'

The older man hesitated, unsure, and then once more shook his head in refusal. 'Later,' he said. 'When this business is all over.'

'Why not now?' said Yuri, exasperated.

'This way it's better,' said Malik stubbornly.

John Willick was finding it difficult to hang on. He knew he had to because if he collapsed – collapsed more than he already had, that is – he would risk discovery and if he were discovered it was a trial and jail, with the key thrown into the Potomac or whatever river ran near whatever penitentiary he was sent to. All he needed was a run of luck: just six months with the market going in his favour, his stocks rising as fast as they had been falling, and the horses being on form, and he'd be out of trouble. That's all it was: bad luck. A lot of bad, cruddy luck, hitting a market slide when that bitch of a wife got her alimony settlement and the horses started running badly and he'd needed three months hospitalization after the ulcer had proven worse than they expected under the exploratory operation and some intestine had to be removed. Jesus, would anyone believe the cost of hospitalization in America! Or such bad luck!

He hadn't given a lot away to the Russians. Well, not at first anyway. Just the sort of assessments and judgements that he'd come to recognize after five years as a senior analyst on the CIA's Soviet desk were nearly always cobbled together from newspaper and magazine opinions: the sort of thing the Russians could have assembled themselves, if they'd taken the trouble. A bit more important when he'd become deeply involved, dependent upon the money, and the fucking stock market and the fucking horses had continued to lose instead of win. Spy-in-the-sky stuff, giving them the chance to realize the accuracy and the precise positioning of the satellites, but that really wasn't such a big deal either. They weren't stupid. They knew the satellites were there and they were technologically advanced enough to know the precision that was possible. He'd never disclosed anything to endanger anyone's life. Important, that. Just facts, never anything life or death.

He was certainly due a change of luck after Burrows getting the supervisor post! Burrows, whose guts he couldn't stand and who couldn't stand his guts in return and was proving it – and his power – by the transfer. It was the transfer that was worrying Willick most of all. He'd had a value on the Soviet desk: known his worth. How valuable would he be in personnel records? Fucking clerk's job, after all.

And then there'd been the switch to Paris of his control, whom he'd only ever known as Aleksandr. Another uncertainty there. He had a kind of trust in Aleksandr. Not friends, of course: more of an understanding. Willick didn't know what to expect from the new guy – didn't even know the new guy – and he felt nervous at the unknown.

Willick had it all worked out, when his luck changed. He'd be straight in six months if he could go on getting the sort of money that Aleksandr paid and the losers became winners, which the law of averages said they had to do soon. Quit then. Explain he wanted to call it a day – say he thought he was under suspicion or something like that – and end the whole episode. No problems. No problem at all, providing he got a bit of luck.

Willick obeyed Aleksandr's parting instructions and joined the perpetual queue feeding into the Washington monument – an untidy, disordered man, scuff-shoed, unpressed, yesterday's shirt fraying at the collar.

'Is this your first visit?'

Willick twitched at the contact phrase, turning to the man beside him: plump, bespectacled, owl-like.

'Yes,' he replied dutifully, with his own contact reply. 'It is strange how you never sightsee in your own city.'

'I didn't expect such a queue,' recited the man.

'Neither did I,' said Willick, filling in his part.

'I think I might come back another time.'

'That would probably be a good idea,' completed Willick.

They walked away side by side in the direction of the Reflecting Pool. The Russian said: 'You must know me as Oleg.'

'My transfer has been confirmed.'

'What division?'

'Personnel,' disclosed Willick apprehensively. Essential as it was to know if his source of income were going to dry up, he said anxiously: 'Will that still be of interest to you?'

'Oh yes,' assured Oleg. 'Of very great interest.'

Willick's relief was a physical sensation. He said: 'There was a regular understanding, between Aleksandr and me.'

'A thousand a month,' acknowledged the Russian. 'I know.'

'It will stay at a thousand a month?'

'Why shouldn't it?'

It was changing! Willick thought euphorically: at last his luck was changing. He said: 'What will you want?'

Oleg looked sideways, briefly, as if he were surprised by the question. 'The sort of things that are contained in personnel records,' he said, simply. 'Names, biographical details, postings, specialities. We'll want all that, John.'

Willick swallowed in uncomfortable awareness, the excited relief seeping away. It meant he would be giving away details of people.

14

Yuri Vasilivich Malik was not prepared: despite all the defectors' lectures and all the videos and the itemizing details of the facsimile houses and streets and cities at Kuchino, he was still not properly prepared for New York. There had been no briefing on the me-first aggress-iveness against 'have a nice day', which anyway had mutated since his instruction to 'have a nice one'. He had not anticipated the perpetual day and night noises and that fire and police sirens *did* shrill all the time, like they did in the films he'd sat through, which were not called films but movies. He had not been told about the parting-at-the-seams decay of Harlem, which he drove past on FDR Drive on his way in from Kennedy airport. Or of the holed and cracked streets, like an earthquake after-math. Or about the permanent, barely moving traffic jam of clogged vehicles, horns wearing out before their engines. The identified-from-photographs skyscrapers ('the Chrysler Building is the one that goes to a point, the PanAm Building straddles Park Avenue, those two together are called the Trade Towers and more people work in them than live on the entire island of Manhattan, and the UN building where you will work is green-glassed') were taller and more awesome than he'd been warned to expect. And he was awed. And excited and impressed. He thought it was wonderful. Not in any imbalanced or ridiculous way, like the defector Levin appeared to have regarded it. Although the experience was only of brief hours, to grow to brief days, Yuri knew quite positively – without the slightest doubt – it would never affect him like that. An immediate – and to become lasting – impression was that New York was going to be like a mistress, something to be enjoyed and explored to the full but never once considered as a wife.

The Moscow-designated position as courier meant

Yuri had greater freedom than any other Russian – and certainly any other KGB agent – at the United Nations. Of which he was fully aware. It was still one of the first things Anatoli Granov raised at their initial encounter, conducted of course during a meandering walk around the UN corridors, away from electronic ears. Granov was a grey man – grey hair, grey suit, grey face – with an unsettling mannerism of beginning a sentence and then repeating the start before the conclusion, as if he wanted to reinforce the importance of every statement. He warned against abusing that freedom – without naming Levin – and of the danger of FBI surveillance, actually referring to the United States as the enemy, which Yuri thought overly dramatic, despite having been trained to consider America the same way. The man told Yuri it was essential he orient himself as quickly as possible against the time he had to adopt his false Western identity, but not so quickly as to risk mistakes from which he might be identified. Throughout the guided tour and lecture Yuri showed no annoyance at being so openly patronized, grateful his function would spare him more than most from the schoolmasterly man. Would Granov be any improvement over Solov, in Kabul? The reflection surprised Yuri. Kabul seemed a million miles and a million years away. And it had not been the disaster posting he'd thought it to be, realized Yuri on further reflection. Without Kabul he would not already have a commendation upon his service record. And had he been posted directly to New York his might have been one of the names identified by Levin, resulting in his recall to Moscow. Yuri was no longer sure he wanted a future in Dzerzhinsky Square. What his future would even be: despite the excitement of his new surroundings the unknowns of Moscow and whatever it was between his father and Kazin stayed as a constant nag in his mind. The brief period he'd spent this time in Moscow with his father had left him disoriented too. It had been like going into the room of a house to which he'd never been allowed access before, a locked place of secrets. It seemed for the first time he'd discovered his father to be a person

130

– someone capable of feelings and fears and fallibilities – and not a robot-like provider of any demand, the aloof miracle-maker who could change anything bad, or imagined bad, into something good, or imagined good. Had he been a spoiled little brat, wondered Yuri. The self-recognition was such a surprise that momentarily he lost concentration upon what Granov was saying and had to stumble a half-question before picking up the caution that unless there were an immediate demand he should not attempt to use apartment 415 on 53rd Street. Yuri promised he would not think of it: he was, in fact, thinking of doing so at once, like he wanted to do every-thing at once.

Confident his impatience would be mistaken for enthusiasm, he asked to be allowed immediately to take up his official United Nations post. And when he was ushered into the public relations section by its deputy head, an Englishman called Smallbone whose name was a perfect description of the man's stature, Yuri decided he was going to enjoy it as much as everything else. The personnel appeared equally divided between male and female and there wasn't one woman to whom he would not have thrown back the bedclothes in invitation: a predictably blonde, clear-skinned Swedish girl whose name he caught as something like Inya had tits rivalling a Himalayan mountain range. The men appeared friendly yet curious, but Yuri did not over-interpret their attitude: he'd been warned by Granov during the carousel parade that all Russians were regarded with some curiosity within the UN.

His desk looked out over the East River with Queens on the other side – with some irony he was never to know it was three floors below but identical by desk position to that which Levin had occupied – but Yuri considered the more important view to be an uninter-rupted line-of-sight vision of Inya, whom he knew to be aware of it. Kabul wasn't a million miles away, he decided; it was light years distant.

Smallbone was solicitous and painstaking in his briefing, like Granov before him although for different

131

reasons, dealing out folders and fact-files and look-up-in-a-moment loose-leaf binders with advice upon how they could be cross-referenced to provide every and any sort of information about the United Nations. Every and any sort of information except the most important, thought Yuri: its use by the Soviet Union and the KGB. At once he rejected the indulgent intrusion. This was his cover, the protection he had to wrap around himself, the way a black-market rich (and Gorbachov-resisting) Siberian *kulak* wrapped around himself the best fur coat against the cold of December. Yuri queried and questioned and qualified, surprising Smallbone by his intense determination.

'You're not expected to assimilate it all in a day!' said the diminutive Englishman, solicitous still, trying for a joke.

'*I* expect to,' said Yuri, not joking.

He couldn't, of course. But he came close: very close indeed. In addition to the other material there were prepared speeches and presentations and within three days of his arrival Yuri believed he could have delivered any one of them and, with the benefit of the back-up data manuals, withstood anything but the most demanding of questions.

Which was not all he did to equip himself. He watched television voraciously, those absurdly frenetic quiz shows and *Dynasty* and *Dallas* and *20/20* and *Sixty Minutes* and *Johnny Carson* and *Oprah Winfrey* and *Donahue*. In the morning he watched *Good Morning America* and in the evening he dodged between NBC and CBS and ABC news bulletins – favouring Dan Rather of the three presenters – to educate and better prepare himself for an environment in which he had to merge as unnoticeably as snow melting into a jostled stream.

He swam in that jostled stream, too. Taking advantage of his unrestricted status, he moved about New York, alert for FBI surveillance which at that moment would not have mattered anyway, but seeking out situations where to lose it really would be important. And decided it would not be difficult with the opportunities that abounded. Grand Central and Penn railway terminals were beehives of places, swarmed with people and with so many entries and exits it would have needed an army of pursuers properly to follow. He imagined a catch-me-if-you-can game employing the commuter helicopter base near Waterside Plaza, from which he could zig-zag – sure of his passenger companions (and therefore able to evade them) – to Kennedy airport and from there to La Guardia airport and from there to Newark airport and then, if he were still doubtful, reversing the entire pattern, knowing as he studied the routes and schedules that it would be a game from which he would inevitably emerge the winner. Even those congealed north to south avenues and east to west streets were a bonus. Buses or taxis could be boarded and then abandoned in apparent impatience, trap-setting for any followers forced to feign the same impatience if they wanted to keep him in sight, unknowing they themselves were being fixed between the cross hairs of a mental sight, to be blown away figuratively if not literally.

And he went to the apartment.

For the first time reconnaissance became reality as he taxi-hopped to Penn Station, ignored the ticket counters immediately to return to ground level and dodge into Madison Square Gardens. He'd chosen rush hour, not just for street traffic but for theatregoers. Yuri merged with people wanting seats for that night's performance and for the future, alert to any recognizable face around him and seeing none, easing himself from the queues and back out on to the street. He was lucky with a cab, screwing in his seat for any hurried pursuit or unmarked car pick-up, and didn't isolate that, either. He staged what the training schools called 'go to ground' on 49th Street, midway between Third and Second avenues, intending to finish the journey on foot if he were clean. It was a local bar and he was glad because the reaction to his entry would be the same for any following stranger and be something he could discern. Yuri walked deep into the bar, wanting to keep the entrance fully in view. He ordered beer, a Miller's Light, not because he wanted such a long drink but because it would give him an excuse to remain there for some time and to study anyone who followed. In fifteen minutes ten people came in and five went out: three entries got the stranger reaction and they were still there when Yuri left. He walked away, but not in the direction of the apartment to which he was heading, openly stopping at the junction with Third Avenue to look for any sudden emergence from the bar or abrupt start-up of a waiting, watching car. Neither happened. Yuri did not walk back the way he came but completed the block, hair-tingling tense for the footfall of pursuit now, finishing the square back on to Second Avenue and then hurrying uptown, to 53rd Street.

Yuri had expected a high-rise but it was not and at once he realized the reason. The five-storey converted brownstone had no foyer and therefore no monitoring, identifying security guard system. The front door led directly into what had been a spacious lobby in its grander days but was now a neglected and foot-marked area of metal mail boxes and discarded or uncollected newspapers, magazines and mail-order catalogues. There was, of course, no elevator and in the shadow of the circular stairwell there was a bicycle that had both front and back wheels removed and chained protectively to the frame, which Yuri thought hardly protective against theft but rather gift packaging to make it easier. There was a permanent, unshaded bulb lighting the entrance area and by it Yuri located the time switch, punching it to illuminate the stairway. He was tensed for sound, wanting to become more accustomed to the area and his surroundings before meeting any neighbours and being forced into small talk about being a staff writer for the Dutch magazine, utilizing company facilities while on assignment. There wasn't any and he reached the fourth floor slightly breathless but free from encounter.

He was pleasantly surprised by the apartment. The American term, he remembered from the Kuchino teaching, was a studio, which meant there was only one main room in which the corner-placed bed was covered to resemble a couch or sitting area during the day. The covering was a blaze of reds and greens and browns on a flamboyant Mexican rug, which fitted the supposed occupation of the apartment. On top was a disorder of cushions and around all the walls were travel photographs and covers of the publisher's magazines: the titles had been removed to make easier the framing. There was a colour television with what proved to be an ineffective indoor aerial when he tried it, a couch with two matching chairs arranged in viewing positions and another bright and vari-coloured Mexican rug occupying most of the wood-block floor. A sideboard contained a small bureau, with a selection of both plain notepaper and envelopes and others in the name of Amsterdam magazines: on the bottom shelf was a small portable electric typewriter. A side cupboard contained glasses and on top there was a tray with a selection of liquor, all American. Yuri poured himself a Wild Turkey and continued the examination. Between the chairs and the couch was a small coffee table. Again there was a selection of the Dutch titles, the most recent one of a month ago, and there was also a stack of *Playboy, Penthouse* and *Hustler* publications. Yuri flicked through them, interested: an exposure to Western pornography had naturally been part of his training and he had enjoyed the sessions more than some of the other instructional sessions. In *Hustler* there was a legs-apart view of a girl who looked remarkably like Inya: it would make for an interesting comparison, later. He arranged the magazines back as they were. Part of the cover for a lived-in ambiance? Or was Granov a masturbator?

There was an adequate kitchen, with a man-high refrigerator that contained some milk he immediately poured away down the waste-disposal-equipped sink, some bread going stale and a single stick of limp celery. In the freezer section there were four ice trays which he emptied and refilled and a frozen TV dinner, veal. He threw that away as well. There was some tinned food, mostly chilli, and a bottle of already ground filter coffee. He found the coffee-making machine, and the filters in an adjoining cupboard, and in another cupboard a teapot, a jar of tea and several pots of preserves.

The bathroom was small but adequate, the shower mounted over the bath which had been badly cleaned after its last use. Yuri, who was a fastidious man, found some cleansing powder in the closet beneath the basin and scoured the bath and basin and then poured some bleach into the toilet bowl. In the bathroom cabinet there was a razor, shaving soap, ordinary soap and an assortment of medicinal aids, things like headache tablets and Band Aids. As with the bath, the razor had not been washed clean after its last use: dried soap and bristles were caked around the blade. He threw everything into the plastic-lined wastebin, not so much offended by Granov's dirtiness as by his carelessness: the stubble detritus, for instance, could have been forensically linked to the man if the apartment had been discovered by any counter-intelligence agency, confirmation of his presence together with the inevitable fingerprints. Yuri paused at the reflection, realizing that his prints would be all over the place: maybe there wasn't that much cause to be critical of the *rezident*.

Back in the main room he sat in one of the easy chairs, whisky cupped in front of him between both hands, aware of the murmur of noise from the surrounding apartments. From one came the sort of screams he associated with quiz shows and there was some music, traditional jazz, from somewhere else.

'Mr Bell,' he said, 'welcome to America,' and smiled at the indulgence of talking to himself. Almost at once the smile went. The American posting was not a problem: the problem was whatever was going on in Moscow.

Yuri was extremely careful with his departure precautions. In the bureau he put a page of the plain notepaper half over the letterheaded sheets, so no search could be made without disturbing it, and on the magazine table he placed *Hustler* again half covering the Dutch magazines. He wedged a corner of the raucous bed-covering just beneath the mattress, as if it had been caught there during the making, and in the bathroom he

136

lodged a fold of the shower curtain against the bath edge, confident both would be disturbed if the apartment were searched. Back at the bureau he put the British passport in the name of William Bell in the top drawer with its edge against the left-hand side of the drawer, but did not immediately close it. He was reluctant to leave the identifying document bearing his photograph but accepted it was too dangerous to carry it with him during his supposed normal duties at the United Nations. A safe-deposit box would be more secure, but that would restrict him to banking hours and he might need to move at once if he were activated for his KGB role. At the door he stopped, professionally examining it. There were three separate locking devices, including a deadlock, and when he slightly opened the door he realized that its edge and the complete surround of the frame were metal ribbed: the effect was to fasten the locks and bolts from one steel base to another, making it impossible to jemmy open. Maybe a safe-deposit box wasn't necessary after all. He smiled with satisfaction at the solid sound of the locks engaging.

'They've withdrawn Dolya,' announced Bowden.

'It would have been obvious I'd identify him,' said Levin. 'What about Onukhov or Lubiako?'

'They're still here.'

'What are you going to do to them?' asked Levin. He was confused by the way Bowden was conducting the debriefing: there had been an insistence on the names of the UN agents but no questioning at all about there being a spy within the CIA.

'They're boxed in,' assured Bowden. 'Neither of them can scratch their arse without us being aware of it.'

They wouldn't have been warned by Moscow, Levin realized. It was going to be a shock for both of them if they were seized in incriminating circumstances. Levin did not feel any particular pity: he hadn't liked either of them. He said: 'Maybe they'll lead you to something.'

'There'll be the usual bullshit about diplomatic

immunity. Or maybe the retaliatory seizure of some of our guys from the Moscow embassy, for a swop.'

'So you're going to let them run?'

'It's the obvious thing, isn't it? At least we'll get their American sources and be able to prosecute.'

'I suppose it is,' agreed Levin. Moscow would have allowed for that, he guessed.

'Just three?' asked Bowden doubtfully.

'Just three.'

'Kind of disappointing that you can't finger more, Yevgennie.'

'You know the way espionage is conducted!' said the Russian, happy at the way the feigned indignation came out. 'Boxes within boxes, everything compartmented.'

'Still would have liked more.'

Why not start asking about the CIA then, thought Levin. He said: 'I've promised always to be honest. I've named the three I *know* to be KGB. I'm not going to start giving names just to make myself appear more valuable.'

'OK, OK,' retreated Bowden. He paused and said: 'There's been a request.'

'Request?'

'From the Soviet mission. Consular access,' said the American. 'They want to meet you. Talk.'

'Meet me!'

'Easy!' said Bowden, reassuring. 'It happens every time. They make a formal request for an interview: try to persuade you to go back, I guess. It's regulations that I have to tell you. Because it's an official diplomatic approach we've got to respond in an official diplomatic way.'

'I don't want to see anyone,' said Levin positively.

Bowden smiled. 'Your decision, buddy.'

'But *I* want access.'

'What?'

'If there's some diplomatic contact, I want there to be an agreement for us to write to Natalia. And for her to write to us.' It would be monitored and hopefully a conduit the KGB had not expected, despite all the planning, from which they could gauge his acceptance.

'I'll ask,' promised Bowden.

138

15

Having buried deep within itself a spy operating for another side is the gut-twisting nightmare of every intelligence organization, so the response of the Central Intelligence Agency to the Paris information was immediate. The empanelled group had no official designation but the codename at the CIA's Langley headquarters was appropriately Crisis and it was in a crisis atmosphere that it met. Harry Myers, whom everyone called Hank, was its head because he was the Agency's security chief and preventing such eventualities was his job. Edward Norris, deputy director of the CIA's Soviet division, was the obvious second member, and the third was Walter Crookshank, the Agency's chief legal counsel: from the beginning the inquiry had to be conducted with a view to eventual criminal prosecution.

'It's a bugger,' declared Myers, a bearded, beer-bellied man who regarded the information as something like a personal insult: if it were true, then he'd screwed up on the job. He didn't like screwing up on anything.

'It's not substantiated yet,' said Crookshank with a lawyer's caution.

'It's got a taste to it,' said Myers obtusely. To Norris he said: 'What about Shelenkov?'

'Provably KGB,' said the Soviet expert. 'Identified first in 1981, in Ottawa. Transferred in 83 to London, where MI5 came within a whisker of making an arrest. He was running a technician from an early warning installation in Yorkshire: just before MI5 swept them up the technician committed suicide, and without an admission from him the legal ruling was there was insufficient evidence. Moved here to Washington in July 1985 . . .'

' . . . FBI put him on a Watch List?' interrupted Myers at once.

'We made the request that they should do so,' said

Norris. He was a swarthy, large-bodied man who on Sundays acted as a lay preacher at his Alexandria church and viewed his role in the CIA in religious terms: someone who knew the truth keeping America clean and free of the atheist non-believers.

'But did they do it?' demanded Crookshank, always needing the legal precision.

'I've asked Pennsylvania Avenue for the complete file records but they haven't come back yet,' replied Norris. 'There was certainly some surveillance: while he was here I got three reports about him, to update our own files. Appeared to be one of the up-front guys. Never missed an embassy party, drank a lot although he seemed to be able to hold it: actually had the balls to mingle with some pinko Democrats up on Capitol Hill.'

'And Kapalet?'

'One of the best guys we've had for years,' said Norris. 'Made his own approach fifteen months ago at an embassy reception. We held him at pole's length for a long time, of course: just in case he was a plant . . .'

' . . . And?' broke in Myers again.

'Not one bum steer,' said Norris. 'He's one of the best we've had in a very long time.'

'No reason to doubt him this time, then?'

'Absolutely not,' said Norris.

'Fuck it!' said Myers vehemently.

'At the moment all we seem to have is a drunken boast,' Crookshank attempted to qualify. 'Just a few words that mean nothing.'

'That's what intelligence is, a few words to go with another few words until you get the whole picture,' came back Myers, venting his irritation upon the lawyer. He snatched up the message that had been telexed from Paris and quoted: ' "We've got the CIA by the balls". That sure as hell isn't just a few words meaning nothing to me. To me that means exactly what it says: that our balls are in a vice.'

Your balls, not mine, thought Crookshank. He said: 'Can't we carry out some sort of investigation here at Langley?'

'Deep vetting, of five thousand people! Strap every one into a polygraph and sweat them, you mean?' demanded Myers. 'You any idea how long that would take? We'd still be doing it when they were swearing in Gorbachov on the White House lawn!'

'What then?' said Crookshank. He thought the security chief's tough-guy repartee was a load of crap; late-night movie stuff.

'We need leads,' insisted Myers. 'We start trying to blanket the entire agency and all we're going to do is maybe warn the son-of-a-bitch and drive him deeper into the woodwork . . .' To Norris he said: 'You briefed Drew, in Paris?'

'Personally, by secure radio patch,' assured the other man. 'Told him to promise Kapalet whatever he wants: top brick off the chimney. Anything.'

'What did Drew say?'

'That he'd already done that anyway.'

'Isn't there anything we can do here?' persisted Crookshank.

'I'm running the character assessment and analysis tests for the last five years through the computer,' disclosed Myers.

'That might throw up something,' offered the lawyer.

'An inconsistency – a problem – should have been thrown up the first time, when they were initially taken and reviewed,' said Myers, refusing to give himself any false hope. 'If the bastard got under the wire that time then the odds are that he will do so again.'

'It's not going to be easy, is it?' said Crookshank, who had enjoyed the sixties hippie movement and still wore his hair long: at weekends he secured it with a coloured bandana and toked pot. In the last year he'd developed a great source, pure sinsimella from California.

Myers looked at the lawyer sourly and made as if to reply. Instead he said: 'What we need is another informant. Some independent confirmation: different – maybe better – leads . . .' To Norris he said: 'When do we expect to hear from Paris again?'

'Nothing's regular,' said Norris. 'When Kapalet's got something he arranges the contact.'

'So it could be weeks?' pressed the security head.

'Months,' said Norris unhelpfully.

'Fuck it!' said Myers again. 'Doesn't that frighten the hell out of you, knowing that somewhere in this complex there is a Commie bastard who could go on operating for months without us being able to do a goddamn thing about it?'

'Yes,' agreed Norris, 'it frightens the hell out of me.'

Definitely late-night movie dialogue, thought Crookshank. More to unsettle Myers than for any other reason he said: 'Imagine, operating even now!'

Which was, ironically, exactly what was happening. John Willick made his way unseeing among the mechanical exhibits in the Smithsonian, uninterested in the revolving wheels and apart-and-together cogs and strange, misshapen forerunner machines that sighed and wheezed, showing their age. Just when he thought he was getting some luck! Just when he thought everything was going to turn out all right – the same money from Oleg as he got from the other guy – everything had to turn sour in his mouth! Fuck Eleanor: fuck Eleanor and her smart-ass lawyer hitting him with a court warning about the alimony arrears, a pay-within-a-week ultimatum. Couldn't they give a guy a break? All he'd needed was a month: just one month, to get another $1,000 payment from Oleg to cover that damned call-in on the gold futures for which he'd pledged himself (who could have calculated the fucking South Africans dumping a huge metal sale when they'd hoarded for months?) and he'd be OK. But no. Eleanor couldn't wait. Never had been able to wait. Pay up or else. Jesus, why had he married the bitch?

'Strange to think that these primitive machines were considered revolutionary just fifty years ago, isn't it?'

Willick started slightly, not having detected the Russian's approach. 'Very strange,' he agreed. Who the hell wanted to talk about cogs and wheels?

'And they made fortunes for their inventors.'

142

Willick was only interested in his own fortunes. He said: 'I've got something pretty good.'

'What?'

Instead of answering, Willick said: 'I've been thinking.' There was a pain in his stomach, on the left, where the ulcer had been, but he didn't think the ulcer had anything to do with it.

'What about?'

'Value,' said Willick. 'My value to you.'

'I've already assured you of that.'

'I want more than assurance.'

'What?'

'A reassessment. I don't think I'm being properly rewarded.'

'A thousand dollars a month is a lot of money, John.'

'Not enough,' insisted the American, tight-mouthed.

'How much?'

'Two.' The pain in his gut was worsening and he could feel the sweat damp on his forehead.

The Russian gave a sharp intake of breath and started to move, taking Willick with him. 'There would have to be higher approval for that,' he said. 'Much higher approval.'

'Get it,' insisted Willick.

The Russian frowned, very slightly, at the rudeness. 'You said you had something pretty good.'

'Wouldn't the confirmed identities of every CIA agent operating out of the Moscow embassy be pretty good?'

'Yes,' agreed Oleg at once. 'That would be very good indeed.'

'Not just names,' expanded Willick, promoting what he had to sell. 'Full biographies. Dependants. Everything.'

'Moscow will be very pleased,' said the Russian.

'We haven't agreed the price,' refused Willick.

The Russian stopped near a moving display of an early steam engine, not immediately replying. Then he said: 'I see. No financial increase, no more information?'

'In a nutshell,' concurred Willick. He was troubled now not just by the nagging pain but by the need for a lavatory.

143

'So it's an ultimatum?'

Like I got from fucking Eleanor and her fucking lawyer, thought Willick. He said: 'The sort of information I can provide now is worth it.'

'Sometimes Moscow resents being pressured like this: being threatened with an ultimatum,' said the Russian mildly.

Dear God, don't let them turn me down, thought Willick, who had no religious beliefs. He said: 'I didn't call it an ultimatum. You did.'

'But if we don't increase the payment to two thousand, you won't help us any more, isn't that what you're saying?' reiterated Oleg. 'To me that sounds just like an ultimatum.'

'Revising the business relationship,' said Willick, trying a definition of his own.

'It would be a great pity if we were to cease being friends,' said Oleg.

'I don't want that to happen,' said Willick. How the hell would he survive without even the $1,000?

'I don't, either,' said Oleg. 'You see, John, Moscow's reaction might be that now we've so positively established what you call a business relationship there really isn't any way you could back away from it.'

At the blackmailing threat the ridiculously grinding wheel's and cogs blurred in front of Willick's eyes. He'd always recognized the possibility of it happening. To remind the other man of his own strength, Willick said: 'I suppose you could force me to go on. But what sort of information do you imagine you would get, if we weren't friends any longer?'

'I'll take it up with Moscow,' promised Oleg.

'Please,' said Willick, belatedly realizing that now he was pleading instead of demanding, like before.

'It would be a gesture of goodwill if you let us have those names now,' encouraged Oleg. 'It might convince Moscow that the increase would be justified.'

As Willick turned to leave ahead of the other man their hands brushed and the details of the CIA's Moscow postings were exchanged. Willick knew that if he didn't get to a rest room quickly he'd mess himself.

'They wouldn't!' insisted Natalia. 'They just wouldn't! I know they wouldn't!' Her eyes were red from the soreness of the operation and there had actually been an injunction against crying but she had not been able to stop herself, so that she wept now from the pain as well as from the abandonment.

'I don't believe it either,' said her grandmother, Galina's mother.

'It's a mistake,' said the girl. 'It's got to be a mistake.'

'No,' said the old woman. 'There's no mistake.'

'But what's going to happen to me?' wailed the girl.

'I don't know, my darling. I wish I did but I just don't know.'

16

The material comprised more than half the blueprints of an IBM mainframe computer being developed for the nineties and stolen on microfilm from the company's headquarters at Armonk, in upstate New York, but Yuri was never to know that. Or how Vladislav Belov wanted to use the recall for other reasons. Yuri was not even told where the microfilm was concealed within the travel writer's camera equipment, the 35mm Nikon, with two spare lenses and three rolls of already exposed film taken in Yellowstone National Park, about which a photographic feature duly appeared in the Amsterdam monthly. There was a further half-exposed role, also of the park, in the camera: the microfilm was secreted within the wind-on spindle by which the camera could be operated quite normally.

Yuri's first proper operation also taught him that remaining undetected was considered more important than the speed of delivery. After being alerted by Anatoli Granov at the United Nations, Yuri had to wait until a necessary excuse for his absence could be manipulated, an address on the international importance and value of the United Nations to a group of lobbyists in Washington DC. It took three days to arrange, three days for Yuri to grow increasingly unsettled by what he might be returning to in Moscow. He wished there had been some way of contacting his father, to be warned if a warning were necessary.

Anxious to extend his knowledge of America as much and as quickly as possible, Yuri travelled to the American capital by Metroliner, gazing from the window, reminded again of the parting-at-the-seams decay of Harlem when the express went through Baltimore. Why was it that trains always seemed to pass the worst back gardens in any city? Only when they began approaching Washington did he concentrate upon the already prepared speech, making the small changes that Smallbone had assured him were permissible for the address to appear his own and not an opinion written by someone else, annotating the main text with reference numbers from his back-up books.

Washington impressed him. He guessed there were exceptions but it seemed a freshly washed and newly swept city. He knew from the Kuchino lectures that Greek architecture had been a predominant theme in its planning and decided it had succeeded, with the broad avenues and massive, squat buildings which also reminded him of Moscow. He'd become accustomed to New York skyscrapers and their absence here was another surprise until he recalled that city ordinance prevented any building higher than the Capitol, which really did look like the decoration at a Western wedding feast which was how it had been described to him by the homosexual defector who'd tried to teach him the idioms of the American language.

It was a breakfast address, important for the necessary timed-to-the-minute operation, and it went perfectly and Yuri was pleased both by his performance and by his reception. As his taxi drew away from the Mayflower Hotel he tried to imagine what the reaction of these people whose vocation was influencing American government thinking would have been if they'd known their lecturer to be a Soviet agent on his way to Moscow to deliver a consignment of American secrets. Mass panic and then mass diarrhoea, he decided. Or maybe diarrhoea first, then the panic. Possibly followed by Congress convening a panel for televised hearings, to impress the folks back home.

Yuri cleared his trail by taking the cab to Union Station, utilizing the covered-in construction work he'd noted on his arrival, sure the boxed and enclosed walkways would hide the initial avoidance manoeuvre. He re-emerged through the side door to catch the shuttle bus back down the hill. He went as far as 13th Street, fascinated by the continuing reflection as he passed the FBI headquarters on Pennsylvannia Avenue; if only they knew, too, he thought. He used the side entrance of the flagship Marriott Hotel, gained the reception area by the escalator and then dodged into the bookshop directly at its top. There he pretended to leaf through the latest publications displayed at the entrance, in reality intent upon any hurried ascent up the escalator by a pursuer momentarily nervous at losing sight of his quarry. No one followed showing that sort of anxiety. Yuri still memorized the faces of the initial five – three men and two women – and was alert for their attention when he crossed the massive foyer to emerge at the main entrance, nodding agreement to the doorman's invitation to another taxi. None of the isolated five followed him.

The driver continued on Pennsylvannia, going by Lafayette Square and the White House, and Yuri had his first disappointment. Set against the grandeur of the Washington public buildings – without even bringing the massive and grandiose Kremlin into the comparison – the official residence of the President of the United States seemed insignificant in size and presence. Just not *important* enough. In front of railings which could have been scaled by a determined ten-year-old (surely there had to be better protection than that!) a bearded, many-coated man was camped beneath a wedge of tarpaulin, surrounded by banners and placards protesting the plight of America's homeless. Yuri reckoned that despite the supposed new freedoms within the Soviet Union it would have taken the KGB internal militia about three seconds on a slow day to find the man very permanent accommodation indeed if he'd attempted the gesture outside the Kremlin's Trinity Gate.

Yuri was ready when the vehicle started to climb the tree-bordered George Washington Memorial Parkway to leave the city, intent for what he had been assured in at least half a dozen lectures existed but which he'd always found difficult completely to accept. And then he saw it, the signpost actually indicating the location of the CIA's headquarters at Langley.

'That's where the spooks hang out,' identified the

driver unnecessarily. 'Must be a strange job, being a spook.'

'I just can't imagine it,' said Yuri.

At Dulles Airport he used the William Bell passport, took the camera bag unhindered and unquestioned through the x-ray examination of the Concorde check-in and accepted the offer of Dom Perignon champagne at the pre-flight invitation. Before his execution the condemned man ate a hearty meal, he thought. How would his father react to a positive demand to explain what the hatred was between himself and Kazin? The temptation was growing in Yuri to make it.

The choice of Concorde was not an indulgence. The three-hour flight got him to Paris' Charles de Gaulle airport with ninety minutes to make the Amsterdam connection, for which he again used the British passport. It was only at Schipol, for the Moscow transfer, that he reverted back to Soviet documentation and he used his KGB accreditation at Sheremet'yevo to avoid any Customs delay. Despite going through two (or was it three?) time changes Yuri did not feel tired, and knew why. The entire identity-switching, pursuit-avoiding journey had been uneventful, not even a flight delay, but all the time he'd known an adrenaline-pumping tenseness, the necessary professional awareness of everything and everybody around him. Would his first mission end with champagne or hemlock, he wondered.

His taxi driver had a full and drooped moustache, a topcoat with the collar black with grease, and emitted a permanent smell of tobacco: closer, inside the car, Yuri saw the moustache was browned with nicotine, so that it looked artificial, as if the man were wearing some clumsy and obvious disguise.

'Come far?'

'Far enough,' said Yuri. In the reflection of the rear-view mirror he saw the man frown at the refusal.

'Know Moscow well?'

'Well enough,' said Yuri. Would his father be at the dacha or the apartment? He should have telephoned from the airport.

'You want anything, you let me know.' The man, who was driving dangerously fast, swivelled in his seat and grinned; his mouth was a graveyard of cracked and stained teeth.

'Want anything?' queried Yuri, concentrating on the man for the first time.

'Man on your own: special company maybe. Nice girls.'

Yuri had forgotten that propelling a vehicle was not considered the primary employment of Moscow cab drivers: would the man have anything to prevent knives going into backs? He said: 'No thanks.'

The car swerved as the man reached across the front passenger seat and stretched back, holding a bottle. 'Take it,' offered the driver. 'Have a drink. See I'm not offering horse piss. It's good vodka.'

Yuri accepted the bottle to get the man's hands back on the wheel but didn't open it. 'I don't think so,' he said.

'Haven't you heard about the alcohol restrictions that Gorbachov's introduced?' demanded the driver, appearing offended at the rejection. 'Lot of vodka stalls have been closed completely and the liquor shops have restricted licences now.'

'I heard,' said Yuri.

'It's a good offer,' persisted the driver. 'Twelve roubles. Cost you more than that on the black market anywhere.'

Yuri saw there was no label on the bottle and that the seal was broken. The liquid inside was reddish, as if something metallic had rusted in it. It probably was horse piss. He said: 'I'm not interested.'

The driver gave the grunt of a frustrated salesman, feeling back for the bottle, which Yuri returned. So much for reforms, he thought.

'How about dollars?' demanded the driver suddenly. 'You come from America, I'll give you the best exchange rate for your dollars? Twice the official price. No argument.'

'I don't want to sell any dollars,' said Yuri.

'That's an American suit,' accused the man, with easy expertise. 'You've come from America.'

'So?'

'Maybe you want to buy some?'

'No,' sighed Yuri.

'You won't get a better rate anywhere.'

'I don't need them.'

'Everyone needs dollars.'

'I don't.' Yuri wished he knew what he did need.

'That luggage American?'

'Yes.'

'You want to sell it?'

'No, I don't want to sell it,' said Yuri. He was grateful for the approaching grey outline marking the beginning of the city.

'American jeans?'

'No.'

'American records?'

'No.'

'You travel between America and Russia a lot?'

Yuri hesitated. 'No,' he said.

'That's got to be a lie, dressed like you are and carrying American luggage,' rejected the driver. 'You like, you and I, we could come to a very profitable arrangement.'

'I said I'm not interested.' In America this man would have been a millionaire, several times over. Perhaps he was here.

'You could make a lot of money.'

'What would you do if I reported you?'

The man snickered a laugh. 'Deny the conversation. Or buy the policeman off. Whatever was easier.'

'I thought that sort of thing was all over?'

'Forget it!' dismissed the man. 'My regular stand is at the airport. You want to come to a deal, you look me up.'

'This is a KGB building,' said Yuri as they halted.

'I know,' said the man. 'Don't forget: the airport stand.'

The Soviet Union lags at least fifteen years behind the West in technology development, so the value of the IBM information fully justified Yuri's courier return, but Belov sought a different, personal benefit in bringing Yuri back. The expected approach from the man's father, at which Belov could have more obviously declared himself, hadn't happened, not even when he'd advised the man of his son's homecoming. Belov knew it could only mean he wasn't trusted, because of his earlier association with Kazin. So it was essential he correct the impression.

Yuri was intrigued, as he was intended to be, to find Belov awaiting him at the directorate headquarters. The division head accepted the already exposed films and the camera and returned unexposed cassettes and a complete replacement camera. The exchange took less than a minute.

Belov said: 'A long journey apparently for so little. It was actually extremely important.' He hoped the hint was passed on, to prompt an inquiry from which he could make his changed allegiance obvious.

'Of course, Comrade Director,' said Yuri. He was as curious at the remark as he was at being received by the man; Belov owed him no explanation. Or perhaps he was trying to make one of a different sort.

'You are experiencing no problems in New York?' Surely an approach as direct as this could not be misconstrued!

'None whatsoever,' assured Yuri. What was the direction of this conversation?

'What effect has the defection had upon the UN mission?'

This was a question for Granov, not him. Yuri said: 'There was the obvious publicity, for several days. It has diminished now.'

'Has there been any indication of greater surveillance from American counter-intelligence?'

If there had been any indication it would have been bad surveillance, thought Yuri. He said: 'None. Of course precautions are being taken.'

'I have advised your father of your return.'

Was it something as simple as being a conduit to his father, Yuri wondered suddenly. But why would the man

152

need a channel to someone heading the division in which he worked? Access was no problem. Yuri said: 'I would welcome the opportunity to see him.'

'Your flight does not leave until ten o'clock tonight.'

'That is extremely considerate,' said Yuri. Which was true. But why?

'Convey my regards to your father.' What the hell more could he do?

Yuri was unsure of his father's attitude when he arrived at Kutuzovsky Prospekt. His first inference was impatience but almost at once he wondered if there were some nervousness involved as well.

'What did you carry back?' demanded the older man at once.

'I don't know. Something in a camera.'

'No difficulties during the flights?'

'None.' What had his father expected to happen?

'Whom did you see?'

'Belov himself.'

'That was unusual: unnecessary.'

'He was almost embarrassingly friendly. Which was unnecessary too. Asked me to convey his regards.'

'He personally told me you were coming back today: a memorandum would have done.'

'Switching from Kazin?'

'Or working with him.'

Yuri felt a flicker of unease. 'You think I was being set up?'

'I'm not sure what to think at the moment,' said the older man.

Seeking reassurance somewhere, Yuri said: 'What about reopening the inquiry?'

'There may be something.'

'What?' demanded Yuri.

'Panchenko's squad were dispersed to other security units,' disclosed the older man. 'The major to Kiev, the others to Leningrad and Odessa. All within three days of the inquiry ending.'

'Hurriedly got out of the way!'

His father smiled, a teeth-bared, humourless

153

expression. He said: 'We'll see. I'm bringing them back. The major should be re-posted within a fortnight. The others about a week after that.'

Yuri recalled his thoughts of making a direct demand of his father. He said: 'When I arrived back from Kabul you talked about an attempt to hurt us both?'

'Yes?' agreed Malik doubtfully.

'Both of us,' insisted Yuri. 'Not just you.'

'So?'

'I deserve to know.'

For a long time Malik did not speak. At last he said: 'I am not sure I want you to know.'

'I want it!' Yuri was surprised at his own force: and frightened, too, that he had gone too far, despite his impression of a closer relationship. His father looked surprised at the outburst, and Yuri hurried on: 'Unless I know I can't understand what the hell is happening: what I should or should not do.'

Still there was no immediate response. Then, almost in conversation with himself, Malik said: 'No, you can't, can you?'

Yuri waited, considering there was a risk in pushing further.

'I loved your mother,' declared Malik bewilderingly. 'You must understand that. And she loved me.'

'Yes,' encouraged Yuri, even more bewildered.

'We were always friends,' continued Malik, still in private reminiscence. 'Kazin and I entered the service together, trained together . . . were together when I met Olga. He was my supporter, at the wedding . . . a friend to us both . . . so it wasn't her fault . . .'

'What?' said Yuri, expectantly now.

Malik did not directly answer. He said: 'I never knew, not at Stalingrad. Not about anything before, either. Kazin's function was liaison, so he flew in and out to Moscow all the time. My job was to remain wherever I was posted . . . She had to be lonely. Never knowing.'

'How long?'

'Something else I never knew: a long time, I think.'

154

Yuri shook his head, still finding difficulty. 'But why does he hate *you?*' he demanded. 'You should hate *him!*'

'Oh, I did once,' said the older man. He jerked his deformity. 'I think if it had not been for this I would have tried to kill him . . . I wasn't able, you see . . . ?'

'But why?' repeated Yuri.

'When the choice came, Olga chose me,' said Malik simply. 'That's what he can't forget: that when she had to choose between us she stayed with me instead of him.'

The Moscow timetable had not allowed for the debriefing to be so leisurely and Yevgennie Levin was worried; by now the demands should have been flooding in from the CIA. Instead all they'd done was discuss his career up to the age of twenty.

'It's going slower than I expected,' risked Levin.

'No hurry,' soothed Bowden. 'No hurry at all. And there's a slight problem anyway.'

'What!' said Levin, immediately alarmed.

'The tutor thought I should know,' said Bowden. 'Petr's refusing absolutely to cooperate: to accept any sort of instruction. Tried to smart-ass the guy by only speaking Russian and when he realized the man was fluent told him to go to hell. That he didn't intend studying anything in America.'

'I'll try to talk to him,' said Levin. It had been a bad miscalculation failing to anticipate Petr's reaction. But there was little they could have done about it if they had gauged it accurately.

'There is some good news to balance it, though.'

'What?'

'Moscow have agreed to a letter exchange between you and Natalia.'

Levin determined to convey as much as possible. The more Moscow realized he was performing in every way they demanded, the more likely they were to release the girl. He still couldn't understand why he'd been activated as he had. Had it been the old days he would have thought of her being a hostage but that was unthinkable now, surely?

17

Yuri was as careful about his return to America as he had been on the outward journey, routing himself from Amsterdam to Rome and from Italy flying back to Washington to complete the journey to New York as he would have done had he remained in the capital to sightsee, which was the cover for his weekend absence. It was late when he finally arrived at Penn Station and he was weak-legged from the exhaustion of the round trip so he deposited the British passport and his small case in a left-luggage locker, for later collection and delivery to 53rd Street.

It was mid-week before he bothered, the trail-clearing virtually automatic now as he crossed town. For part of the way, for the first time, he used the New York underground and was staggered by its dirt and its graffiti, literally confronted with the most direct contrast he'd so far encountered between the two countries. He thought it looked like an art gallery in Hell. So what did that make the marbled and chandeliered and daub-free mausoleums of the Moscow system? Something like a waiting room to the other place, he supposed: Comrade God has a season ticket on the Moscow underground! He got off after just two stops, grateful to return to street level. As he reclaimed the contents of the locker Yuri relegated the metro system to a last resort in any future surveillance evasion.

Yuri planned for it to be dark by the time he reached 53rd Street, which had the benefit of concealment but the disadvantage of enveloping the interior lobby in complete blackness. He groped out, locating the time switch, and was actually inserting the first of the apartment keys into its separate lock when the voice said: 'Hi!'

The surprise grunted from Yuri as he jerked around, seeing the girl.

'I made you jump,' she laughed. 'I'm sorry.'

She had, and it irritated Yuri. Not because it was so immediately obvious that he'd been startled but that he had been unaware of her, so close: his training was supposed to make that impossible. Automatically he looked down, seeing the rubber-soled training shoes visible beneath the cuffs of some sort of baggy trousers. Still no excuse. He said: 'You certainly did.'

'So you're one of our mysterious writers, coming and going like ships in the night!'

'I'm moving around on assignment, yes,' agreed Yuri. Who the hell was she! And how did she know the cover by which he was using the apartment? She had not been behind him in the street: he was sure she hadn't. But then he'd not been conscious of her when she was directly behind him. Writers, she'd said: more than one. How did she know more than one person used it? He said: 'You live here?'

She thrust her hand out and said: 'Caroline Dixon. I've got the apartment directly above yours . . .'

His door open and he clicked on the light. She looked beyond him, into the room and said: ' . . . and it's identical.'

Yuri remained in the doorway, his uncertainty a comparison to her smiling self-assurance. Becoming involved with anyone in the apartment block was positively precluded, for every obvious reason. But to shut the door in her face risked her becoming curious as well as affronted. Mysterious, she'd said. So she was *already* curious. Yuri took the offered hand and said: 'Bell, William Bell.'

'Bill? Or William?'

Before he could reply the time switch went off, plunging the hallway into darkness. Positively forbidden, he thought. Despite which he said: 'Why not come in for a drink?'

'It's really too late to jog anyway,' she accepted, at once. 'So what is it?'

'William,' said Yuri, donning the false persona as he would put on a familiar jacket. 'I guess it sticks from

157

having the name on the articles in the magazines.' He gestured to the table, realizing as he did so that uppermost were the hard and soft porn publications he'd carefully arranged as a warning if the apartment were entered in his absence.

'You write for skin mags!'

'No,' he said quickly, hot with discomfort. He collected up *Hustler* and *Penthouse* and *Playboy* and said: 'It's a company apartment. These were left over by someone else. Not mine.'

'It's not a crime to read them,' she grinned, aware of his embarrassment.

Yuri was aware of it too. He was surprised, because it was strange that he should be, but not unhappy, because it might be the sort of reaction she would expect. Forbidden though such encounters might be, Yuri realized that the soft-walking Caroline Dixon, whose jogsuit top bulged most interestingly, would be a useful and necessary test, like all the others he had set himself. At the United Nations he was identifiably Russian, at the Washington lecture he had been identifiably Russian, and during the flight to and from the Soviet Union William Bell had been nothing more than a false name to which he responded. Which made this the first time he had been in any sort of situation where he really had to *be* William Bell: to act out a passing social encounter without for one second it appearing to be an act, to avoid the silly, small mistakes that he'd been taught were invariably those which lead to discovery. He picked up the Dutch magazine and said: 'I work for this. Travel. Nature stuff. That sort of thing.'

Politely she took them and Yuri studied her more closely as she flicked through. Sufficiently confident to confront a stranger without any make-up, her face actually shiny, the blonde hair he guessed to be about shoulder length caught up under some wrap-around band. She looked as if she really had been setting out to jog. She smiled up and said: 'I can only just detect it.'

'Detect it?'

'The accent,' said the girl.

Definitely a useful test, Yuri decided, feeling the apprehension rise. He said: 'I didn't think I had one.'

'It's hardly discernible,' she said. 'You're not offended?'

'Of course not,' he said. The training schools would be, though. Quickly he added: 'I'm not getting you that drink, am I?'

'You got anything else?'

The query seemed a pointed one and he didn't know how to respond: he felt the perspiration forming along his back, glueing his shirt, and hoped it was not showing on his face. He said: 'I've been on the road for quite a while. I need to get things in.'

She said: 'I thought you might carry but then I guess it could be difficult, in and out of airports.'

Yuri was baffled by the conversation, the apprehension lumping in his stomach. What did carry mean? Floundering, he said: 'I will try to be more prepared next time,' and she picked him up at once and said, coquettish and enjoying his discomfort, 'Next time so soon!' and Yuri recognized he was floundering more than he realized. This had been a ridiculous experiment, contravening every rule and instruction, and he had a stomach-wrenching awareness that the ice beneath his feet was thin and melting. Melting fast. He decided to utilize the embarrassment she was enjoying, adopting the pose of the hapless and ingenuous innocent. He said: 'So what can I get you?'

'I've got some,' said the woman. 'It'll take me a minute.'

She was gone without any further explanation, leaving the door ajar, and almost at once Yuri thought he heard her go into her own apartment. Only a minute, she'd said. He wanted more than a minute: he wanted . . . what did he want? Yuri realized the ice was sagging, about to give way: and there was a very real danger of his disappearing over his head into the cold water of suspicion. So what about all the lectures from the supposed experts, the precautions against just such a thing happening? Apart from the slight accent not their fault, he answered himself rationally. The training had been to infiltrate and assimilate gradually. But in his conceit – the conceit he had imagined he'd lost – he had not thought he needed any infiltration or assimilation to be gradual: that he knew it all. Not just a spoiled brat but an over-sure, conceited one as well. But with a separation. There had not been any personal danger in being spoiled, as a kid. But he was no longer a kid and no longer under his father's protection in Moscow and he feared there was a very real danger of his being caught out in his encounter with this discomforting woman.

When she re-entered the apartment Yuri saw that Caroline had taken down her hair, which did reach to her shoulders, and only bothered with the minimal amount of make-up, just a suggestion of lipstick. She held out her hand and he saw the kit and Yuri felt the pop of relief at his belated understanding. It still should not have taken him so long, so maybe the training school were to blame.

'I don't,' he said.

'You tried it?'

'Sure,' he lied.

'Why not, then?'

'Just doesn't do enough for me.'

'It does enough for everybody.'

'Not me.'

'Mind if I do?'

'Go ahead.'

Yuri appeared to concentrate upon preparing his drink, busying himself with getting ice into a bucket and then making his choice of liquor, all the time intent as the woman chopped the lumps out of the tiny pile and from it made ready her line with the razor's edge. Balancing his most recent thought, Yuri supposed there were some things never to be learned at a spy college. He hoped the accent would flatten out with his constant exposure and use of English.

'You sure?' she said.

'Positive.'

She took a thin metal tube from its fastenings in her case, which was chamois, blocked off her left nostril to

160

inhale half the line and then changed, gently breathing out between times, to complete the line in her right nostril. Almost at once she said: 'Whee!'

Caroline was pressed back into the chair more directly in front of the ineffectual television, her eyes closed, but as Yuri carried his drink – Wild Turkey again, which he'd taken without interest or particular choice – to the adjoining seat she opened them and smiled at him. She appeared bright and alert, not soporific as he thought she might have been: more gaps in the training. Anxious to settle other uncertainties, he said: 'How did you know I was one of the mysterious writers?'

'Everyone knows,' she said.

The concern settled deeper in Yuri's stomach. 'It's hardly a big deal,' he suggested, pleased with the way the sentence formed.

'No big deal at all,' she agreed. 'Someone learned from the janitor that a Dutch publishing house were the lease-holders. I've only been here two years but there's been quite a few of you guys through: the one before you was a miserable bastard, ignored everybody . . .' She looked across at the rearranged magazines. 'Just imagine what he got up to in here with that stuff!'

Yuri gauged it to be the normal sort of gossip, within an apartment block like this, but it would unquestionably require a warning to Moscow. Disconcerted though he had been – and could still easily be again – it definitely had not been a mistake to invite her in. Sat as she was, the sweatshirt was tighter, emphasizing her figure: he guessed her tits were easily as good as Inya's. He said: 'That's the problem. We're moving around so much there's rarely the chance to be friendly.'

'You're being friendly,' she said archly.

'I'm glad we met,' said Yuri, with mixed feeling.

'So am I,' she said.

A silence developed and Yuri didn't want silence, he wanted to know what else was gossiped knowledge within the block. Calling upon his legend and his early concentration on American morning television he said:

161

'I've just finished an assignment in Yellowstone Park. Never saw Yogi once.'

'I'd be interested to read some of your stuff some time.'

So would I, thought Yuri. He said: 'You get to know any of the other guys?'

Caroline shook her head. 'That's what makes this apartment so interesting: a place of strangers.'

Too much curiosity, thought Yuri at once. 'Not any more,' he said, to carry the conversation on.

'Do you want to know something?'

'What?'

'I hid,' admitted the woman. 'When I heard the door open downstairs and the hall light went on I actually hung back on the stairs hoping it was someone from this apartment.'

'Why?'

She shrugged and said: 'Just because.'

The idiom didn't mean anything to him but Yuri decided against challenging it. A safe house with a nosy neighbour living directly above (the smallest of drills, the most imperceptible microphone or lens) hardly qualified for the description of safe house. Except that the microphone or lens would hardly capture anything embarrassing, unless it focused on the lavatory where Granov hunched over his magazines. He said: 'What would you have done if it had been the miserable bastard before me?'

'Probably still said hello.'

Would Granov have been crept up upon so easily? That he hadn't detected her still irritated Yuri. Time for curiosity of his own. He said: 'We're spending a lot of time talking about mysterious writers, who aren't really mysterious at all. Just hacks. How does Caroline Dixon earn a living?'

She was in advertising, actually on Madison Avenue, completely responsible for five accounts and senior consultant on an additional four. 'You know the ad where the plants don't get fed the proper fertilizer so they all pull up their roots and walk to the next-door garden?'

'No,' said Yuri blankly. It would be necessary to

confirm that Caroline Dixon did work for the Madison Avenue agency and was responsible for some nonsense involving walking plants. And not just *a* Caroline Dixon: *this* Caroline Dixon.

She seemed disappointed. 'I got nominated for an award for it.'

'I'll watch out for it,' promised Yuri.

'You're going to be here a while then?'

Yuri was instantly cautious, unsure of an answer sufficient to account for his infrequent use of the place. He said: 'Away tomorrow. I don't know for how long. But I'm assigned to America for the moment, so this is going to be my base.'

'It'll be nice, knowing my neighbour at last.'

Was the ice beginning to creak again, for different reasons? What real, positive danger was there? No schooling, no matter how intense, could properly equip him undetectably to mix as he was mixing now into the sort of Western environment in which he had to merge if he were to survive. Surely more advantage than danger, then? And he was sure those breasts would be spectacular. He said: 'Are you in any hurry to go anywhere?'

'No,' she said at once, almost too quickly.

'I've only just got back, so there's nothing in,' he apologized. 'We could go out to eat, if you'd like.'

She smiled and said: 'I think I'd like that very much . . .' She looked down at her jogging outfit and said: 'I'll need fifteen minutes.'

'Take as long as you like.'

Before she returned Yuri unpacked his carry-on case and positioned the William Bell passport again in such a way that he would know if it were tampered with while he was out of the apartment. This time he rearranged the magazines with the Dutch publications uppermost, in a recognizable way, but left the other signals as he had set them before. Finished, he considered another Wild Turkey and decided against it. The effect of the cocaine upon Caroline had not been as he expected; there had appeared no loss of control or lack of awareness at all: the opposite, in fact.

She wore pumps and jeans and a tighter sweater that confirmed Yuri's impression, with a short jerkin jacket over it, and her hair was held back by a simple band. She still had not bothered with anything more than lipstick. 'Didn't need fifteen minutes,' she said. 'Where are we going?'

'I don't know Manhattan particularly well,' he said. There was protection is playing the role of a stranger and it would not be a difficult part.

'My choice?'

'Your choice.'

In the street outside Caroline slipped her arm familiarly through his and although it surprised him he gave no reaction, actually cupping his hand over hers. Were all women in the West as immediately friendly as this? On Second Avenue she hailed the cab and he heard 'Brooklyn', but no more, so when he was inside he said: 'Where are you taking me?'

'Tourist stuff,' she said.

Utilizing her earlier friendliness, Yuri put his arm along the back of the seat behind her, the movement enabling him to check through the back window for any pursuit. He didn't detect any but the road was thick with vehicles so it was impossible to be completely sure: certainly the taxi appeared a genuine vehicle, not some counter-intelligence mock-up. Caroline maintained a constant babble of conversation, pointing out landmarks, insisting he lean forward for a better view of the skyscraper when they went by the United Nations, which he did in apparent straight-faced interest.

'Costs millions and is complete crap,' judged the woman. 'Just a lot of supposed diplomats living tax free of the fat of the land telling countries to stop fighting each other and being given the straight middle finger in reply.'

What did 'supposed' mean? Thinking of his own country's use of the organization, Yuri said: 'It must serve some purpose.'

'Yet to be discovered,' Caroline insisted.

When the car started to cross the bridge, Yuri said: 'We're going to eat in Brooklyn?'

'Wait,' she insisted.

The driver was unsure so she leaned forward to give directions before they left the bridge, gesturing for the immediate right turn, which again enabled Yuri to look back. There was still no indication of any following vehicle but the packed road made it as difficult as before to be sure.

'The River Café,' she announced when the car stopped. 'Recognize anything?'

'Not at once,' said Yuri doubtfully.

'Better inside,' she said.

Yuri followed her into the restaurant, intent on everything around him, straining for the recognition she apparently expected but unable to find it.

'There!' she announced, when they reached the bar.

Yuri looked across the river to the illuminated skyline of Manhattan, at once relieved and then thankful at last for the training-school videos and the television. 'The famous view,' he said.

'Isn't it great!'

'Terrific,' agreed Yuri. Caroline had to be too ingenuous to be any sort of counter-intelligence plant!

'Just the beginning,' she said.

He imagined they were going to eat there but she said they'd only come to drink, matching him martini for martini and then guiding the new cab driver back across the bridge and downtown to a Mexican café in Greenwich Village, which was an area of the city he had not explored. Ordering nearly became a problem because Caroline announced she would defer to an experienced travel writer: he recognized tacos and chilli on the menu and chose for both of them and was lucky, too, with Margueritas, which she declared to be a drink she liked. Yuri was confident she had not detected his hesitation. Caroline continued to lead the conversation and Yuri was happy to let her: it gave him the opportunity to study her, seeking the slightest hint to warn him that she was part of some entrapment operation. She talked of a

San Francisco upbringing and of a Berkeley education and a marriage that lasted two years ('we woke up one day and couldn't understand why we'd done it in the first place; we send each other Christmas cards') and of coming to New York to make a clean break and of loving advertising ('you sure you haven't seen the advert with the walking plants!') and slowly Yuri began to relax. He offered scraps of his carefully prepared legend, improvising a Dutch father for his English mother to account for the newly discovered accent and of never having had time to get married, aware as he talked of Belov's wisdom in choosing a European background to account easily for any further slight mistakes he might make.

Yuri thought the Margueritas were bland and suspected the tacos would give him heartburn; Caroline said wasn't everything wonderful and Yuri agreed that it was. After the meal they walked aimlessly through the village and Caroline took him to a bar called the Lion's Head because it sounded English. She went to the toilet while he ordered and as he did so Yuri realized Soviet security would already have alerted Granov of his failure to return at the expected time. After Levin's defection they'd be very nervous of unaccountable absences but regulations forbade his making any contact from an insecure telephone. They'd just have to sweat. It would mean an inquiry and an official report the following day but Yuri was not really concerned, sure of a satisfactory explanation. Besides which, he was enjoying himself.

They left after only one drink, and in the uptown cab to their apartments Yuri wondered if Caroline were as curious as he was at what might happen when they got there. She did not appear to be. She went into the block ahead of him, pumped the courtesy light automatically and said: 'You won't have any coffee, having just got back. So it looks like my place.'

As he entered her apartment Yuri saw that it really was exactly like his, but without the strident colour of the Mexican rugs and bed covering. Instead the focal point of her decoration was a series of blown-up photographs and prints of what he presumed to be advertising promotions with which Caroline had been associated. He couldn't see any illustration involving walking plants.

The coffee was excellent and she had French brandy and insisted he take the enveloping easy chair while she settled herself upon the bed, legs screwed up beneath her. She said: 'I've had a great evening.'

'So have I,' said Yuri. Had it been the test he'd set it out to be? He thought so. Successful, too. Nothing positive, producing guidelines. What then? An attitude, he decided: a feeling of becoming comfortable – at ease and apparently accustomed – in what could have been an uncomfortable situation. And he *had* been uncomfortable, beyond the nervousness that Caroline's pick-up had not been as casually accidental as it initially appeared. He was at least quite sure now about that: she was an adoptive New Yorker, nothing more.

'Where are you off to tomorrow?'

He'd already told her he was leaving the following day so it was an innocent enough question. Prepared, he said: 'Canada. Life-in-the-Rockies type of article.'

'How long do you expect to be away?'

Yuri hesitated: innocent enough again. He said: 'It's never possible to be sure: as long as it takes.'

'Oh.' She seemed disappointed.

'Weeks rather than months.' Why had he said that, making some sort of promise? Tonight had been a test, an experiment, and valuable even though it was officially forbidden. He should not – could not – consider anything more.

'So there'll be other times?'

'Yes,' he said. No! he thought.

'You think I'm a pushy broad?'

Broad had certainly been a word taught him by the disillusioned American defector. He said: 'No, I don't think you are a pushy broad.'

'Want to know something?'

'What?'

'I was trying to impress you, with the coke and the tour of New York. All that stuff.'

Yuri supposed she had succeeded. He was unsure how to respond. He said: 'Why?'

She shrugged, seeming embarrassed at the blurted confession. 'Don't know. Nervous I guess.'

'And the coke helped?'

'Didn't do a lot for me, actually. It was a gift, from a client: sort of thing they do in Madison Avenue and Wall Street. I've had it a long time. I wasn't really sure how to do it.'

Yuri said: 'It's not really important, is it?'

'It's just . . .' She stopped, shrugging once more. 'There seems to be a way of behaving here,' she started again. 'Everything's brittle and finger-snapping; this minute is the last in my life, to hell with the sixty seconds coming next. I guess I behaved instinctively, imagining you'd be the same . . .'

The anxiety flooded back. Needing movement, Yuri put the half-finished coffee on a side table but retained the brandy snifter. Forcing the casualness, he said: 'And?'

'You're not,' she said, simply.

'Really so different?' Yuri realized, gratefully, that there was no shake in the hand holding the brandy glass.

'Pleasantly so different,' she said. 'You're . . .' She halted again, smiling hesitantly up at him. 'I don't know how this conversation got started: it's embarrassing.'

'I want you to go on,' said Yuri, with more sincerity than she would ever know.

'You're straight,' she said. 'Straight and nice. Not acting at all.'

The snorted laugh, of apparent modesty, fitted her compliment but it was really a sigh of relief, the amusement that of irony. He *had* passed the test. Completely. He said: 'Straight and nice sounds boring.'

'I didn't find it so . . .' She sniggered to what was becoming one of her familiar hesitations. She said: 'I'm coming on like a pushy broad again, aren't I?'

'I'll tell you when to stop.'

'Do you want another drink?'

'No.'

'Coffee?'

'No.'

They remained looking at each other, eyes held, for several moments unspeaking in a loud silence. Then Caroline smiled and said: 'Your move.'

All the much-considered words – like precluded and forbidden and prohibited – crowded in upon Yuri, along with others like madness and stupidity and insanity. He put the brandy glass on the convenient table, edging on to the bed beside her but avoiding any contact, just leaning forward to kiss her and she leaned forward to meet him but also without her body touching his. They stayed that way for a long time, mouth searching mouth, but when he finally reached out she snatched for him eagerly, pulling them together so that they fell back against the bed. Each started to undress the other, clumsy in their eagerness, so they became impatient and they stopped with each other and stripped their own clothes off, unable to wait. He explored her again with his mouth, her nipples hard to his tongue atop those spectacular breasts, and then tasting her wetness and she ate him too. He was too far gone when he entered her but so was she. They climaxed practically at once but he didn't have to stop and the second time took much longer, settling to a rhythm, and again they came together.

'We forgot the rules,' she panted.

'Rules?'

'In the age of AIDS we're supposed to use condoms.'

'You're safe,' he said,

'How do you know you are?'

Yuri laughed with her, taking the remark beyond her intended joke. How safe was he, in this situation? How safe in any situation? The inevitable reflection about Moscow brought another thought, jolting him. Was this how it had been for the grotesquely fat Kazin and a woman he had never known but who had been his mother? Yuri tried for some feeling, the disgust or hatred of which his father felt incapable, but could not manage it either. How could he feel any emotion about people he had never known?

The following morning he left early, before she got out

of bed, promising to call as soon as he returned and careful to stop off at his own supposed apartment to collect a case to carry from the building if she looked out of her upstairs window and saw him in the street. It meant the delay of storing it again in a left-luggage locker but he used Grand Central instead of Penn Station, which was nearer to the UN building.

He ignored his own official section at the United Nations, going directly to confront Anatoli Granov, who stared bulge-eyed at him but held back from any open demand in surroundings of which they were unsure, waiting until they began the corridor perambulation. Even then the man's fury – mixed, Yuri was sure, with relief – had to be muted by their being in a public place.

'Where the hell were you?'

'I had no choice.'

'Moscow want an explanation.'

Yuri knew that was an exaggeration, an attempt to frighten him: Granov would not have raised any alarm this quickly. He recounted the confrontation with Caroline, stressing her remarks about mysterious strangers and the janitor's gossip about the leaseholders, conscious as he talked of Granov's anger deflating.

'She was suspicious?' demanded the *rezident*.

'Curious,' qualified Yuri. 'Quite obviously it was necessary for me to remain overnight in the apartment.'

Granov nodded in reluctant agreement. 'I will recommend to Moscow that we dispose of it: find somewhere else.'

'To do that, because of a passing encounter, would too easily create suspicion,' argued Yuri at once. Why was the protest so important? It had only been a one-night stand, like all the others.

'You think we should do nothing?'

'Some eventual contact was inevitable,' said Yuri. 'To run would be quite wrong.'

'What is she like, this woman?'

'Quite ordinary,' lied Yuri easily.

'How long were you together?' pressed the older man.

'Maybe an hour: perhaps a little longer. To have

avoided the conversation would have been as suspicious as it would be to close up the apartment,' said Yuri.

They were at that part of the corridor overlooking the main entrance. Granov stopped abruptly, jerking his head to look directly at Yuri. He said: 'You didn't get involved with her?'

'Involved?' queried Yuri, quite relaxed under the questioning.

'Sleep with her?'

Yuri stared directly back at his superior. 'Even to have considered such a thing would directly contravene all my training!'

Granov retreated under the imagined outrage. 'Quite so.'

'I have a question, Comrade Granov.'

'What?'

'Some of those magazines, showing unclothed women,' said Yuri, with open-faced innocence. 'Most decadent, I thought.'

'I considered them essential, to give the impression of typical male occupation,' said the *rezident*, flush-faced.

'They're *yours!*' said Yuri, in apparent surprise. 'Would you have me return them to you?'

'Of course not!'

'What about the ass on the blonde in *Hustler!*' said Yuri. 'Wasn't she something?'

The local KGB controller stared at him and abruptly walked away without speaking.

'You've been sweating us, Sergei,' protested the American.

'That's not true,' rejected Kapalet, sure of his strength. 'The only purpose of a meeting is to pass on information: with no information there was no reason for us to meet. It would have been dangerous, in fact.'

'So you've got something!' demanded Drew eagerly.

They were in the Crazy Horse Saloon, Wilson Drew hunched over the bar, uninterested in the stage, the Russian looking in the opposite direction at the floor show in which a girl with disappointingly small breasts

171

was stimulating herself with an eighteen-inch length of thick rope. Kapalet said: 'I'm really not sure.'

'What!' said the American.

'Shelenkov is a difficult sod,' said Kapalet. 'Talks in riddles.'

'Just tell me what he says,' insisted Drew with forced patience. 'We'll solve the riddles.'

'Washington is worried, then?' The information was important to send back to Moscow.

'What do you think?' said Drew. 'They've established a special committee.'

Definitely important to relay back to Moscow. Kapalet said: 'It comes out in bits: nothing connected.'

'Just tell me!' begged the American.

The woman on the stage definitely seemed to be screwing herself with that rope. Kapalet said: 'You know about Semipalatinsk?'

Drew turned to him, frowning: 'Your development complex?'

Kapalet nodded: 'According to Shelenkov you think you've got a source there . . .'

'*Think!*' interrupted Drew, isolating the important word.

'Shelenkov got drunk, three nights ago. Said something about all those crosses over Semipalatinsk on the CIA maps being kisses, to America's oblivion.' Reluctantly Kapalet turned momentarily from the girations on the stage, to assess the reaction from the American. It was possible to see the tension stiffen through the CIA officer.

Drew said: 'I'm not sure I'm getting this right.'

'I'm not sure that I have, either,' said Kapalet, turning back to the stage. It wasn't possible to see the rope at all now. He said: 'The way it sounded to me was that having established someone within the CIA to disseminate the reports as Moscow wanted, Dzerzhinsky Square installed someone inside Semipalatinsk to leak out whatever disinformation we wanted you to swallow.'

'Holy shit!' exclaimed Drew. 'You any idea what that could mean?'

'No,' said Kapalet, whose limited knowledge anyway made it an honest answer.

'It means that if we've been misleading the President about Soviet space technology, Star Wars is just so much wasted money,' said Drew. He gulped at his drink and said again: 'Holy shit!'

'I think that's too positive an assessment, on just those remarks alone,' said Kapalet.

Drew shook his head, locked into some inward reflection. 'What a fuck-up!' said the American. 'Jesus H. Christ what a fuck-up!'

'It's been useful?' queried Kapalet, not forgetting the need to be paid.

Drew turned at last away from the bar, using the cover of his open jacket completely to conceal the passing of the money to the Russian. Drew said: 'What else?'

'That's all,' said Kapalet. Feigning the grievance, he said: 'I would have thought that was pretty good, from your reaction.'

'It's terrific, Sergei: just terrific,' placated Drew immediately. 'You're doing good, real good.'

There was a drum-roll crescendo on stage and the person whom Kapalet had for thirty minutes believed to be a woman engaged in self-intercourse with a piece of rope was triumphantly and explicitly revealed to be male.

'It was a man,' said Kapalet, disappointed.

Drew looked finally towards the stage. 'Nothing's what it seems,' he said.

'You're right,' agreed Kapalet.

18

The major entered the office with military precision but the respect of authority was there and Malik determined to maintain it, wanting the man nervous. To heighten in Chernov's mind the importance of the recall and the interview Malik had assigned an official car to bring the man to Dzerzhinsky Square directly from the airport. It also denied any opportunity for prior contact between the man and Panchenko, to prepare an agreed account.

Malik kept the security officer standing and nodded through the ritual of Chernov formally identifying himself, not actually looking at the man but appearing to study the files and dossiers carefully arranged over the desk, purposely to convey the impression of a detailed and widespread inquiry. When he looked up at last Malik said, intentionally curt: 'You were part of a squad assembled on 9 September to arrest Comrade Deputy Agayans?'

'I was,' agreed Chernov. He was a small, clerk-like man.

'Describe to me what happened.'

'With Comrade Colonel Panchenko and others I went to Gogolevskiy Boulevard . . .' began the major but at once Malik cut in, stopping him.

'No!' said Malik. 'From the beginning: the very beginning. From the time the squad was assembled.'

Chernov swallowed, pausing in the effort to recollect and when he resumed it was haltingly, which Malik decided was understandable because until ten minutes earlier the man would have had no idea why he had been brought back to Moscow. Malik actually did have Panchenko's revised report before him, following through it as Chernov talked, accepting there was no important disparity between the two accounts about the beginning of the arrest assignment.

174

'Nightclothes?' interrupted Malik again, when Chernov reached the point of Agayans opening his apartment door.

'A robe, over pyjamas.'

'What time was it?'

'Nine.'

'You are sure of the time?'

'Positive. I checked at the moment of the door opening. It is procedure.'

Which Panchenko appeared to have ignored, remembered Malik: still not an important disparity. He said: 'What was Agayans' demeanour to find himself confronted by a uniformed squad?'

Again Chernov paused, frowning to find the appropriate words. Then he said: 'There was hardly any reaction at all. I had never encountered such a response before.'

'He did not even appear surprised?'

'More as if he were dulled,' said Chernov after a further pause. 'As if he were uninterested in our being there.'

Quite a variation from Panchenko's account, decided Malik. He said: 'What happened then?'

'Comrade Agayans asked what we wanted and Comrade Colonel Panchenko said we had orders for his arrest, upon your authority.'

'How did Agayans react to that?'

Chernov shifted with discomfort and said: 'I thought he was going to laugh.'

'You thought a man about to be arrested was going to laugh!' echoed Malik.

'I mean no disrespect, Comrade First Deputy,' said the security man. 'I was trying honestly to answer your question.'

This was emerging very differently from Panchenko's account, thought Malik. He said: '*Did* he laugh?'

Chernov shook his head. 'He said he had done nothing wrong and that he wanted to get dressed, to sort it out . . .'

' . . . Sort it out . . . ?' stopped Malik. Something else not in Panchenko's report.

'Yes,' said Chernov uncertainly.

'How did he say he was going to sort it out?' insisted Malik.

'He didn't,' said Chernov and Malik felt a sink of disappointment.

'What happened?'

'He and Comrade Colonel Panchenko started to walk in the direction of a corridor which I assumed to lead into the bedroom. I started to follow . . .'

' . . . *You* followed?'

'It is procedure to accompany an arrested person at all times,' said Chernov. 'At the entrance to the corridor they stopped. There was a conversation and Agayans turned, as if he were coming back into the room.'

'The conversation!' seized Malik. 'Did you hear what was said!'

'Not completely.'

'How much!' demanded Malik.

'Odd words,' said Chernov. 'I thought I heard him say nonsense. And then something about sorting it all out.'

'Did Agayans come back into the room?'

'He definitely took one or two steps back – I'd halted, not sure what was happening – but Comrade Colonel Panchenko stopped him.'

'Stopped him!'

'Physically reached out, holding him by the shoulder. There was some further conversation and then Agayans turned away from where we were and went back along the corridor.'

The questions jumbled in Malik's mind but he refused to go out of sequence. He said: 'What did you hear of this further conversation?'

'Again just odd words,' said Chernov. 'I thought I heard Agayans say "settled" and I'm sure Comrade Colonel Panchenko said "bedroom" . . . something like "in the bedroom" or "to the bedroom".'

'During this time,' said Malik, speaking slowly, 'did you hear any names mentioned?'

Chernov appeared to give the question some consideration and then he said: 'None.'

176

'Think about it,' persisted Malik desperately. 'Are you *sure* there was no name mentioned apart from mine during the conversations between Panchenko and Agayans?'

'Quite sure,' insisted Chernov.

Malik was reluctant to leave the insistence upon names but decided that he had to. He said: 'What happened when Agayans turned away from the main room a second time to set off down the corridor?'

'Colonel Panchenko *did* come back into the room,' said Chernov. 'Actually turned me back to where the others were standing.'

'*Turned* you back?'

'Yes.'

'Did you find that unusual?'

'Yes. As I have already explained it is procedure always to accompany a detained man.'

Malik said: 'What conversation was there when you and Panchenko returned to the rest of the squad?'

'Comrade Colonel Panchenko gave orders how we were to travel back to the First Chief Directorate headquarters . . . who was to occupy which car and who was to accompany Comrade Director Agayans.'

'And then?'

'Comrade Colonel Panchenko told us to remain where we were and said he was going to check the bedroom.'

Malik looked back at his crowded desk, isolating the disclosures the major had made. He said: '*Told* you to stay where you were?'

'Yes.'

'Told who? Just you? Or the rest of the squad?'

'The remark was generally made but Comrade Colonel Panchenko appeared to address the remark to me.'

'Were you surprised by that?'

'Regulations do not stipulate the precise number of people who should accompany a detained person in these sort of circumstances,' said Chernov unhelpfully.

'What time elapsed from the moment Agayans went towards the bedroom, the discussion about the cars, and Panchenko following the man along the corridor?'

'Three minutes,' said Chernov at once.

Curbing any excitement in his voice, Malik said: 'How can you be sure it was three minutes?'

'I checked my watch,' said Chernov simply.

Which Panchenko also claimed to have done, recalled Malik. And recorded the interval as ten minutes. He said: 'There is no possibility of your being mistaken about the time?'

'Absolutely none,' insisted the man.

'When he left you a second time did Panchenko hurry towards the bedroom?'

'Yes,' said Chernov.

'Did he say anything as he left the room?'

'Nothing.'

'You could not see Panchenko enter the bedroom because the corridor bends?'

'That is correct.'

'So what did you hear?'

'A voice. Someone shouting "No!" '

Slowly again Malik said: 'How long after Panchenko had gone out of your sight did you hear the shout?'

'I did not record the time but it would only have been a matter of minutes.'

'One minute? Five minutes? Ten minutes?'

'Nearer one minute.'

'And then?'

'There was the sound of a gunshot,' said Chernov. 'We all ran along the corridor, to the bedroom.'

'What did you see when you entered the bedroom?'

'Comrade Colonel Panchenko was kneeling over Agayans. The body was on the other side of the bed, half hidden, but it was obvious he'd shot himself: half his head had been blown away. The bedside table had collapsed, where he'd fallen against it.'

'What did Panchenko say?'

There was a pause for recall. Then Chernov said: 'My recollection is that the Comrade Colonel said: "He's shot himself, the bastard." And then he said: "This isn't going to look good on my record." And almost at once, again, "The bastard." '

'Who shouted "No!"?' asked Malik.

'Comrade Colonel Panchenko,' replied Chernov at once. 'After calling Agayans a bastard and saying that he'd shot himself, the Comrade Colonel said: 'I shouted for him to stop but I couldn't get to him in time.'"'

'Yet you said a few moments ago "a voice",' reminded Malik. 'You didn't say it was Panchenko.'

'It could not have been anyone else, could it?'

'Could you positively identify it as Panchenko's voice?' persisted Malik. 'Could it not have been that of Agayans?'

'Agayans!'

'Answer the question, don't pose one.'

'The voice was indistinct,' conceded Chernov.

'Could you swear to the fact that the protest was made by the Comrade Colonel if required to do so by a tribunal?'

'No,' said Chernov, in further concession. 'I could not.'

'Was there any talk of calling a doctor?'

'He was obviously dead, as I have already said.'

'Or the civilian militia?'

'Comrade Colonel Panchenko ruled that it should remain an internal KGB matter.'

'Were any technical experts called to the apartment?'

'Not during the time I was there.'

'Any evidence assembled at all for a possible inquiry?'

'I took the gun to our forensic department here and made a report to the medical expert examining the body at the mortuary.'

Upon the sheet in front of him Malik wrote the word 'gun' and put a query against it. He said: 'So there was an autopsy?'

'I believe so,' said Chernov. 'I was not called upon to attend.'

Alongside the query about the gun Malik wrote 'autopsy' and queried that, as well. Enough to reopen the inquiry, he wondered. Without doubt sufficient to have brought about a stronger rebuke at the original hearing but, alone, the further indications of negligence

179

were scarcely grounds for a reconvening. He said: 'Did Agayans at any time in your presence seem suicidal?'

'No,' said Chernov without any hesitation.

'Did you expect to be transferred to Kiev?' demanded Malik abruptly.

Chernov frowned at the unexpected question. 'No, Comrade First Deputy.'

'Did you request it?'

'No.'

'Were you surprised to be transferred?'

'Yes,' said the man at once.

'I've given orders today for you to be reassigned back here, to Moscow,' announced Malik. 'I may wish to question you further about the incident.'

Malik had held back from issuing such instructions, wanting Chernov in the capital for questioning before Panchenko learned of the recall. The security chief did so within an hour of the encounter, with the arrival in his office of Malik's official but delayed edict. Panchenko had already made the alarm call to Kazin when the second notification reached him, this time from Major Chernov strictly obeying the earlier directive issued by the security chief that any interview or approach concerning the incident involving Igor Agayans should be immediately reported.

So Malik had not given up, Panchenko realized. The man intended sniffing on, like some dog searching for a half-detected scent. Except that there was not one dog but two, Kazin as well as Malik. And Panchenko recognized he risked being chewed and torn between them, like some disputed rabbit. Panchenko confronted the fact that he was already too committed and too exposed. It was time he started taking what little precautions still remained open to him.

David Proctor kept the monthly appointment upon which Levin had insisted, striding hand outstretched into the debriefing den and repeating 'Yevgennie, it's good to see you, Yevgennie' several times before releasing the Russian. As soon as the FBI man sat down, his spectacles began their on-off movement, to be polished and repolished.

'What news about Natalia?' demanded Levin at once.

Proctor frowned towards the debriefer. 'Didn't Billy tell you about the letter agreement?'

'Sure did,' said Bowden at once.

'I meant about her coming here.'

'Give us time, Yevgennie!' pleaded Proctor. 'We're practically moving at the speed of light as it is.'

'It doesn't seem so to me.'

Proctor put his spectacles briefly into place and said: 'It's come good, Yevgennie.'

'What do you mean?'

'We caught Lubiako, red-handed,' announced the American.

'When?'

'Two nights ago,' disclosed Proctor. 'We were letting him run, as you know. But keeping him under the tightest surveillance. Our people followed him directly from the United Nations and out to Newark airport. Nabbed him actually making the exchange with a junior technician at a company holding a whole bunch of defence contracts with the Pentagon.'

Dzerzhinsky Square were prepared to sacrifice a very great deal, Levin thought. He said: 'What happens now?'

'Moscow is making a song and dance. We'll arraign Lubiako but I guess we'll have to agree to a swap. We usually do. But it means we've taken some bastard traitor out of circulation at one of our defence plants.'

'I'm glad it worked out for you,' said Levin.

'Time to move on a little now,' announced Proctor.

'Move on?'

'We're going to tell the CIA what you told us,' came in Bowden.

Levin kept any reaction from showing, the almost immediate excitement balanced by his finally understanding why the delay had occurred. They had wanted one of the KGB agents he had identified positively to be proven an operative – and by so doing provide further proof of his own genuineness – before making any approach to the sister agency. Cautiously he said: 'I am surprised you kept it from them.'

'Reasons, Yevgennie, reasons,' said Proctor. 'It'll mean they'll want to see you.'

Time for awkwardness, decided Levin. He said: 'I've been promised a letter from Natalia. But I haven't received one yet. And we don't know what to do with those we've written to her.'

'Why I'm here,' said Proctor glibly. 'Your mission . . .' He hesitated, smiling again. ' . . . Your *old* mission,' he qualified, 'have agreed to the correspondence being exchanged through the United Nations. Give me what you've got and I'll take them back to Manhattan with me tonight.'

'And Natalia's, to us?'

'I'll come up as soon as anything arrives. My word.'

'I had expected to hear by now,' protested Levin. It was not difficult for him to appear disgruntled.

'I'm sure it'll be soon,' soothed Bowden. 'What we'd like to settle today is cooperation with the CIA.'

'What sort of cooperation?'

'Your telling the Agency everything you know. We can assure them that you will, can't we?'

'It will be safe?' demanded Levin, maintaining the pretence of a nervous defector.

'You surely don't need any proof of that?' said Proctor. 'You're armour plated.'

'How will it be done?'

'Still to be decided between us,' said Bowden. Imagining the reassurance was necessary, he said: 'But you're not to worry. You'll be absolutely protected whatever the arrangement.'

'Of course I'll cooperate,' said Levin, apparently conceding. Guessing how much the FBI would want it, he added hurriedly to Proctor: 'But however it's done, I want either you or Billy with me. I don't want to be with people I don't know.'

From the other men's immediate and smiling response Levin knew he'd guessed correctly.

Proctor said: 'You're going to insist on that?'

'Definitely.'

'Then we'll be with you, every step of the way,' guaranteed Bowden. The FBI would have sought positive involvement: Levin was their catch, to be shared but not taken over.

'You will bring anything from Natalia, the moment it arrives, won't you?'

'My word,' promised Proctor again.

Always a quick undertaking, thought Levin. He said: 'And something else. We're cooped up here like prisoners. Aren't we allowed some sort of outing?'

'Why not?' agreed Proctor at once.

At last things were moving, thought Levin. Literally.

Establishing that *a* Caroline Dixon worked at an advertising agency occupying three floors of the skyscraper block near Madison and 46th Street was almost overly simplistic: Yuri telephoned the number, was assured an executive of that name was employed there and was available and hung up before he was connected to her extension.

He snaked his zig-zag way from the UN, doubly, redoubly and then again retracing his own route. Finally satisfied he was alone he was in position just up from the cross-street junction by 4.30 in the afternoon, aware as he established himself he had no idea what time she would leave.

It was 6.45 before she did, by which time he had had to shift positions four times to avoid drawing attention to himself by loitering, which was not the immediate focus of anger. The woman who left, laughing, was *the* Caroline Dixon. And she was hand-in-hand with a bespectacled, three-button-suited, clip-collared, club-tied man with a short haircut and vacation-determined tan. Why irritation? he demanded from himself at once. The purpose of the expedition was to confirm that the person whom he had encountered at the 53rd Street safe house was who she claimed to be. Nothing else apart from being sure: ridiculous to be irritated.

He was lucky to halt a cab almost in procession to

theirs, stumbling his uncertainty about a destination by saying he was unsure of the address he wanted, gesturing the man in pursuit of the vehicle one hundred yards ahead and saved any positive difficulty by their stopping at a bar just two streets and three blocks away. There was another bar, practically opposite, and he got a window bench and sat with a club soda growing warm between his hands as Caroline and the man encountered a group that seemed to expect them and with whom they drank, for another hour. Yuri stayed with the one club soda. It was more difficult to follow them the second time, because it was later into the evening and the taxis were not so frequent but again they only went three blocks and on the same avenue this time, so it was a straight-line journey and he never lost sight of them. He thought of following them into the restaurant, confident he could conceal himself in the bar, and then decided it was a pointless pursuit and so he abandoned it, but not at once, lingering for almost an hour for no reason, knowing he was behaving foolishly. Maybe he'd already behaved foolishly, he thought, as he finally hailed yet another cab: maybe he should have taken some precaution against AIDS. It was followed quickly by another thought. How was it that his father couldn't hate, at being cuckolded as he had been?

19

Panchenko had hinted the emergency was greater than before – and definitely sounded more alarmed – which made avoiding the First Chief Directorate building even more essential than after that other panicked call. Kazin decided against using the car again, instead designating the gazebo overlooking the metro station from Izmaylovo Park. Kazin still travelled there in his official vehicle. It had been years since he'd deigned to use any sort of public transport: ten at least, maybe fifteen. He could still remember the stink of too many bodies crowded together.

Panchenko was already waiting, once more ill at ease in civilian clothes, the same dark topcoat over the same dark suit. Away from the warmth of the car, Kazin shivered in his own overcoat, thinking the vehicle might have been more comfortable after all. He pulled into the rotund garden house, glad of the partial protection from the worst of the evening chill.

'So what's the problem?' Kazin demanded at once.

'Malik's still investigating,' announced Panchenko.

The familiar chill Kazin experienced now had nothing to do with the evening's cold. He said: 'How do you know?'

'He withdrew Chernov from Kiev. I've just had two hours of the man telling me all about this afternoon's interview with the bastard,' said Panchenko.

'How the hell *could* Chernov have been withdrawn without your knowing?' demanded Kazin.

'Malik withheld notification of authority until Chernov was back. Had him taken directly to Dzerzhinsky Square from the airport.'

'It is a problem,' conceded Kazin. 'A serious problem.'

Panchenko snorted an empty laugh, openly careless of Kazin's superiority. 'Serious! You're damned right it's serious! It could be disastrous . . .' The pause was achingly posed. ' . . . Disastrous for both of us . . .'

Still not the time for correction, thought Kazin; but then it had not been on the previous occasion, either. As insistent now as he had been then, Kazin said: 'Tell me everything, from the very beginning: nothing left out.'

Panchenko did, from the discovery of the recall notice and the coincidence of Chernov's almost immediate approach, and throughout Kazin listened head slightly bowed but surprisingly – illogically – all the time conscious of the flow of people in the street outside, funnelling white-breathed towards the underground station. Small people with small fears, he thought, almost enviously.

'How could Chernov have told a story so different from yours?' Kazin said when the security chief finished.

'How could he do otherwise?' came back Panchenko, as irritated by that remark as he had been by the earlier reflection. 'It was to avoid any contradiction that we had him posted to Kiev!'

'I never imagined Malik would be this determined,' said Kazin, reflective again. But why not? Hadn't the misshapen pig been this determined when he'd returned from Stalingrad, the whey-faced, bemedalled war hero, to discover his wife didn't love him any more?

I love you.

Leave him then.

I can't, not like he is now.

You must.

I can't!

Momentarily Kazin closed his eyes, shutting out the memories. Urgently he said: 'So what was Chernov's impression? Why did he think he was being questioned at all?'

Panchenko replied carefully. He said: 'Chernov talked of a lot of files and documentation on the desk. And said Malik kept making notes. Chernov felt it was an official inquiry: Malik is reassigning him to Moscow to be available for more questioning.'

'And Malik knows the rest of the squad were drafted

186

away from Moscow?' demanded Kazin, wanting absolute clarification.

As he spoke, Kazin shifted, needing movement against the cold, and Panchenko followed him, so that they resumed in the same position as that in which they had earlier been talking. Panchenko said: 'Chernov was quite explicit about it. Said Malik asked him if he knew of the transfers, which he didn't of course. And then queried if Chernov had requested his move.'

'Any indication of the others being recalled?'

'No,' said Panchenko at once. Just as quickly, he said: 'But then we didn't know about Chernov until it had happened, did we?'

'You could specifically inquire,' suggested Kazin.

And have my name upon an incriminating document, thought Panchenko. He said: 'What legitimate reason would I have for doing so?'

Kazin again avoided a direct reply. Instead he said: 'So Malik has brought back to Moscow a man who's given an account different from yours. And might possibly interrogate the others. But so what? Every recollection *has* to vary.'

'Can you take the risk of his probing until he finds the evidence you know is there to be found?' asked Panchenko.

So much about this encounter appeared a repetition of the first, thought Kazin, recognizing the qualification. Responding to it and wanting to correct the imbalance in their positions, he said: 'No, I don't suppose I can take that risk. I don't think that either of us can take that risk . . .' Now he staged the artificial pause. 'But my understanding was that the evidence, such as it is, incriminates you?'

'I was following your orders, not Malik's, in doing what I did that night at Gogolevskiy Boulevard,' insisted Panchenko.

'I don't remember anything being written down: any provable documentation,' said Kazin with ominous mildness.

For a long time Panchenko stared unspeaking across the narrow space separating them. 'I see,' he said.

'No,' said Kazin, with forced patience. 'I don't think you do see. Perhaps I was wrong, a few moments ago, in trying to minimize the dangers. Something has to be done, to protect us both. Permanently to protect us both. But before we consider that, let's consider something else that would be wrong. It would be a very stupid mistake for us to fall out: to start making threats against each other. I think you are dependent upon me and I am dependent upon you. Have I made myself clear?'

'I think so,' said Panchenko. In the half light the man's expression seemed something like a smile. 'What can be done to protect us both? And permanently?'

Once more Kazin wished there had been an opportunity, an hour at least, for more consideration. He said: 'Something *very* permanent.'

There was no expression resembling a smile upon Panchenko's face now. His voice cracking with the strain, the man said: 'You can't seriously mean that!'

'What's the alternative?'

'I don't know,' said Panchenko. The words still groaned from him.

'We can't go on, always threatened like this,' urged Kazin.

'How!'

'An accident.'

'No!'

'You did it before.'

'Which is why I don't think I can do it again.'

'Disastrous,' said Kazin.

'What?'

'Your word,' reminded Kazin. 'You said the continuing investigation could be disastrous. And it will be.'

Panchenko shuddered. Weakly he said: 'I really don't think I can. Not again! There must be some other way.'

'There isn't,' insisted Kazin.

'Mine is always the risk, never yours,' protested Panchenko.

'You're trained, I'm not.'

'It can't be another shooting.'

'I said an accident.'

'When?'

'Soon. It has to be soon. Before he has time to dig any deeper.'

'The last time,' said Panchenko, an insistence of his own.

'There won't again be the need,' assured Kazin. And if there were Panchenko would have to obey whatever order he was given because he was not in a position to do anything else. Despite which, once Malik was out of the way, Kazin determined to disassociate himself from Panchenko. Not discard him, of course: appear to remain his advocate, in fact. But to limit their contact and association. Panchenko had been useful this time and doubtless would be again but it would be wrong for the man to imagine any permanent situation. Kazin had not enjoyed having so openly to concede the dependence.

'You know you're telling me to kill a First Chief Deputy of the KGB, don't you?' said Panchenko.

Kazin shook his head across the tiny pavilion at the security chief, inwardly contemptuous of the man's almost catatonic demeanour. Most definitely limited contact in future, he thought. He said: 'I'm telling you how to save yourself from destruction. How to save us both.'

Panchenko, who had feared the other man might become suspicious at the almost awkward repositioning when he'd shifted in the cold, decided he had been wise to equip himself with the sound equipment and the directional body microphone to record everything that had been said between himself and Kazin. He tried to think if there were anything he had failed to manipulate on to the tape and decided there wasn't. He said, finally for the benefit of the recording: 'I obey your orders, Comrade First Chief Deputy.'

Natalia's maternal grandmother lived on the outskirts of Mytishchi, in a forever stretching development of identical high-rise after identical high-rise. It was a neglected estate. The elevators were invariably broken and the smell along the therefore necessary stairways, cavernous by design and dark from the further neglect of unreplaced bulbs, was of sour damp and even sourer cooking. But it was an unshared apartment and therefore luxurious by Soviet standards and so from the moment of Levin's defection the old woman and the girl had lived in daily apprehension of eviction. So when the official envelope was delivered both were initially too terrified to open it, staring fearfully at it on the table between them, as if in some way it were contaminated. It was Natalia who moved at last, the bravery of youth coming slightly ahead of the resignation of age, and when she read its contents the girl's bewilderment deepened.

'I can write,' she announced simply. 'The Foreign Ministry are permitting us to exchange letters.'

'Nothing about having to get out?' demanded the old woman, unimpressed and still suspicious.

'Nothing.'

'It doesn't make sense,' she insisted. 'Retribution is always exacted against the families of traitors.'

Natalia winced at the word but didn't challenge it. She said: 'Being able to write is practically a favour.'

'It *is* a favour,' insisted the old woman. 'That's what doesn't make sense.'

Natalia sat for a long time, paper and pen untouched before her, trying to envision an ordinary sort of letter and then decided that nothing she wrote could be ordinary and that it was ludicrous trying to formulate any normal sort of correspondence. At last, almost impulsively, she snatched up the pen, scribbling hurriedly.

'My Darling Mamma and Papa and Petr,' she wrote, lower lip trapped between her teeth, 'I love you so much and thought you loved me and so I cannot understand why you have abandoned me . . .'

Inya suggested the United Nations Plaza, because it was the hotel closest to the UN building from which it got its name and because, she said, it epitomized the glamour and glitter of New York. Yuri agreed, really uncaring at the choice. When they settled in the cocktail bar, he decided it was well chosen anyway.

'Well?' she said.

'Very glitzy,' said Yuri. It was a new word he was trying out.

'Very much New York?'

'Very much New York,' he agreed. She really did have a spectacular body. So why wasn't he more interested than he was?

'I have a question,' she said.

'What?'

'You are Russian?'

'You know I am.'

The woman giggled and said archly: 'No, it's ridiculous.'

Yuri thought it was, too, but was curious at his irritation. This was seduction coquettishness, the familiar pre-mating ritual, and before he'd always accepted its necessity without impatience. So what was different this time? Forcing himself into the expected response he said: 'Go on: what is it?'

Inya sniggered again. 'You know what they say about Russians, at the United Nations?'

'What?' he asked expectantly.

'That you're all spies!'

She put her hand to her mouth, as if shocked by her own outrageousness, and Yuri hoped it was all worthwhile when they finally got to bed. It was, he reflected, still a useful test of sorts: not so many weeks – even days – ago a challenge like this would have tightened him like a spring. Tonight he just smiled back at the woman, quite unworried. He said: 'Do they?'

'So *are* you?'

Was there an aphrodisiac for her in the knowledge? Yuri said: 'Of course I am. Everyone knows that!'

'Now you're mocking me!'

He pointed towards the olive in her drink and said: 'That's a bug recording everything we say.'

'You *are* mocking me!'

'I'm telling you the truth,' said Yuri. 'All Russians are

191

spies and we've got snow permanently on our boots and we eat children and we can hardly wait to press all those red buttons to launch the missiles at America. The only reason we haven't fired them already is that we've got so many they'd all collide with each other and explode over Minsk.'

Inya laughed, genuinely enjoying herself, and said: 'OK, so I apologize. You're not a spy. I was curious, though, that you seemed to have more freedom than a lot of other Soviets in the building.'

Yuri experienced a slight stir of unease, wondering at the extent of the talk about him. He said: 'Can't you guess the reason?'

'What?'

'I'm so unimportant I'm not worth worrying about.'

'I don't think you unimportant,' said Inya heavily, moving on to another part of the ritual.

'I don't think you are, either,' said Yuri, another matching response.

Yuri guessed she expected to go at that moment but although he was impatient with this untouching foreplay he found himself strangely – inexplicably – reluctant to move on to what was the purpose of their being together anyway. Conscious of her surprise he suggested they remain in the bar, which really did epitomize the glamour of New York, like the staggering view of the Manhattan skyline from the River Café. Yuri wondered what Caroline Dixon was doing at that moment. And with whom. He forced the conversation and the lightness, making Inya laugh at least, and insisted on a further drink, aware as he did so of her curiosity.

She lived downtown, so he'd booked at Harvey's, and as the cab took them there Yuri thought of the last time he'd travelled in this direction and with whom. Throughout the meal Yuri feigned interest in her stories of Scandinavia and United Nations gossip – concentrating momentarily to isolate the hint to pass on to Granov that Smallbone, the head of their section, had homosexual inclinations – and felt another positive reluctance when he could not any longer delay their leaving.

Inya had a loft on a secluded street near Gramercy Park and so they walked. As they set out Inya slipped her arm through his and Yuri was given another reminder of another time.

Her room was high, with a view of the river, and decorated and furnished in stark Scandinavian attractiveness, contrasting blacks and whites and light furniture and a lot of space. Yuri was later to realize how hard she tried. She served chilled aquavit and put a soft jazz combo on a player, and when he kissed her – the ritual continuing – she came back at once, actually leading, which until this moment Yuri had always found arousing. Her body was as lithely exciting as he had imagined it would be and her breasts wonderful. She knew and tried every lovemaking trick and technique and throughout it all he remained limp and flaccid. He brought her off, of course, with his hand and tongue but he knew she had expected more, like he had of himself.

'You do not like me?'

'Of course I do,' he said. 'I'm sorry.'

'I'm not attractive?'

'You're beautiful.'

'Why then?'

'Drink,' he lied. 'Too much to drink.' Would Caroline be with her three-buttoned advertising executive, he wondered.

Bowden drove in his battered, muddied car, with Petr beside him and Levin and Galina in the back.

'The grand tour!' he announced.

No one made any reply.

Levin noted the road was numbered 202 and saw signs to places called Woodville and Bantam and Grappaville before they entered an obviously preserved township which Bowden identified as Litchfield. He said it was named after a town in England, but spelled differently, and pointed out the curious verandahs around the tops of some of the colonial-style houses, which he called captain's walks, and explained they were traditionally to give the wives of sail-masted, whaling seafarers vantage points to watch for the return of their husbands. Appearing to enjoy the role of historical guide, Bowden pointed out the house in North Street once occupied by Colonel Benjamin Tallmadge, whom he smilingly named as the American chief of intelligence during the war of independence from England. On the way back to the safe house Bowden pointed out the still scarred and in places naked hills, where an infestation of gypsy moth caterpillars had a few years before destroyed huge tracts of Connecticut forests.

Throughout it all Levin sat forward, intent upon his surroundings and possible landmarks.

So did Petr and for the same reason, although he was as careful as his father to disguise his interest.

20

Finally it had all emerged so easily, reflected Vasili Malik: so stupidly, incriminatingly easy! And now he had them! Panchenko definitely. And Kazin as well. Not so definitely but enough: enough to convict them both. But this time he had to move more carefully than before. He'd failed once by initiating a premature inquiry and he did not intend losing the second opportunity by making the same mistake. And he *was* being more careful this time. Like establishing his own duplicate records, strictly illegal though it might be, of everything he uncovered, to prevent any later interference or change. And the forensic evidence, or rather lack of it, was unquestionably sufficient to reinvestigate Panchenko's account of the supposed suicide because if Agayans had killed himself the way Panchenko recounted there would have been extensive powder burns to the head, where the gun had been held close. Which there weren't. Any more, any longer, than there was still in secure custody the alleged suicide weapon. Which further forensic and ballistic examination had intriguingly discovered, before its disappearance, had fired the same-calibre bullet as the type of weapon officially issued to Lev Konstantinovich Panchenko. One of the first actions when the inquiry was reconvened would be to seize Panchenko's gun for comparable ballistic assessment against the fatal bullet. And prove, as he could from official records, that Agayans did not have a gun of his own. This time they wouldn't escape: he had them!

Near the centre of the city Malik dismissed his driver, as he habitually did every night, to walk and to think on the final half mile home but again habitually he did not set out at once in the direction of Kutuzovsky Prospekt. Instead he turned towards Red Square, striding in his uneven gait in head-bent thought, oblivious to the cupolas and the onion domes of St Basil's or the cloud-reflected scarlet stars blazing from the Kremlin towers.

Malik doubted the contradictions of the rest of the squad would be as telling that those which Chernov had already disclosed. It would be a week, possibly longer, before they arrived in Moscow. And take perhaps a fortnight after that to cross-reference the interviews for further disparities. Frustrating but necessary, he decided, aware that he had reached Novaya. This time, once and for all, he was going to rid himself of Victor Kazin. After so long, he thought. And breaking the promise to Olga, who'd begged and pleaded in those last, pain-racked days for him once again to become friends with the man. An impossible promise, he thought; one she should not have sought. Malik stared around, recognizing the Ulitza Oktyabrya and aware he'd practically completed the square.

Malik looked for and found the cross street for the shortcut to pick up Kutuzovsky Prospekt, stumping off with his mind filled again with the past and its part in the present. There was still no hate. Not for what happened before nor for what he believed Kazin had attempted, since Malik's transfer to the First Chief Directorate. He was actually surprised, disappointed even, *wanting* the consuming emotion he had once known: shouldn't he, of all people, have found that easy! He should, but he didn't. All he wanted was to be rid of the man, to remove an irritation.

He wished now he had not told Yuri: could not understand why he had. It had always been a promise to himself – and to Olga who had never known the baby was to be a boy – that the child should never know. It had been a mistake, a ridiculous weakness to blurt it out.

At least, Malik tried to reassure himself, Yuri did not know it all. Nor would he ever know.

The cross street by which Malik was limping to regain the broader thoroughfare to Kutuzovsky was dark and ill-lighted, hardly more than an alley, and enclosed in himself as he was Malik was abruptly disorientated. His first outward impression was of light going to darkness, which could not be right because it was already night and therefore dark. His continuing reaction was that he'd suffered some optical aberration, having come so recently from such a highly illuminated highway into a street sombre in comparison. And then he realized, further confused and not understanding, that it was not an optical aberration at all and that behind him a vehicle *had* entered the alley with its lights full on. But that now they were extinguished, plunging the car into an indistinguishable gloom, so indistinguishable that it was difficult to delineate it as a car at all: certainly it was not possible to see precisely where it was or guess the direction it was taking. And clumsy as his injury made him, it was quite impossible for him to attempt to get out of the way.

The following seconds – those last, brief seconds – were a chaos of thoughts too quickly brought together to form any cohesive sense. There was the horror of an approaching black mass and the recollection of a conversation with Yuri, about killing, which he knew the boy had not believed, and an instant fear of pain, of agony, and then there *was* agony, a searing, tearing anguish which incredibly – miraculously – lasted only seconds, hardly sufficient for the scream blocked in his throat to burst out. He had the disembodied sensation of being thrown against something solid – a wall, his mind was clear enough to guess – but there was no fresh jab of hurt. Rather he was suffused with a feeling of heat, a warmth almost too hot to bear. Black was crowding in and he did not feel himself fall, although there was another sensation of hardness and the black became blacker and he thought it was the vehicle again, because there was an enormous, crushing pressure, which was the last conscious awareness that Vasili Dmitrevich Malik had before he died.

There had been a shouted argument between Levin and the boy after Bowden's warning of Petr's refusal to cooperate with his tutor and another yelling dispute when Bowden reported no improvement after a fortnight, and

Levin was worriedly aware that the hostility hardening between himself and his son was stretching to create a deeper division between himself and Galina. He was desperate for something with which to break down the barriers and so he was fervently grateful to Proctor for delivering at once the letter from Natalia. He bore it like a talisman before him into the kitchen in which it had become their custom to live, in some unacknowledged preference to the other, more comfortable rooms of the safe house.

'From Natalia!' he announced.

For the first time since that outburst on the night of the defection Petr's attitude faltered in his inability to control the excitement at contact from his sister. Father and son deferred to Galina to open it. Levin discerned almost at once Galina's near-tearful collapse and Petr's instant retreat behind the accustomed wall of antagonism when the boy became aware of the effect upon his mother.

Galina tried her best at control, unspeakingly handing the letter to Levin, whose own eyes misted when he read it and who then gave it, again without speaking, to the boy.

'Abandoned!' accused Petr, the letter half read, at once picking up Natalia's accusation.

'I have not abandoned her!' said Levin. He knew it was quite the wrong reaction but felt a boredom at the persistently repeated defence.

'Convince her!' sneered the boy.

'We've written to do just that.'

'I bet that'll be a terrific comfort to her.'

'Don't you realize what this correspondence means, you stupid little idiot!' exploded Levin, exasperated.

Petr smirked, happy to have angered his father. 'Why don't you tell me!'

'It means she's not being victimized . . .' Levin snatched the letter back, gesturing to the address. 'She's being allowed to stay where she is, without any pressure being exerted upon her . . . she's being allowed to write to us and we are being allowed to write to her, in return.

198

Which is a concession which further indicates that no pressure *is* going to be imposed upon her . . .'

'Big deal . . . !'

Levin lashed out, stopping the renewed, Americanized sneer. It was an unthinking action, fury moving him, shuddering both at what he'd done and at the physical pain as the flat of his hand slapped against the side of Petr's face, which whitened and then almost at once reddened, at the force of the blow. The boy's eyes flooded at the pain and he clamped his lips between his teeth, literally biting against a breakdown. Just one tear escaped, meandering lonely down his cheek, and Petr ignored it, pretending it wasn't there.

It was Galina who was openly crying, the sobs groaning throughout the room and careless of the FBI-approved staff who remained quiet and apparently embarrassed near the stove area. Galina rocked back and forth, physically holding herself, saying 'No, oh no!' over and over again.

'Don't question me!' hissed Levin to the boy, inwardly conscious of the danger of an anger he'd been trained always to subdue. 'Don't question me or treat me with contempt or doubt it when I say that a way will be found for Natalia to come here, to us!'

For several moments Petr remained staring at his father, arms tight to his sides against the impulse to reach up to the sting in his flushed face.

'Fuck you!' he said at last. And he intended to, thought the boy: he intended to fuck his father completely for what he'd done to wreck the family as he had.

By the time Alexandr Bogaty arrived at the scene the
street was sealed, with closed-sided trucks drawn across
either end and the technicians of death, the forensic
experts and photographers and a pathologist, busy
around the body, scraping and measuring and picturing
and examining. There were two uniformed militia men
at either end of the street, reinforcing its closure, and
four more by the body. Accustomed to unexpected and
violent death, they were uninterested in the mechanics
of its cause: two were smoking cardboard-tubed Prima
cigarettes and the other two huddled close together,
stamping their feet against the cold, breath puffing
whitely from them as if they were smoking, too.

The captain, one of the two who was not smoking,
saw Bogaty's approach and broke away from the group
to meet him.

'Thought you should see this from the beginning,
Comrade investigator,' he said.

The man's name was Aliev, Bogaty remembered: a
good policeman but nervous of responsibility and so
inclined to summon superior officers when something
appeared difficult. Bogaty said: 'If it's important, I'm glad
you did.'

'It's important,' insisted Aliev.

Bogaty moved past him, towards Vasili Malik's body.
Arc lamps flooded everything in harsh white light and
Bogaty saw from the chalked outline how the man had
lain when he had been found: the body was shifted on
its side now for some pathological probe. There had been
a lot of bleeding. Bogaty said: 'What's it look like?'

'Struck from behind,' recounted Aliev. He gestured to
a bloodstain that Bogaty had missed. 'Thrown against
the wall, hard, then fell where the outline is . . .' As the
man spoke the pathologist returned the body to its orig-

inal position and Aliev said: 'It was the tyre marks . . . see?'

'Yes,' said Bogaty, 'I see.' Aliev had been right: it was important. Not that he would have been irritated if it hadn't been: given the opportunity to work meant he did not have to go home to Lydia and a diatribe of complaints about the conditions of the apartment and what she could afford or not afford upon an MVD investigator's salary and when was he going to be promoted to a senior investigator of the homicide division to get the salary increase they need just to exist, let alone live. Without the summons here he would have been drinking in some café and lied about a fictitious assignment when he got home.

'It could have been a panicked reverse to get away, of course,' suggested Aliev, guarding himself against a mistaken summons.

'Why reverse?' said Bogaty. He was a fat but tidy man who cared about his appearance. He'd been oversized since he was a child and long ago abandoned diets: Lydia complained about what he spent on clothes, as well. Once the complaint had been about how heavy he was when they made love. They didn't any more, which was a small relief.

'That's what I thought,' said Aliev, relieved.

'Who was he?' said Bogaty.

'Important: the reason for calling you,' said Aliev, offering the investigator the identification documents which had been taken from Malik's body.

'Shit!' said Bogaty. He supposed the KGB caused him more annoyance than Lydia did, if that were possible. There were frequent occasions when investigations in which he had been involved overlapped on to what they regarded their territory – which was everything – and Bogaty resented their arrogance and despised their supposed ability as competent investigators. He said: 'Have you told them?'

'I waited until you arrived,' dodged Aliev.

'Witnesses?'

'None.'

'Who found the body?'

'A motorist.'

'What's he say?'

'He turned off Oktyabrya and his lights picked up someone lying on the pavement. He was going to drive by, thinking it was a drunk, but then he saw blood. So he stopped.'

'And?'

'He halted with his lights on the body, checked that the man was dead and called emergency.'

'Where is he now?'

Aliev jerked his head in the direction of one of the obstructing trucks. 'Making a fuller statement.'

'Could he have done it?'

'No,' said Aliev positively. 'He's not showing the sort of panic there would be, if he'd done it. His car is not marked . . .' The man nodded towards the tyre tracks. ' . . . And his tyres are different from those.'

Bogaty sighed, slump shouldered, and said: 'I suppose it's time we alerted Dzerzhinsky Square: saw how the big boys operate.'

As Aliev moved away, the pathologist straightened from the body, nodding to Bogaty. 'Crushed,' the man announced unnecessarily. 'Dead almost at once. Back was broken, too. Looks like the poor sod had already suffered enough as it was, before this.'

'Couldn't have felt much, then?' said Bogaty.

'He felt a lot,' insisted the pathologist.

The doctor's departure signalled the end of the technical examination. The photographer started packing up his equipment and the forensic expert tidied small, see-through envelopes into a special wide-bodied briefcase.

'Anything?' Bogaty asked the man.

'Glass fragments,' reported the forensic examiner. 'Some paint, too . . .' He gestured towards the blood-stained wall. 'I think the car scraped it.'

'What about those tyre marks?' asked Bogaty.

'Definitely a reverse,' judged the man. 'Bloodstained from the initial impact, which registered when it came back.'

'Could the car had been jammed against the wall so that the driver needed to reverse?'

'Possibly,' said the man. 'But if it had jammed I would have expected more evidence of damage . . . more glass, more paint. Maybe some broken-off metal.'

'But there was some damage to the vehicle?'

'Certainly a broken light and a scraped wing.'

With Bogaty's arrival, the uniformed men had stubbed out their cigarettes. To one Bogaty said: 'Get the trucks moved to let the mortuary ambulance in.'

He stood directly at Malik's feet, plump chin against plump chest, staring down, moving his head left to right and right to left, tracing the passage of the hit and run vehicle. Not simply hit and run, he decided. Hit and hit again. Then run. The bloodied outline and tread of the tyres were very obvious in one direction, but there were no brake marks from what must have been the approach. Rigor mortis was already stiffening the body: the man's arm was thrown out, hand extended in a pointing gesture, and the lips were strained back from the teeth in a seized grimace of agony. Poor bugger, Bogaty thought: like the pathologist said, he'd been through enough already. Bogaty wondered how he'd suffered the earlier, appalling injury.

What would the KGB response be? Not his concern; he guessed there was very little that would be his concern. Still, excuse enough to avoid the nightly tirade from Lydia. Bogaty, who knew himself to be a very positive policeman, recognized that in his private life he was contrastingly ineffectual. One day, he reflected, he would divorce her. One day. Recalling the name of the corpse before him, Bogaty wondered if Vasili Dmitrevich Malik had been married. It would be the KGB's job to advise any widow. He would have liked to have known what the man's position had been in the Committee of State Security. Something further not to be his concern. He supposed most investigators would be grateful for such an apparently difficult case shortly to be taken from their hands, but Bogaty wasn't. He enjoyed detective work, discovering what people did not want to be discovered,

203

and would have liked to find out why a crippled giant of a KGB man had been intentionally run over and killed. Maybe not so difficult to discover: Bogaty's guess was someone with a grievance. And there were certainly enough people in the Soviet Union with grievances against the KGB: the majority of the population, he guessed.

Bogaty looked sideways, conscious of someone approaching and expecting to see Aliev but instead recognized the uniform of a KGB colonel. Instinctively he straightened and at once, irritated at the gesture of respect, relaxed again. In self introduction, he said: 'Investigator Bogaty. MVD homicide.'

The man nodded without bothering to reply, gazing down at the body.

'And you?' pressed Bogaty.

The colonel turned and for a moment Bogaty imagined the man was not going to identify himself. Then he said: 'Panchenko. Security. KGB First Chief Directorate.'

'He must have been important for a colonel to be involved?'

'It is none of your business,' rejected Panchenko curtly.

Supercilious shit, thought Bogaty: they were all the same. He said: 'He was deliberately run down. You can see where the car reversed over him.' He saw the uniformed man shiver from the cold: the feeling had practically gone from Bogaty's own hands and feet.

Panchenko said: 'It will be a KGB investigation.'

'I anticipated it would be.'

'What examination has there been?'

'Pathological, forensic and photographic,' listed Bogaty.

'It's all to be handed over.'

Why was politeness always so difficult for KGB personnel? Bogaty said: 'It will be.'

'Immediately.'

'When it's available,' qualified Bogaty. It was hardly independence but it was something, at least.

'And all your notes.'

'I haven't made any,' said Bogaty.

'Anything your officers might have.'

'The motorist who found the body is being interviewed.'

'I definitely want that.'

'That's all there is.'

'Sure?'

'Of course I'm sure!' Bogaty wasn't impressed or frightened, even if the man were a KGB colonel.

'I want everything.'

'You already said that.'

'Just so you understand.'

'He *was* killed,' insisted Bogaty.

'It is no longer your investigation.'

'You said that, too.'

There was the sound of engines from the end of the street and the blocking vehicle moved to admit an ambulance. Panchenko said to the attendants approaching with their wheeled stretcher: 'To the First Chief Directorate mortuary, not the civilian militia.'

The rigor-hardened body was easy for the men to manoeuvre on to the stretcher: briefly, for no more than a second, the one rigidly outstretched arm pointed directly at Panchenko, who looked abruptly away, back to Bogaty.

'Don't forget the official reports,' he said.

'Is it likely I would?'

'What was your name again?'

To show he was not intimidated, Bogaty spelled it out instead of saying it.

'I'll remember it,' bullied Panchenko.

It wasn't difficult to imagine why people wanted to run KGB officers down. Trying to end the encounter on his terms and not be dismissed by the man, Bogaty said: 'If I were you I'd start checking garages before whoever did it has a chance to get his car repaired,' but it didn't work because Panchenko had already turned away and was walking back to the entrance to the street, without any farewell. Bugger the man, thought Bogaty: he wouldn't get the expert reports until he asked for them. And asked for them politely. Still too early to go home to Lydia. Just one drink, in the café on Sverdlova. Maybe two.

As always Kazin insisted on caution on unsecured telephones so when Panchenko called the man said, simply: 'Safe?'

'I did what you ordered,' replied the security chief, which was not the arranged reply. But it was necessary for the tape recorder Panchenko had attached to his receiver.

Yuri approached the apartment on the opposite side of 53rd Street so that he could establish from her lighted window directly above the Soviet apartment whether Caroline were home, which she was. He closed the outside door loudly and ascended the stairs slowly, but there was no shout from above. He slammed his apartment door loudly, too, and then stood in the middle of the room feeling stupid, which he decided was appropriate because stupidly was how he was behaving. Positively childlike and juvenile, he told himself. He strained to hear her moving about, but couldn't. He started towards the uncertain television to watch it with the volume high, but halted determinedly. Time to stop being stupid. He'd come to see her and the way to see her was to call, not stumble about like some immature seventeen-year-old with wet dreams and a romantic crush. He didn't need to look up the number because he'd checked it before he left the United Nations building.

'Where have you *been!*' she demanded, at once.

'The job took longer than I expected,' said Yuri. The excitement in her voice sounded genuine.

'Are you coming to me or am I coming to you?'

So the button-down man wasn't with her. Yuri said: 'Why don't I come up?' There might be some indication of his being there.

'Hurry! I've missed you.'

She appeared to have done. She was waiting by the open door when he climbed to the next storey and when he got to her she reached out, pulling him to her, holding her face up to be kissed. When they parted she refused to let him go, clutching his hand and leading him back into the apartment, pushing him into a chair and then settling at his feet.

'It's good to see you again,' he said sincerely.

'No call!' she complained. 'Not even a postcard!'

'I'm sorry,' he said. He wasn't handling it as he intended.

'I said I missed you. What about you?'

'How are walking plants?' he avoided.

'Still walking,' she said. 'And who gives a fuck?'

Yuri looked around the apartment for some sign of occupation apart from Caroline's but could not see any. It did not mean she had not slept with the man. Yuri said: 'So what's new?'

'I had a visit,' she announced.

'A visit?'

'My brother, from California. I hoped you'd be back in time to meet him.' She swivelled, taking a small photograph frame from a ledge, and offered it to him.

Yuri stared down at the picture of the man he'd watched escort Caroline from the advertising agency. The inscription said: 'To Carro, from Peter'.

Looking up at him, Caroline said: 'What are you grinning at?'

'Nothing,' said Yuri, returning the photograph. 'I didn't know that I was.'

'I told him I'd met you.'

'Told him what?' The question only just stopped being abrupt.

'That I had a new guy who was a journalist. He asked what the magazines were but I couldn't remember.'

Dangerous, thought Yuri. Like coming here at all. So why had he, without a proper, professional, KGB-approved reason? He said: 'What does Peter do?'

'Cameraman at Universal Studios.'

'Does he visit often?' queried Yuri cautiously.

'Once or twice a year.'

Hardly likely to be a problem, Yuri decided. No more than the problems he was creating for himself, anyway.

He said: 'I still haven't got anything in. Do you want to go out to eat?'

'No,' she said positively.

'What then?'

'You really want to know?'

'I really want to know.'

'I want to go to bed and eat you.'

Which she did. Fleetingly Yuri wondered if he would have the difficulty with Caroline that had embarrassed him with Inya, but he didn't. The first time was hurried in their eagerness for each other, like before, but the next time it was slower and better and she screamed out when she came, driving her nails into his back, scratching him. Afterwards they lay quietly, locked together and unspeaking, her head against his chest.

It was Caroline who spoke first. She said: 'You sure you're not married?'

'I told you I wasn't.'

'I know what you told me.'

'So what sort of question is it?'

'The sort of question that a girl asks a guy when she wants to be sure.'

Unseen above her, Yuri swallowed. He said: 'No, I'm not married. And I'm sure about it.'

'Good.'

'Why good?'

'Just good.'

'Isn't this conversation getting a little heavy?' he said. Instead of replying, she said: 'How long are you back this time?'

'It's not definite,' said Yuri, avoiding again. He was glad her posturing with the cocaine appeared to be over.

'I want it to be a long time.'

Yuri thought he heard a telephone ringing in the apartment below but decided he had to be mistaken. He said: 'Maybe it will be.'

'Stay with me tonight? Sleep I mean.'

'If you'd like me to.'

'I'd like you to.'

They made love once more, before they slept, and

during the night Caroline awakened him and they made love again. He said: 'You're going to exhaust me,' and she said: 'That's what I'm trying to do, tire you out so you won't have the energy to go with any other girls.'

Yuri had the account already prepared when he entered the United Nations the following day, the explanation that he'd gone to check the apartment and encountered a neighbour again, smiling expectantly when Granov hurried towards him, serious-faced.

'Where the hell have you been!' demanded the *rezident* before Yuri could speak. 'We've tried everywhere to find you!'

'What is it?' said Yuri.

'Your father's dead,' said Granov.

Panchenko stared at the scraped and dented wing of the car and the gaping emptiness, where the light had been, remembering Malik's stumbling, last-minute attempt at avoidance and how he'd had to twist the wheel to hit the man and by so doing made it impossible to avoid the glancing collision with the wall. Nothing more than a minor problem, he decided: now that he had taken the investigation away from the civilian militia there was no danger of any damaging inquiry. Still essential that he take precautions. Repairs through the Directorate motor pool were logged and he had to avoid official records. So it had to be a back-street, no-questions-asked garage: from those same KGB records he wanted to avoid, Panchenko knew the name of every one. But first the car had to be cleaned: there was a surprising amount of blood.

22

The sleet started as the cars approached the Novodevichy cemetery, neither snow nor rain, just adding wet to the cold and making everything greyer. The colour – or lack of it – was one of Yuri's most positive impressions: dark cars, dark-clothed men, dark-earthed burial place. Even the sprigs and flower arrangements on the other, existing graves seemed withered and old, bleached of any brightness.

The uncertainty at the line-up to the grave was not from any respect for the man they had come to bury but one of protocol because Victor Chebrikov was attending. The KGB chairman chose his own place actually alongside Yuri: earlier the man had nodded, once. Yuri knew that anything further, like conversation, had to be initiated by Chebrikov, so he didn't speak. He supposed the man's presence indicated a great honour in memory of his father, like his signing the obituary in *Pravda*. It seemed immaterial. The self-awareness surprised Yuri. Very recently being in the presence of Victor Chebrikov would have mattered to him a very great deal.

The cortege set off through the graveyard with appropriate slowness and Yuri, who had never before been in a Soviet cemetery, became conscious of the size and ornateness of the burial place. The markers were nearly all elaborate slabs of stone or marble and many were fronted with huge, glass-protected photographs of whoever had died: the monument to a bemedalled soldier whose name Yuri could not read was actually in the shape of the five-pointed stars which adorned the Kremlin towers. More important in death than in life, thought Yuri.

Except in his case, he decided, in immediate and necessary contradiction. The formation at the graveside put Chebrikov and Yuri directly opposite the other mour-

210

ners, with the coffin in between, and Yuri gazed across the separating gap at six expressionless men for whom he was sure the ritual was a required political act, like putting their names as well to the *Pravda* report. Apart from Chebrikov the only other people he knew were Vladislav Belov, director of the American section through which he worked and Victor Kazin, from the inquiry. He'd spoken only to Belov, who had mumbled regret and at once shown up the insincerity by hurrying on immediately to practicalities. Because of his father's rank Yuri would be allowed to retain Kutuzovsky Prospekt until he could arrange the disposal or storage of his father's possessions, but the Lenin Hills dacha had to be vacated at once, that afternoon if possible. He would, of course, be allowed to remain in Moscow for a few days. Completely missing was the reaching-out attitude of their previous encounters.

Yuri was only passingly interested in his division chief, his concentration entirely upon the twitching, grossly fat Victor Kazin. His initial, extraneous thought was not of what had happened to his father and of this man's part in it but that his mother – any woman – could have gone to bed with such an ogre. Yuri thrust it aside, annoyed. That was past and this was present. He accepted now that he had been wrong in dismissing his father's talk of killing. Belov had talked of a hit-and-run accident being investigated by their security division and Yuri knew that security division to be headed by the man against whom his father had also warned. The bastards had killed him.

Kazin was gloating. So much so that as they filed into the cemetery a few moments earlier he'd abruptly had to bring himself up short, conscious that he was smiling his satisfaction. And there was every reason for satisfaction. He'd only thought of Malik's death as removing the potentially disastrous threat. Definitely not beyond: not of being summoned before Chebrikov, as he had been the previous day, and told that the experiment had been abandoned and that he was once more sole head of the First Chief Directorate. *Everything!* reflected Kazin, bursting with excitement: he'd achieved everything!

More, even, if more were possible: not only had he defeated Malik but he had emerged unchallengeable. It was very difficult not to smile; not to laugh aloud.

The son was very different in appearance to the father. Shorter, slighter and definitely of the necessary Western appearance. Kazin, who recently and sometimes worryingly experienced difficulty in remembering precisely the chronology of events, particularly those affecting the now dead man, tried to recall a previous reflection about the son, relieved when it came. Like father like son: that was it. Except that they were not alike, physically. Not important. Still the bastard son of a bastard father. And he *had* been a bastard, the person whom the inquiry had proved to have interceded in Afghanistan: caused most of the difficulty in the first place, in fact. Maybe not in the first place, Kazin corrected, straining again for the right chronology: but definitely someone who had brought about a lot of trouble. If it hadn't been for his interference, the Afghanistan entrapment would have worked. And there would not have been any condemning, although now thankfully forgotten, inquiry. Deserving of punishment then; thoroughly deserving. Like father, like son.

The idea came to him complete, without any need for refining consideration, and Kazin needed every degree of control he possessed not to smile this time, in anticipation. It was perfect: absolutely perfect. Destruction of the younger Malik and further, positive, proof to the Americans that Yevgennie Levin was a genuine defector. It was almost the moment anyway to disclose to the chairman the complete details of the Levin operation. It was going to be an impressive coup, to mark the resumption of his absolute and proper control of the Directorate. Kazin turned to look further along the line towards the head of the American section. Could he trust Belov to initiate the idea he'd just had? The man would object, he guessed: argue there was no reason to provide further proof to support Levin, like he'd argued against triggering the defection while the girl was still in the Soviet Union. Kazin decided he wasn't sure about Belov any more; not as sure as he had once been. Better to set it up himself. There would even be some vicarious pleasure in personally briefing Yuri Vasilivich Malik. Like father, like son. To be removed, like father; permanently.

Belov was conscious of Kazin's attention and answered the look, but Kazin turned away immediately. Belov accepted it had been fortunate that he'd been kept at arm's length by Vasili Malik. If the dead man had responded to the obvious invitations, Belov knew he'd be in a bad position: more so now that Kazin had been reconfirmed in the previously shared leadership, entrusted with unfettered and unquestionable control. Lucky then: but still uncertain. Kazin had survived the political jungle of Dzerzhinsky Square by judging, practically instinctively, his supporters and his opponents. So Belov anticipated the man would be conscious of his distancing himself, particularly after the inquiry. For some time he was going to have to take every precaution, every care: at least until the Levin operation was disclosed and he was identified as its architect. Maybe then he'd be less exposed. Belov felt a stir of relief: that couldn't be much longer. A month or two, hopefully.

The coffin was lowered unsteadily into the grave, almost disappearing by the time it reached the bottom. Yuri watched its descent, wondering what was being buried with it. His safety, he decided; the protection the old man had always given him in place of love and of which, until recently, he had been so absolutely unaware. So what did he feel? Hardly sadness: not the grieving-son-for-lost-father sort of sadness. Their relationship had never been one for that sort of emotion. Hadn't had time to develop, in those last few months of vaguely proper awareness. Regret, of course, but not the normal regret in such circumstances, either. It was for himself that he felt sorry. At the complete knowledge, yawning before him like the visible hole that was now being filled with sticky black earth, that for the first time in his life he had no one to look after him in perhaps the most bizarre environment in the world, fulfilling perhaps the most bizarre function in the world: that people he was sure –

he *knew* — had killed his father now controlled him, as a puppet master controlled a marionette. And that there was nothing whatsoever he could do to protect himself, to avoid jumping when a string was pulled. Or to prove the truth about what had happened to the old man. At last Yuri accepted the sensation he had so rarely known in the past and so far always refused to acknowledge, because this time it was stronger than it had ever been before and he could not ignore it any more. He was frightened; very frightened indeed.

A trowel was handed to him, to make the token gesture, which he did and then moved away from the graveside. Chebrikov was already ahead, striding more quickly now, and Yuri accepted that the chairman's presence had been as symbolic as that of the others and that there was to be no conversation between them, not even an empty phrase of sympathy. As he followed, Yuri supposed he would have to consider a headstone. He decided at once against anything as ostentatious as the majority of the monuments. For the first time he realized his father had been buried separately from his mother. When she'd died, the man had not occupied such an exalted position, he guessed: so she hadn't qualified for a place in Novodevichy. Where, he wondered, was her resting place? So much he didn't know; would never know.

'You are to remain in Moscow for a few days?'

Yuri turned at the question, startled to find himself addressed by Kazin. Despite the cold and the continuing sleet, the man's face had a glisten of perspiration. 'I am being allowed to settle my father's affairs, Comrade First Deputy,' he said with strained politeness. Less than a metre separated them, Yuri judged: irrationally he wondered if he could reach out and throttle the other man before there could be any intervention. Yuri gripped and ungripped his hands, annoyed at the reflection: he was thinking like the plots in those absurd adventure series on American television.

'Quite so,' said the Directorate chief, as if he already

knew. 'Before you return to America I want a meeting between us.'

The fear that Yuri had experienced at the grave engulfed him again, worse this time. It would be wrong for him to ask the reason, he realized. 'When, Comrade First Deputy?'

'Tomorrow,' decided Kazin. 'Make yourself available at three.' The man turned after the peremptory demand but almost at once looked back. 'Precisely at three,' he bullied. As he continued towards his car, Kazin thought that absolute power was like an aphrodisiac. Better than an aphrodisiac, in fact.

Yuri watched the man get into his car, conscious that he had an advantage in the warning from his father of which Kazin was unaware. It was a fleeting attempt at self-assurance. What good was the warning to him now, Yuri asked himself. He was quite exposed: quite exposed and helpless.

Yevgennie Levin wrote carefully and in as much detail as he felt was possible. Anything from the debriefing was obviously precluded but there was a lot from the outing through the Connecticut countryside. He did not identify any township by name, of course. He referred to Litchfield simply as an historic place, although he described the rooftop vantage points ('to watch the sea where there is no sea') and talked about the strange defoliation ('like the horrific pictures that came from Vietnam') of the elms and spruce and firs as he had travelled along the Naugatuck Valley, although he did not identify that, either, because he did not know its name. He wrote about the house, too, setting out its size and fittings and assuring Natalia that her mother and Petr were happy, fully aware as he wrote that it was a lie.

It was not until the last page – the fourth – that he tried to answer the accusation that had reduced Galina to tears and caused Petr's outburst when Natalia's letter had arrived.

'I have not abandoned you, my darling,' he wrote. 'None of us have abandoned you. We would never do that; could never do that. I have been promised that you will be able to join us here, one day . . .' Levin halted, realizing the exaggeration but deciding to leave it, guessing her need. 'That day – that one day soon – we will all be together again as a family, loving together as a family, complete as a family. Please have patience. Trust me. Know that I love you.' Levin stopped again, eyes blurred over the paper. Moscow should not have done this to him: to any of them. Presented with the situation again, Levin knew he would have abandoned the entire project and returned to Moscow, to whatever awaited him there. Quickly he stopped the run of thought. Had he returned to Moscow, wrecking what had taken so long to establish, the destruction of the family would have been even more complete, his being parted from them for years in some corrective *gulag*. Levin blinked, clearing his vision, reading the letter through and deciding there was no more he wanted to say. He repeated his love and was sealing the letter when Petr came into the den in which Levin spent most of his time; Bowden had left for the day only an hour before.

'I've just written to Natalia,' said Levin.

'When's Proctor collecting it?'

'Some time this evening.'

'Would he take one from me as well?'

'Of course.' Levin was curious, detecting the absence of the animosity to which he had now become accustomed from the boy.

As if in confirmation of his father's thoughts, the boy said: 'I want to talk to you.'

'About what?'

'Mistakes: my mistakes.'

'Doing what?'

'Behaving as I have.'

Levin smiled, hesitantly but hopefully. 'It hasn't been easy, for any of us,' he encouraged.

'I haven't made it easy for anyone,' confessed the boy. 'I want you to know that I'm sorry.'

'I didn't expect this,' admitted Levin.

'I'll never lose the feeling about being Russian,' said

Petr in apparent qualification. 'I've just come to realize that my attitude is ridiculous. What's happened has happened.'

'I never expected it to be so difficult for you,' said Levin in further admission. 'You always seemed to like everything about America: clothes, television . . . things like that.'

'Because I'd never known it before,' explained the boy. 'I used to fantasize what it would be like, going back to Moscow with things that none of the other boys had: imagine the impression I would create.'

'Now you can have them permanently,' reminded Levin.

'I've apologized to my tutor as well,' disclosed Petr. 'Did you know he used to teach at Forman School in Litchfield, that little town we went to the other day?'

'No,' said Levin. 'I did not know.'

'He says I'm doing well now.'

'It's good to hear,' said Levin. 'In fact everything's good to hear. Your mother will be pleased.'

'Natalia will be able to come one day, won't she?'

'I promise she will,' said Levin. He wished he were sure.

'Why did you do it? Defect, I mean.'

Levin hesitated, wondering if there would ever be a time when he could tell the boy the truth. One day, maybe: but not for a very long time. Inadequately, he said: 'I felt it was best.'

Petr appeared about to speak when David Proctor entered the room, earlier than Levin had expected. Levin said at once: 'Petr and I have been having a conversation. About his being here.'

'I'm apologizing for the way I've behaved,' came in Petr, unprompted. 'I'd like to say sorry to you, too, Mr Proctor. I haven't been very pleasant.'

The FBI supervisor began his habitual spectacle cleaning, smiling short-sightedly in the boy's direction. 'I've been waiting for you to accept things,' he said. 'Took longer than I expected but I knew you'd get there, in the end. Well done.'

They were stupid, all of them, thought Petr. He wasn't the least bit sorry for the way he'd behaved. Just that it had taken him so long to realize the restrictions he was imposing upon himself, by the constant opposition. From now on he was going to be the best son and the best pupil imaginable, until he was able to get away from this prison of a place to a proper classroom that the Forman lecturer had said, three days before, was essential if he were to learn properly. And he was going to be the ideal student until the first day they relaxed. Then, knowing now where he was, he was going to catch the first train from the first station back to New York and to the Russian delegation at the United Nations there. His fool of a father might have defected, but Petr Levin hadn't. And they were going to know it – his father and Bowden and Proctor – when he denounced them all, as publicly as the Soviet mission would allow him to denounce them.

23

Yuri was astonished how few of his father's personal possessions there were to remove from the dacha: from the bedroom a jacket, two pairs of trousers, some underwear and a smock, the photographs of his unknown mother; some winter boots and a frayed greatcoat, also for the winter, which he found in the outhouse. Truly a transient occupation, decided Yuri, recalling his impression the last time they had been there together: the last time he had seen his father alive. There was no mark of the man whatsoever, anywhere: as if he had never existed. Caught by the thought, Yuri wondered if at Kutuzovsky Prospekt there would be any photographs of his father: he couldn't remember there being. If there weren't, there would be no tangible memory of him at all: the pictures here were all that he wanted to keep. Everything else could be thrown away: hardly worth the trip out of the city.

Yuri bundled everything, even the greatcoat, into a single suitcase and stood above it, gazing around the main room of the country house. Who would be the next occupant? Would he – or they – make it a home, rather than a temporary resting place? He looked back to the suitcase. So little, he thought; not enough.

It was almost without thought that he mounted the stairs to make a final search for anything he might have missed, checking first the cupboards and drawers of the room he'd occupied and finding nothing apart from the government-supplied linen, and after that his father's room and finding the same. It was when he left the second bedroom that he glanced upwards, again without thought, and guessed from the slope of the ceiling above him that there was probably a loft: certainly a space between the peak of the roof and the covering above his head. Curiously, with closer concentration, Yuri looked for a trap door throughout the length of the landing but there was no evidence of one. He went back, staring upwards this time, into both bedrooms but there was no entry from either.

If there were an attic it was sealed, Malik concluded, going out again on to the central corridor: another aimless search. He was practically at the head of the stairs when he stopped, parallel with the door to the narrow storage cupboard which he'd already checked and knew to contain only more government-owned material, mostly bedcovering. He opened it again, looking for something else this time.

It was a narrow hatchway, seeming to be tightly cut from the planking after it had been laid, so that only by looking positively was it possible to detect the likelihood of an opening. And impossible to reach anyway because of the serried layers of slatted shelves upon which the sheets and towels lay. Yuri removed the contents and after the contents the wooden strips, which was difficult because they were sized differently. At first he took them all out but then realized he would have to replace one at each level, to provide some sort of ladder to reach the entry. He had to climb with his back pressed against one wall, with no handhold, and strain to push the overhead hatch open, so snug was its fitting into its surround. He had not thought of the need for illumination until the planking moved and then saw he would not need it; there was a window, invisible from the ground, actually set into the roof.

Yuri hauled himself through the gap, sitting with his legs dangling over the edge. His immediate thought was that it had been a wasted effort and that the angled room was as empty as everywhere else in the house. And then he saw the trunk, quite compact but with a curved top, wedged into the darkest corner, at the furthermost point from the window's light.

It was a small room, restricted by the roof's drop, so Yuri crawled towards the box, pulling it out directly to be under the window. There was a stir of dust and a cobweb snagged across his face, but the container appeared quite clean. For several moments he gazed down, not attempting to open it, the strange reluctance to intrude briefly stronger than his absorbed curiosity. There was a lock, but no key. To have to break it open seemed . . . he didn't know what it seemed but he didn't want to do it. But he didn't have to: the lid lifted quite easily and held, kept up by hinged metal struts. His initial reaction was one of disappointment. Yuri had expected it to be full – of what he didn't know – but it wasn't: only a third, maybe less, was taken up. There were several stacks of papers, all appearing to be aged. Tentatively he reached out, feeling their brittleness to his touch. He lifted the topmost document cautiously, conscious of tiny cracks at the edges, knowing it would be most fragile at the fold, so he was even more careful straightening it.

'My Darling,' he read. 'I am still warm from you, wet from you, feeling so much loved by you: I touch my sex to feel where you have been and want you there again. You consume me, my own darling. Make me live . . .'

Yuri jerked his eyes away from the yellowing paper, face burning and aware that he was physically blushing. He'd already guessed anyway but he still looked to the second, final sheet of what he held, for the inscription. His mother had signed it, strangely formally, 'Olga', which surprised him: he'd expected something else, a love-name, and was absurdly disappointed. Still with the first letter in his hand, Yuri went to another, separate bundle, aware at once of the different handwriting and recognizing it just as quickly. His mother's letters to his father, his father's letters to his mother: before him, on cracked and frail paper, was set out their love, their life. He felt like a child – which in reality he could never remembering feeling – peering through the keyhole of their bedroom, shocked by their nakedness and by what they were doing. But like the peeping child, he did not stop looking, despite the discomfort. The correspondence was carefully arranged by date, so that it was easy to follow, to chart the progress of their relationship. The first letters *had* been formal – his father had signed off three 'Your respectful and obedient servant', at which

Yuri openly sniggered – the intimacy gradual, almost imperceptible. As he read, Yuri's embarrassment seeped away, replaced by another surprise. His mother had only ever been a frozen image, encompassed in a frame. But he'd known his father . . . no, not known: been aware of. Familiar. He would never have believed – still could not have believed but for the letters he held in his hands – that the aloof, white-haired, uneven-shouldered man who had always found any expression of affection so difficult could have brought himself to write the sort of intimate, exposing words he was reading.

There was too much for him to read sitting up here in the darkening attic. Yuri flicked through, finding the photographs halfway down the pile of his father's letters, obviously in their special place. Four were of their actual wedding, his father not disfigured then, towering above her, thickly dark-haired. There was a shot of his mother staring adoringly up at the man and another of her placing her wedding flowers traditionally upon the monument to the unknown soldier. And then Kazin. It was not a good photograph, blurred by poor focus, but Yuri knew it to be the man: much thinner than he was now, smiling towards her. Kazin's expression appeared proprietorial, which Yuri knew it could surely not have been, not on the day that she married someone else. There was a further photograph of his mother alone, demure and not actually facing the camera, looking instead into what Yuri guessed to be the stream running past the dacha and which he preferred to the framed ones he had already packed. And a close-up, full-faced shot of his father, still uninjured. The man had on what appeared to be the same suit he'd worn at the wedding but Yuri didn't think it had been taken then: this looked more like the sort of formal portrait for some KGB accreditation, stern and expressionless. At least he would not have to worry about any photographs being available at Kutuzovsky Prospekt, thought Yuri; he wished there had been more.

He reached out, touching the unread correspondence again. How much more, beyond the fuzzy photograph, was there here about his mother's involvement with Kazin? And how much better would he know her – understand even – when he'd read everything? It was difficult to know. It would be like trying to understand someone from the pages of a book and Yuri had always found that difficult: from the contents of this box he would always be someone outside the window of his mother's and father's life, able to look in and catch the occasional word but never truly able to understand what really occurred between them.

Yuri replaced everything within the box exactly as it had been arranged when he opened it – even the photographs precisely where he'd found them – and depressed the hinges to lower the lid. He had his . . . had his what? Memories was not the right word. Legacy either. Momentos, he supposed, although that did not seem proper, either. Maybe a combination of all three. A small box (why did everything always seem inadequate?) that contained the life and the innermost secrets of two strangers who had been his parents. Maybe, after he'd read everything, they would not seem quite such strangers.

Yuri scraped the trunk across the floor after him and lowered himself ahead of it through the trap door, feeling about blindly for the foot-supporting slats. When his foot connected he eased through until he was supported by one arm, leaving his other hand free to pull the box finally to the lip of the hole. He was actually beneath it, feeling up to get a hold on its bottom, when his fingers encountered the unevenness. He managed to wedge the box on his shoulder to get it back on to the landing and having done so turned it over.

The concealment was very clever and almost perfect; Yuri guessed only his jerked hauling of the box across the attic floor had dislodged the intricately tooled wooden sleeve that formed an envelope for more papers and which was cut to fit as a false but very narrow base. He tugged at it, gently, freeing it completely and then tapping the papers into his lap. It was too dark to read them on the landing, so Yuri carried it all downstairs into the room in which the already packed suitcase lay, and lit a lamp near the stove.

I've made copies, of everything.

His father's words, that freak late summer day here at the dacha, echoed in Yuri's mind as he looked down at the documents in his hand. It had not been an exaggeration, Yuri decided. Here *was* everything: a memorandum in his father's name, within days of the GRU debacle in Afghanistan, a bundle of decoded messages to and from Kabul, aborting the insane retribution, the request for the inquiry in which he had been so disappointed and the result of that inquiry. And much more. There appeared to be a heavily annotated and queried report, from Colonel Panchenko, and another account, just as heavily marked, to point up apparent contradictions from a major named Chernov. And a top page which Yuri supposed to be some sort of index, a prompt sheet. There was a list of three men beneath the heading 'Squad' and a date, in two weeks' time. Against Agayans' name was written 'gun' with a query against it and there were question marks after notes about a post mortem and forensic examination.

Yuri sat as still as he had upstairs in the loft, this time gripped by a fury, an anger he consciously felt move through him. It was a sensation not of heat but of coldness: implacable coldness. He'd been sure his father had been killed and now he was equally sure he knew the reason; that he was physically holding it, in his hands. His father had continued to probe, as he'd said he would. And was uncovering the lies, as he'd said he would. And somehow they – Kazin or Panchenko or maybe both – had become aware what he was doing and killed or had him killed before he could obtain sufficient proof to reopen the inquiry and expose them.

And now he possessed it, Yuri recognized. So what? His fury deepened at the self-demand, because of the immediate awareness of his impotence. What he had was half an investigation, maybe more than half, but what could he do with it? He could only pass it on to be continued to someone in higher authority. And Kazin was that higher authority, the person through whom regulations decreed he always had to move, to any ultimate superior. And continued by whom? Those same regulations dictated that internal Directorate irregularities and crime be investigated by the security department headed by Colonel Lev Konstantinovich Panchenko. Helpless, thought Malik bitterly: he was absolutely and utterly helpless.

A question of choosing the greater or the lesser risk.

Something else his father had said that day: actually praising him for making the choice about intercession in Kabul. Different then, though. Then he had acted knowing he had the power and the prestige of his father behind him; had actually bullied the Kabul *rezident* with that power and prestige. Which he no longer had. Any more, as he had already frighteningly realized, than he no longer had the old man's protection.

He would do something! The conviction came quite rationally, not spurred by unthinking anger or I-will-avenge-my-father bombast. He did not know how – or what – it would be but Yuri determined to expose the two men as his father had intended to expose them.

The greater or lesser risk, he thought again. His father had taken the risk and now his father was dead. Objectively, but strangely without the fear he was finding it easy to acknowledge at last, Yuri greeted the realization without concern. He felt that knowing the danger gave him some sort of advantage: like possessing everything his father had discovered – but which Kazin and Panchenko would never suspect – gave him some sort of advantage.

He returned the file to its wooden envelope and slotted it snugly and imperceptibly into place in the base of the trunk, balancing the weight of it in one hand against the suitcase in the other to walk out into the complete blackness of the night.

So what, he asked himself, was he going to do?

As always the meeting was to be in a public place, this time the Museum of American History, and Willick hurried early in off Constitution Avenue, anxious for the encounter with the Russian. Had he been too greedy in demanding $2,000? He needed the money – Christ how he needed the money! – but he wished now he'd tried to get it a different way. Asking, in fact: not demanding. The man he knew only as Oleg had been right in reminding him of the pressure they could exert, if they chose. What was he going to do if they refused? And not only refused the increase but held back the $1,000 upon which he had become so dependent, blackmailing him into working for nothing? He'd be destroyed, Willick accepted: utterly destroyed. Christ, what a mess!

'In reality, the life of an American cowboy was very dirty, wasn't it?' said the Russian, approaching as Willick stood unseeing before some original photographs of a cattle drive to Chicago.

'Very,' agreed Willick. Who the fuck wanted to talk about dumb-assed cowboys!

'You were early.'

'Found a parking place first time,' mumbled Willick, trying not to disclose his anxiety.

'Moscow were extremely pleased with the names you provided,' announced the Russian.

Hope flared at once through Willick. He said: 'It has proved my worth?'

'Oh, absolutely,' said Oleg mildly.

'So what was their reaction?'

'They've agreed the increase as from this meeting,' said the Russian, quite matter of fact.

Willick had to bite his mouth closed to prevent the mew of relief. He'd made it! Everything was going to be all right! 'That's good,' he said tightly.

'But in return we want very specific things,' said the man.

'Like what?'

'The complete structure, names and biographies . . . on everyone possible within the CIA. From the Director downwards . . .'

'That's not all held in the records to which I have access!'

'Everything that there is,' insisted the Russian. 'For the increase to $2,000 we want absolutely everything. Do you understand?'

'Yes,' said Willick emptily. 'I understand.'

24

Yevgennie Levin had never before travelled in a helicopter and the moment it lifted off he decided he didn't like it; his stomach dropped with the sudden upward movement, so that he had to swallow against the risk of being sick and when that passed he grew uncomfortable at the fragility of everything. There seemed to be more glass than protective metal. The control panel did not appear big enough and the constant vibration jarred through him, shaking a machine too flimsy to withstand that sort of disturbance. He forced himself to concentrate upon landmarks, trying to lose himself in tradecraft. From above he saw again the withered, stripped-bare trees he had described to Natalia and then the black snake of the Naugatuck and realized there was river along the valley floor. From its direction he was able to isolate Litchfield and because the pilot initially took a south-easterly route, to pick up the coast, Levin knew how accurate he had been in describing the captain's walks as look-outs to watch the sea where there was no sea.

Bowden, who was sitting to his right, gestured and mouthed the name when they approached New York but it was an unnecessary identification: Levin had already isolated the sprawl of Queens and Brooklyn and New Jersey and the jammed-together centrepiece of Manhattan. From the air there hardly looked to be any roads or avenues at all between the stuck-together skyscrapers, as if all the buildings had been neatly packaged up to be shipped elsewhere. It was easy for him to pick out the United Nations, its greenness obvious even from this height. What would have happened to Vadim Dolya? And Lubiakov, the other sacrifice? Would the FBI surveillance still be on Onukhov, for when he made his mistake? Always questions.

The pilot continued to fly south with the shoreline in view and Levin stared down, thinking how vast a country America was. Of course the Soviet Union was as large – larger – but Levin had never flown over it like this, from literally a bird's-eye vantage point. My home now, he thought. Forever. Providing he did not make any sort of mistake: never relaxed. At least the worry – and distraction – with Petr was over. He had actually begun to fear that the rift between them was permanent and would worsen, and knew Galina thought the same. Her mood had visibly improved with Petr's acceptance of the situation. Only one major distraction remained. Would Natalia have got his last letter? Was there one on its way from her? More questions. It was important to go on stressing the concern over Natalia when he got to Langley.

Which would not take much longer, Levin guessed. The pilot made a circular approach, looping over the Capitol and then coming back upon himself, giving Levin a tourist's overflight of The Mall and the Washington Monument, and the Reflecting Pool in front of the Lincoln Memorial, before picking up the Potomac and flying parallel with it to the headquarters of the CIA. There were three cross-marked landing areas; they came down upon the first, the nearest to the hotch-potched building, wings and extensions obviously added to the original, inadequate structure. With objective comparison, Levin supposed the additions here had been made with slightly more success than those built on to Dzerzhinsky Square by Stalin's prisoner-of-war slaves.

They were expected, Levin guessed from some radio warning from the pilot. Two unidentified men approached and nodded to Bowden and Proctor, but made no gesture towards Levin. The Russian walked in the middle of the group not towards the main complex but to a small, separate building to one side. He was not surprised to be kept from the most secret centre of America's external intelligence organization; his surprise, in fact, was at being brought here at all. It would not have been the way a defector's debriefing would have been conducted in the Soviet Union, even a defector apparently with information as important as his. The encounter would have taken place somewhere far removed from the organization headquarters.

The route took them in front of the main building and directly by the statue of Nathan Hale, the American patriot hanged as a spy by the British during the American War of Independence. The history had naturally been part of Levin's instruction, which was why he had immediately recognized the name of the American chief of intelligence during that war when they had toured Litchfield with the attendant Bowden as a guide, aware that Benjamin Tallmadge had been a friend of Hale's.

Levin glanced towards the memorial, showing no particular interest, recalling as he did so a forgotten part of that long-ago basic training. As he ascended the English gallows, Hale was supposed to have said: 'I only regret that I have but one life to lose for my country.'

Which was all he had, acknowledged Levin. Remembering his helicopter reflection on the journey from Connecticut, the Russian thought again how careful he was going to have to be, now he appeared to be within finger-touching distance of making work the operation he'd been sent to perform. If they found out what he was really doing then he really could lose his life, he realized.

At the entrance to the outbuilding Proctor and Bowden went through the required identification and screening and Levin guessed he was being photographed by various unseen cameras positioned in the foyer. When the security officials completed their checks of the two Americans they took prints of Levin's every finger and thumb, photographed him with an instantly produced Polaroid – which Levin thought created a very bad picture – and had him sign against it and the prints on a large, official-looking form. Levin wondered with whom or with what the details were going to be compared in a further effort to confirm his bona fides.

The unspeaking escorts took them to a ground-floor room at the back, overlooking a packed car park which Levin thought larger than the square separating the KGB headquarters from the GUM department store, back in Moscow. A Cona coffee machine steamed on a side table and Levin nodded acceptance to Bowden's invitation.

'Feel OK?' asked Proctor.

'Fine,' lied Levin. Persist with his genuine concern over Natalia and volunteer no more than the very minimum to any question, he thought. String it out, in fact: ideally there had to be as many sessions as possible.

Harry Myers led the committee into the room, with Norris immediately behind and Crookshank coming last. The formation told Levin that Myers was in charge, although no introductions were made, which he did not expect. Myers jerked his head to Proctor and Bowden with the familiarity of the earlier escorts and then smiled, with surface politeness, at the Russian.

'Appreciate your coming here today, sir,' said Myers. 'Believe you might have things to tell us that we'd find extremely interesting.'

Although he hoped for more meetings between them, Levin studied the three CIA officials with instinctively intense professionalism, trying to memorize in one interview every personal detail for later recall and possible – although now unknown – use. The chairman was a huge bear of a man, obese with neglect and indulgence, flowing beard unkempt, strained suit sagged and bagged around him. Maybe an intentionally careless appearance – as he judged Bowden's appearance to be intentionally careless – to inculcate ill-judged contempt. Just like it would be ill-judgement to infer respect by the man's use of the word 'sir', which Levin had come to recognize from his time in America to be a verbal mannerism, the equivalent of a comma or a full stop in a sentence and nothing to do with respect. The man to his right was contrastingly neat, crisply suited, crisply barbered, open-faced. The third member of the panel wore a suit and a club-striped tie but Levin was intrigued by the hair, long enough practically to reach his collar. Of the three only the last set out pens alongside the yellow lawyer's pad, to take notes.

Nodding towards Proctor, Levin said: 'I have promised to help, in any way I can.'

'You've said you believe there to be a spy within this agency?' demanded Norris, direct.

'I have also been promised help,' avoided Levin, smoothly.

'Sir?' said Myers.

'What progress has there been getting my daughter Natalia from the Soviet Union to join me?'

'We've gone through all this, Yevgennie,' came in Proctor. As he spoke he shrugged apologetically in Myers' direction. Back to the Russian he said: 'You know we're doing all we can.'

Ignoring the FBI supervisor, Levin said to Myers: 'Have you heard anything from your sources?'

Myers sighed. He said: 'We know your concern – can understand your concern – but until today we haven't been involved . . .'

' . . . Can you do anything now that you are involved?' interrupted Levin, finding no difficulty with the urgency.

'Like what?' demanded Norris, recognizing that the matter of the man's daughter would have to be disposed of before they could go any further.

'You've got a CIA residency at the American embassy in Moscow. Assets, presumably,' said Levin. 'Can't you find out what's happening to her?'

'You're getting letters telling you what's happening to her,' responded Norris carelessly. 'She's not under pressure.'

The reply told Levin several things. From it he knew there was some liaison concerning him between the FBI and the CIA. Which therefore meant here at least there was not the animosity that existed in his own country between the KGB and the GRU. And that if they knew she was not under pressure they were opening and reading the letters before passing them on. Monitoring the correspondence was to be expected, he supposed: the KGB would be doing the same in Moscow. There would be a lot of curiosity about him in the American section of the First Chief Directorate. He would have liked to

232

convey some message but knew any attempt at a code was impossible; particularly now he had confirmed the tampering. To extend the conversation, he said: 'Couldn't you make some inquiries?'

'But would that be wise?' demanded Myers at once. 'You are trying to get her out, right? Can't you see the danger, of Moscow discovering the CIA inquiring about her? They could stage a trial over something like that.'

To explain the apparent thoughtlessness of the demand, Levin said: 'I'm very worried about her. Desperate.'

'We know, sir, we know,' soothed Myers.

'Will you tell your State Department how I'm helping: add to the FBI pressure?' persisted Levin.

'Sure,' said Myers, the promise as glib as Proctor's had been, that first day.

'What is it that makes you think there's a spy here?' demanded Norris, maintaining his earlier insistence.

'Things that happened when I was at the United Nations,' started out Levin.

'What things?' It was the first time the long-haired man had spoken: Crookshank had an oddly high-pitched voice.

'There was a KGB man, here in Washington . . .'

' . . . Name?' broke in Crookshank, pencil ready.

'Shelenkov,' identified Levin, as he had been instructed all those months ago, in Moscow. At that moment he was more alert than at any time since the interview began and was aware of the look of recognition that passed between Myers and Norris.

'What do you know about him?' said Norris.

'He was ranked number three at the *rezidentura* . . . regarded as a good operator.'

'How was he involved with you at the United Nations?' asked Myers.

'That's it,' said Levin, intentionally obtuse. 'He wasn't.'

'I'm not following this,' protested the CIA lawyer.

'There is occasional liaison, between the embassy here and the UN mission,' said Levin. 'Just very occasional. There was a standing instruction, which could not be ignored, that Shelenkov should never, under whatever circumstances, be involved in any contact.'

'Why not?' asked Norris.

'For the risk of being compromised, in something else.'

'Something else?' It was Crookshank who asked the question.

'It was understood that Shelenkov was completely seconded to just one job: that he could be considered for no other operation.'

'Understood by whom?' demanded Myers.

'Everyone in New York.'

'The mission in New York were told this?'

Levin shook his head, conscious of the trap. 'That is not the way intelligence is conducted . . . not KGB intelligence, anyway. Individual operations are boxed, agents working quite separately and unknown to each other.'

'So how was it understood?' said Myers.

Levin allowed the impression of slight irritation. 'Because of the hands-off order. A KGB officer is never . . . well, rarely . . . allowed the luxury of just one assignment. There are always several ongoing.'

'If Shelenkov were so removed from everything, how do you know he was not active in several, ongoing operations?' said Norris. 'You explained yourself a few moments ago that the very principle of espionage is limiting the knowledge of operations.'

'People talk,' said Levin. 'Other agents in the Washington embassy said he was removed from any normal, day-to-day functioning. Actually complained at the extra work load it imposed upon them.' To convey the impression of strain, which he was genuinely feeling, Levin looked in the direction of the coffee and Proctor took the hint and moved to refill his cup.

'We're dealing with disgruntled gossip?' said Crookshank with a lawyer's dogmatism.

Levin shook his head. 'With good reason for their being disgruntled,' he said, in insistence of his own. 'You must believe me when I say it's unheard of for anyone

234

in a *rezidentura* to be allowed to operate like that, without good reason.'

'Gossip,' said Crookshank dismissively.

Concern moved through Levin at the thought that in his keenness to protract the interview over a period, to impress them sufficiently, he might be risking the panel rejecting what he was saying. Before he could speak, Myers picked up: 'What sort of good reason?'

'An exceptional source,' said Levin simply.

'You think Shelenkov had such a source?' said Norris.

'I know he did.'

'Know!' The demand came simultaneously from Myers and Norris.

'There are three ways of transmitting to Dzerzhinsky Square,' recounted Levin. 'The first is electronically, from the embassy. Secondly there is the diplomatic bag. Moscow are suspicious of both. Anything electrical can be intercepted, monitored . . .' He paused, looking sideways at Proctor. 'And the diplomatic bag is not regarded as being completely safe: there have been tests and from them we know that the FBI open them, although they are supposed to be protected by international agreement . . .'

'What's the third way?' intruded the lawyer impatiently.

Levin did not respond at once, staring across the intervening table and realizing that of the three, this long-haired man was the one he had to convince. He said: 'Personal courier. It's practice for people personally to transport things . . . encoded and concealed in microdots or hidden in some way. This was always the way that Shelenkov's material was moved to Moscow.'

'How do you know, if he were kept so separate from you?' said Crookshank.

'I was told, by people in Washington . . .'

' . . . Gossip again,' interrupted the lawyer.

'Fact,' rejected Levin, prepared. 'On occasions the courier was from the United Nations. Always it was to move what Shelenkov had.'

'Who was the courier at the United Nations?' The question came from Bowden but the CIA group showed no annoyance at the questioning being taken away from them.

'Vadim Alekseevich Dolya,' identified Levin, the lie already prepared, knowing from Bowden's disclosure in Connecticut of Dolya's withdrawal to the Soviet Union that he could not be challenged.

'Let's accept for a moment that Shelenkov *did* have an exceptional source and that Dzerzhinsky Square were prepared to operate in the unusual way you've described,' explored Norris. 'You haven't so far given us any indication why that source should be CIA.'

'Moscow identify the CIA by the same name by which you call yourselves,' disclosed Levin. 'The Company . . .' He smiled apologetically. 'It amuses them, I think. On every occasion when material was carried through UN personnel, Shelenkov used that phrase. "Company business" or "Secrets from the Company".'

'You told us he was regarded as a good operative,' reminded Myers. 'Number three in the *rezidentura*, you said. A good operative would not have been as indiscreet as that.'

Levin appeared to hesitate, before responding. 'Shelenkov had a problem,' he said. 'He drank too much. The story that filtered back to us at the UN was that Moscow specifically moved him because they were frightened by his indiscretions: that he might reveal his source, through carelessness.'

'You're saying that he used the expression about the Company when he was drunk?'

'Yes.' It was all coming out more quickly than intended and they'd missed something upon which Levin had expected them – wanted them – to pick up. He shifted laboriously in his chair, to give the impression of discomfort.

'UN personnel?' said Crookshank.

Levin was sure he concealed his relief. 'I am sorry?' he encouraged.

'A while back you identified . . .' The lawyer paused, consulting the legal pad. ' . . . Someone called Vadim

Dolya as the courier. Then you used an expression about UN personnel, as if more than one man were involved.'

'There were,' said Levin. He spoke simply, as if surprised at Crookshank's confusion, glad it was this man who had initiated the questioning.

'This isn't coming easily, is it, Mr Levin?' demanded the lawyer.

'I have promised to help,' reminded the Russian. 'I am responding as best I can to what I am asked, how I am asked it. I do not have a prepared statement: there was no way I could anticipate what you were going to ask me, apart perhaps from the first, obvious question.'

'I'm sure my colleague was not trying to sound critical,' said Myers, soothing again. 'It's all going to come out in time.'

From the look that Crookshank gave the unkempt man it was clear he had very much intended to sound critical, but Levin only gave that impression passing thought. He was more intent upon what Myers had said, indicating further sessions: at last! Levin thought, further relieved.

'Did you ever have any direct contact with Shelenkov?' asked Norris.

'Yes,' said Levin, conscious once more of the looks that went between the three men he was facing.

'Maybe you'd better describe the system, so that this stops coming out like we're pulling teeth,' said Crookshank.

'As I thought I'd already made clear, the primary consideration was to avoid Shelenkov's activities being compromised in any way. Which meant, naturally, the use of cut-outs.'

'You acted as a cut-out?' pressed Norris.

'Yes.'

'How often?'

Levin hesitated, seeming to give the question consideration. 'Maybe three or four times.'

'You know the importance of what we're asking!' erupted Crookshank at once. 'So how many times was it? Three? Or four?'

'Four,' said Levin.

'How?'

'Dolya was the courier to Moscow. So the break had to be between him and Shelenkov, minimizing the risk of any connection if the FBI targeted either of them,' recounted Levin. 'I had to travel down here from New York, on some pretext, make the pick-up and then transfer it to Dolya in the complete security of our mission when I got back.'

'Did you ever know what you were carrying?' said Myers.

'Of course not.'

'*How* did you carry?'

'Once a specification catalogue, about a tractor . . . the sort of thing always available at agricultural shows,' said Levin. 'Twice sealed letters. The last time it was a holiday postcard.'

'Microdots,' said Norris, a remark more to himself than anyone else in the room. 'Somewhere on material absolutely ordinary and unremarkable in itself.'

Levin was about to respond, confirming the man's guess, but Proctor spoke across him. 'I'm curious, Yevgennie,' said the FBI man. 'How come you never told me any of this before?'

The Russian was grateful there had been so much preparation before he left the Soviet Union. Turning to the man who had acted as his control, Levin said: 'Don't you remember what I said, the day I asked to come across?'

'Remind me,' urged Proctor.

'Insurance,' said Levin. 'I regarded it as my insurance, to ensure my acceptance by you.'

'I think we've got a lot to talk about,' said Myers. 'That this has only been the start: the absolute start.'

The satisfaction flowed through Levin. He said: 'I believe there is much to talk about, certainly.'

'Enough for today,' concluded Myers. 'There is more than enough for us to think about.'

And check, guessed Levin.

The CIA committee remained in the room after the others

left for the return flight to Connecticut, momentarily unspeaking. Then Myers said: 'Well?'

'Looks good enough to me,' said Norris.

'I'm not sure the presentation is properly disjointed,' disputed the lawyer, whose early career had included courtroom cross examination.

'What the hell's that mean?' demanded Myers, who'd found some difficulty curbing his language during the encounter with the Russian.

'There were occasions when I thought he responded in a rehearsed manner.'

'He would have rehearsed some responses, wouldn't he?' said Norris. 'He knew what he was here for.'

'He said he didn't have a prepared statement,' reminded the lawyer.

'He would have anticipated some things . . . thought them through,' insisted the Soviet expert.

'We've obviously got to take it further,' judged Myers. 'It's too soon to make an assessment one way or the other yet.'

'What if he's a plant?' demanded Crookshank.

'We've checked out Kapalet in Paris,' said Norris. 'We know he's one hundred per cent and we got Shelenkov's name from him, first.'

'And through Kapalet we might still have some sort of link to Shelenkov,' said Myers. 'Levin would look pretty kosher if we managed to get confirmation of the courier system, wouldn't he?'

'*If* we could get confirmation,' agreed Crookshank reluctantly.

Alexandr Bogaty tapped and patted all the expert evidence assembled at the scene of Malik's killing into an orderly pile and replaced it on the desk in front of him, nodding at what he'd spent three hours reading and digesting. He had not had any doubt, from his initial impression, but this was positive confirmation that once having been knocked down, the man had been intentionally run over a second time by the reversing vehicle. The medical evidence was the most positive, two separate points of impact, the first which had broken Malik's back; the second when the car had come back and gone over the chest, crushing the chest wall. And the photographs were corroboration of what Bogaty had discerned that night: no brake marks which there should have been, just before the collision, but heavily bloodstained tyre impressions showing the reversing pattern. Bogaty looked to the specimen envelopes, separate from the reports. The paint scrapings – fawn – by themselves would have proved the vehicle to be a Lada saloon, but there was additional corroboration from the recovered headlamp glass, practically enough to recreate the entire light assembly.

Bogaty sighed, regretting it was all being taken away from him. How many garages would that arrogant prick of a KGB colonel have checked out, by now? He was surprised the demand had not come for the evidence that lay on the desk in front of him. Perhaps, reflected Bogaty, he was being infantile in withholding it until the request was made. But what the hell? They *were* arrogant. All of them. So they could wait.

The sigh of regret was more heartfelt the second time, as Bogaty stood to leave his office. Not straight home, he decided. A drink or two on the way, partially to numb himself against Lydia.

25

By the time Yuri entered Victor Kazin's office suite at the
First Directorate headquarters he had studied his father's
dossier so closely that there were long tracts – particularly
of the encounter with Panchenko set against the
conflicting interview with the major – that he had memorized verbatim. So he was well prepared for the confrontation. And not just from his knowledge of the secret
and unknown file: further prepared by the arduous and
painstaking psychological instruction at those KGB
training centres in Metrostroevskaya Street and Turnaninski Pereulok, always to be able to conceal his true
feelings or emotions from anyone with whom he came
into contact. There weren't going to be any mistakes this
afternoon: the determination somehow to expose Kazin
and the security chief obsessed him to the exclusion of
everything else. He just wished he could take that determination beyond more than an amorphous resolve.

Kazin remained seated, finding easy the reserve from
superior to subordinate. He thought – as he had at the
cemetery – how different the man was from his father.
But only in appearance: once more Kazin reminded
himself that this was the person directly responsible for
what had occurred in Afghanistan. So he had to be just
as devious and just as cunning. An enemy, like his father
had been. Kazin said: 'I would like to express my
personal condolences over this tragic affair.'

There were several available chairs in the room but
Kazin did not indicate any of them. Yuri acknowledged
the refusal as demeaning but was unaffected by it: small-
man behaviour, like the *rezident*'s similar stupidity in
Kabul had been small-man behaviour. In direct contradiction to the intended effect, it gave Yuri a feeling of superiority. He said: 'Thank you, Comrade First Deputy.'

'He was a brilliant and much admired colleague,' said

Kazin. He wanted to protract his enjoyment of power over this helpless man he was going to destroy. A pawn, he thought, remembering his chess analogy: a sacrificial pawn to be played in an unbeatable game.

'I appreciate your condolences,' replied Yuri. What the hell was there behind this graveside summons! He tried to think of what the other man reminded him, strangely but obviously vibrating beneath the desk from what he guessed to be some nervous mannerism, that part that was visible above the table swarthily fat, chins puddled on chins, polished with sweat. A toad seemed somehow too trite but that was the impression Yuri had. How could his mother have done what she did!

'I have studied your personal file. It is impressive.'

And the most impressive endorsement of all the commendation from an inquiry which got you censured, thought Yuri. It was a nonsensical remark for the man to have made: so he was sure of himself to the extent of open contempt. It was an important realization. Conscious before he spoke of the cant, Yuri said: 'It is my hope always to be of service to the Committee for State Security.'

The younger man was a conceited, pedantic prig, concluded Kazin. It was almost going to be too easy; time to move you, little pawn. He said: 'I have a function for you to fulfil.'

'Which I will do to the best of my ability,' responded Yuri, in apparent eagerness. It's going to be more difficult to destroy me that it was my father, you bastard, he thought.

'You replaced Yevgennie Pavlovich Levin at our mission to the United Nations?' demanded Kazin.

'Yes.' said Yuri, intrigued. Even posed rhetorically it was a fatuous question.

'The man is a traitor to his country,' declared Kazin.

Yuri was unsure how to keep his side of the conversation going. 'I understand that,' he said. But little else so far.

'I want him found,' announced Kazin. But you detected

first, he added, mentally. One little pawn exposed to the knights and kings of America's counter-intelligence.

Yuri was well enough aware of the attitude towards defectors – there had been several warning lectures on retribution at Turnaninski Pereulok – but seeking out and punishing members of the service who went across to the West was not the responsibility of his department. Those who chased defectors were attached to that most secret of divisions, the Executive Action Department. Not to challenge would indicate his suspicion of the other man and at the moment his foreknowledge was the only protection he had. Cautiously Yuri said: 'That would be a corrective assignment?'

'It is a particular assignment with which you are being entrusted,' said Kazin: the game plan did not allow any escape.

Necessary to protest further, decided Yuri: but clumsily. He said: 'Throughout my training I was instructed to refrain from physical violence.' Which was true and Kazin would know it: physical violence attracted attention, always the most essential thing to avoid.

Was this man really as devious and cunning as he suspected from the Afghanistan episode? It was difficult to believe from these responses. Kazin said: 'I was not aware of any discussion of physical violence.'

'I apologize, Comrade First Deputy, but I am having difficulty in understanding what it is you wish me to do,' said Yuri. Would he be able to prolong this apparent briefing sufficiently to guess the tripwires, anticipate the trap? He had to try.

'I wish you, with the ability which you have to move freely around the United States, to find where the Americans have hidden Yevgennie Levin,' said Kazin, a teacher spelling out an instruction to a dull pupil. 'Having done so, I want you to report directly to me.'

'Having discovered the location, report directly back to you? Nothing more?'

Did the fool want it spelled out on paper in words that his lips could move, to follow! Kazin said: 'Precisely that.

243

Your part in the operation will cease, from then on . . .' He smiled patronizingly. 'No physical violence.'

Maybe not exactly a tripwire, but an indication that they were being laid with some carelessness. What Kazin was ordering was still not something in which he should become involved, despite the apparent qualification. So the man was underestimating him. Good, thought Yuri. Time to attempt erecting hazards of his own. He said: 'The Americans will have put Levin under deep cover.'

Frightened and apologizing in advance for failure, decided Kazin: a chance to frighten him further. He said: 'I do not regard it as an easy assignment. Nor one, however, upon which I expect you to fail.'

There'd been enough assurances of dedication to the service, Yuri decided. Instead he said: 'There will have been an investigation into Levin's defection?'

'Of course.'

'It will be made available to me?' As he asked the question, Yuri wondered suddenly and for the first time why – having destroyed his father as he was sure Kazin and Panchenko had – they had not carried out some search of Kutuzovsky Prospekt or the dacha, seeking any private, incriminating file the man might have maintained. That he might have done so would have been a reasonable surmise. And then Yuri remembered his own reaction that day, to his father's revelation that he was copying official documents. To do such a thing was criminally forbidden by every regulation and edict governing the KGB. Not a reasonable surmise then, for men whose lives were constantly governed by those regulations and edicts.

In answer to Yuri's question, Kazin patted the folders already laying on his desk and said: 'Correspondence has also been permitted, between Levin and his daughter.'

'There is a relation still in Russia?'

'In Moscow.'

'I should see her,' said Yuri. It would have been a reaction the other man would expect.

Kazin touched the file again, 'The address is here. Copies of all the letters, too.'

Yuri decided upon another snare. He said: 'I am to communicate directly to you?'

'Only to me: this is an absolutely restricted operation,' said Kazin at once.

Kazin had become entangled in it, Yuri judged. The reply had been too quick, almost urgent, and the insistence meant the cutting out of Vladislav Belov, the Director of the American Department, through whom all traffic should normally have been channelled. Another inconsistency. No, corrected Yuri at once. Not at inconsistency. A further indication, if he needed one at all, that this was not the operation it was being made out to be. He said: 'How is that communication to be conducted?'

'Diplomatic bag,' instructed Kazin.

Was there anything else upon which Kazin would snag himself? At once Yuri thought he saw a chance and said: 'Regulations are that any communication in the diplomatic bag should be authorized and vetted by the on-base *rezident* . . . Comrade Granov, in my case.'

Kazin pressed down upon his twitching knee, unsure if he had been right in doubting the other man's deviousness, realizing the implication of the question. He said: 'I will issue special instructions to Comrade Granov in New York.'

So there would be some formal record that he was involved in a specific operation masterminded by the head of the First Chief Directorate, acknowledged Yuri. Insurance of a sort, he supposed. Against what? He decided to prod in a more positive direction. He said: 'Has the driver involved in the accident with my father been found?'

No reason for apprehension, thought Kazin. They were absolutely safe. This was nothing more than a natural, predictable question. He said: 'No. But I assure you he will be. The investigation has been taken over from the civilian militia by our own Directorate security.'

Re-introducing his father's death into the conversation had been throwing a stone into a pool, hoping to make ripples, and Yuri decided there had been a tidal wave. Until that moment he had not known of any civilian involvement in the investigations into his father's death. He said: 'Thank you, for the assurance' And for more, much more.

The man was definitely not as clever as he imagined himself to be, decided Kazin.

The man was definitely not as clever as he imagined himself to be, decided Yuri.

This time Kapalet chose Le Vivarois restaurant, taking as much care as he always did, remaining concealed in the Avenue Victor-Hugo until he saw the CIA man enter and waiting until Drew was seated before going in himself.

They went through the formality of ordering – Drew on this occasion impatiently selecting the wine – and as soon as the chevalier left the American said: 'Well?'

'It hasn't been easy,' avoided Kapalet.

Drew sighed at the accustomed bargaining, slipping the envelope into the Russian's hand beneath the concealment of the table.

'I managed to ask,' said Kapalet, which he had, but from Moscow, not the reassigned Shelenkov.

'And?'

'He saw sometimes a man named Dolya, who acted as the courier to Moscow.'

'What about the other name?'

The Russian nodded in affirmation. 'Levin,' he said. 'From the UN mission as well. Performed as a cut-out, between New York and Washington.'

'How many times?'

'Four, as far as he could remember.'

Drew smiled, gesturing with his wine glass as if he were offering a toast. 'You've done well, Sergei. You always do well.'

'There's something else,' said Kapalet, as he had been specifically instructed by the head of the First Chief Directorate himself.

'What?'

'Levin's defected, hasn't he?'

'Yes,' agreed Drew cautiously.

246

'The order's gone out,' said Kapalet. 'A general instruction to all *rezidentura*, in case you people move him abroad, but concentrated directly to America.'

'What order?'

'Levin's to be traced,' said Kapalet. 'Traced and killed, as an example. As assassin has already been assigned in America.'

'Who?'

'I don't have a name,' said Kapalet. 'But you'd better take special care of Levin if you want to keep him alive.'

26

Yevgennie Levin held back from any immediate inference, guarding against mistakes, but the attitude of the CIA group appeared different from the first occasion. Friendlier would have been an exaggeration. Perhaps more relaxed. The long-haired man with the legal pad might provide the indicator. They arranged themselves in the same room as before, positioned exactly as before: the bearded, shaggy man was still wearing the abused, strained suit.

'Maybe we could get into a little more detail today, sir?' opened Myers.

'In what way?' responded Levin cautiously. Don't over-respond, don't anticipate, he thought.

'Tell us about Shelenkov?' urged Crookshank. 'What did he look like, for instance?'

Not the personal antagonism of the previous session, assessed Levin; not yet, anyway. He said: 'Quite a small man, balding at the front. It seemed to embarrass him, because he was careful to bring his hair forward. Some facial coloration, from blood pressure I always thought. Maybe from the drinking.'

'Good English?' prompted Myers.

'Very good. Fond of Americanism.'

'Americanism!' seized Norris – as he was intended to – remembering the original warning from Paris of the man having had the Agency by the balls.

'Slang. Things like that. Said it provided cover.' Levin was aware of Norris scribbling and then passing a note to Myers, curious at what it said.

It was the lawyer who took up the questioning again. 'So you had some extensive conversation with him?' suggested Crookshank.

'I do not know that I would have called it extensive. More social exchanges.'

Imagining a weakness, Crookshank said: 'You travelled down from New York for one purpose only: you were a messenger, sent to collect something?'

'Yes,' agreed Levin guardedly, not sure which way the interrogation was going.

Crookshank took a long time shuffling through his pad, a courtroom trick to unsettle a witness. He looked up and said: 'A tractor sales catalogue, two letters and a holiday postcard?'

'Yes.'

'Which would have taken no more than seconds to pick up?'

Levin thought he knew the thrust but refused to anticipate. 'Yes,' he said, for the third time.

'Why the need for social exchanges?'

It was a bad point, decided Levin: almost desperate. Easily he said: '*Because* the handover only took seconds. If I had been under FBI surveillance and entered and left the embassy so quickly, the purpose of the visit would have been obvious. I would practically have been confirming myself as an agent of the KGB. Having made the collection there was the need to remain at the embassy for a reasonable period.' He was conscious of Myers' barely perceptible nod of agreement.

Crookshank refused to give up. He said: 'As a member of the Soviet mission to the United Nations you are an international civil servant. You had no purpose being at the Soviet embassy in Washington in the first place.'

How thorough and all-encompassing the preparations had been, reflected Levin. He said: 'My attachment to the United Nations was in the mineral division. The Soviet Union has the largest deposits of minerals anywhere in the world. Had there ever been a challenge – which there never was – the explanation was to be that I was actually *using* my position as a Russian to obtain Soviet mineral data for UN use and benefit. I always brought back with me some statistical documentation, to substantiate such an account . . .' Completely to out-argue the long-haired man, Levin turned sideways to Proctor, who had again accompanied him in the helicopter from Connecticut, and said: 'My approach to you was the first indication the FBI had that I was KGB, wasn't it? I was not suspect until then?'

Proctor did not directly answer the look, forced into an admission of oversight. 'No,' he agreed. 'You were never suspected.'

'Always clever!' said Crookshank, almost petulantly.

Always, echoed Levin, in his mind. He said: 'I thought I had made it clear how important Shelenkov's position was regarded. How he had to be protected, at all times.'

'And we've rather drifted away from how we began this conversation,' came in Myers, appearing irritated at his colleague's digression. 'So you've told us what Shelenkov looked like and talked about social chit-chat. *As* it was social chit-chat, where did you meet?'

'Always in Shelenkov's office, within the *rezidentura*.'

'Never elsewhere.'

'Certainly never outside of the embassy. Once . . . no I think it was twice . . . we had a drink in the embassy mess.'

'Why?'

'To pass a period of accountable time. As I said last time, Shelenkov liked to drink.'

'To go to the mess was his idea?'

'Everything always had to be initiated by him,' said Levin. 'He actually ranked as my superior officer.'

'What did he drink?' asked Norris.

'Scotch whisky, usually. Sometimes vodka,' replied Levin. He knew none of the questions were as inconsequential as they seemed: obviously they had another source, with which or with whom everything he said could hopefully be checked. Still very much on trial then: and would be, for a long time.

'What can you remember of these conversations?' pressed Myers.

'Even in conversation I had to defer to Shelenkov, of course,' embarked Levin cautiously. 'He was a boastful man . . .'

' . . . Tell me some of his boasts,' interrupted Norris.

'He would always laugh, sneering. Say he had never been suspected,' said Levin.

'He was wrong,' insisted Crookshank, smarting from the earlier exchange. 'He was suspected in Canada and came near to arrest in London, before he was transferred here, in 1985.'

'From which time he successfully ran a spy accorded the highest priority in Moscow without once being detected by you, didn't he?' came back Levin. The remark was intended to deflate his constant antagonist but it was Proctor who was embarrassed by the immediately critical attention of the CIA committee. The Russian realized there might be protection in fomenting discord between the representatives of the two agencies: it was something to keep in mind.

'What other boasts?' persisted the CIA's Russian expert.

'He said something once about Latin America . . . the Caribbean Basin Initiative . . .'

'One isn't linked to the other,' argued Norris.

'Shelenkov linked them,' insisted Levin.

'How?' demanded Myers.

'Said something about it being inconceivable that you relied upon the sort of people you did in Latin America,' recounted Levin. 'Then he said he thought it was madness, the type of people whose word you accepted in the Caribbean. Said they were all drug dealers who only knew how to cheat.'

'Wait!' stopped Myers, actually holding up his hand. 'This is important: very important. "You". That's the word you're using. What or whom did you understand Shelenkov to be talking about? America as a country? Or the CIA, as an agency?'

'The CIA of course,' said Levin, as if he were surprised by their need for clarification. He spread his hands apologetically. 'I am sorry,' he said. 'I was paraphrasing and that was wrong. What he said was that he thought it inconceivable that the Company relied upon such people in Latin America. Like I said last time, he used that expression . . .'

'. . . I remember what you said last time,' stopped Myers. On his own pad he wrote 'Latin American desk' and followed it with a hedge of exclamation marks, and Norris nodded back in agreement.

'He definitely mentioned both: Latin America and the Caribbean?' said Norris.

'That is my recollection,' agreed Levin. 'You will appreciate that at the time I did not attach particular importance to it. Not as I do now.'

'It's important all right,' said Myers, a personal remark.

'What about countries: any countries?' pressed Norris. There were sub-divisions and departments for each geographical unit and island, so without more definite leads it would still be a haystack hunt.

'Never,' said Levin, at once and unhelpfully. 'It was a general remark, not specific.'

'What did you infer from what he said?' came in Crookshank. 'Could the remark not have been that he knew the quality of our informants from your own Soviet presence in the regions? Not necessarily that he had a source within this Agency?'

'I do not think that would have been possible,' said Levin.

'Why not?'

'The KGB division of which Shelenkov was then a member – of which I was a member – is limited entirely to the United States,' lectured the Russian. 'There is no liaison with other divisions concerned with the Caribbean or Latin America. So therefore no way he could have known. It had to come from somewhere here, internally.' He was aware of Myers nodding, in agreement again. He would have thought he had by now given them enough to check and to investigate but they gave no indication of wanting to end the session. Levin wished they would. The concentration of remembering the rehearsed disclosures and revelations was physically draining him and he was frightened. Just one mistake, one slip, he thought, the perpetual warning litany.

'Sure Nicaragua was not mentioned?' persisted Norris, reluctant to give up.

'I do not recall it.'

'Honduras?'

Seeing a way to end the interrogation, Levin shrugged and said: 'It doesn't trigger any recollection.'

'San Salvador?'

'I don't think so.' Levin made himself a bet and won.

Crookshank said: 'That's neither a negative nor an affirmative, to the last three questions.'

'It is difficult to be positive,' protested Levin. 'I need time to think, to recall . . .'

Once more Myers held up his hands in a placating gesture. 'There's no hurry, no pressure,' he said reassuringly. 'We got all the time in the world.'

'I've been here for five hours,' reminded Levin. He'd found the helicopter ride easier this time than on the previous occasion: he'd have to describe it in tonight's letter to Natalia.

'Let's break,' decided Myers, moving his hand again in a halting gesture when Levin started to rise. 'Think on it, Yevgennie,' he urged. 'Try to remember as much as you can.'

'I will,' promised the Russian.

On their way back through the Langley grounds to the waiting helicopter, Proctor said: 'I felt pretty stupid in there a couple of times, Yevgennie.'

'You know why I held back about what I knew in the CIA,' said Levin. 'Nothing I did was intended to embarrass you.'

'No more surprises about possible mistakes the FBI might have make. OK?'

'OK,' agreed Levin. Poor man, he thought.

'I don't like it,' insisted Crookshank.

'I sure as fuck don't like it either,' said Myers. 'I'm supposed to be head of internal security, don't forget. This isn't a can of worms: it's a whole fucking drum full.'

'I mean Levin himself,' argued the lawyer.

'What's not to like?'

'The last time we talked of gossip and rumour, so that we have to drag from him the fact that he was a go-between,' reminded Crookshank. 'From what he said today, he was hugger-mugger enough with Shelenkov to be best buddies.'

'That's an exaggeration and you know it,' disputed Norris. 'I don't find any difficulty at all in accepting his nervousness, the first time, against what he told us today. Kapalet came back with every confirmation we asked for. And look what more has come out today . . .' The Soviet expert extended his hand, ticking the points off by collapsing his fingers one by one. 'He said Shelenkov prefers Scotch whisky, which from Kapalet we know he does. He said sometimes Shelenkov shifts to vodka, which from Kapalet we know he does. He said Shelenkov is a boastful son-of-a-bitch which from Kapalet we know he is because that's how we started this whole affair in the first place. He describes Shelenkov as Kapalet describes him, physically . . .' He was aware of Crookshank about to speak but shook his head against interruption. 'Don't tell me they're small, unimportant points. They're exactly the sort of small, *important* points which convince me that Levin is genuine and he's got a lot to tell. And if you don't like the unimportant points, don't forget the most positive proof yet to come from Paris. According to Kapalet, Moscow has issued a kill order against the guy. You're telling me they'd do that if Levin were a plant! Come on, Walt, for Christ's sake!'

'I agree, one hundred per cent,' said Myers. 'I just wish to hell he'd hurry up and show us the way to go.'

'What can we do about the Caribbean and Latin America?' asked Norris.

'Check the desks, like you suggested,' said the security chief. 'But discreetly: I don't want to drive anyone into the woodwork.'

'What about analysis divisions?'

'Those too,' agreed Myers.

'We could play it back to Paris, in the hope Kapalet can offer something?' suggested Crookshank.

'It's worth trying,' said Myers.

'At this stage anything is worth trying,' said Norris. 'What about the hunt that Moscow's started for Levin? Do you tell the FBI?'

'I don't want to,' said Myers. 'There's a risk of it spooking the Bureau. I don't want them running all over the country, trying to find a new place to hide and delaying our access to him.'

'It would be a bigger problem if the Russians did get a lead and blew him away before he told us what we need to know,' said Norris.

'I guess you're right,' said Myers reluctantly. 'If they get jumpy, volunteer some protection from us.'

'The improvement – the change – is remarkable,' praised Sylvester Burns. Petr Levin's tutor was practically a caricature of an academic, fair, disordered hair almost to the collar of a suit of expensive material and cut but seeming to have been tailored for someone at least two sizes smaller: the sleeves rode up his forearms and the trouser cuffs were ankle length. There was a hole in the heel of his left sock.

'I'm glad you're pleased,' said the boy.

'Pleased!' echoed the man. 'I'm delighted. I'm sure your parents will be, too. Everyone.'

Never once during their one-to-one lessons had Burns referred to the FBI by title, used the word defection or shown any reaction to the unusual circumstances of his teaching. Petr supposed Burns was a contract employee of the agency. He said: 'You think I'll have no difficulty, achieving my grades?'

'I'd be shocked if you didn't.'

'I'll be able to do it all, from here?' asked Petr, directing the conversation the way he wanted it to continue.

'Tutoring like this most definitely has its drawbacks,' said Burns. 'Apparatus for science, particularly. And there's a physical limitation on the number of textbooks I can transport.'

'I've not found it easy, denied reference text,' said Petr impromptu.

'Maybe I should speak to someone,' said the tutor.

As soon as you like, thought the boy; as soon as you like.

27

Knowing the side road off Novaya Street in which his father had been killed made it easy for Yuri to identify the nearest civilian militia post from which officers would have been summoned and his impulse was to go there immediately to find and question whoever had initially been called to the scene that night. But he didn't. Although he was conscious of the convoluted irony, Yuri decided the best way to discover what really lay behind Kazin's instruction to locate Yevgennie Levin was actually to attempt such an investigation and by so doing set himself up as a knowing bait. And having done that, to spend more time looking behind than in front. So Natalia Levin had priority.

Before setting out for Mytishchi, he went through the material Kazin had made available, almost at once disappointed. And then equally quickly irritated at himself for expecting a lead where to start in America. If Russian security attached to the UN mission had suspected the remotest contact with the FBI, Levin would have been arrested and hauled back to Moscow on the next available plane. Muddled thinking – and he couldn't afford muddled thinking. He concentrated upon what information there was, memorizing the biographical details that were available and particularly studying the photographs: Levin and his wife both fat, heavy people, the black-haired fourteen-year-old girl he was going to see squinting myopically at the camera through thick-lensed spectacles, but quite pretty apart from them, the boy smirking self-consciously, dressed up for officialdom.

It was not until he got to the copies of the correspondence between the girl and her family – and then not until, according to the date, he was halfway through the first letter that Levin had been allowed – that Yuri thought he'd found something. He stopped and went back to the beginning and then read steadily through in the order in which they had been written and replied to, building up the points in his mind, his reaction a mix of curiosity and bewilderment. Illogic upon illogic, he thought: if he resolved the doubts about these letters would he get any nearer to discovering what Kazin intended? A possible route, maybe; at the moment the *only* route. He wished there were more clearly marked signposts.

Accustomed always because of his father's position to the accommodation of the Soviet elite, Yuri was repelled by the concrete forest estate at Mytishchi. Apart from the absence of any spray-canned graffiti, it could easily have been one of those worn-down, worn-away parts of Manhattan he'd found it so easy to criticize when he'd first arrived in New York. How much his thinking and his attitudes about everything had changed: how much everything had changed.

The blocks were identical and unmarked, so it took him thirty minutes to locate the section where Natalia Levin's apartment was listed. He waited a further five minutes for the lift to arrive and when it didn't climbed the stairs instead: there were puddles on a lot of the steps and tiny lakes on two of the intervening landings, where the roofs leaked. The pervading odour was of cabbage and paraffin and maybe urine and Yuri decided some of the landing wet was not all rainwater. On the wall at the second level someone had crayoned 'Raisa for Minister of Fashion' and Yuri decided the similarity with America was complete: American graffiti-writers had just served a longer and wittier apprenticeship.

There was no immediate response to his knock but Yuri detected a sound, a shuffling movement, beyond the door and so he knocked again. When it opened it was only by a crack. The apartment was dark, so that Yuri had difficulty in seeing: an old lady, a *babushka*, heavily shawled, all in black.

'I want Natalia Yevgennova Levin,' he said.

'Who are you?'

'Komitet Gosudarstvennoy Bezopasnosti,' Yuri

announced formally. He found the effect startling. The old woman jerked back, as if she had been physically slapped, and despite the gloom the fear was immediately visible, not just in her face but in her eyes. It was the first time Yuri had witnessed the reaction of an ordinary Russian to the KGB. It was unsettling.

'I knew you'd come. Said so,' stammered the woman. 'Knew it would happen.'

'Natalia Yevgennova?' repeated Yuri.

The old lady stood back, saying nothing more, and Yuri walked past her into the apartment: the outside smells seemed to follow him in. The girl whose features he had earlier studied stood in the middle of the main room, hand up to her face, knuckles against her teeth. The spectacles appeared thinner-lensed than in the photograph and her eyes were red beyond, but she was not squinting.

'What is going to happen to me?' Natalia said. Her voice was cracked, difficult to hear from behind her hand.

While Yuri was searching for some response, the old woman's voice came from behind. She said: 'When do we have to get out?' and Yuri partially understood their apprehension.

He said: 'I am not here about the apartment.' It was minimally but comfortably furnished, he saw, and the impression of the outside smells had been mistaken. It was clean and there were flowers, in two separate vases. On a side table and a ledge that ran the length of one wall there were four separate photographs of Yevgennie and Galina Levin – in one of which they appeared dressed as he'd so recently seen his parents dressed, for the ceremony at the Hall of Weddings – and two of the boy, Petr. In both of them Petr was wearing American-style clothes and was clearly older than the official file picture.

'We're not being expelled?' It was the old woman again, distrustful and suspicious.

'Not by me,' assured Yuri. Why hadn't they been? he wondered, focusing on their concern. Yevgennie Levin *was* a traitor who had betrayed his country. Basic though it was, this was still a favoured apartment – and unshared, so therefore further favoured – and Yuri would have expected the privilege to have been withdrawn.

'When?' persisted the woman.

Yuri realized the supposed positions were reversed: he was being interrogated instead of interrogating. He remembered the reaction at the door and decided he did not want to be cast as an interrogator. These two had done nothing wrong. Ignoring the question, he said to Natalia: 'I want to talk about your father.'

'I am being allowed to go to America!' The girl's hand came away from her face, abruptly relaxing into a tentative, hopeful smile.

Levin's apparently confident hope and Natalia's seeming expectation to be allowed to leave the Soviet Union had been one of the first points to register with Yuri when he read the letters. Wanting to move the exchange on to his terms, he avoided the direct answer and said: 'It is under consideration. We have to talk first.'

'What about?' asked the girl, the smile leaking away.

'I want to know what it was like when you were in New York.'

'Like?'

'Where did you live?' asked Yuri, who knew anyway but wanted to conceal the real question. 'What did you do? What friends did you have?'

Natalia frowned and Yuri hoped she was as confused as he wanted her to be. She said: 'We lived at Riverdale, of course. Everyone does.'

'You went to school there?'

The girl shook her head. 'The Soviet mission academy.'

'What about friends?'

'Of course I had friends.'

'What sort of friends? Russian friends? Or other friends?'

'Russian friends.'

'Only Russian?'

'Yes: that's the way it is. The way it has to be.'

'No others? American perhaps?' Natalia's face had closed against him in uncertain suspicion, Yuri saw.

'No others,' said the girl.

The old woman came by him at last, going supportively to the girl's side. Uninvited Yuri sat in the chair he guessed to be the old woman's because it was in the dominant place in the room, a place he needed now to occupy. 'Sit down,' he said to both of them, an order rather than an invitation. He was not enjoying the part of a bully, either. They hesitated and then did as they were told. Yuri said: 'What about your parents? What sort of friends did they have?'

Yuri saw a further tightening of her face and guessed she had not been confused at all. 'The same,' she said.

'No Americans?'

'No.'

He would have to bully further, Yuri realized uncomfortably. He said: 'You realize, don't you, that the possibility of your being allowed to go to America . . . your being allowed to remain here, in this apartment, depends upon you cooperating?'

Natalia's eyes filmed and Yuri thought she was going to cry, and gripped his hands against her doing so. She didn't but he knew it had been close. Natalia said: 'Yes, I realize that.'

'You never saw your father with an American?'

'Never.'

'Overheard any conversation, between your mother and your father about any Americans?'

'No.'

The conversation had gone into a cul-de-sac, Yuri accepted. He said: 'Tell me about your operation.'

The girl hesitated, unsure how to respond. Then she said: 'I had a cornea deformation, from the time I was born. The specialists said it could be corrected when I was old enough.'

This could be a useful direction, gauged Malik. He said: 'So it was planned, for a long time?'

'Yes.'

'To be carried out now? Or was the date suddenly given to you from the Moscow clinic?'

'There was about six weeks' notice,' said the girl.

'What did your father say?'

Natalia looked quizzically at him. 'That I had to have it done: that it was what we had been waiting for!'

'He was anxious for you to have it done?'

'Very anxious.'

Yuri was reluctant to ask the question but knew it was necessary. Prepared for her reaction from what he'd read in the letters, he said: 'Your father loves you?'

This time she did start to cry, tears building up and then bursting by her glasses. Very carefully she removed them, tried to dry her eyes and then just as gently replaced them. Unevenly she said: 'Of course he loves me.'

'What did you think, when you learned he had defected?'

'I couldn't understand it. I still can't understand it.'

Neither could he, decided Yuri. He didn't doubt the affection in the letters or what she had just said, about love. Which made it inconceivable that Levin would have moved with her out of the country, beyond reach. So six weeks prior to the provable date of her operation, the man had not intended to cross. Yuri wondered if it had any significance. 'What have you come to think since?'

'I haven't,' mumbled Natalia. Her lips quivered. She made a determined effort at control and said: 'Will I be able to join them?'

Another imponderable, isolated Yuri: like their being allowed to maintain this apartment. And the constant references in the letters to their being reunited, which this girl clearly expected. What made Levin imagine it could – or would – happen? Unable to answer the girl's question, Yuri said: 'That is being decided.'

'How soon?'

'I don't know,' said Yuri. Before there was the chance of another demand from her, he said: 'Did you like America?'

'It was different,' said Natalia, imagining he had the power of letting her leave or not and anxious against any offence.

'What about your father?'

Her struggle for the right reply was pitifully obvious

and Yuri felt a further wash of pity. Natalia said: 'It was his job to be there.'

'Were you able to travel at all?'

'Once,' she said. 'To Disney World, in Florida.'

'Did your father like it?'

'He said it was for us,' she avoided.

'Sometimes your father went away without you, didn't he?'

'For his job at the United Nations,' she insisted defensively.

'Did he ever talk about it?'

'That would not have been correct.'

'Did he ever talk about a particular part of America: somewhere he preferred more than anywhere else?'

'No,' she said again.

Another cul-de-sac, accepted Yuri. It was hardly likely anyway that already the FBI would have settled Levin under a new identity in a location of his choice. At this stage there would be interrogations far harder than this, bleeding the man of everything he knew.

'When she goes will I be able to go too?' demanded the old lady. 'I'm Galina's mother. I've got no one else.'

Another confident expectation, thought Yuri. Improvising, he said: 'There'll have to be the proper application.' It was the first time he'd known she was a grandmother. Which made incomplete the dossier Kazin had provided. What other more important things had been omitted, to entrap him?

'Why are you asking all these questions?' blurted Natalia, abruptly and with forced braveness.

Yuri momentarily hesitated, seeking an answer. Then he said: 'You can't understand why your father defected and neither can we: it could be that he was forced, in some way.' The reply was not as good as he would have liked it to have been but Yuri thought it was adequate. He didn't anticipate the development from it.

'The letters don't indicate he is being forced to do anything he doesn't want to,' said the girl.

Which was true, Yuri accepted, another shapeless, unformed image from the correspondence hardening into a positive shape. Yevgennie Pavlovich Levin was a senior KGB officer with twenty-five years' service to his country. He had defected to a country regarded as the Soviet Union's chief enemy, subjecting himself, his wife and a son to a lifetime of false indentities in hideaway homes. And by so doing abandoned a daughter he unquestionably loved. Yet apart from Natalia, the letters showed no uncertainty or regret. Surely there would have been? If not uncertainty or regret, then at least an effort at justification or attempted explanation: I have taken the decision which makes me a traitor because . . . But there was nothing. Yuri made the decision to study them again, for that specific detail, but he was sure he was correct. It was, of course, an exaggeration but rather than the outpourings of a man who had taken the most momentous decision of his life, the tone of the letters could equally come from the back of a 'wish you were here' holiday postcard.

Before Yuri could speak further the grandmother said: 'I have read in *Pravda* and *Izvestia* of defectors being tried *in absentia*.'

'I am not involved in such things,' said Yuri.

'What will happen if he is tried?' asked Natalia.

'That is a matter for the courts.'

'I meant to me?'

'That is not my decision either,' said Yuri, avoiding again.

At the possibility of some action against her father, Natalia's defiance leaked away as abruptly as it had come. Blinking against a fresh outburst of tears, she said desperately: 'I want to be with my mother and father.'

Yuri recognized he had lost control of the encounter by feeling sympathy when he should have shown sternness. But this was not the sort of intelligence for which he'd been trained and was proud to perform: this was brutality and he had no stomach for it. Not against innocents like these anyway. What about other people in other environments? His father's words intruded into his mind – *I think I could kill someone who tried to kill me.* And someone had. So would he be able to consider

264

killing, by proxy? Striving for the attitude he'd so far failed to achieve, Yuri said: 'Your difficulties are of your father's creation, no one else's.'

'He loves me!'

For the first time since he'd entered the neat apartment, Yuri detected an indecisiveness in the insistence. Illogically Yuri thought of Caroline, in a New York which seemed at that moment to be part of another planet. The Caroline whose sympathy had obviously been sincere when he said he was having to go away because of his father's death (the least danger is in the least lies) and told him to get back as soon as he could and that she'd ache for him until he did. He searched for a comparison between the two, knowing there was not one. Not physically, at least. Natalia *was* reasonably pretty, despite the glasses, but the dark hair was untrained and a figure that one day might be desirable still bubbled with puppy fat. Wasn't there a possible connection, though? Levin had abandoned Natalia. Shouldn't he abandon Caroline? Too tenuous. No way comparable, either. He said: 'Don't tell your father in letters of this visit.'

Natalia seemed about to respond but then closed her mouth tightly. If she did write about it Yuri knew he could intercept and prevent the letter.

'What else must I do?' she asked obediently.

'Tell him it's cold here.'

The girl looked blankly at him. 'I don't understand.'

'There's no reason why you should,' rejected Yuri. 'And write frequently. I want there to be a lot of letters from you.'

As he splashed down the odorous steps Yuri tried to sift in his mind what he had achieved by the encounter. A lot, he decided. But still not sufficient to warn him where Kazin was setting his trap.

The questions routed to him from Paris, requiring the confirmation that Washington sought, was the signal to Victor Kazin that Levin was being debriefed by the CIA. Kazin felt dizzy at the immediate realization, passingly worried that he often felt dizzy lately and that thoughts

265

seemed to wriggle away before he could grasp them. But then his head cleared, becoming clearer than it had been for longer than he could remember.

It had worked!

Now, at last, it was time fully to brief Comrade Chairman Chebrikov on his brilliant concept. There was too little remaining of Vladislav Belov's proposal for any shared credit. And as the unassailable head of the First Chief Directorate the credit was deservedly his anyway, as a matter of right.

Kazin prepared graphs and progress sheets for a formal presentation and felt the dizziness again at Chebrikov's ecstatic endorsement of everything that had been done. Not even Kazin anticipated that the KGB chairman would recommend he be awarded the Order of Lenin and when Chebrikov announced his intention Kazin relented and disclosed Belov's minimal involvement.

The Director of the American division learned from a memorandum of praise from the KGB chairman, congratulating him upon his 'help and assistance', how the idea that had taken years to formulate had been stolen from him. Briefly Belov came close to physical collapse, slumped over his desk like a man suffering a stroke or a seizure: for a while his vision was actually hazy and blurred.

He'd been robbed, Belov acknowledged: robbed after five long, wearisome, jigsaw carving years of the recognition he had been sure would rocket him through the promotion ranks to at least the leadership of a Chief Directorate.

The next immediate awareness was worse. He knew that, trapped beneath Victor Kazin, there was nothing whatsoever he could do about it.

28

Yevgennie Levin was disturbed by the tightened security, some of the men in the guardhouse visibly having guns and clattering helicopters frequently overhead, but was glad it had not interfered with the altered system for Petr's tuition. Professionally the Russian felt an enormous satisfaction at having apparently succeeded, but there was an equal relief at Petr's adjustment. Straight As in every subject, without exception, and a completely changed demeanour, too: polite and respectful, both to him and Galina, actually ready to laugh, which had been impossible for them all, for too long. He seemed anxious, as well, to make friends with the FBI and CIA protective personnel whose now increased presence was almost claustrophobic. Only about Natalia did there remain a difficulty and even here there was no longer from the boy the resentful, hostile attitude of the early weeks. He talked of when, not if, she would be able to join them, actually boasting of what he would show her in that part of Connecticut he was getting to know, now that he was going daily into Litchfield to school.

Levin felt Galina slip her arm through his at the door of the house as they watched the car carrying Petr crunch down the drive and go out of sight, between the trees that concealed the largest of the guardhouses.

'I never thought he'd settle,' she said.

'Neither did I,' confessed Levin.

He felt her pressure, urging him further away from the house and people who might overhear. Having got far enough away from the house to talk it was momentarily impossible because of the overhead stutter from one of the guarding helicopters. The woman grimaced up in its direction, her free hand trying to hold her hair in place, and when she was able to speak said: 'Why the supposed hunt?'

'I don't know,' said Levin, in further confession.

'Was it ever discussed?'

'No.'

'Natalia was supposed to be allowed to come with us. And she wasn't. Now this,' protested Galina. 'I don't like things happening that we're not prepared for. It's difficult enough as it is.'

'It can only be to make me seem more important to the Americans,' said Levin.

'Was that really necessary?'

'What else can it be?' he demanded.

'I worry about Petr going out alone, to school.'

'He isn't alone.'

'OK, so he's driven there and back,' Galina conceded. 'But there's no guard when he's there: we decided that to avoid the curiosity of the other kids.'

'Darling,' said Levin patiently. 'Not fifteen minutes ago we both agreed we never thought Petr would settle down. Now he has. And he's doing exceptionally well. You telling me you want me to risk it all by insisting he's tutored back in the house again?'

'I suppose not,' she said.

'Everything is going fine,' assured Levin.

There was the sound of another helicopter, this time the machine that was to carry him to Washington. Galina tried to protect her hair again and said: 'Any idea what time you'll be coming back?'

'No,' said Levin.

'You *will* come back?' she said. 'You won't be kept in Washington?'

She really was nervous, Levin recognized irritably. Why the hell had Moscow introduced something for which they were unprepared! He said: 'There's never any suggestion of my staying over.'

David Proctor ran towards them, bent double under the rotor blades, blown by the downdraft which flattened the grass. How deafening would the sound be on those unseen sensors, wondered Levin.

'All set?' shouted the American.

Levin nodded, making towards the machine. Because

of his size it was more difficult for Levin to bend than it was for Proctor and by the time he belted himself in he was panting. Levin was no longer worried by helicopter travelling: in fact he rather enjoyed it. He gazed down at the bulging hills of the immediate Connecticut country-side, seeing how much thinner the tree covering was now from how it had been the first time he had made the trip, only the firs and some of the maple retaining any thatch. He switched his headrest button, enabling him to talk to Proctor during flight and said, nodding downwards: 'Looks cold.'

The FBI supervisor nodded back and said: 'You ski?'

'Not any more.'

'What about Petr?'

'Yes.'

'There are some great ski lodges in Connecticut,' came in Bowden, sitting on his other side. 'When the snows come we can make a trip.'

'When will that be?'

'A month,' promised Bowden. 'Maybe six weeks.'

'Any news about Natalia?' demanded Levin predictably.

'Still pressing,' said Proctor, giving the usual reply.

Levin went familiarly from the Langley helicopter pad towards the debriefing building, mentally parading what he had to disclose today. It was difficult for him to be absolutely sure but he believed himself to be precisely on the schedule devised by the KGB. At the entrance to his debriefing room Levin glanced back to the main CIA complex. There'd never been an indentity – a protection against his revealing it under hostile, drugged interro-gation – but somewhere in there was a man who was going to cause a volcanic upheaval within America's over-seas intelligence agency.

'It's names we want, Yevgennie,' opened Myers at once. 'What you're telling us is invaluable but we need better direction.' The checks were continuing through the personnel on both the Caribbean and Latin American desks and extending on into the analysis sections but so far there had not been the slightest breakthrough.

'I know,' said the Russian. Don't hurry, he thought; let it come bit by bit, as it would from a deeply searched memory.

'Let's go back to those mess hall meetings with Shelenkov,' suggested Norris patiently. 'What time of year was it?'

'Summer. June I think. Then the Fall. September, maybe October,' said Levin.

'Hot then, the first time?'

'Very,' agreed the Russian. 'Humid, too.'

'Always a bitch,' coaxed Norris. 'Guess you felt like a drink when he suggested it?'

'I hadn't thought about it,' said Levin. 'When he did it seemed a good idea.'

'He drank Scotch?'

A comparing question, Levin recognized: they were still testing him. He said: 'Yes.'

'A lot?'

'Difficult to remember.' Frighteningly, Levin saw the trick when it was almost too late and added: 'He must have done, mustn't he?'

'Why's that, Yevgennie?' came in Crookshank. There was no antagonism yet.

'I told you before, he used to boast when he got drunk.'

'So you did,' said the lawyer. 'So how many do you remember his having?'

'I can't be positive, about an actual number. Five or six perhaps.'

'Five or six Scotches!' echoed Crookshank. 'The guy must have been on a bender?'

'He drank like a Russian.'

'How's that?' asked Myers.

'Quickly. It's custom to drain a glass, when there's a toast.'

'There were toasts?'

'The second time.'

'To what?'

Levin feigned the difficulty. He said: 'Shelenkov was given to being melodramatic.'

'Want to spell that out for us?' said Norris.

'He toasted the progress of communism . . .' Levin paused for effect, and said: 'I found it embarrassing. He was very loud: I thought it all unnecessary.'

'Where, exactly, to the progress of communism?' isolated Crookshank.

The man might be the least convinced but he was the one who picked up the carefully dangled carrots, decided Levin. He said: 'That was how Latin America came into the conversation.'

Both Myers and Norris came perceptibly forward in their seats. Myers said: 'Let's get this into sequence, Yevgennie. What did he begin talking about first, Latin America or the Caribbean?'

Levin appeared to give the question consideration. Then he said: 'I think Latin America . . . yes, it was definitely Latin America.'

'Think you could remember the exact words?' suggested Norris.

Levin laughed, guessing at another disguised pit. 'How could I possibly remember the exact words after all this time!'

'Paraphrase it then,' shrugged Norris.

'He lifted up his glass— showing off, like I said – and toasted the progress of communism. He said Latin American. Then Nicaragua . . .'

'Nicaragua!' Myers spoke lightly ahead of Norris but it was the suspicious Crookshank who pounced with the question.

'We asked you specifically about countries last time!' he challenged. 'You said you couldn't remember!'

'You asked me to try to remember,' corrected Levin. 'I've done so, as best I can. I recall Shelenkov making that toast and mentioning Nicaragua. He was laughing, like I told you, about the people you trusted. He said there was no danger to the Sandinista regime while the main opposition was the Nicaraguan Democratic Force. And then there was a name.'

'What name!' demanded the lawyer.

Levin shook his head, in supposed apology. 'That's it,'

271

he said. 'I've tried to recall it precisely, but I can't. I'm not sure which it was.'

'Give it to us!' said Myers.

'It was either Hernandez or Fernandez,' offered Levin. 'They both seem to be among the commonest names in the region, so I don't think it means anything . . . I'm sorry.'

The identity was, in fact, Ramon Hernandez and he was deputy operational commander of the CIA-backed Democratic Force and regarded by the Agency as their leading asset in the attempted overthrow of the Sandinistas. All of which Moscow knew from their support and infiltration of the Managua government and none of which had come from any encounter with Shelenkov, whose sole responsibility had been running the CIA spy John Willick.

Already on the pads in front of them Myers and Norris had a ring around the name Hernandez. On his sheet Myers wrote 'We've got a trace' with several exclamation marks and thrust it sideways, to Norris.

'Great, Yevgennie. You're doing great,' encouraged Myers. 'What else?'

'Shelenkov said Nicaragua was going to be a communist success and then he said he thought there would be some success in the Caribbean, like there had been with Cuba . . .'

'Another country you've specifically remembered!' cut in Crookshank.

'Having remembered one, I remembered the other, because of what was said,' replied Levin.

'I don't follow that,' complained Norris.

'A lot of it was history,' said Levin. Despite the hours and weeks of rehearsal and training, he was beginning to ache again, from the strain of necessarily presenting everything piecemeal and convoluted and jumbled.

'Take us through it,' said the soothing Myers. 'Your pace, your way. Just so that we get some idea of the picture.'

'It was confused; I still don't fully understand the significance. Even if it's significant at all,' set out Levin.

'He talked about the missiles that we put on Cuba and how President Kennedy was able to face Castro down and get them removed. Said American strength was not in the U–2 overflight photographs that you obtained, here at the Agency. It was in having as an asset in Russia Oleg Penkovsky, who was able to confirm that at that stage of development our rockets had ineffective guidance systems . . . that there was no real danger and that Krushchev had to back off . . .'

'You've lost me,' interrupted Crookshank. 'I haven't a clue where we're supposed to be going here.'

'I said I did not know if it had any significance,' apologized Levin once more.

'Don't stop,' urged Norris. 'Let's hear it all, no matter how confusing it seems.'

'He said it would never happen again. That we were aware exactly how much you knew about our main rocket centre at Semipalatinsk . . .' Levin was conscious of the reaction from the three men, unknowingly coordinating the supposed information passed on weeks before by Sergei Kapalet, in Paris. ' . . . And not just in Semipalatinsk . . . at our other installations, too . . .'

'I've got to stop you here, because it's important,' broke in Norris. 'What, exactly, did you think Shelenkov was telling you at that moment? Was he telling you that we were being fed disinformation, from assets we think we've got within the Soviet Union? That we were getting it all wrong?'

Almost there, thought Levin. 'Oh no,' he said. 'That was something else Shelenkov laughed about. I can't remember the precise words, of course. But he said something like "And it's all coming from the Company themselves" and then added that you were never going to know it.'

'But now we do,' said Myers distantly. 'And we're going to screw the motherfucker into the ground.'

John Willick felt better than he had in weeks; months. More months than he could remember; wanted to remember. The last $2,000 had got Eleanor and her flesh-stripping piranha lawyer off his back at least for a while, he'd picked three out of five winners at Aqueduct during the weekend trip to New York, and today the metals were showing two points above what he'd bought in at. He intended to gamble up to a four-point increase and sell. Maybe just take the profit and sit back a while, not be in a hurry to get back into something too quickly. Money in the bank. It was wonderful to be free of pressure. He'd always known it would get better, one day. Just taken longer than he'd expected, that's all. Christ, he felt good.

Willick joined the line and filed behind the guide on to the viewing gallery of the Library of Congress, looking down at the readers at their circular reading benches and listening to the hushed commentary of the number of books stored in the honeycomb vaults of Capitol Hill. He thought the woman said twenty-four million, but he wasn't sure. At her suggestion they all gazed up at the intricate mosaic ceiling and Willick did so in genuine admiration, able at last to think of something outside his own personal problems. Didn't have any personal problems, not any more.

'It's magnificent, isn't it?' said Oleg, arriving beside him.

'Wonderful,' agreed Willick.

'Ever been to Rome?'

'No.'

'There are some roofs and mosaics there that remind me of this.'

Willick filed after the Russian from the gallery, down the steps to the ground floor and across the zodiac-signed marble floor to the exit. The wind howled up the hill, biting into them, and both men huddled down into topcoats. Oleg went into the direction of Independence Avenue and the CIA man caught up, falling into step.

'Moscow were very pleased with that last batch,' praised Oleg.

'I'm glad.'

'What else have you got?'

'Files on a lot of the senior analysts. Twenty-four.'

274

'But not all?'

'I warned you my Records Section wouldn't have everything, for Christ's sake!'

'We're not complaining,' placated the Russian. 'That's very good. But you'll try to get more, won't you?'

'Yes,' sighed Willick.

'The biographies are complete of those you have got? Particularly their specialities?'

'Yes,' assured the American.

'That's good, John. Very good.'

Willick passed over the envelope to the other man and said: 'Don't I get something in return?'

'Money,' agreed the Russian, handing over a smaller envelope. 'And advice.'

'Advice?'

'We want you to be careful, John. Very careful.'

'Why?' demanded Willick, feeling the beginning of that familiar stomach churn.

'Nothing unusual happening up there at Langley?'

'No,' said Willick doubtfully.

'You sure?'

'Unusual like what?'

'We listen to a lot of radio traffic at the embassy,' said Oleg, which was true although not the source of this conversation, which was specifically timed instructions from Moscow. 'The way we read it there's a pretty intensive investigation under way.'

'Investigation?'

'One intercept talked of Agency penetration.'

'Oh dear God!' said Willick. Why couldn't the feeling of relief, of well-being, have lasted longer! It wasn't fair; why wasn't anything ever fair!

'Don't panic,' said the Russian. 'Panic and you'll give yourself away. There's no reason to think it's directed at you.'

'It's got to be, hasn't it?'

'Not necessarily.'

'It is!' insisted Willick, already convinced.

'Remember something,' urged Oleg. 'Whatever happens, we won't abandon you.'

'What's that mean?'

'That we're your friends. And that we'll go on being your friends.'

Kapalet was irritated that the floor show at the Crazy Horse was unchanged, wishing they'd chosen a different meeting place. He turned away from the transvestite and the rope trick and said: 'It looks as if Shelenkov knows things about Latin America.'

'Like what?'

'No specifics, like names.'

'What then?'

'Says you guys don't stand a chance in Nicaragua. That you didn't, even before Irangate.'

'Why?'

'I don't know.'

Wilson Drew jabbed impatiently at the drink coaster on the bar with his cocktail stick.

'Who's he talking about when he says there's a foul-up in Nicaragua?'

'The Agency. It's always the Agency.'

'Shit!'

'I wish there were more.'

'I must have a name!'

'You know there's no way I can get that.'

'Something . . . anything!'

'That's why I asked for this meeting,' disclosed the Russian, grinning.

The huge American looked savagely sideways at him and said: 'Don't jerk me about, Sergei! This ain't no fucking game we're playing here!' If it hadn't been so necessary to keep the guy sugar sweet he'd have stuffed that ass-sweaty piece of rope from the cabaret act down the Russian's stupid throat.

'It seems he was being moved,' announced Kapalet.

'Who?'

'Shelenkov's source.'

'Where from?'

'I don't know.'

'To where?'

276

'I don't know that, either,' said the Russian. 'Shelenkov simply said, two nights ago, that his man was being shifted, within the Agency.'

There was another trace, maybe the best way, Drew realized. He said: 'When was it happening?'

'There wasn't a positive date,' said Kapalet. 'He said the move almost coincided with his transfer.'

'When did Shelenkov arrive here in Paris?'

'June thirtieth.'

'We've got him!' said Drew triumphantly. 'All we've got to do is sift all the Agency movements, a month before and a month after June thirtieth.'

'One more thing,' said the Russian. 'Shelenkov said where the man was going could be as useful as where he had been.'

'Where he was going was as useful as where he had been?'

'That's what he said.'

'Sorry I ran off at the mouth there just now, Sergei. I was out of order.'

'No offence,' said Kapalet. 'Be good to get this thing resolved, won't it?'

'You wouldn't believe how good,' said the American.

29

Militia Post 20 was on a corner, with the majority of the building extending along Petrovka Street, a gloomy, grime-windowed, barrack-like construction. The entrance hall was bisected from wall to wall by a separating barrier, elevated in its middle. Behind it sat an officer whose rank Yuri could not identify from his shoulder designations. On either side of him were men in civilian clothes, clerks hunched over ledgers. Yuri expected it to be a noisy, bustling place but it was strangely quiet: although he had never entered one, Yuri thought the atmosphere had to be something like a church. On the wall behind the division was a large photograph of Mikhail Gorbachov: it was an early, pre-*glasnost* picture upon which the birthmark on the leader's forehead had been brushed out by the printer, unlike today's photographs. There was a large noticeboard with very little on it along the wall to Yuri's right. To the left were unmarked doors to three offices. There was a smell, although different from that at Mytishchi: here it seemed to be an odour of chalk, which he didn't understand, and dust and bodies, which he did.

Yuri had not determined his approach before he entered and was still undecided as he walked to the barrier. Once there, he had to look up, because of its height. The uniformed man continued reading something unseen behind a ledge and the clerks went on writing. Why was some sort of intimidation so important to so many people? With the word in mind and remembering the effect upon the woman at Mytishchi, Yuri announced: 'Komitet Gosudarstvennoy Bezopasnosti.'

The clerks wrote on and it was several moments before the officer looked up. 'So?' he said.

'So I want information.'

'I thought the KGB already knew everything.'

Yuri refused to pander to the man's pretension. He said: 'Vasili Dmitrevich Malik.'

Close now, Yuri realized that the man to whom he was talking was contributing heavily to the body smell of the building. The officer's slight straightening in his chair was the only perceptible change in his attitude. He said: 'Criminal division handled that.'

Yuri did not know what the differentiation signified. He said: 'They are not here?'

'Of course they are here.'

'Where?'

The desk officer gestured vaguely behind him, to the rear of the building.

'Who?' demanded Yuri.

'Investigator Bogaty.'

Yuri moved to speak, about to make it a polite question. Instead, responding to the hostility, he said: 'Tell him I am here.'

The man did not move at once and briefly Yuri thought he was going to refuse. Then he lifted what must have been an internal telephone, leaning back to talk behind a cupped hand, so that Yuri was unable to hear all that was said. He managed to detect the identification of the KGB. The man replaced the instrument and gestured behind him but positively to the left this time. 'You're to go back. Room 12b.' He seemed disappointed the meeting had been granted.

Yuri pushed through the swing gate, picking up the numbering halfway along the open corridor. He hoped the deskman's attitude was not indicative of a general feeling about the KGB within the militia headquarters. At 12b Yuri knocked politely, and heard at once a muffled 'Enter', which he did.

It was a pristine, almost antiseptically clean office: there was even an antiseptic smell which Yuri saw came from a deodorizer device on top of a filing cabinet, arranged against two other filing cabinets in absolute symmetry, every drawer closed. There were two windows at which the blinds had been half pulled precisely to a matching level and a desk the top of which shone. On it were seried In and Out trays, both empty, with a telephone directly in line and an unmarked blotter measurably in its very centre. Behind sat an overweight man neatly encompassed in a well-cut suit with a colour-coordinated tie and a white shirt as pristinely clean as everything else around its wearer.

'Investigator Bogaty?'

'At last!' Bogaty said.

The reply confused Yuri: it could only have taken seconds – two minutes at the outside – for him to have walked from the front hall desk! He said: 'I have come about Vasili Dmitrevich Malik.'

'After nine days, five hours and thirty-five minutes!' said Bogaty, with a policeman's contempt of a neglected investigation.

'I do not understand,' said Yuri, who didn't.

'It's taken nine days, five hours and thirty-five minutes for the KGB – for Colonel Panchenko – to say please. And then he couldn't do it himself,' said the investigator.

Yuri understood the reply little better than he had anything else, but he didn't think comprehension was immediately important. For an unknown reason he had an apparently angry man talking by name of someone he believed to be connected with the death of his father. He said: 'I am sorry, if it has caused you difficulties.'

'Hardly me,' said Bogaty. 'Have you been put in charge of the investigation?'

Yuri searched desperately for a reply he could regard as safe and couldn't find one. So he said: 'Not exactly.'

'You know it's too late, don't you?'

What was the response to that! Yuri said: 'I hope not.'

'You haven't checked the garages, have you?'

A negative question invites a negative reply, thought Yuri, remembering the interrogation lectures. 'No,' he said.

'So it's too late!' insisted the detective. 'I told him! That night, when it happened, I told Panchenko to check the garages, before there was time to get the damage repaired.'

Stoke the apparent outrage, decided Yuri: let the man

boil over so he could pick up a lead to what this was all about. He said: 'I don't know anything of this.'

'If you people can't do the job you're supposed to do, why don't you leave it to others who can?' demanded Bogaty.

'What would you have done?' asked Yuri. Lecture me, patronize me, be contemptuous, he thought.

'Gone through all the garages, particularly the back-street, cash-in-the-hand junk houses,' said Bogaty. 'There aren't any I don't know. Hassled them until I found a circa 1984 Lada with a smashed light and a crumpled wing . . .' Bogaty breathed heavily to a halt. 'A week,' he resumed. 'That's all it would have taken me. A week. Now you don't stand a chance. Not a chance in hell.'

What exactly was the man complaining about? A botched inquiry, obviously. But how could he know whether any inquiry had been botched or not? Despite the bewilderment, details were registering with him: a 1984 Lada, with a smashed headlight and a damaged wing. Yuri decided to pique the man's obvious pride. He said: 'It certainly seems we should have sought your help sooner.'

Bogaty did not reply at once. Instead he opened an unseen drawer to the right of his desk, extracted a manila folder which he threw towards Yuri, without disarranging the carefully positioned blotter, and said: 'What good do you imagine this is going to be so late?'

Now it was Yuri who did not respond at once, realization at last crowding in upon him. The folder was a metre away, close enough for him to reach out and touch. And how much he wanted to touch it: snatch it up and devour everything that was inside! But he didn't. Forcing the calmness into his voice, he said: 'What's it say?'

'What do you think it says?'

Shit! thought Yuri. He said: 'Facts, not supposition.'

'The man was hit from behind by a Lada car, which from the glass fragments and paint samples is shown to have been manufactured around 1984,' said Bogaty. 'The initial impact broke his back. Tyre marks, in the poor bastard's own blood, show the vehicle reversed over him,

281

crushing the rib cage and all the organs, including the heart. Died instantly.'

Yuri swallowed at the dispassionate recital, needing fresh control. My father, he thought: that's my father you're talking about, like he was a piece of meat in an abbatoir. He said: 'Run down deliberately?'

'No question about it,' insisted Bogaty.

'And the proof's there?' said Yuri, indicating the folder between them. He was hot, flushed, and hoped it was not showing by the colour of his face. So this was why the inquiry had come under the aegis of the criminal division!

'Of course it's all there. I told Panchenko at the time it would be.'

'I didn't speak directly to him,' risked Yuri. *At the time.* Did that mean Panchenko had physically been at the scene? Should he extend the risk, telling the detective who he was and openly seeking the man's help? No, rejected Yuri, conscious of the neatness of Bogaty's office. It was inconceivable that someone to whom order was so important would knowingly breach a different sort of order.

'By taking so long it's virtually useless,' insisted Bogaty. 'Is this how it is in the KGB?'

'You know how things are,' shrugged Yuri invitingly.

Bogaty gestured around his sterile office. 'I know how things are here,' he said. 'And I know that if I was aware of technical evidence available I would not have waited nine days, five hours and thirty-five minutes before I collected it.'

Bogaty believed him to be Panchenko's messenger! The complete and incredible comprehension flooded in on Yuri and he fought against it mentally overwhelming him, recognizing the opportunity it represented but conscious how, by the smallest error, he could be destroyed by it. Hopefully, he said: 'Was the way it happened obvious, at the scene?'

'To me it was.'

He had to take the chance, Yuri decided. He said: 'Did the comrade colonel take the same view?'

'The comrade colonel did not express any view,' said Bogaty stiffly.

He had it! There was still the need to proceed with one foot placed just inches in front of the other. No accident, he thought: deliberately run over – the evidence in front of him like a mockery – and Panchenko provably at the scene. More, in every respect, than he'd imagined possible. Would he be able to get out of here with that file? Reaching out, grateful there was no shake in his hand, Yuri said: 'I'd better be getting along.'

'I'll need a receipt,' announced Bogaty.

'Of course,' responded Yuri. Who? he wondered desperately. The name came and Yuri decided it was ironically appropriate, scrawling 'Igor Agayans' across the formal hand-over document that Bogaty pushed across the desk at him. He was guilty of forgery, recognized Yuri. Deception and theft, too. Positively committed from this moment on into doing something, although he still did not know what. *I think I could kill someone who tried to kill me*, he remembered.

'Best of luck,' said Bogaty. 'You're going to need it.'

'I know,' said Yuri, with feeling.

He had consciously to walk at a normal pace back through the militia building, the dossier tight against his side, ears strained for some belated challenge from behind. Incredible! he thought exultantly: incredible and unbelievable but it had happened because of the investigator's simple assumption, from his desk officer's introduction. And that for nine days, five hours and thirty-five minutes – no, fifty-five minutes now – Bogaty had been expecting a courier from Panchenko to collect promised technical evidence. He would even perform the function of a courier, decided Yuri. But only after reading and copying everything that was here.

Which was what he did, the following morning, in a public duplicating booth in the GUM department store – actually within view of the KGB headquarters in Dzerzhinsky Square – with the exception only of the photographs which he decided were too gory to risk their being accidentally seen in such a public place. The photographs had given Yuri most difficulty the previous night, when he had got back to Kutuzovsky Prospekt, each brutally taken to show up and expose rather than to minimize. He'd had to swallow against the sensation that rose in the back of his throat, lips moving in a private promise to himself. There were twelve photographs, and Yuri removed just one of the originals, the least horrific, but showing most clearly the delineated tyre tread outlined in his father's blood. The rest he returned to the master file, which he delivered to the central document receiving desk at the First Chief Directorate headquarters, for internal distribution to the office of Colonel Lev Konstantinovich Panchenko.

From the forensic evidence he now knew in such detail, Yuri recognized the investigator's insistence upon checking garages to be the next obvious step, but he held back from taking it, ingrained KGB professionalism overriding personal impatience. He illegally possessed a police file and he possessed a dossier illegally assembled by his father. Neither complete, perhaps, but both in terms of his training invaluable intelligence. And he'd been lectured about invaluable intelligence at the KGB training academy on Metrostroevskaya. Protect had been the dictum: protect absolutely, secure absolutely. Neither of which he could do here in Moscow, in an uncertain apartment, subject at Kazin's or Panchenko's whim to search. Absolutely to protect and to secure meant, almost absurdly, that he had to get both sets of records out of the Soviet Union. Which he could do, he realized, without the slightest risk of interception or detection; his return to Russia this time had been official, on compassionate grounds. So he could openly travel on United Nations documentation as the international diplomat he was supposed to be and which relieved him of any Customs or immigration check upon his re-entry into the United States.

The time difference between Russia and America meant it was still early afternoon when Yuri landed at Kennedy Airport. He took the taxi to central Manhattan and although he was sure from the journey into the city that

284

he was unfollowed he still spent an hour on foot clearing his trail before entering the Chase Manhattan Bank on Second Avenue. He opened the safe-deposit box in the name of William Bell, using the passport for identification, and put into it everything with which he had returned from Moscow, including the unread letters between his mother and father.

He was reluctant to go immediately to the UN building, needing to unwind from the constant tension of the Moscow journey. He went to the UN Plaza Hotel directly opposite and the glittering bar to which he had taken Inya that failed night, able at that time of the afternoon to get a place at a concealing corner table.

So he had his invaluable intelligence and now it was protected and secure. But so what? There was still nothing, in any of it, positively linking Panchenko to a crime or departmental infraction: and even less positively a provable link to Kazin. Like trying to fit together an intricate jigsaw puzzle without knowing the picture it would represent, thought Yuri. No, he contradicted at once. He was sure he knew the picture: it was the necessary completing pieces that were missing. What would he do – could he do – if he found the pieces and made up his picture? Always questions, never answers, he thought. Now the most pressing unanswered question of all: was the Kazin-ordered assignment, to try to locate the recent defector, part of the same picture? Or something altogether different? About that, at the moment, he was only certain of one thing. That unquestionably it represented a personal danger: the sort of personal danger that had destroyed his father.

Colonel Panchenko read through the experts' reports and then studied the photographs with a professional detachment, nodding admiringly in the solitude of his office at the well-assembled and obvious evidence of a crime. His initial feeling was to destroy everything, as he'd had removed by the garage off Begovaya any trace on the Lada's nearside wing of the collision with the wall. And then he hesitated, because there was a difference. The car had been one of the dozens used for unsuspected KGB surveillance, with an untraceable civilian registration, MOS 56–37–42. The definite association with him came from the listing in the records of the Directorate motor pool. But there was nothing personally incriminating in what the militia had produced. No danger, therefore, in retaining it in the safe on the far side of the office to which only he had the combination: the safe which already contained the tapes of his car and gazebo conversations with Victor Kazin.

30

The Crisis Committee reacted to the persistent and impatient demands of the CIA director that speed of detection was the foremost consideration and tried to shortcut when they got the apparently vital leads from Paris. And disastrously delayed the identification of John Willick.

Their mistake – which they were intended by Moscow to make – was to try to combine the name supposedly remembered by Yevgennie Levin with the provable date and transfer intentionally disclosed by Sergei Kapalet.

Cots were moved into the debriefing building for Myers, Norris and Crookshank to work around the clock to scour the CIA records to find an internal relocation one month either side of 30 June of any Langley-based official or officer who had the remotest links with Ramon Hernandez in Nicaragua. The CIA station in neighbouring Honduras, through which Hernandez was run, was warned against the man and ordered to carry out an investigation into his loyalty. Additionally the station was instructed to relay back each and every name within the Agency of people through whom Hernandez operated – or thought he operated – in the hope one might be different from those listed on those same records as being members of the man's headquarters control group.

There weren't any. Neither was there the slightest evidence to doubt Hernandez' commitment. And nor did the personnel records show up an internal transfer of anyone connected in the remotest way with the man's activities or reports in Latin America. Refusing to be deflected, Myers extended the transfer period to two and then three months either side of the June date. Still there was no one who could be linked with the Nicaraguan.

'It doesn't make any fucking sense!' erupted Myers.

'It has to, somehow,' said the more controlled Norris.

'How!'

'If I knew that, I would not be sitting here looking at a blank wall, would I?'

'We've approached it the wrong way,' realized Crookshank.

'What wrong way?' demanded Myers, whose decision it had been.

Instead of replying, Crookshank said: 'What's the most positive thing we have?'

Neither of the other two men replied at once. Then Norris said: 'The date?'

'The date,' agreed Crookshank. 'And the fact that there *was* a relocation.' With a lawyer's pedantry, he searched through his papers, then smiled up. ' "He said the move almost coincided with his transfer," ' he quoted. 'Drew's verbatim record of Kapalet's account. Two months and three months isn't almost coinciding. We've confused ourselves, trying to involve Hernandez.'

'What have we got, without him?' demanded Myers, irked at the criticism.

'What we've just agreed to be the most positive lead there is,' lectured Crookshank. He went back to his papers again, coming up with a single sheet. 'The first list,' he said. 'Of internal transfers one month either side of June thirtieth. Fifteen people: five seconded to overseas stations, six retired, four departmental moves.'

'I think you're right,' agreed Myers reluctantly.

'We could sweat them all on a polygraph in a week,' accepted Norris.

'But no advance warning,' agreed Crookshank.

John Willick didn't need it. He'd handled three of the Crisis Committee's requests for names and biographical details of people affected by internal movements. And knew from casual gossip over coffee and two hurriedly sought-out cafeteria lunches on successive days with others in the personnel department that there had been at least five further inquiries, all for precisely the same sort of material. That by itself, after Oleg's warning, would have been sufficient to alarm the American. But it was not by itself. The requests clearly specified move-

288

ments either side of the date when the controller he knew only as Aleksandr had been moved from Washington. And came from an unspecified committee sufficiently important to qualify for a scarlet-classified, respond-this-day security designation. So it was not alarm Willick felt; it was terror.

He used the number he had been given by Shelenkov and had reconfirmed as an emergency contact by the man's successor, careless of the panic he heard in his own voice when he demanded an immediate meeting, refusing in even more panic to wait until the following day for the opening of any of their customary public monuments or places and agreeing at once and without thought to a bar he didn't know in Georgetown.

It was not where he expected it to be, on M Street, but against the river and directly beneath the skeleton of the overhead railway. Eager for omens of protection, Willick was relieved to get a seat at the bar directly abutting a corner, so that he could sit without the possibility of anyone approaching him unseen. How long would it be, before they *did* approach him? Try to rationalize, he told himself, striving for control. Try to assess. Couldn't have isolated him yet: the request was general, for *all* the transfers. One of several then. But how many? Impossible to know, because he could not risk asking around any more than he already had. Eight, of which he knew. Probably more. Pointless attempting a possible figure. How were they being investigated? Alphabetically or . . . ? Or how? Couldn't think of another way. Had to be something like alphabetical, he supposed: they hadn't got to him yet and from what he knew the first request had arrived three days before. Could have been earlier, of course. Thank God his name began with the initial letter that it did. When then? Tomorrow? The day after? No way of knowing. Jesus, where was Oleg? He gestured for a refill and when the barman came asked for a large one. Finished, he thought: he was finished. Christ, wouldn't Eleanor laugh! Actually enjoy it. Keep cuttings of newspaper reports and go on all the breakfast TV shows. Bitch would probably write a book: My

Unsuspecting Life with a Russian Spy. Make a fortune. Jesus, where was Oleg! He held the glass up, as a signal to the barman.

The Russian came bowed-headed into the bar and directly to the corner where Willick was sitting: the two adjoining bar stools were empty and Oleg sat on the furthest one, so there was a gap between them.

'Where the hell have you been?' demanded Willick.

Instead of replying Oleg ordered draught beer from the returning barman and waited until it was served and the man moved away before he spoke. He said: 'You were extremely careless. Foolish.'

'What are you talking about?'

'There is an inquiry going on at Langley?'

'You know damned well there is.'

'And you are suspect?'

'All the transfers, around the time of Aleksandr's recall, have been pulled from records.'

'Yet you come directly here without checking in the most rudimentary way whether or not you are under surveillance and complain when I don't immediately join you!'

Instinctively, feeling stupid halfway through the gesture, Willick jerked around towards the door and back again.

'You're not being followed,' assured the Russian. He took the top off his beer, making a loud sucking sound. '*We* followed you.'

'They're on to me,' insisted Willick impatiently. 'They're checking transfers, around the June date.'

Oleg drank further, nodding in calm agreement as he replaced the handled mug. 'I think you're probably right.'

'I don't know what to do,' protested the American. 'You said you were my friend. Wouldn't abandon me.'

'And we won't,' said Oleg.

'So what can I do?' moaned Willick.

'Cross, whenever you want.'

'Cross?' The American looked blankly at the hunched roly-poly figure beside him, genuinely confused.

'To the Soviet Union,' expanded Oleg.

Willick continued to look blankly at the other man. Never, once, had the idea of defecting – of leaving America – occurred to him. He'd made the approach to the Russians because he was desperate for money. But naively he'd only ever regarded it as a temporary expediency, something he would be able to abandon once he straightened himself out. Jagged-voiced, unable to stop the giggle, he said: 'Defect! To Moscow!'

'Have you thought about what would happen when they arrest you?' demanded the Russian. 'You're a traitor, John. The worse kind of traitor. There won't be any rules, any kindness. They'll stretch you anyway they feel like – lie detector, chemicals, whatever – and when they've got all they want they'll put you up before a court and you'll get life. Can you imagine that, John? Life inside some penitentiary. Fresh meat, to be passed around and raped. Or maybe you'd get lucky: find someone with power inside who'd want to keep you for himself. Still have to sleep with him of course. Be his wife. Better than being gang-banged, though. Less chance of catching a disease: lot of disease in American jails, so I believe. AIDS.'

'Stop it!' pleaded Willick. 'Please stop it!'

'You like another drink?'

'Yes.'

'Large?'

'Yes.'

As the fresh glasses were put before them the Russian said: 'Not much of a choice really, is it?'

'What would I have to do in Moscow?'

'I don't know,' replied Oleg honestly. 'I was simply told that we would accept you, if you asked.'

'When?'

'How much time do you think you've got?' asked Oleg.

'I don't know,' said Willick despairingly.

'Tomorrow might be too late,' said the Russian. 'What's to stop you coming now?'

Nothing! thought Willick, in mounting excitement. All he here were debts and hassle and an ex-wife in two weeks' time due alimony that he didn't have. It would be wonderful to turn his back on it all! Actually dump on Eleanor. He said: 'How would I do it?'

'You've got a passport?'

'Yes.'

'There's a plane leaving here at eleven tonight, for Paris. Just go to our embassy there and you will be told the rest.'

'You planned this?' demanded Willick.

'I told you before that we were your friends,' reminded Oleg. 'When I got your call I found out how it could be done. You've got a lot of time.'

'I don't have money for a ticket,' remembered Willick.

Oleg passed a sealed envelope across the intervening chair, his hand concealed beneath the bar top. 'Enough for first class.'

'I could do it,' said Willick, like a child trying to encourage its own endeavours.

'Of course you could do it,' supported Oleg.

'I *would* go to jail, wouldn't I?'

'For life,' said the Russian positively.

Willick shuddered and said: 'I'll never be able to repay you.'

'I'm sure you will,' said the man.

On the credit side Yuri decided there were advantages to being assigned special duties by the head of the First Chief Directorate. Unquestioningly Granov granted him monitoring authority to the UN-channelled correspondences, but more importantly the *resident* did not object to Yuri living more at the 53rd Street apartment than at Riverdale. It meant Yuri was able to spend as much time as he wanted with Caroline, which he did rarely thinking of the breach of regulations or of any inherent dangers. He was guilty of so many breaches of regulations and faced so much inherent danger that the nights they were together seemed by comparison oases of normality and safety.

In no way, however, did he neglect the search for Yevgennie Levin because he realized that an obvious attack if he failed could be the accusation under some disciplinary code of professional incompetence in carrying out an order.

He grew convinced that the letters were the key. He assembled the family's to Natalia and hers to them separately by date but connected them through a central graph upon which he listed what he regarded as potential clues to Levin's whereabouts.

The punctuality of their replies confirmed what he regarded as the most positive indicator that Levin was on the east coast of America and not too far from New York. Because he controlled the letter flow, he was able to time precisely the handover of Natalia's first letter after his return from Moscow, at three o'clock on a Wednesday afternoon. The intercepted response – from Galina – was not only dated the same day but timed, at eight o'clock the same evening. There had to be subtracted, of course, some unknown time against the delivery not being initiated immediately and for the period it would have taken for the mother to have read it, even guessing that she would have done so at once. And for the possibility that it had gone from New York by air and not by road, which he doubted but for which he had to make allowances because in a letter from Levin there was reference to a helicopter journey and of having flown directly over Washington landmarks like the Capitol building and the Washington obelisk and Lincoln Memorial. On his chart, Yuri wrote 'Five hours' but was prepared to adjust either higher or lower. In the same letter Natalia had obediently followed his instruction to complain about the coldness of Moscow and from Petr it prompted the sort of reply for which Yuri had hoped.

'It is cold here, too,' the boy wrote. 'We are told there are a lot of ski lodges and that the snow will be here in a week or two, a month at the outside.'

From the date on the letter Yuri wrote 'November, first or last week?' recognizing it as an indicator hopefully as positive as the timing of the replies. It definitely ruled out at least twelve of the southern or mid-west states, where snow never fell. And also the mountain or western states where it did, because on such high ground the snow was permanent and not dependent upon the seasons. And to none of them, even by aeroplane, could a letter have been delivered from New York and prompted a reply in such a short time. There was winter skiing in the Catskill Mountains, Yuri knew. Throughout New England, too. Still a vast area: too vast.

At the first reading Yuri underlined Levin's listing of the Washington landmarks, seeking a significance but not immediately finding it. Caught suddenly by an idea, Yuri posed as the journalist he was supposed to be and telephoned the Federal Aviation Authority in Washington using his legend name of William Bell and the title of his Amsterdam cover publication to be told that no civil or commercial winged aircraft would be permitted low-level overflight of the sort he described. It would, however, be possible by helicopter, the spokesman helpfully added. Before ringing off Yuri established the average cruise speed of small, passenger-carrying helicopters and by computing speed against time came up again with a travelling period of around five hours, four at the minimum. Levin had not only described Washington from the air. He'd written of flying over New York. Which indicated an approach from the north. Marking the American capital as the extreme of one sweep of the compass Yuri halved his equation and completed the circle with Washington as that one outside marker. It created a radius that stopped just short of Boston but reached out to include huge tracts of Virginia, West Virginia, practically all of Pennsylvannia, and further daunting areas in Connecticut, New York State and Massachusetts. Too much, he thought. Too much while he possessed too little to enable him to narrow the boundaries.

On his graph he created a box, in which to list the references he considered important but which he could not understand. What did the passage in Levin's earliest letter mean, referring to trees that appeared from the air to be defoliated, like the Americans defoliated Vietnam? Or the phrase about apparent vantage points to the sea where there was no sea? Or even more intriguing, the paragraph that read of spies in statues and spies in history.

Still too many questions against too few answers. When was it going to change, the other way? Another question, Yuri recognized.

31

John Willick felt like he had that special day, when he'd been a kid of fourteen. His father, who had been first mate on an oil tanker and away from home for months at a time, had returned from sea and taken him to the amusement park at Coney Island and told him he could go on as many rides as he liked; do what he liked. Willick didn't think he'd missed one, not a single one. And he'd eaten ice cream as well and candied apples and cotton candy and then he'd been sick, violently, the man standing behind him and holding him around the waist, to stop him falling over. It had been wonderful.

Willick was sure he was not going to be sick this time, although the chance seemed there from the moment he seated himself in the first-class section of the Air France 747, immediately to be handed champagne and then foie gras and after that a white wine and a red wine he'd never heard of, to go with the seafood and the beef prepared in a way he'd never heard of, either. Wonderful, like that day at Coney Island. Only better. He was grown up now.

He celebrated during the flight but was careful not to get drunk, aware despite his euphoria that he'd escaped disaster (would he really have been so sexually abused, in prison?) by inches or by minutes and not wanting to endanger that escape by a mistake until he was completely safe, in Moscow. He still had a slight headache when the plane landed at Paris, at breakfast time because of the time change, and felt gritty-eyed and stubble-chinned. From Charles de Gaulle airport he took a taxi into the centre of Paris, chose a café at random actually on the Champs Elysées that he'd seen in all the movies and on television and sat over coffee that was too bitter, watching the city wake up around him. Free! he thought: I'm free. Free of Eleanor and free of horses that don't win and stocks that don't rise and free of pay-or-else letters and most important of all free of fear. He knew – was absolutely certain – that Moscow was going to be terrific. A new start, with the slate wiped clean and his being treated properly, like he should be treated, with respect. No one had ever treated him properly, with respect. Not Eleanor or those bastards in the CIA. Never. Served them right, all of them. Bastards. Bitches and bastards. Good, to be free.

Willick felt a twitch of apprehension when he came to pay but the waiter, who spoke English, accepted the American money and thanked him politely for a three-dollar tip, which was twice what it should have been, and Willick set off for the Soviet embassy buoyed by the gratitude. Being treated properly, he thought; with respect.

He had to ask twice for directions to the street address Oleg had given him in the Washington bar (could it really have only been last night, less than twenty-four hours?) and when he located it at last Willick's uncertainty worsened at the sight of the uniformed gendarmes on duty around the embassy, with a police truck that looked like a shed on wheels obviously drawn up in a side street.

The American loitered on the far side of the avenue, watching the arrivals and departures, realizing with relief that there was no entry challenge from the French policemen. Stomach in turmoil, wishing now he had not eaten the seafood and the beef in that rich sauce on the aircraft, Willick forced himself to cross the road and walk as confidently as he could past the guards and into the compound, ears ringing for the demand to stop, which never came. Wet-palmed, he handed the letter that Oleg had given him to the unsmiling clerk at the vestibule desk, praying there was a lavatory nearby that he could use. Damn the seafood; shellfish had never agreed with him.

The letter was dispatched with a guard, the response was instantaneous, and Willick's nervousness ebbed away just as quickly. Being treated properly, just like he knew he'd be. Respectfully.

Sergei Kapalet, who never identified himself, strode arm outstretched from somewhere at the rear of the building, retaining Willick's hand to guide him back beyond the entrance. Willick expected an office but instead was led into a kind of apartment, with couches and easy chairs and even fresh flowers in a vase. There was not just a lavatory for Willick's immediate need but a shower and a complete toilet kit, for him to shave, and a robe he was able to wear while his suit was pressed and his shirt laundered. In his excellent English Kapalet maintained a constant and relaxing stream of small talk, inquiring about the flight and wondering about the delay in Willick's expected arrival at the embassy (there is nothing like the first *petit déjeuner* on the Champs Elysées, he agreed) and promising the American he'd chosen an excellent restaurant for lunch.

The idea of leaving the security of the embassy surprised Willick. Kapalet laughed at the doubt and said: 'Why not?' and Willick smiled back and agreed: 'Why not?' He was free, after all. Still difficult to adjust.

They ate at the Taillevent, on the Rue Lamenais, Willick deferring completely to the Russian's obvious familiarity and expertise around a French menu and wine list. Willick could not remember ever having eaten or drunk anything that came remotely close to what Kapalet ordered. Just twenty-four hours earlier, for that nerve-jangled lunch in the CIA cafeteria, there'd been meat loaf and coffee, he remembered, disgusted. Not something to remember; something to forget. Like so much else. America – his life there – was over, Willick recognized. It was his future that was important now, the thing to think about: his wonderful, free, rewarding future.

His mind on that, Willick said: 'When am I to go to Moscow?'

'There is an Aeroflot flight tonight. Seven o'clock,' said Kapalet.

'Yes,' accepted Willick. It was a ridiculous reaction – he was tired, he told himself – but there was the vaguest feeling of regret. It would have been nice to have stayed in Paris for a day or two. Not that he had any doubt about Moscow: of course he hadn't. Just liked to have seen a bit more of Paris – eaten in a few more restaurants like this – that's all.

'Moscow are anxious for you to get there,' said Kapalet.

'I am regarded as important, then?' said Willick, wanting to hear the words actually spoken.

'Very important,' assured the Russian.

After lunch, because Willick requested it, Kapalet took him on a motor-car tour of the Paris sights, to the Arc de Triomphe and the Eiffel Tower, and to get to Notre Dame they drove the complete length of the Champs Elysées and around the Tuileries Gardens, and once again Willick started to think how good it would be to stay a few days longer, but refused to finish the reflection. This wasn't a vacation, for Christ's sake!

Kapalet concluded the sightseeing early, refusing to risk any rush-hour traffic delay, and led him directly to what looked like a closed Aeroflot counter. At once a plainclothes official appeared.

'He will escort you through immigration: see that everything is as it should be on the plane,' promised Kapalet.

'Thank you, for what you've done,' said the American.

'Thank you, for what you are going to do,' replied Kapalet.

The Aeroflot man stayed to one side and slightly apart while Willick went through French immigration but once that was achieved – without difficulty – the man closely escorted him directly through the embarkation lounge and on to the aircraft, ahead of anyone else. Willick was seated in the front, in a curtained-off section separating him from the other passengers. At once a stewardess offered him champagne, which Willick, feeling he was getting accustomed to the life, accepted.

The meal was not as good as it had been the previous evening but his treatment was. The greeting stewardess appeared to be exclusively assigned to him and halfway through the journey the pilot came back to invite him on to the flight deck. Willick went, although he was not particularly interested, unable to see anything in the darkness except for an occasional straggle of lights. But the view – or lack of it – was not what mattered. What mattered was the indication of his importance: Willick liked that, very much indeed.

And it continued, when the plane landed. Willick was led off once more ahead of anyone else to a waiting limousine drawn up close to the aircraft, without any hindering formalities. The driver opened the door for him and Willick began to enter but then stopped abruptly, momentarily startled by the figure of Vladislav Andreevich Belov already waiting in the rear seat.

'It's good to see you in Moscow,' greeted the director of the American division of the First Chief Directorate.

Willick got in beside the man and said: 'I'm glad to be here.'

The vehicle moved off immediately, around an airport perimeter road to pick up a multi-laned highway along which it began to move at a speed which surprised Willick, accustomed to the rigidly enforced limits of the United States. Sixty, maybe seventy miles an hour, he guessed; the first obvious difference, between his old and new life. Good, like everything else was good.

'You'll be tired?' anticipated Belov.

'I am,' agreed Willick. He'd dozed on the Air France flight and again on this final leg but it had to be almost forty-eight hours since he'd slept in a proper bed.

'Accommodation is already prepared for you,' promised Belov. 'We won't talk about anything tonight.'

'Has there been any announcement from Washington?'

'No,' said Belov.

Willick felt oddly disappointed. 'I thought there would have been, by now.'

'It's still only early afternoon, in Washington,' reminded the Russian. 'You'll only have been absent from your desk for a few hours.' The disclosure the Soviets intended was calculated to catch the main NBC, ABC and CBS TV broadcasts. There were still precisely three hours to go and Belov was anxious against the Americans revealing it first: a confirmation was going to have far less public impact than Moscow being first with the news.

'Everything seems to have happened so fast,' said Willick. 'It's still difficult to think in terms of hours, which is all it's been. Impossible, in fact.'

'It will seem real, soon enough.'

Willick was conscious of moving through streets which vaguely reminded him of Washington, expansive although matchingly low-rise buildings positioned either side of even more expansive but similarly matching highways. The only difference seemed to be in their lack of bustle and the corresponding absence of noise. Willick wondered what he was listening for and then realized it was a fire or police siren. Another immediate difference, between old and new: neither a cultural shock, so far. The street in which they stopped was deserted and Willick's comparison now was not with Washington but with Paris because the entrance to the building was through huge, pavement-abutting gates into an inner courtyard off which led the main entry door. Although he was not sure, it seemed to be an apartment complex. The ground-floor area was unidentified and, obediently following Belov, Willick ascended to an upper level and went through a secondary entry door into a suite that literally made him gasp. His immediate impression, coming through the courtyard, was that it was a pre-revolutionary building and everything about the apartment confirmed it. The furniture was gilded and tapesty-upholstered, the walls were covered in flocked wallpaper, there were reflecting chandeliers – two in the main room and others in the two bedrooms – and the floor-to-ceiling windows were draped in heavy, tasselled silk curtains. The flowers were not in vases but bulge-bellied bowls and on a circular, claw-footed table in the main room there was a frosted ice bucket containing yet more champagne and alongside it a silver bowl, iced again, of beluga caviar and a side dish of black and white bread.

Belov continued the conducted tour, into the chandeliered master bedroom where the curtaining design carried on with the bed canopied in matching material

301

and off which led a marbled bathroom that Willick guessed to be roughly the size of the main living room of his never-returned-to Rosslyn apartment. The shower stall was separate from the bath and there was a bidet as well as a toilet, in an enclosed stall. White towels fountained from differently sized wall holders and everywhere there was the smell of some flower-like fragrance.

The dining area was as lavishly furnished but a comparatively small alcove, compared to the remainder of the apartment and into Willick's mind came the question as Belov answered it.

'There is no kitchen on this level,' said the Russian. 'On the ground level are the people who will look after you. The kitchens are there. Whatever you want, they can provide. Just lift the telephone and ask. Whatever.'

'I understand,' said Willick, overwhelmed.

'You will be comfortable here?'

'Oh yes,' assured Willick hurriedly. 'Very comfortable indeed.' He'd hoped to be feted but never like this. If this weren't the former home of a Grand Duke it was something pretty close. What was close to a Grand Duke? Maybe just an ordinary Duke. He wished there had been identifiable ancestral portraits on the walls from which he could have tried to work out whose home it had once been.

'Get some rest,' urged Belov. 'There's a great deal to be done in a very short time.'

'What?' asked the American at once.

'Tomorrow,' said Belov. 'Everything can wait until tomorrow, when you're rested.'

Willick walked with the Russian to the exit and turned immediately inside it as the man left, staring into the apartment with his back pressed against the door, trying to recapture the emotion of his earlier entry, a junkie trying to repeat the high of his first fix. Not precisely the same, but close. Incredible. Not good enough: not expressive enough. Spectacularly incredible: that didn't sound right, either, grammatically or in any other way. Why try to find words for it? He guessed his value was being assessed for the years he had spent upon the CIA's

Soviet analysis desk, years from which he was aware of the divide – the Grand Canyon or Mississippi Delta? – between the haves and the have-nots of the Soviet Union. Never, in his most speculative assessment, had he considered anything like this. This was ... His mind blocked, unable to cope. Wonderful was the word which danced in his head, like a child's toy on the end of an elastic string. Inadequate, like every other superlative, but it would have to do. Absolutely wonderful.

He was sagging from fatigue but like a child again, unwilling to leave the best birthday party it's ever known, he spooned some of the red eggs upon some black bread, although he wasn't hungry, and tugged open the champagne, although he was not thirsty nor did he want to drink. Glass in one hand, spilling caviar in the other, Willick went to the window, gazing through the misted gauze curtains at the darkened, hushed and deserted street beyond. Who would his neighbours be, he wondered. Doubtless get to know them, in the way one got to know one's neighbours. Hadn't happened in Rosslyn, though. Not his fault. Eleanor's fault. Everything was Eleanor's fault: stand-offish, snooty bitch. Different this time. Wouldn't rush it – no need to rush or be in a hurry – but respond properly when the invitations came, accept theirs and respond to theirs, after the proper length of time. Wouldn't be able to say what he did, of course. Hadn't been able to in Washington, either. I work for the government: the customary reply, so customary that everyone knew he worked for the CIA. Get guidance about that. Plenty of time and he didn't want to offend, through ignorance. Would he be awarded a car? Certain to be, if he were allocated accommodation like this. And a driver? Almost certain again. Have to drive himself sometimes, though. Enjoy that. Especially at the speed at which the driver had come in from the airport. Seventy miles an hour at least: maybe eighty.

Willick looked at his watch, blinking to focus, trying to work out the difference between Washington and Moscow, and realized he had not altered the time from his departure from Dulles Airport. He frowned, surprised

303

at the oversight. Five, he saw. They'd be worried now. Checking with the section head to see if he'd called in sick, panic rising from his name being on the list of internal transfers, then the hurried swoop at Rosslyn. To find nothing: empty fridge, empty bottles, empty bed, empty everything. Lots of bills, though. Who'd be responsible for those now? The Agency? Or Eleanor? Supreme but fitting irony if Eleanor were judged responsible for all the shit he'd left behind and ordered by some court to clear it up. He belched and had to swallow, quickly: have to be careful against being sick. Where had that been? Coney Island, he remembered. Long time ago. Didn't live anywhere near there any more. Lived here. Had champagne and caviar. Didn't want any more though, not right now. Tired. Wanted to sleep.

When the KGB attendant entered the suite the following morning he found Willick lying in his underwear across the bed, which had not been opened, half a glass of champagne and the remainder of his caviar and bread on a side table, upon which the light still burned. The debris was cleared away and the clothes were collected to be valeted and Willick was rolled, grunting, between the covers for two more hours' sleep before being properly roused. He took the proferred robe but refused any breakfast, his stomach still loose from the excesses of the previous day. Pain was banded around his head and a shower didn't help.

Belov arrived carrying a briefcase, smiling broadly, and said with immediate briskness: 'And today we work.' The smile, like the briskness, was forced. They'd succeeded in making the announcement of Willick's defection and from the overnight Washington embassy playbacks he knew all three national television networks had led their main newscast with it. It had also been the major item on subsidiary programmes throughout the nation, and in newspapers and on radio occupied major segments after the CIA confirmation that the man was missing. So now – today – should have been the start of his being acknowledged the architect of one of the most brilliant

KGB coups ever. And would have been, but for the bastard Kazin.

'What?' asked Willick.

'Your defection has been made public,' disclosed Belov, without saying how.

Willick frowned at the word: until this moment he had not thought of what he'd done as defecting. He said: 'When?'

'Last night.'

'Has a lot been made of it?'

'Lead item throughout the media.'

He'd be famous, thought Willick. He said: 'You didn't tell me what you meant, by saying I had to work.'

'You're going to give a press conference,' announced Belov. 'The Ministry has been inundated with press inquiries. We've said you'll be made available this afternoon.'

'I don't want to give a press conference!' protested Willick. He'd shouted and he had not meant to. But why did it always happen to him? Why, when things looked good, did it always have to crumble? He'd be attacked, he knew: sneered at and called a traitor.

'We want you to,' said Belov with quiet, contrasting insistence.

'No!' said Willick. It was a plea more than an outright refusal. 'I won't be any good at it; won't know what to say.' He'd be like some exhibit, a freak at a funfair. Like Coney Island.

Belov patted the briefcase beside him and said: 'We'll prepare everything, you and I. So you'll know the answers to give.'

'How, before we know the questions?'

'Everything will be on our terms,' said Belov. 'You'll make a statement . . .' He patted the briefcase again. 'That's here, all ready. There will be people on the platform with you during the questioning. They'll help you, before you have to answer.'

'Will I be on television again in America?'

'Of course you will,' said Belov. That's the whole object, you stupid fool, the Russian thought.

305

Eleanor might see him: realize how important he was. Willick said: 'No one will be allowed to attack me? Criticize me?'

'We will control everything,' repeated Belov patiently.

'I'm still not sure I can do it,' said Willick. What if he broke down halfway through; couldn't think of anything to say and made an idiot of himself while the cameras were running?

'A doctor is coming,' said Belov, conscious of the other man's nervousness. 'He'll give you something.'

'A shot?' Willick did not like injections.

'Pills.'

He could do it then, Willick decided. Pop a couple of pills, just to settle his stomach: appear on television right across America, show everybody just how important he was. He said: 'All right. I think it would be OK if I had some pills.'

'Of course it would,' encouraged Belov. He took the prepared statement from the briefcase and said: 'You don't even have to learn it: just familiarize yourself. You can read it from the platform.'

It was shorter than Willick had expected, just two sheets, double spaced. There was an insistence that the CIA was an organization involved in illegality against every nation in the world, even its allies, and the assertion that it was working actively in several of those nations to undermine and subvert democratically elected governments. The document claimed Willick had become sickened by his growing awareness as a CIA analyst at how the Agency ignored its own country's laws and the restraints of Congress, and that his coming to the Soviet Union was as a protest against their pervasive control. The last paragraph read: 'I know – because I have seen and handled the evidence practically every day of my working life – that America is controlled by a government within a government, a government about which the country I love is not aware and which remains in power despite any supposed election. Just as I know, within the Agency, there are others who feel as I do. That I am not,

306

nor will be, the last to try to expose the Agency for the evil that it is.'

'This isn't what I think,' said Willick weakly.

'Would it sound better if you said you betrayed your country for money?' demanded Belov brutally. 'That you didn't give a damn about anything, apart from how much you got paid?'

Willick winced at the abrupt change. 'But I don't think it's true. It *isn't* true.'

'That is the statement you will make,' ordered Belov. 'And although there is no need to learn it all you *must* memorize the last two lines and not forget, under any circumstance, to say them.'

'But it sounds . . .' Willick began and then stopped, nervous of offending the other man. ' . . . strange,' he picked up. 'Artificial.'

'How it sounds is no concern of yours,' said Belov dismissively. 'Learn it.'

The two men sat opposite each other for another hour until Belov was satisfied that Willick was familiar enough with the statement to utter it as if the views were his own and not as a recitation prepared by someone else. His valeted clothes were returned just before a lunch of cold, unidentified meats and boiled cabbage and potatoes. Belov refused Willick either booze or wine, reminding the American he was going to be prescribed a drug and that he needed to retain a clear head.

The doctor arrived unannounced as they were finishing the meal. He gave Willick a cursory examination and then tapped out three orange tablets from a sweet-shop array in the case he carried with him. He watched while Willick took them and said something in Russian to Belov.

To the American Belov said: 'He says you are actually going to enjoy it.'

Belov led the way from the suite to the waiting car of the previous night. The streets were definitely busier but there seemed to be a reserved central lane along which they travelled again at a very high speed. A lot of the buildings *were* squatly monolithic, like Washington; at one junction, where they had to slow, Willick looked to his left and thought he saw the walled Kremlin and the oriental tips of St Basil's Cathedral, with the vast square in front. The drug began to work, the sensation at first unsettling but very quickly not disturbing at all. Willick was absolutely conscious of where he was and what he was going to do and what he had to say – large tracts of the statement came easily to mind – but there was none of the hollow-stomached fear he knew so well. He actually felt confident: eager, even. He was important, admired.

They entered the quadrangle of a huge, square building through gates that opened and closed immediately, and at once dipped into a long, darkened tunnel, from which they emerged into an inner courtyard. Willick followed Belov through a small door beyond which waited four men who were identified without name as the people who would help him through the press conference.

'Aren't you going to be with me?' Willick asked Belov.

'I'll be waiting,' said the Russian.

The journalists were already assembled when they moved on to the stage. The moment Willick appeared the television lights burst on and there were flashes from still cameras, and Willick found it difficult to see beyond the glare, to establish how many people there were wanting to interview him. From the noise, it seemed a lot.

A thin bespectacled man whom he'd met at the entrance unnecessarily introduced Willick ('a brave American') and announced he had a statement to make. Willick cleared his throat, looking directly out to where he believed the television cameras were placed, and delivered the prepared speech perfectly, consulting the sheet occasionally but more frequently staring directly out at the journalists. The effect of the pills strangely seemed to make it possible for him to hear himself, as he talked: he knew he sounded calm and forceful. He enunciated the sentences upon which Belov had been most insistent with his eyes unblinkingly out into the room.

There was an immediate babble of questions when

308

Willick stopped. The thin man held up his hands, quieting the uproar, pointing to individuals whom the American still had difficulty in isolating.

'How long have you been a spy?' was the question and unprompted the Russian alongside cupped his hand over the microphone and leaned sideways to Willick.

'It is not a sudden decision for me to come to the Soviet Union,' recited Willick, grateful for the prompt. 'It is a process that has taken some time.'

'That's not an answer,' protested the questioner but the Russian was already selecting someone else.

'Have you told the Soviets of your work within the CIA?'

'I have already outlined in my statement how I regard the operations of the Central Intelligence Agency,' replied Willick, guided again. The pills made him feel fantastic: he wondered if it would be possible to get some more.

'Haven't you endangered the lives of fellow Americans by what you have done?'

'The Central Intelligence Agency endangers the lives of fellow Americans' was the prepared reply.

'Do you regard yourself as a traitor?'

'I regard myself as someone driven by despair, at what I know, forced to speak out.' Willick thought that sounded good, if a little melodramatic.

'How did you get here?'

'Openly, by aeroplane.' Willick hadn't needed help that time.

'Did your recent divorce have anything to do with your decision to defect?'

Willick supposed they would have delved into his background but the question surprised him. 'Nothing whatsoever,' he said. Who would Eleanor get her alimony from now!

'Do you have any involvement with anyone here, in Moscow?'

'No.' Another question he found easy.

'Were you blackmailed into defecting?'

The thin man came sideways but Willick was confident enough to reply by himself. 'Certainly not,' he said.

'What evidence do you have – can you give us – about the claims you've made about the CIA?'

Willick listened attentively to the whispered advice and said: 'That is a demand that should be made by the American people to the CIA. And admitted by the CIA.'

'What did you mean by the remark about others in the Agency feeling like you . . . that you will not be the last to expose the evils of the CIA?'

The assistance was immediate and Willick said: 'I do not feel able to expand any further upon that remark. I think it speaks for itself.'

Willick was searching the blur of faces, enjoying himself like the doctor had promised, but the thin man rose abruptly, cupping his hand beneath the American's elbow to bring him up as well, and led him away to a cacophony of protests.

'I'm prepared to go on,' protested Willick.

'We're not,' said the man.

The American television networks only showed edited highlights, of course, but using the State Department as a front the Crisis Committee obtained complete transcripts from CBS and NBC and from their own wire services they got a full transcript from Associated Press.

'We've got a wholesale fucking disaster on our hands,' judged Harry Myers.

It was an assessment confirmed within two days, when KGB-supplied names of Central Intelligence Agency personnel whom Willick had identified were published in left-wing newspapers and magazines in Spain, France and West Germany.

In Bonn the deputy head of the station was assassinated by a group claiming to be the Red Army faction.

Petr Levin felt physically limited in his frustration, as if he were enclosed in some sort of straitjacket. He wanted so badly to let Natalia know she had not been abandoned in Moscow. And that it would not be long now before he was with her. And it wouldn't be long. He'd made the checks carefully over several days and knew that having dropped him off at school the CIA driver did not

310

hang around Litchfield but returned to the house. Which meant he was unescorted for six hours: six whole hours, to get to New York! They'd never even miss him, until it was too late. Petr knew he'd been equally clever discovering the necessary railway route, disputing it with a girl called Janie who thought he was interested in her until to prove an apparent argument she brought him the timetable of the New Haven Line which actually set out the stations. Not quite sure which one yet. Waterbury, maybe. Or Naugatuck. Then straight south and right into Grand Central. He would be able to walk to the United Nations in minutes.

Petr grimaced up through his bedroom window at the noise of the patrolling helicopter, catching a faraway sight of one of the armed patrols. Was there really a Soviet assassination search going on for his father, like they all said? They seemed to be taking it seriously enough. But then they seemed permanently to take themselves seriously. What would he say, if the Russians at the United Nations asked him where his father was? Tell them, he thought at once. He was a traitor, wasn't he? His father had deserted Natalia, so he couldn't love her, despite all the shit that he did. Couldn't love any of them. Deserved all that was coming to him. Even to be killed.

The boy returned to his letter, bored with the emptiness of it. He scribbled a few more lines, describing the widow's walk he could see from the schoolroom window and then recounted, because he thought it was funny, that the locals called the rock that was everywhere not granite, but ledge, and signed off as he always did that he hoped to see her soon, hoping she would read into the last line what he really meant it to convey.

And it would be soon, he told himself again, in familiar litany. Very soon now.

32

With desperate hopefulness the CIA attempted a damage assessment by expanding the Crisis Committee, not at executive level but administratively. Everything upon which John Willick had ever worked or been associated with was computer located, withdrawn from records and subjected to the most intensive scrutiny. And then independently double checked, to confirm or challenge that first analysis of likely or unlikely harm. The three original members remained in permanent session and in permanent occupation of the ground-floor room in which they had interviewed Yevgennie Levin, whose debriefings were temporarily suspended on account of the assessment priority. Because of the urgency, the reports were delivered individually, immediately they were released after the second clearance, and with each arrival the despondency of the three men worsened.

'You know what I think?' demanded Myers, not wanting an answer. 'I don't think we're ever going to be able fully to estimate how much injury the bastard's caused.'

'A lot,' said Norris in agreement. 'Incalculable.'

'He was employed for fifteen years,' reminded Crookshank. 'We're going to have to assume he let the Soviets have everything, throughout those fifteen years.'

'We might as well shut up shop and put the Boy Scouts in charge of external intelligence,' said the security chief bitterly. He guessed he was being retained because he had been involved in the inquiry from the start, but expected to be retired when the committee made their eventual report to the Director. And then what the fuck was he expected to do, become a nightman at some all-night store? After watching Willick's Moscow press conference he'd physically thrown up in the toilet, sick to his stomach.

312

'We've got to set ourselves guidelines,' argued Norris, refusing absolute dejection. 'We know from the bank records and from what we found in Rosslyn that Willick was hopelessly in debt. And from the interview with the wife that those debts became practically impossible after their divorce, because of the alimony he had to pay.'

'So?' demanded Crookshank.

'So, from those bank records we know he had a credit balance until late 1984,' reminded Norris. 'That's when, according to the wife, he began gambling on the stock market to make up for losses at the track. And when, because of their money problems, the arguments began and got so bad she decided to leave him. Which increased his money problems after they got divorced.'

'And Aleksandr Shelenkov arrived here in Washington in July, 1985!' remembered Myers in belated awareness.

'Why couldn't Willick have had a control before Shelenkov?' demanded Crookshank. 'He certainly had one afterwards because Shelenkov was moved before Willick's shift to Records. And we know from what happened in Spain and France and West Germany that he's been identifying agents left, right and centre.'

'We don't,' agreed Norris. 'But the financial difficulties fit the pattern.'

'I think it's too speculative,' said the lawyer.

'Maybe it's a question for Levin,' said Norris.

'There's a barrel of questions for Yevgennie Levin,' said Myers.

'I think the agent identification is the most serious aspect,' said Norris. 'As of this morning we've had to recall a total of thirty-eight men from overseas postings.'

'And we still don't know how many more he's fingered,' said Myers. 'Christ, I'd like to get my hands on the fucker! I'd kill him. I really mean I'd kill him.'

'I think there is something equally serious,' ruminated Crookshank, customarily consulting his notepad against the reports stacked up alongside each of them. 'Maybe more so.'

'Like what?' asked Norris.

'Levin told us of some conversation with Shelenkov

involving Soviet space installations. And Kapalet in Paris said the same thing,' reminded the lawyer. 'And we know from backtracking on Willick's work thus far that when he was in Analysis that was his speciality.'

'So it fits,' said Norris.

'Sure it fits,' agreed the lawyer. 'It fits and it means a lot of things. That Shelenkov wasn't boasting when he said he had us by the balls, because Moscow will know precisely how many of their sites and silos we've located by satellite and precisely how we've designated then. And that they can move them and make everything we know – every Star War assessment – not worth a bucket of spit. And that both Levin and Kapalet are guaranteed, one hundred per cent reliable informants.'

'What else?' prompted Myers.

'We've heard a lot, too, from both of them about Latin America and the Caribbean,' said Crookshank, in further reminder.

'Oh Christ!' said Myers, realizing. 'Oh Jesus H. Christ!'

'Nowhere, in any file so far considered or double checked, has there been anything connecting Willick with Latin America or the Caribbean,' acknowledged Norris, understanding too.

Myers pulled forward the tattered, over-handled Associated Press transcript of Willick's press conference. 'I know, within the Agency, there are others who feel as I do. That I am not, nor will be, the last to try to expose the Agency for the evil that it is,' he quoted.

'He as good as told us, in his reply to the later question,' came in Norris, taking up his own copy. 'When he was asked what he meant by that he said he did not feel able to expand further; that it spoke for itself.'

'It does, doesn't it?' said Crookshank. 'Unless, in something we haven't yet seen, there's an assignment connecting Willick to Latin America or to the Caribbean then we know that Willick wasn't the only KGB source, within the Agency. That there's someone else still buried deep somewhere here at Langley.'

'I don't want to think about it,' said Myers, who genuinely didn't.

314

'We've got to think about it,' said the lawyer. 'We've got to think about it being a practical possibility and not imagine it's over, by Willick's defection.'

'Thank God for Kapalet and Levin,' said Myers.

'They're the best chance we've got,' agreed Norris.

There was nothing in the KGB file that had been made available to him – the file he anyway instinctively felt to be incomplete – connecting the defector Yevgennie Levin with the American paraded at the Moscow press conference, but Yuri wondered if there had been any association. Not that it would have helped him to find Levin. Very little seemed to be helping him to locate the man. His central graph connecting the exchanging letters had started out so promising – too promising, upon reflection – but all he had now were incomprehensible phrases and expressions, followed by a growing number of frustrated question marks. There was an additional one, after the reference to a widow's walk which had appeared in the latest communication from Petr to his sister and which Yuri had ringed and joined to captain's walk, the phrase which had appeared in Levin's first letter. And an additional unknown, also from Petr's letter. When he'd read the word Yuri had felt a spurt of excitement. Looking up 'ledge' in two separate and unabridged dictionaries, he'd been unable to find in either it being used to describe granite, which seemed to be the commonest rock along the entire eastern seaboard. According to the geological gazetteer, which he'd also consulted, the island of Manhattan was just one solid block of it.

If Kazin's move against him were to be made through an accusation of professional incompetence it could not be long coming, Yuri guessed. He wished that, in those bank-vaulted dossiers, there were something he could regard as a defence, instead of just more sheets of paper with more question marks upon them.

Although he'd studied the letters and his charts until his eyes ached – until, he feared, he was so familiar with it all that he risked missing something of significance even if it were there – Yuri again poured over them in the 53rd Street apartment, with an hour before Caroline was due to arrive home. This time he started out from the very beginning, querying his own notes, and almost at once stopped, aware of a possible oversight. He'd assessed so much from the punctuality and until now not realized how differently it could be used! Maybe he was guilty of professional incompetence!

'Eight days,' said Caroline, later, after they'd eaten the meal she'd prepared in her own apartment.

'What's eight days?' he said.

'How long since you've had an assignment. And how long I've been able to have you to myself. I think it's great.'

'It won't last,' predicted Yuri.

It didn't.

33

The letter from Natalia arrived the following day, giving Yuri an earlier than expected opportunity to test the idea he'd had. He read it, deciding at once there was nothing of importance, but still took a copy for his files before re-sealing it. The mission official whose duty it was to liaise with the Americans over the correspondence was a Ukrainian named Votrin who was not a member of the KGB but who knew that Yuri was, and listened with nervous attention to the instructions he was given.

Yuri wanted the response from someone senior, in direct contact with Levin, so – aware from the correspondence and of his meeting with the girl how much it mattered – he ordered Votrin to relay that in addition to a letter there was some reaction from Moscow to Natalia's exit request. And that it had to be collected from the UN building. David Proctor came personally.

Votrin positioned himself on the delaying second-floor corridor as Yuri instructed and the moment he witnessed the contact Yuri moved, needing to get outside, hoping the American would be held for at least five minutes by Votrin's assurance that Natalia's departure from the Soviet Union was being favourably considered.

Yuri walked as fast as he reasonably could without attracting attention across the vast forecourt of the UN building, dodged through the traffic on the Plaza and went two at a time up the Shcharansky steps, ironically named after the Jewish dissident whose emigration to Israel the Soviet Union had prevented for so long. The geological bump directly opposite the skyscraper gave Yuri the perfect elevation from which to see Proctor emerge from the buildings: using the camera that was part of his William Bell legend, Yuri took two photographs of the man for later possible identification and a third of the green Buick he was obviously approaching, in the car park. Precisely on time Votrin came from the UN, calling to halt and delay the man once more and again Yuri moved, this time to the car hired and parked within an hour of the letter arriving.

He drove impatiently out on to Second Avenue, took the immediate right on 44th Street and was at the junction with the UN Plaza when the green Buick nosed out opposite, its indicator showing the necessary right turn. The lights were in Yuri's favour and he managed to get out two vehicles behind the other car, which he considered dangerously close but unavoidable on such clogged streets if he were not going be separated and lose it at yet another set of traffic lights. He gambled on the jammed traffic actually protecting him because there was no alternative but for one car to follow another: so near, he was able to see that the American was travelling alone. He thought the continuing blink of the indicator was a failed cancellation but then saw the car begin to move to the right and realized it was making for FDR Drive. Yuri allowed another car to intervene between them before following, deciding that his timed and distanced ring upon the map, calculated from the Washington destination Levin had disclosed in his letter, had already been enormously reduced. This could only be a northerly direction: upstate New York, Connecticut, Rhode Island or Massachusetts. And a large proportion of that area could be excluded by the time frame. He thought Long Island unlikely, because of the reference to the abundance of trees and skiing. And was proven right when Proctor ignored the turning, making instead for the Hutchinson River Parkway when he cleared the Bronx.

On the Interstate the traffic thinned more than he wanted and Yuri saw an additional risk of his being detected because of the slowness with which it travelled. He fell further back, tucking himself behind an enormous truck proclaiming that Habcocks Chicken Breasts were the best in the world, daring to emerge only occasionally to see the Buick remaining distantly in front. At White Plains, Proctor picked up Interstate 684 and Yuri mentally eliminated Rhode Island from his list. And when it divided and the Buick took the easterly route on Interstate 84, he erased New York State as well. Which left a limited section of Connecticut or a small area of Massachusetts. His protective lorry pulled off at Danbury, leaving him exposed, and the Russian decreased his speed further, so far back it was only just possible to distinguish the colour of the vehicle he was pursuing.

Yuri drove conscious of the frequent rock outcrops and of the denseness of what seemed to be perpetual forests, thinned though they were by the approach of winter. He decided later that it was the natural thinness which initially made him miss it, one of the references of hopeful significance he had isolated from the letters. And then it registered and he remembered the phrase – *like the horrific pictures that came from Vietnam*. It had been an exaggeration of Levin's because Yuri's recollection of the films that had been shown so often on Soviet television was that the American defoliation in Vietnam had been far more severe than this, but there it was, on several of the ridges when he looked closely, long swathes of stripped-bare trees whose absence of leaves had nothing to do with the nearness of winter. Close, thought Yuri: he was getting very close. But not close enough, he realized, in different awareness. He had concentrated too much, for too long, upon the surrounding countryside and not enough upon his quarry. When Yuri looked back to the road he could not locate the vehicle he was following. He jabbed his foot on the pedal, abruptly accelerating up to the clump of cars in which the Buick had been moving and when he reached it saw, sickeningly, that it was not there any more. There was a Buick in the group but it was brown and contained an entire family, the rear seat jostled by squabbling children.

Yuri let the cars pull away, looking for some identification and almost at once saw the turn-off sign indicating the next exit to be for Marion. He left the highway before that, at a rest stop, and using Marion as a marker on his map worked out where he was. And from there traced backwards along the Interstate, for possible earlier exits, over a distance of ten miles. Four, he concluded. With

319

Waterbury the largest and most obvious. But in which direction from that turn-off, north or south? And why, necessarily, Waterbury? He'd been careless, Yuri recognized, irritated with himself. And hadn't he decided he couldn't be careless, about anything? He doubted that the encirclement on his map reached as far north from this point to include Massachusetts. So out of every state in mainland America he had achieved a remarkable pinpointing. And although he lost the man this time, he had not lost the eventual opportunity. He could use the letter delivery ploy again but next time carry out the initial pursuit differently now that he knew at least the route to Danbury, able to drive undetectably ahead of the American while keeping him in the rear-view mirror, with no need to reverse the positions until after that point.

Yuri used the Marion exit to loop back on to the Interstate and return to New York, but at the Waterbury turn-off he impulsively left the road again and for no other reason than that northwards had been the general direction in which he'd followed the American, Yuri drove towards Torrington.

What were the references that still baffled him? Rooftop verandahs *to watch the sea where there is no sea*, he remembered. *Widow's walks*, which he guessed to be the same thing and of which Petr had written in his last letter. Ledge, which meant granite, but was a definition he could not substantiate. And perhaps the most incomprehensible of all, *spies in statues and spies in history*. Who was a spy commemorated by a statue and what was the link with a spy in history? Two separate people? Or one and the same?

Because Torrington was the name he'd chosen to follow, Yuri drove into the town. It was early afternoon and very empty. He had a choice of parking meters and stopped in the main street, not immediately getting out of the car. It was, he realized, his first time in small-town America and the comparison with the New York he now knew well and the Washington he'd briefly visited was absolute. There was none of the noise to which his ears were so accustomed that he closed it out, no longer hearing it, and there were no teeth-jarring breaks and holes in the road or any strewn rubbish, at least none that he could see. And the construction seemed to be equally divided, between brick and concrete and wooden clapboard. It occurred to him, as it frequently did on the journey into Manhattan from Kennedy Airport, that wooden buildings always gave the appearance of being insubstantial. So why didn't he feel the same about such houses in Russia? Yuri shrugged, finally leaving the car: he had enough unanswered questions without encumbering himself with more.

The sign on the side of one of the wooden houses gave him the idea and when it came Yuri grew as annoyed at himself as he had been earlier, because it was so obvious. The place identified as the local historical society was closed, but the adjoining tourist office was open and Yuri pushed his way in to be greeted by a white-haired, apple-cheeked woman around whom clung the vague aroma of lavender and cooking. Adopting his protective persona, Yuri said he was an Englishman touring the area and she said it was late in the year to be doing that and he agreed that it was, but that it was the only time his job allowed. He waited for her to ask about it, but she didn't.

'What are you looking for?' she asked.

'Nothing particular,' said Yuri casually. 'Local colour. History. That sort of thing.'

'Plenty of history around here,' said the woman. 'Connecticut has always been a pretty important state in the Union.'

'One phrase I have come across that intrigues me is widow's walk,' chanced Yuri. 'I think it's got something to do with houses.'

'Sure has,' she agreed at once. 'It's the way the old whaling captains and shipowners used to build their houses, with a walkway around the roof so that the returning sailships could be seen on a horizon and registered home. The story grew that their wives used to walk there, on the day their husbands were due in port, to see whether it had been a safe voyage or not. If it hadn't been, they would have been widows, wouldn't they?'

Yuri felt the bubble of hope but balanced it against the phrase: *to watch the sea where there is no sea.* He said: 'Built on the coast then?'

'Still see quite a lot around Boston,' she assured him. 'Heard there are some in Providence, too.'

'None around here?'

'Oh sure,' she said. 'Litchfield. It's the cutest place: colonially preserved. I guess they just copied the idea.'

The bubble ballooned and then popped. Yuri said: 'And that's close?'

'Fifteen minutes, due south on the 202 . . .' She gestured through the window. 'That way.'

'Save me a journey to Boston, won't it?' said Yuri, turning to go and then stopping. 'What's the rock called all around here?'

'Ledge,' said the woman. 'It's granite really but it's always been called ledge. No one knows why.'

'You've been very helpful,' thanked Yuri sincerely.

'Like to buy a local guidebook?' asked the woman, remembering her function.

'I'd like very much to buy one of your guidebooks,' said Yuri, in small but literal repayment.

His car was even pointing in the direction she'd indicated and Yuri got to Litchfield in ten, not fifteen minutes. It was cute and preserved, like she'd promised, a place of all-wooden houses painted in uniform white and set amid barbered lawns around a central grassed area. He thought it looked as if it were kept permanently under the protection of glass. He counted seven rooftop verandahs within a hundred yards of the pointed-roof church and found the tourist office in the middle of the central reservation. He bought the guidebook at once this time, from a waistcoated man with white hair and metal-framed spectacles, but asked about the township's history without opening it. He heard about it being named, but wrongly, after a town in Staffordshire, in England, and listened patiently about someone called Tapping Reeve who'd opened the first law school ever to exist in America and of another academy that had been the first to provide higher education for women. Then the man pointed to a road he identified as North Street and said it was possible to see the house that had been occupied during the American War of Independence by Colonel Benjamin Tallmadge, who had been chief of intelligence for the American rebels. Who had been, finished the man, a friend of Nathan Hale, who had actually been hanged by the British for espionage. Complete, thought Yuri. Almost.

'Does it have a school?' he asked.

'One of the best,' assured the man. 'Forman. Down that street, about three hundred yards. Can't miss it.'

Yuri didn't. The boy he recognized as Petr Levin from the photographs with which he had been provided in Moscow was the third to come out when school ended that day, lingering for a moment with a blonde girl and then entering a car in which the driver sat waiting. It was a Buick, blue this time.

The solitary waiting – and not knowing what he was waiting for – got on Willick's nerves, and the second day he went through what he regarded as the ridiculous charade of lifting the telephone and asking to be allowed to go out of the apartment for a walk at least. The man said, simply, 'No', and put the telephone down, and when Willick tried to go out anyway he found that the gates leading from the courtyard were locked. When he turned the man who had earlier refused him was watching from a ground-floor doorway. He didn't do or say anything and Willick slowly climbed the stairs back to his suite feeling like an admonished child.

A supply of Scotch was maintained and thin red wine was made available at midday and in the evening, and so Willick drank a lot. On the third day the alcohol stopped and when he asked for it the man, whom he'd first thought of as an attendant and now, properly, regarded as his guard, shook his head in refusal, not even bothering to talk this time. On the telephone Willick yelled for someone in charge to come to see him, but nobody did, not for a further four days.

'Why am I being treated like a prisoner?' Willick demanded the moment Belov entered the room.

'Because it is necessary,' said the American division chief.

'Why?'

'Some of the Western correspondents might have tried to find you: it is doubtful they would have succeeded but we had to take precautions.'

'There's still a lot of publicity about me?'

'There was, for a few days. Not any longer.'

Willick felt disappointed. 'I was impressive, at the conference though, wasn't I?'

'I told you so at the time.'

'I can go out now?'

'That's what I'm here for,' said Belov. He didn't like the American and was glad this was the last occasion he'd have to deal with the man.

Willick trailed respectfully behind the Russian and in the courtyard smiled in some imagined triumph at the attendant who'd refused to let him out. Surprisingly, the man smiled back. The car was smaller than it had been on other occasions and Willick felt further disappointment. Belov sat pulled away in the far corner, looking out of the window, apparently uninterested in him, so Willick looked out too, conscious that everyone was bundled up against the weather and realizing he would have to get some thicker clothing. There was so much he had to do. They drove for what seemed a long way and Willick saw that the grandiose architecture of central Moscow was giving way to smaller buildings, a sprawl of suburbia.

'Where are we going?' asked the American.

'Karacharovo.'

'What is that?'

'An area of Moscow.'

'What's there?'

'Your home.'

'My what!'

'Your home,' repeated the Russian.

324

'But I thought . . .' said Willick, foolishly twisting in his seat, as if the luxury building beyond the gated courtyard would still be visible, like Coney Island had been that day when they drove away.

The man beside him laughed. 'Don't be ridiculous!' he said. 'Gorbachov himself doesn't live in a place like that!'

'I don't understand,' said Willick, weak-voiced.

'We wanted you comfortable to perform a particular function, which you did,' said Belov.

'And now?'

'You are being allocated an apartment of your own in a block at Karacharovo,' disclosed Belov. 'That in itself is a concession: housing is not easy in Moscow. Each day be ready at 8.30. A car will call for you: there are a lot of questions we need answering, upon the information you provided over the years.'

It was crumbling again, like it always did, thought the American desperately. 'What happens after I've answered all your questions?' he asked.

'You will be allowed to attend school to learn Russian.'

'How will I live? Money, I mean,' said Willick.

'A job will be found when you are considered qualified. There'll be a pension, for what you've done in the past. And a salary when you start working. You really will be treated extremely well.'

The apartment was in an isolated block on what looked like the beginning of a new housing estate. A lot of side roads were unpaved, puddled and rutted, and a second block stood half finished, girders and metal rods sticking up like a giant rib cage. No one was working on it and the impression was of desolation. They had to balance on planking because the outside pavement was not completed and the area hollowed out for it was one huge, water-filled ditch. The elevator shaft was an empty, unprotected hole, but Willick's flat was fortunately only on the second floor. Belov handed him a key, for the American to admit himself. In contrast to its outside appearance everything inside the apartment seemed old and worn. The scrap of carpet was threadbare and the seats of two chairs either side of a small dining table were greased by previous use. The kitchen led directly off. The stove was slimed and black and there were several rings grimed around the sink. There were further rings around the bath and the toilet and the similarly stained mirror over the handbasin was cracked so that it reflected a distorted image. The bedroom had a mirrored dresser, a small wardrobe and a narrow single bed, covered in thin, grey linen.

Willick turned, face twisted in disgust, and said: 'I can't live here!'

'Where else can you go?' asked Belov.

The grinning son of a bitch at the other place would have known what was going to happen, Willick guessed.

The meeting was at Wilson Drew's request, in response to the panic from Washington, and he chose Le Duc. As always Kapalet watched the American enter and waited a sufficiently safe time before entering off the Boulevard Raspail.

'Washington is wetting its pants,' announced Drew.

'They've got good reason,' goaded Kapalet.

'I need a hell of a lot of help,' pleaded Drew.

'That's not going to be as easy as it has been,' warned the Russian.

'Why not?' asked Drew, immediately worried.

'I'm being recalled to Moscow,' announced Kapalet.

34

The chances of his being detected were appalling. On the Interstate there had at least been other concealing vehicles but on the country roads Yuri was utterly exposed. The one car separating him from the Buick carrying Petr turned off after only a mile and Yuri decelerated, letting the distance increase between them, protected only by the rise and fall of the road and its too occasional bends. Because it was ingrained from his training he'd precisely started to check the distance as he'd driven away from the school: so far two and three eighths of a mile. It seemed like a hundred. The wheel was slippery in his hands and the perspiration stuck the shirt to his back. Streets and road signs registered, because they could be important: Meadow and Little Pitch and New Pitch and Heron Pond and Marsh Pond. Far to his right the treeline was abruptly broken by the defoliation he'd detected earlier, a brief baldness, and Yuri added that to the attempted landmarks. Webster Road and Cranbery Pond and Scharmerhorn Hill. Four miles exactly from the school. The humps and dips in the road were becoming more frequent: still not enough cover. They seemed to be climbing. He'd have to stop soon, abandon this attempt: exchange the car overnight, a different model and a different colour and try to evolve another system of pursuit, the following day.

And then the car in front turned. It was abrupt, with no signalled warning, and Yuri braked hurriedly, jerked forward against the wheel by the suddenness of the manoeuvre. And because he was closer against the windscreen he saw the helicopter. It was hovering some way to his left but as he watched it began a series of gradually expanding circles in the middle of one of which it pulled away in his direction. Yuri's instant fear was that it was coming towards him but sharply it turned upon itself and from its position Yuri guessed it had isolated the car he had been following, minutes earlier, and was flying some sort of aerial escort. It stopped practically at once, hovering again, and Yuri memorized a clump of trees darker than the forest around them.

Hurriedly Yuri put the car back in gear, knowing he had to move before the machine resumed its circling and expanded the survey sufficiently to isolate him on the road. It only took him minutes to reach where the other car had turned; Yuri had hoped for a driveway but it was not. It was a minor dirt raod and at the speed he passed Yuri was unable to see any name sign. It wasn't necessary: he wouldn't have any difficulty finding it again. And he would locate it again, he thought, the decision hardening in his mind. He still needed to understand why Kazin had given him the assignment, but having got this close Yuri determined to complete it absolutely.

Yuri's intention had been to drive back to Torrington for what he wanted but he saw the signpost to Thomaston giving a closer mileage, so instead he headed there. A part of his KGB instruction he'd never imagined he would need, reflected Yuri. But perhaps the most vivid to recall, and not just because of its savagery. It had been the nearest he'd come to failing any of the tests: how near only he knew. The parachute drop had been twenty miles from Bryansk, which was one of the few map references he had been given, because that was the city he had to reach undetected in an exercise which purported him to be a denounced agent pursued by a hostile enemy. And his pursuers *had* been hostile, *spetsnaz* commandos whose own fail-or-be-dismissed exercise had been to prevent his reaching the sanctuary of the city. To achieve which they were permitted to employ every and any method they chose. There had been a hunt from behind and a cordon ahead and the bullets and the booby traps had been real, not faked. Yuri had not intended the commando to be maimed in one of his own traps, after he intentionally triggered an alarm: merely to create a diversion sufficiently distracting for him to get past the country road barrier. The mine had been specifically placed to prevent that being possible. Had the man not stumbled on it himself, Yuri would have trodden upon it and been crippled, if not killed. Later, at the KGB academy in Moscow, he heard rumours that deaths were very frequent during such exercises.

In Thomaston he protectively spread the purchases, buying the waterproof rucksack and hiking boots from the obvious sports store but obtaining the other things – the thick socks, jeans, anorak, torch, sports shirt, woollen hat and binoculars – from various shops. He parked the car in a multi-storey park on a deserted level where he was able quickly to change, packing his suit in the rucksack, and left by the least conspicuous side entrance.

He forced himself at the beginning of the walk back, knowing from his careful observance on the way into the town that there were seven miles to cover and anxious for the maximum amount of remaining daylight. Sure of the way, he did not need the map he'd taken from the car and put in a side pocket of the rucksack, along with the camera. Yuri was confident he had followed the first rule of that murderous field exercise and merged inconspicuously into the background. This was going to be much easier than Bryansk.

He reached the humped road in just under an hour and slowed, trying to find as much cover as possible from the bordering trees, which was not as easy as he had hoped it would be. There was a wide, separating verge and in places a ditch. Before he rounded the corner just prior to the dirt road into which Petr Levin had been driven, Yuri saw the helicopter: it was making tight circles now. Wanting to establish its pattern, Yuri jumped the ditch and ran into the treeline, entering only far enough into the forest to be hidden from the road, equally sure he was sufficiently concealed from the air. He squatted on the rucksack, back against a moss-covered fir, focusing upwards with the binoculars, the adjustments of which were stiff with newness and difficult at first to move. Gradually the machine widened its sweep, as it had been doing when it picked up the boy's returning car. Yuri calculated it to be five minutes from the point of stationary hover until the helicopter was directly over the road and a further seven minutes before it reached the apogee of its manoeuvre and tightened the circle to return to what had to be directly over wherever the Levin family were being kept. Yuri acknowledged that aeronautically the surveillance was absolute and therefore professionally expert: unprofessionally it provided an almost perfect method of identification.

Yuri watched the manoeuvre twice more, to confirm his timings, and at the instant of hover went back to the road and managed to get within ten yards of the turning before having to run again into the trees to avoid detection. Near enough, he decided: from that point he would go entirely through the forest, avoiding any open area. And even here be careful: the eye follows movement, not stillness, had been another field edict. He chose a fir again because of its permanent covering and waited patiently beneath it for the helicopter to fly outwards and then in again, only moving when it neared the unseen house. From the outset the gradient was increasingly uphill and matchingly steep. With the self-imposed stop-start precaution and the snagging thickness of the undergrowth, it took Yuri almost a further hour to reach the peak and having done so he was still much farther away from the now visible building than he had expected to be. There was an odd, U-shaped rift caused by a river and although it was not a barrier between him and the house the land broke sideways, creating a valley before him.

With nothing intervening he had a perfect view of his objective, however. And was able, too, to see that the sun was already close to a mountain top beyond. The last hour before darkness, Yuri estimated: maybe a little more.

From the map he decided that the mountain later to obscure the sun was called Prospect and that the river was named Bantam: it appeared to feed into a huge lake of the same name, but he could not see that from where he crouched. He had slight difficulty again adjusting the binoculars but through them finally obtained a greatly enlarged view of the mansion-like house. And more. As he watched he saw two men come from a coppice within the ground, one with a telescopically-sighted gun crooked under his left arm. The other waved to the helicopter pilot on a return run and Yuri followed the path of the machine. Into view came a separate group of guards, three this time, one with a Doberman restrained tightly on a leash. The downdraft of the helicopter upset the dog, which began to fight against the lead and to bark: the sound did not reach Yuri.

Another man in the group made a gesture of greeting to someone out of Yuri's vision and he shifted direction, perfectly to see the boy he'd observed leaving the Litchfield school. Yevgennie Pavlovich Levin was by his side. Yuri was just in time to see the defector respond to the wave. Yuri snatched his camera from the rucksack and managed three exposures, despite the focus being blurred. He tried the infinite setting but was still unsure if the man would be identifiable from that distance.

Yuri was about to press the button again when he heard the sound, the soft noise of something moving carefully against detection. Momentarily he stayed motionless, seeking the cause within his immediate vision, not daring even to turn his head. There was nothing. He lowered the camera, but to the cushion of pine needles and not the rucksack where it might have scraped against the canvas, looking as he did so to the left and then the right. Still nothing. It came again, closer this time. Behind him then. Yuri pressed himself against the bole of the tree, trying to assess his vulnerability. Bad, he decided; very bad. Wrong to make the slightest shift; safety in stillness, he remembered. He swallowed, thinking he could hear himself do it.

The doe snuffled into view from his left, nuzzling beneath the leaf mould. The animal saw Yuri as he saw it. Its head came up, in startled alertness: for several seconds it regarded him with brown-eyed curiosity and then hurried away, not panicked but at a trot. Yuri released his breath, shivering with the tension.

He looked back to the faraway house, still able to see Levin and his son. He needed to be closer, he thought. There would be just enough light, for about another half an hour. He let the helicopter clear the house and started at once down the hillside, not waiting for it to get as far away as he had earlier, finding an animal path and using it instead of trying to make his way through the delaying undergrowth. As he descended lower, where the trees were thicker, Yuri occasionally lost sight of the house and realized he could not descend too far, because he needed the elevation. Twice he had to halt when the aerial surveillance was directly overhead and on the last occasion, waiting, Yuri confronted his error. The dusk was making it difficult to see more than a few yards in the fast-darkening forest: the helicopter was already using lights. Just ahead was a knoll, from which he was sure he would be able to see over the valley floor into the house for the last opportunity.

And in deciding to make that one final attempt Yuri made his greatest miscalculation. The helicopter had passed and the Russian was actually starting up the incline when the siren screamed and the searchlight stabbed out from above, whitely illuminating the animal track only yards behind him.

Yuri kept going, to increase their mistake and get further away from the light, pulling into the undergrowth when the probe began splaying back and forth, gauging the sweep when it went uphill to plunge on down into the valley, fleeing from it. No safety in stillness now, he decided, panted breath burning into him: the only thing now was to run. But towards what? The siren sounded again, an obvious alert to the armed and dog-handling guards below, towards whom he was running.

He thrust sideways, off the track, stumbling over roots and fallen wood he could not see, face whipped by branches that stung and tore at him. He could actually feel the torch against his hip, through the rucksack, the light he needed but could not use because it would immediately show where he was. Going in the proper direction, he told himself: parallel with the slip road but away from its junction with the larger highway, the obvious place to block. Was there another linking road, the way he was heading? He could not remember, from the map: possible but the line could have indicated another tributary into the lake he'd not been able to see. And if it were a road, wouldn't they block that exit, too? The rucksack was an encumbrance, the straps and buckles easily entangled, but Yuri refused to discard it, not wanting to leave any evidence of his detecting Levin.

Not easier than Bryansk. The same: surrounded by a hostile enemy, guns that weren't fakes. As the thought came Yuri believed he heard shouts from the road below and a dog, perhaps several dogs, barking. The helicopter's lights still darted and searched above him, once so close in front that he had to stop against a tree, to prevent stumbling into it. Definitely voices. And dogs. The dog sounds were closer: he guessed the animals had been let loose, to hunt him down. He'd forgotten a knife: anything at all that might have served as a weapon. He needed a stream, any wetness, to blur the scent. Wouldn't be tracking him by scent, he realized, starting forward again. All they'd need would be his noise. The barking was definitely closer: he thought he could hear their crashing through the undergrowth.

Yuri was fleeing with both hands outstretched, to detect the trees, but only his right hand struck the obstruction and it wasn't wood and he stopped, frightened by the unknown, feeling out and touching the coldness with both hands. It was, absurdly, the seeking helicopter light which briefly illuminated it and even showed him the commencement of the culvert, where it opened to the stream. He groped along its length, in the darkness again, to its beginning and felt around it, trying to assess the size. Big, he determined: huge, in fact. He'd have to bend but it would be possible to walk in. Maybe even run. No, couldn't run. There was the stream. Water. What he needed to defeat the animals whose yapping and barking was very close now. The water's flowing would actually disguise any sound.

The helicopter returned, again briefly illuminating. The

stream emerged from somewhere above, about a foot across, but a much wider path and a concrete receiving sluice had been built at the entrance to the pipe which ran in the open for about fifty yards. And then disappeared into the hillside. The wideness of the stream had given Yuri the clue: it was a drainage pipe to carry off the melted winter snows ('there are lodges and good skiing all around') from a river that had been eroding the hillside through which it passed. How far was it buried, before re-emerging? Yuri definitely heard a man's voice this time; an irrelevant question, then.

He slipped out of the rucksack and, thrusting it before him like a shield, entered the total darkness of the pipe. The water came up above his ankles, soaking very quickly through his boots and numbing his feet. He scuffed along, bent double, feeling the slime underfoot. It was greasy to his touch when he reached sideways for support to the wall of the drain and he pulled his hand quickly back again, offended. He was aware of a sound above the hiss of the water, a squeaking, and recoiled when something brushed against his leg, above the waterline. The smell – wet decay and decomposing rot – was so repugnant Yuri gagged, choking back vomit. After several hundred yards he turned but was unable to see the slightly lighter circle marking the entrance so he decided at last to risk the torch.

Dozens of reflective spots of light came back at him. Eyes. He'd expected rats but not so many. They swarmed either side, unafraid, but were avoiding the water. Just rats? He couldn't see anything else. Surely the water would have prevented it being habitable to snakes! The slime virtually encircled the pipe, showing the volume of water at the height of the snow thaw. How did the rats survive then? Yuri put the rucksack back on, to free his hands, and waded on, directing the torchlight straight ahead, desperately anxious for some sign of the tunnel's end. Total blackness stretched ahead of him. A rat squeaked and made as if to jump at him and Yuri whimpered away, shuddering. And not just with revulsion. The coldness was moving up from his feet, actually making it difficult for him to walk properly and he clamped his mouth closed against the distraction of his teeth chattering. He moved the torch up again, away from his immediate path. Still total blackness but at least there were fewer rats: far fewer. He supposed it was obvious they would congregate around the beginning of the tunnel because of the need to forage outside for food.

Attuned as he was to sound after the forest manhunt it was the change in the rush of water which registered first, louder and faster, and expectantly he pointed the torch again, looking for the outlet to the river into which the stream fed, but couldn't see it. He drove himself forward, wanting to get out of the foul place, and had there been more feeling in his feet and legs he might have detected the change underfoot, because it was not abrupt but graded. It was not until he began to slip on the slime that he became aware that the pipe was curving increasingly downwards. And realized the sound wasn't a river but the fall of water and that was why there were no longer any rats. By then it was too late. Yuri clutched out but there was no purchase in the slippery walls and then he fell, awkwardly, losing the torch. The rucksack became a float beneath him and the rush of water hurried him down the now virtually perpendicular pipe. Everything was black. He was engulfed in rushing, choking water but he fought against choking because he could not breathe, either. Yuri was not conscious of hurtling out of the pipemouth. The indication was a lessening of the water's push, where it spread into a man-created waterfall and of falling differently and helplessly through space, without the hardness of the concrete tube around him. He tried to correct himself, to get as near as he could into the parachute landing position he had been taught, but the rucksack unbalanced him and he cartwheeled, out of control. It was only later, in daylight and from the bank to which he hauled himself, that Yuri realized how close – hardly more than a foot – he had come to being thrown against the sharp-ridged granite cliff face that would almost certainly have killed him. Instead, propelled from it by the thrust of the water, he

335

landed actually in the river, but from the height from which he fell it was practically the same as striking solid ground. His left wrist twisted under him and he felt a sear of agony and what little breath he still held was knocked out of him.

It was the rucksack, still acting like a float, which prevented his drowning in those first few minutes. He groaned breath back into his body and, unable to use his left arm, paddled instead with his right, combining the rucksack's support and the river's current to get himself to the pebbled bank.

Yuri lay for a long time unmoving, recovering, at last with his right hand groping along his left arm, trying to assess the damage. The wrist was already swelling but he could just move his fingers: sprained, not broken, he decided. He tore the sleeve of the shirt away at the shoulder, soaked it further in the water, and then bound it as a cold compress around the wrist with his good hand and his teeth before pulling himself further away from the river to drier ground.

Not like Bryansk at all, he thought. Worse. But there was a comparison. For the Bryansk exercise the *spetsnaz* had been alerted to what he was attempting. Just as the helicopters and the armed men and dogs – unimaginable protection but for one obvious reason – had been forewarned, back there.

He knew, at last, what Kazin intended by the instruction to locate the defector. *I think I could kill someone who tried to kill me*, he thought. So it hadn't ended with the death of his father: destroy or be destroyed, he accepted.

'What was it?' demanded Levin. They were in the main room of the house, Galina nervously close by his side, Petr by the window watching the car lights of the returning searchers.

'False alarm,' assured Proctor. 'The observer in the helicopter thought he saw someone but it couldn't have been. We've covered every inch.'

'What then?' asked Galina, unconvinced.

'An animal,' insisted the FBI man. 'We've had them trigger the sensors before. The observer is a new guy: too jumpy.'

'You can't be sure,' argued the woman.

'Isn't there something more important to think about?' reminded Proctor, who had brought Yuri's false message. 'Moscow are actually thinking of letting Natalia out!'

Petr turned away from the window, back into the room. His decision would be the same, if his sister were allowed to come. It wasn't a melodramtic exaggeration that he hated his father. That genuinely *was* his feeling for what the man had done. Betrayal for betrayal, he decided. God, how he hated the man.

The rucksack had admitted some water, at which Yuri was not surprised, but the clothes inside were damp, not soaked. Yuri changed into them and let them dry on him as he followed the river bank at first light, locating the lake and from it picking up the avenue that bordered its western side. It was still early, not yet six, when he got to Thomaston, which was deserted, still sleeping. He recovered the car and got to New York by ten. He telephoned Caroline's apartment, not to speak to her but to ensure she was not there and likely to see him in the condition he was. Having ensured she had already left for Madison Avenue, Yuri illegally parked the car against a fire hydrant very close to 53rd Street, knowing the vehicle would be towed back to Hertz and the penalty automatically charged to his William Bell credit card. In the apartment he stripped himself naked, searching for the damage in the full-length bathroom mirror. His face was scratched but not as much as he had feared and the swelling in his wrist was diminishing. Far better than he had expected.

'What happened?' asked Granov the moment he encountered the *rezident* at the United Nations.

'An accident,' said Yuri.

'You've got to go to Moscow,' announced the man. 'Orders from there!'

'Courier from here: the function you are supposed to

be fulfilling,' said Granov, who resented not being officially informed of the mission to which Yuri had been assigned by the Kazin message. 'I've already advised them.'

So Kazin had not instigated the recall. There would have to be an acceptable excuse to be away from the UN. Time enough then to go to the safe-deposit box at the Chase Manhattan Bank. Destroy or be destroyed, he thought. Which would he be?

35

'So there has to be another one, buried deep?'

It was Myers who voiced the inevitable conclusion, on the day the Crisis Committee agreed from the review of the final computer analysis that neither Latin America nor the Caribbean had featured in any assignment with which John Willick had ever been associated from the time of his recruitment into the Agency.

'Inevitably,' said Crookshank.

'We can't reassign every bloody agent in the two regions!' protested Norris. 'It would come to hundreds.' Another twenty people disclosed to the KGB by Willick had been recalled from Finland and England after being identified as CIA operatives in left-wing publications. At least there had been no further attacks, as there had been in Bonn.

'We'll have to do exactly that, over a period. We can't do anything else,' said Myers.

'And every analyst working out of here on raw material coming from anywhere in the area will have to be moved, as well,' insisted Crookshank.

'You know what you're saying, don't you?' asked Norris. 'You're saying that the Agency has got to undergo the biggest agent turnover it's had in its entire history. And it's not just a question of moving people around. Some of these guys have been specifically trained for nothing else: cultivated for a lifetime's career. Most speak Spanish better than English.'

'Then a lot more are going to have to be specifically trained,' said Crookshank, unimpressed.

'I know Ramon Hernandez appears to check out but I think he should be isolated, too, until we're one hundred per cent sure,' said Myers.

The other two men nodded in agreement, effectively

closing off from the CIA its best and most loyal source in Nicaragua.

'And we mustn't lose Kapalet, just because he's being withdrawn to Moscow,' said Crookshank.

'I don't intend to,' said Myers. 'I'm recommending to the Director that because of their special relationship Wilson Drew should be shifted there from Paris to continue as control.'

'It's not going to be easy for Kapalet, is it?' said Norris, recalling the warning that had come from France after Drew's last meeting with the Russian.

'Nothing's easy about this whole fucking mess,' said Myers. 'We can't judge until we know the department or division to which he's being posted but he could be even more important there at headquarters than he was in France.'

'What about Levin?' asked Crookshank.

'Vital,' replied Myers at once. 'There isn't anyone more important. I still think we might shortcut the search for the Latin American source through him.'

'How?' asked Norris.

'He's Russian so let's use his knowledge of the way they operate and react,' proposed the security chief. 'Let's get as much and as many electronic intercepts of Soviet traffic as we can, from the National Security Agency. Use our own stuff, too. And put him to work on them. Working from source backwards, we might be able to find the spy without all the turmoil we've been talking about.'

'It's an idea,' agreed Norris doubtfully. 'But it would mean disclosing all our sources. And those of the NSA as well.'

'That's a minimal consideration,' argued Myers. 'Levin's on our side now. He's proved that, unquestionably.'

'If it's a shortcut to discovering who our second spy is, then I'll go for it,' endorsed the lawyer.

'It would require taking him on,' pointed out Norris.

'We've made consultants out of defectors before,' reminded Myers. 'Yuri Nosenko was appointed when he came across and told us the KGB had no part in Kennedy's assassination.'

'Not as quickly as this,' said Norris.

'Time we don't have,' said Myers.

'I don't think we can bring Levin properly aboard soon enough,' said Crookshank.

Yuri made more than one trip to the Chase Manhattan Bank. On the first, by himself, he retrieved and recopied both sets of files, including this time the tyre-mark photograph. The originals he sealed and addressed in an envelope. The copies he put in the briefcase he intended taking with him, back to Moscow.

Caroline accompanied him on the second visit, frowning with curiosity as they went through the formality of signatory and withdrawing authority being extended to her, and then looking more puzzled in the vault itself, when she saw the envelope addressed to the New York *Times*.

'I thought you worked for an Amsterdam magazine?'

'I do,' said Yuri. 'This was a very special assignment.'

'Special enough to be kept in a bank vault!'

'That special,' assured Yuri. 'You understand completely what I want you to do?'

'Not exactly the intelligence test of the decade, is it?' she said. 'You're going away on an assignment tomorrow and if you're not back within a week I'm to collect the package from here and post it to the *Times*.'

'Right,' said Yuri. It was incomplete and bewildering and he had no idea if the newspaper would make any use of it arriving anonymously. But if anything happened to him this time in Moscow and they did publish, it might just conceivably cause Kazin and Panchenko harm.

'Why not just give it to them now?'

'It would be too soon.'

'Remember what I said, that first night?'

'What?' he asked.

'That you were mysterious,' she reminded him. 'And you are. I still don't know a damned thing about you, with one important exception: how I feel about you.'

The safe-deposit box also contained the still unread letters between his father and mother, Yuri realized. It was preposterous – insanity – to go on with Caroline like this. He would end it shortly, he promised himself. But not quite yet. He needed her now.

Kazin was surprised that Vladislav Belov had not volunteered the open commitment he had once shown, particularly now that the control of the First Chief Directorate was undisputed and beyond challenge. The man was a fool, like Panchenko was a fool although for different reasons. Kazin decided he didn't need supporters or sycophants any more. His position *was* beyond dispute: he was unassailable.

Kazin gazed across his desk at Belov and said: 'The New York courier is being recalled?' One of Kazin's new edicts, since his sole appointment, had been that he was advised of all agent movements.

'Yes,' said Belov. Why so much interest in Yuri Malik? 'Why?'

'Some time ago we obtained partial copies of a new IBM computer design: he is bringing back the remainder.' It was the man's function in the United States, scarcely requiring a personal explanation, surely?

The idea was a sudden one. Kazin said: 'Are you satisfied with his performance in New York?'

'Completely,' said the chief of the American division. 'He's carried out everything asked of him and in addition successfully identified the head of the publicity division to which he's attached as a homosexual. We are instigating a blackmail entrapment.'

'I am unsure he was not prematurely promoted,' declared Kazin. A decision of his father's, after the inquiry embarrassment: proper that it should be rescinded, then. And Kazin was having second thoughts of trying to manipulate the man's embarrassing discovery by the Americans. A feint, in the attack of his own personal chess game. The game – the pleasure of the torment – would be far better if the man were withdrawn here to Moscow, to be prodded and goaded. Making the decision, Kazin said: 'See him yourself when he gets here. Tell him he is being reassigned: that he is to settle whatever is outstanding in America and prepare to return permanently.'

'To do what?' asked Belov. The permanent recall was ridiculous, an order with no logical reason or purpose.

The man's attitude was dangerously near contempt, discerned Kazin. Perhaps someone else who needed reassigning, into oblivion. Savouring his power as if he could actually taste it, Kazin said: 'Whatever I decide.' He would have to devote more thought than he had to that hurriedly conceived idea at the graveside. Definitely too rushed: he'd do better next time.

It was as if Kazin were paranoic about the son of the former joint Chief Deputy, thought Belov. He said: 'The last batch of CIA identification is going to be the most embarrassing. We've got the names of forty headquarters officers at Langley: every division chief and most of their deputies.'

'And the chaos has only just started,' mused Kazin.

'The Foreign Ministry have confirmed Washington's application for a diplomatic visa for Wilson Drew,' disclosed Belov.

'Maintaining Kapalet's control?'

'Obviously.'

'Through whom we can go on feeding them what we like, for years,' said Kazin, reflective still. 'This really has been the most brilliantly devised and executed disinformation coup!'

The megalomaniac appeared sincerely to believe he was its architect instead of its on-the-sidelines approver, Belov realized, incredulous. Kazin *had* to be mentally unstable: there wasn't any other explanation.

36

Yuri routed himself through Spain and Germany, so it was a long flight, but up to the last hour before the Moscow touchdown he had not properly worked out how he could advance into the necessary destructive indictment the information he carried in the briefcase at his side. Or even into the unquestionably more necessary protective one. And then he remembered rust-coloured vodka and body odour and a contemptuous disregard for authority and coupled it to the militia investigator's insistence upon the importance of back-street repair shops in discovering who had killed his father. And decided, in rare assurance these days, that he had nothing to lose.

Yuri walked slowly along the line of waiting taxis, peering in and ignoring the inviting gestures, finding the man he wanted five vehicles from the front. He got into the car, ignoring the hornblasts of protest from the others ahead, which the driver did as well. The lead taxi protested the loudest and as he passed Yuri's driver thrust up a single middle finger and said: 'Fuck you.' As they negotiated the exit loops from Sheremet'yevo the man said: 'Come far?'

Yuri was too impatient to endure a full repeat of the sales pitch of the previous journey so he leaned forward against the seat in front, the fifty-dollar note folded upward and almost directly in front of the man.

The driver said: 'What's that?'

'What's it look like?'

'Fifty American dollars.'

'That's what it is.'

'Piss off,' dismissed the man. 'Is that how you get promotion in Gorbachov's anti-corruption militia? By entrapment! Amateur: fucking amateur.'

'Last time you offered me girls and vodka and said I

wouldn't get a better rate anywhere for my dollars,' reminded Yuri.

He was conscious of the man's attention in the rear-view mirror and moved, to make himself more visible.

'Who are you?' demanded the driver.

Yuri didn't reply to that question, either. He let the note drop and said: 'It's yours.'

'You haven't asked the rate.'

'I don't want to know the rate.'

'You're not making sense.'

'I want help: the sort of help I think you can give me.'

'You notice I'm not touching that money? Don't know it's there,' said the man. 'You've got to get up much earlier in the morning to trick me, asshole. You know what I think I'm going to do? I think I'm going to stop here and throw you out of the cab. That's what I think I'm going to do.'

As close as he had to be, Yuri saw that the collar of the driver's coat was even blacker than before from his greased hair and the miasma of tobacco appeared stronger, too. As the car began to slow and move to the side of the highway, Yuri took another fifty-dollar note from his pocket and held it up, like the previous one. 'You know whose portrait that is?' he said. 'That's Ulysses S. Grant.'

The man looked from Yuri to the money and back to Yuri again. He said: 'I asked you who you were.'

'And I said I wanted help.'

The driver's eyes went back to the money, briefly, and he said: 'What sort of help?'

'Garages which repair cars that have been in accidents that can't be reported. For unaccounted money.'

'You . . . ?' began the man and then stopped, looking back at the airport and shaking his head. He said: 'I don't know what you're talking about.'

Yuri let the fifty-dollar note drop beside the first and said: 'I'm talking about money.'

'Who told you?'

'About what?'

'Me.'

'This isn't a trap.'

'Convince me.'

'Look closely.'

The tobacco breath was disgusting as the man turned fully to him. 'So?'

'Recognize me?'

'No.'

'Try harder.'

'Why should I?'

'For the hundred dollars beside you.'

'I don't know anything about a hundred dollars beside me.'

'You weren't so careful last time. You wanted to deal in anything American that I wanted to sell or barter.'

'I don't remember any last time: there wasn't one.'

'You wanted to sell vodka and to buy dollars and anything American that I had,' repeated Yuri.

'I've never seen you before.'

'You took me to the KGB building on the ring road.'

'I did not.'

'I could have reported you then to the anti-corruption militia,' said Yuri, remembering how strong the temptation had been and glad he had not succumbed to it. 'I didn't. If I had done and you'd been intercepted how would you have explained the vodka? And all the cash you were carrying as a money black marketeer?'

'There wasn't another time,' insisted the man.

The denial was weak and Yuri knew the man had at last remembered him. He said: 'I didn't do it then. I am not going to do it now. Not unless I have to.'

'What's that mean, unless you have to?'

'It means there's two ways,' said Yuri. 'One way makes you money. The other way makes you unhappy: subject to stop and search and harassment, whenever, however.'

'I'm supposed to be frightened?'

The bravado was weaker than the denial. Yuri said: 'What would a search squad find right now, where you live?'

'Two hundred dollars,' capitulated the driver.

'If it's worth it.'

346

'Now.'

'Later, when we find the garage.'

'There are a lot: the anti-corruption campaign is a joke.'

'Keep the meter running, all the time.' The man's physical presence could be an advantage.

'You looking for engine damage? Engineers?'

Yuri hesitated. 'Bodywork,' he said.

'What happened?'

'No need for you to know.'

There appeared to be a lot, as the man said. Because it was on the way into Moscow from the airport they stopped at Khimki and after there near the Dynamo sports stadium and crossed to the northern river terminal, where they unsuccessfully checked two places from which the driver, who by now had identified himself as Leonid ('like Brezhnev: he enjoyed living well, too') said stolen cars were sold as well as unrecorded repairs carried out. At every garage there was a wall of rejecting hostility towards him and Yuri quickly realized just how much he needed the man with him. The pattern developed of the questions being put through the driver rather than directly from him. Yuri became hopeful at a service station on the road to Krasnogorsk when a paint-sprayer remembered a 1984 Lada and was just as quickly disappointed when he said the colour had been green.

'Sure you want to go on?' asked Leonid as they turned off the ring road to appraoch the centre of Moscow.

'Quite sure.'

'You see what's on the clock?'

'It doesn't matter.'

'This must be pretty important to you.'

'It is.'

There were four more garages and two more wrongly coloured Ladas before the taxi pulled into Begovaya Street. It appeared to be a three-man business, one of the owners the sprayer himself, anonymous behind a protective mask, his overalls multi-coloured from previous jobs. From the attitude Yuri guessed he knew

Leonid personally: instead of answering the first question the man nodded in Yuri's direction and said: 'He OK?'

'Yes,' said the driver.

'How OK is OK?'

Yuri didn't understand until the driver said: 'Of course he'll pay; he's with me, isn't he?'

'A 1984 Lada?' queried the garageman. He had lifted the visor of his mask but it was still not possible to see what he really looked like.

'Around October fourteenth,' prompted Yuri.

'Fifteenth,' said the man at once.

He'd got this far before, thought Yuri, curbing the optimism.

'What was the damage?' asked Leonid.

'Scraped nearside wing,' said the man. 'And the light assembly was smashed.'

'What colour?'

'Fawn. Managed a good match.'

A feeling of satisfaction engulfed Yuri. Abandoning their established system and taking over from the driver, he said: 'Remember anything about the man?'

'He was a soldier,' declared the sprayer at once.

'A soldier!' demanded Yuri. 'You mean he wore uniform?'

The man shook his head. 'The way he walked; held himself. Always tell a military man.'

The fit was there, decided Yuri. He said: 'What else about him? Anything at all?'

Instead of replying, the sprayer said to Leonid: 'You sure this is all right?'

'Dollars,' promised Leonid.

'How much?'

'Twenty,' opened Yuri.

'Fifty,' bargained the man.

The ultimate satisfaction would be charging it to KGB expenses, Yuri decided as he handed the money over: 'payment for essential information' perhaps. He said: 'So what else about him?'

'Nothing about the man: just that he had a positive military bearing.'

348

Yuri felt a flare of irritation, imagining he had been tricked into parting with money upon the promise of something more, and then recognized the qualification in the reply. He said: 'What else, if it wasn't about the man?'

'You sure this isn't official?'

'You often get paid in American dollars by the police?'

The man hesitated and then went into the cubby-hole office in one corner of the paint shop, re-emerging at once with a ledger-sized book. 'Wouldn't have mattered if it had been official,' he said, offering it already opened at a page.

Double book-keeping, as a protection against any police raid! Yuri realized. He took the book eagerly but before he could study the work record, the man said: 'Everything is properly detailed. Everything. Even the registration.'

'Registration!'

'On the first line.'

Yuri didn't ask, unwilling to risk a refusal. He walked to the cubby-hole and copied MOS 56–37–42 on to a scrap of blank paper on the desk top, put it in his pocket and left the account book there. He could actually feel the throb of his own heartbeat and wondered if he were flushed with the excitement. He'd got the most positive evidence yet. And already knew how he could use it further! He was close, he decided: close enough to reach out and touch!

'Thank you,' he said, with more sincerity than either of them knew.

'You ever need a car resprayed, you know where to come.'

'I'll remember that.'

'Where now?' asked Leonid, back in the car.

'The ring road building,' said Yuri.

When they got there Yuri handed over the additional hundred dollars and settled the meter fare, which registered a hundred and seventy-five roubles. Yuri guessed it had been tampered with, to run quicker.

'By the time any search squad gets to where I live, there won't be anything there,' said Leonid.

'You're safe,' said Yuri.

'You really KGB?'

'What do you think?' said Yuri.

'What I've always thought,' said the man, turning the remark. 'You can't trust the KGB: they're assholes. Money's good, though.'

Yuri did not report at once to the reception area. Instead he took the elevator to the basement garage, where he'd once regarded the people who'd cleaned and looked after his father's car – the car in which he'd lost his virginity – as allies if not friends. His luck held. The duty clerk was a man he recognized: Andrei, he thought. The smile of recognition was returned but faded at once, embarrassment at a misplaced expression. 'Sorry about your father,' Andrei said.

'It's being investigated,' said Yuri.

'Let's hope they get the fucker.'

'Let's hope,' said Yuri. He produced his official accreditation and said: 'I want to know from records if a Lada numbered MOS 56–37–42 is one of our cars. And if it was booked out on fourteenth October.'

With a positive date to work from it took the clerk only minutes. 'Colonel Panchenko,' he said. 'He kept it a week.'

'Is it here now?'

The clerk consulted a chart on the wall and said: 'Bay 38.'

The paintsprayer had not been exaggerating, acknowledged Yuri: the colour was an excellent match. Like another positive match, the provable tread of the tyres compared against those outlined in his father's blood, at the scene of the killing: outlined in the photograph he possessed.

He had it all, thought Yuri, taking the elevator back up to the reception area. Now what was he going to do with it? He imagined the question answered when he identified himself and was told he had to report to Vladislav Belov.

*

350

The despair lumped in John Willick's throat and he swallowed against breaking down, although there was no one in the Karacharovo apartment to witness his crying. No one anywhere. The drivers taking him to and from the debriefings appeared unable to speak English and his interrogators rotated and every one treated him with an attitude bordering on contempt anyway, so he was resigned against any possibility of acquaintanceship, let alone friendship. The system had been established for him to be paid but he had been granted no concessionary facilities. He had not yet been able to buy anything without lining up for hours and having to use sign language when he'd bought the purchase ticket and then moved into the second queue to reclaim what he wanted, against the price already paid. He found the language sessions impossible. The instructor was impatient with him and Willick knew it would take him months – years – to get even a limited mastery of Russian. He was so miserable, he thought; more miserable than he'd ever been in his entire life. He didn't know what to do; there was nothing he could do. He choked, unable to hold on any longer, sitting at the stained table, the sobs shuddering through him.

The revelation of the CIA headquarters personnel was as devastating as Vladislav Belov had predicted during the last interview with Kazin. The identities were disclosed over a period, for maximum and sustained impact, were published throughout Europe, and from the outlets there picked up and carried on television and in newspapers across America.

Harry Myers was named as the Agency's security chief and Edward Norris as the deputy controller of the Soviet Division in the second batch released.

'Holy Mother of Christ!' exploded Myers.

'I know,' anticipated Crookshank, uncertain if the disclosures were over and fearing his name could still come. 'If you could, you'd kill him. I would, too.'

37

It took Yuri the time to pass through the entry formalities on the ground floor and reach Belov's quarters on the sixth storey to evolve his approach. Where he was almost immediately off-balanced. The reception from the other man was different again from what it had been before, neither the surprising affability of their earlier meetings nor the frozen reserve of the cemetery encounter. Yuri searched for the word and decided it was weariness: Vladislav Belov appeared bowed by some sort of fatigue. The remainder of the IBM mainframe computer blueprints had once more been carried in a film cassette and as before Yuri went patiently through the hand-over ritual, waiting.

'I am seeing you personally to inform you of changes,' announced Belov. He had decided to do exactly as he was told; recall the man, announce some unknown reassignment and avoid getting involved from then on. That was the way to avoid any difficulties for himself: just see his time out. Fifteen years, he thought, agonized: a lifetime! What else could he do?

'Involving me?'

'You are being withdrawn from New York.'

'Upon the instructions of Comrade Directorate chairman Kazin?' anticipated Yuri.

Belov blinked at the astuteness of the question. With stiff formality, he said: 'It is not permissible to discuss or question reassignments.'

'I would like to show you something,' said Yuri, going to the documentation that bulged his briefcase. He handed across the table the photograph he had taken of the defector and his son in Connecticut: the pictures were blurred and grainy but brought up under a magnifying glass it was just possible to make an identification, which Yuri knew because he had done it.

'Who are they?' demanded Belov, examining them first without enlargement.

'The man is Yevgennie Pavlovich Levin. The boy is his son, Petr,' said Yuri simply.

'What!'

Yuri was tensed for the response from the other man, whom Kazin had instructed could not be told, wanting to learn from it. But he learned nothing: it sounded like outrage, which Yuri could not understand. There could be no turning back, not now. He said: 'When I was in Moscow on compassionate leave after the death of my father, I was ordered by the Comrade First Deputy to locate Levin, which I did. He and his family are near a small township called Litchfield, in Connecticut . . .' He paused and then announced: 'The American authorities were warned, in advance.'

Belov sat shaking his head and once again Yuri's inference was of overwhelming tiredness. 'Why?' said the man, his voice exhausted like the rest of him. 'Why?'

Defectors *were* pursued, thought Yuri curiously. He wished he could infer more from the other man. 'I would also like to present to you irrefutable evidence that my father was murdered,' Yuri plunged on, producing the police files, with what he had discovered himself that day uppermost. 'And by whom,' he finished.

Belov read, head bent, for a long time, the sound of concentrated breathing the only noise in the room. Yuri could see the traffic streaming around the peripheral road but not hear it through the double glazing. Would the taxi driver by now have cleared anything incriminating from his home? Yuri guessed he probably had: already converted the incriminating dollars, too.

The lassitude had gone from Belov when he finally looked up. In its place was an attitude of intense wariness. He said: 'Who else has seen this?'

'No one, not in its complete form.'

'There are no copies?'

'Not in its complete form,' reiterated Yuri, wary himself.

'Is there anything else?'

Yuri hesitated, unsure. But why unsure? If he'd made a mistake it was irreparable so there was no safety in holding back what his father had accumulated. He passed over the second dossier and again there was uninterrupted silence for a long time. When Belov looked up again he did not immediately speak but remained gazing blank-faced across his desk.

Say something! Do something! Yuri thought desperately. Anything! As forcefully as he could, Yuri said: 'My father was killed to prevent his pursuing an inquiry that would have proven the involvement of Colonel Panchenko in the death of Igor Agayans.'

'Yes,' said Belov at last. It was not so much an agreement with Yuri's insistence but a personal acceptance of all that he had read during the previous hour. He went on: 'How did you trace Levin?'

'Through the letters between the family and the daughter.'

'He stopped her leaving, didn't he?' said Belov, again in some private conversation. Concentrating more, he said: 'Did you realize Levin was trying to convey as much as possible, about his acceptance?'

'Acceptance!' queried Yuri, baffled once more.

'An incredible man,' said Belov admiringly.

'The man is a traitor.'

'Yevgennie Levin is carrying out a service to his country unparalleled in Soviet intelligence,' corrected Belov. 'All the indications are that he has succeeded brilliantly, although we will not get confirmation for many months, when he can make contact.'

'Make contact?' said Yuri weakly.

'After his absolute infiltration into the CIA,' announced Belov. And he talked on, in complete and chronological detail, a catharsis for the impotent frustration he felt at being cheated by Kazin. Belov recounted the manipulation of John Willick and explained how the apparent disclosures by Levin coordinated with those of Sergei Kapalet, in Paris. And how they were to get a secondary benefit by the recall to Moscow of Kapalet to continue as an apparent source, through which they could feed whatever disinformation they chose to Washington.

'Unbelievable!' said Yuri, in genuine awe.

'On the contrary,' said Belov, wanting to boast. 'From what the CIA have done already we know it is all believed. Absolutely.'

'Your idea?' said Yuri, guessing the man's need and wanting to bring the conversation back to his father.

'It took years to formulate and put into practice,' confirmed Belov. 'And Kazin has taken the full credit: I was congratulated, for peripheral assistance. I believe Kazin is paranoic: certainly mentally unstable in some way.'

Pleased with the direction of the remark, Yuri indicated the material lying between them on the desk and said: 'And now you can bring him down.'

Belov snorted a laugh that had no humour, shaking his head bitterly. 'Panchenko, certainly. But there's no proof of anything against Kazin except for the negligence for which he's already been found culpable and apparently forgiven. It will be his word against Panchenko's.'

'You can't be serious!' said Yuri, aghast. Everything wasted! he thought: everything! He said: 'Kazin *is* involved!'

'I don't have any doubt either,' said Belov. 'But there's not enough here to do anything about it: certainly insufficient for me to go to Chebrikov himself.'

It was more than just lack of evidence, Yuri guessed. Belov was unwilling to become linked to an attack that might misfire: headquarters survival politics about which his father had lectured him before his posting to Afghanistan. Exasperated and not caring that it showed, Yuri said: 'So no action is taken against him! He goes on doing what he likes, to whom he likes! Someone you think to be paranoid!' What sort of nightmare would he be coming back to, if he were brought back from New York with Kazin still in control?

'Nothing can be done against him: nothing that is sure to succeed,' said Belov, confirming Yuri's thoughts.

'There is,' insisted Yuri, as the idea came.

'What?'

Yuri found it easy to explain and Belov was nodding, in growing agreement, before he finished.

'Yes!' said Belov, excited. 'Yes, it could succeed that way!'

Their contact procedure was arranged before Kapalet's transfer from Paris and Wilson Drew responded instantly the Russian initiated it, hurrying early to the Museum of Early Russian Art at the monastery on Pryamikova. Despite the American being ahead of time, Kapalet was already watching, although the need for self-protection no longer existed as it had in Paris.

He approached Drew in an icon room dating from the time of Peter the Great and said: 'Very different from France.'

'You can say that again!' complained Drew. He thought Moscow was the pit of all pits.

'I'm not enjoying it either,' said Kapalet, which was true.

'Is it always going to have to be this sort of place?'

'We'd be far too obvious in any restaurant.'

'You got something about Latin America or the Caribbean?' asked Drew eagerly. There were daily demands from Langley and there had been six separate messages from the Crisis Committee when he'd advised them of the contact summons in advance of the meeting.

'I don't think I'm going to be able to help about that: not immediately anyway,' said Kapalet. 'But I think I've got something better.'

'There couldn't be anything better,' said the American, disappointed.

Kapalet gazed around, apparently to check that they were unobserved, and handed Drew the plastic carrier he held.

'What is it?' asked Drew.

'Part of an internal security investigation,' disclosed Kapalet, as he had been instructed by Belov. 'It's creating absolute pandemonium at headquarters. It's all in

356

Russian, obviously, so you'll have to get it translated to make your own assessment. I think it's dynamite.'

Dynamite was actually the word Langley used in the cable of congratulation to Drew, within twelve hours of the dossiers arriving in the diplomatic pouch. The cable also said he'd been promoted two grades, which meant a salary increase of $2,000 a year. Drew conceded Moscow had some advantages, after all.

John Willick knew himself well enough to accept he would not have the courage unaided, so he queued at various liquor stores, hoarding the vodka. He bought the cheapest, because he guessed he'd need a lot, and when he tried it before the real attempt, a sort of rehearsal to ensure everything would go right, its harshness caught his breath, making him cough. Which in itself was a useful test because it meant he'd have to take his time, drinking it.

He chose a Friday night because there was no debriefing on a Saturday, so no drivers would be calling for him. There were six bottles and he lined them up like pins in a bowling alley, starting from the left. The alcohol burned at first, making his eyes water, but it was easier once he became accustomed to it. He didn't feel drunk at all after the first bottle and worried he might not have collected enough, but his head began to go before he reached the end of the second, so he knew it would be all right. He began to belch so he stopped drinking for a few moments, not wanting to risk losing the effect by vomiting.

Willick decided he was ready halfway through the third bottle. He felt quite rational – knew exactly what he was doing – but there was no nervousness, none of the usual snatch in the guts.

He'd bought the rope on another shopping expedition, thick, heavy-duty stuff that he'd tested to carry his weight by hanging from it by his hands, looped around the curtain support which was high enough for the purpose. He'd assembled it and prepared the knots before he'd started drinking and moved the chair over now, needing it to climb up. He tugged, needlessly, ensuring the strength again and slipped the noose over his head, hesitating at the very last moment. And then he kicked the chair away.

He was even unsuccessful in killing himself properly. He'd tried to get the knot behind his ear, the way he'd thought it was done, but it slipped around so his neck didn't break, killing him instantly as it should have done. He choked to death, instead. It took twenty minutes for him to die, ten of them conscious and in agony.

38

From the moment he entered the now familiar debriefing room at Langley, Levin was aware of an apparent but inexplicable attitude between the three men with whom he had spent so much time. Lightness was the word that came to his mind, but he dismissed it because it had to be wrong.

'We've made some assessments, from what you've told us. Compared it against the defection of Willick,' announced Myers.

Levin wondered how Willick was being treated in Russia. Cautiously he said: 'I'm glad if I have helped.'

'You've been invaluable,' said Crookshank.

'And we're anxious for you to go on helping,' said Norris.

Levin controlled any reaction. He said: 'Of course.'

'We are offering you the position of a contract consultant with the CIA,' announced Myers. 'In effect you will be permanently employed.'

Levin was not concerned at his difficulty in immediately replying because they would expect him to be surprised. Forcing himself to speak, the Russian said: 'I would be delighted to accept.'

'And we would be delighted for you to be with us here at Langley,' said Crookshank, critic-turned-supporter.

'Welcome to the CIA,' endorsed Myers.

'I hope to be very useful here,' said Levin, a remark for his own enjoyment, the only celebration he could allow.

'What will it involve?' asked Galina, that night, when he made the announcement back in Connecticut.

'Moving to the Washington area, I suppose,' said Levin. 'Being able to get a house of our own, instead of living like we do here: in a goldfish bowl.'

Petr, who was in the same room as his father, accepted

it was time that he made his move. Which he did the following day. It coincided with Yuri Malik's arrival at Kennedy Airport, after a circuitous flight through Canada.

Petr's escape went as smoothly as he had known it would. He waited thirty minutes after being deposited at school and then complained of feeling unwell. He rejected the offer of the school recalling his car and was walking up Litchfield's North Street before the hour was out. The lack of public transport was a minimal problem, because the first lift he picked up was going all the way to Nauga-tuck and from his map and timetable Petr knew there was a station there. He caught a train just after eleven, settling in a corner seat, bunched with excitement at what he had already done and in expectation of what he would soon be doing. Would they have him make some immediate public denunciation of his father? Or want to interview him at length first, to find out what had happened since their defection? Whatever, the boy decided: he'd do whatever he was asked. And enjoy it. God how he was going to enjoy it! His voluntary return showed he had no part in the defection and certainly Natalia hadn't: important to make it clear that his mother was not involved, either. He could remember how bewildered she had been, that night at the Plaza. Only his father: his father the bastard. Puffed with imagined importance, boasting of some consultancy or job with the CIA: soon to be taught a lesson, though. His father would know something to be wrong, when he wasn't there to be picked up from school that evening. Served him right. Bastard.

Petr mentally ticked the stations off his list, each one bringing him closer to New York, excitement building on excitement. He was free! In complete realization Petr decided the Connecticut house with its armed guards and suspended helicopters had been as much a prison keeping them in as a safe house keeping pursuers out. Hadn't kept him in, though: he'd beaten them. They'd never suspected him; didn't have a clue. He laughed openly, in the carriage, stifling the outburst at once to avoid drawing

360

attention to himself. How surprised they'd be! What else? Angry, of course. Frightened, too. He hoped so much they'd be frightened, not knowing what he would do. What to do themselves. He wanted them to be frightened: his father particularly.

Old Greenwich, he saw. Only fourteen more stops and only then if they halted at each one. He consulted his timetable and saw that they didn't: bypassed six. And from the schedule he calculated they were precisely on time for the noon arrival. Ten minutes, down 42nd Street and he would be there! Less than two hours. The expectation built up and he shifted impatiently in his seat.

The problem came to him abruptly and there was a twitch of annoyance that it had not occurred to him before. The United Nations was not a public place: certainly there were public tours but they were tightly controlled so he would not be able to walk in and roam the building until he found a Soviet delegate he could ask for help. There were guards who would demand his accreditation: and they would be Americans, who could intercept him and warn Proctor or Bowden or someone and get him hauled back to Connecticut. The resolve came, as quickly as the problem, and Petr smiled to himself again, pleased with the way he was thinking. Nothing was going to stop him: nothing could.

At the cavernous, echoing Grand Central terminal Petr found the telephone bank by the exit on to 42nd Street and politely, in English, requested the number of the Soviet delegation. He was confused when the telephonist demanded a reason, blurting without thought that he wanted information, which was how he came to be given the extension not of the delegation he sought but the public affairs department.

The call was taken, by further coincidence, by Inya who since that failed night had spread the story of Yuri's impotence through the department. When Petr repeated his request she signalled to Yuri that it was for him.

'You are Russian?' asked Petr, still in English.

'Yes.'

The boy switched immediately to their own language.

361

'I am the son of Yevgennie Pavlovich Levin,' he announced. 'I was forced to go with my father. I want to return, to expose him.'

Yuri was astonished, for the first few seconds completely unable to respond. In Russian, too, he said: 'Where are you?'

'New York. I have escaped. I want to come in but I know I will be stopped without the proper documentation.'

Could it be a trick, some trap being set by the FBI or the CIA who had become suspicious of Levin? Yuri said: 'Where have you been held?'

'Connecticut,' said the boy at once.

'What was the nearest town?'

'Litchfield. I was attending school there.'

That checks out: I know it checks out, thought Yuri. Other impressions tumbled in upon him, the most important being the recollection of Vladislav Belov only twenty-four hours earlier describing to him a KGB operation regarded as the most brilliant ever conceived. He said: 'Whereabouts in New York?'

'Grand Central.'

The right station, Yuri recognized. If it were Petr Levin on the telephone the last place in New York – in the world – where he could publicly reappear was at the UN. Where then? No time to plan or prepare, like any encounter should be planned and prepared. He said: 'Do not come here. I will come to you.'

'To the station?'

It was as good a place as any, decided Yuri. 'Yes,' he said. 'Just wait in the main concourse.'

'How will I recognize you?'

'I'll recognize you,' assured Yuri.

To walk was the quickest way and it enable Yuri a few moments to try to rationalize what was happening. The first consideration had to be the personal risk in going to meet the boy at all. Very little, accepted Yuri. None, in fact. It would be quite understandable for someone attached to the Soviet delegation to go to see a member of a defector's family seeking help. More suspicious to refuse, in fact. So where could the danger lie? That it was the trick he'd already considered, an attempt either by the CIA or the FBI to check the genuineness of the father's defection. How? He couldn't know that until they'd talked. What other danger? The greatest of all was that it *were* Petr Levin, that he was disaffected and by doing what he had done risked destroying a KGB infiltration that had taken years to evolve.

Yuri did not enter through the 42nd Street entrance but off Lexington, so that he was at the top of the stairs, high above the main concourse. He saw Petr Levin at once. The boy was walking back and forth at the very centre, behind the ticket queues, concentrating upon the 42nd Street doorway through which he expected his contact to enter. But Yuri was not looking for that sort of concentration. The boy hadn't been trained. If this were something set up he'd be accompanied and, amateur that he was, there'd be some indication, glances or smiles for reassurance. There was nothing. Yuri could not isolate, either, anyone obviously keeping Petr under observation but in a place with so many people that was practically impossible.

Yuri descended the stairs, went straight up to the youth and said: 'How can I help you, Petr Yevgennovich?'

'Who are you?'

'The person you spoke to on the telephone.'

'I want to come back. To Russia. To my sister,' declared the boy simply.

It was too crowded, too bustling, for there to be any sensible sort of conversation. Through the doors Yuri saw the Howard Johnson snack bar on the opposite side of the road and said: 'Let's sit down and talk.'

Petr Levin needed no prompting. Ignoring the coffee Yuri bought to justify their occupation of the booth, the boy poured out an uninterrupted diatribe against his father. The most frequently used word was hate. He hated his father for the abandonment of Natalia and he hated the man for forcing him to defect and he hated him for betraying his country. It all appeared to be utterly

363

sincere, without any indication of rehearsal or training for which Yuri was constantly attentive.

'So what do you want to do?' asked Yuri.

'Come back to Russia. And something more.'

'What?'

'Expose my father for what he's done. And what he's going to do. Utterly destroy him.'

The potential trap, guaged Yuri. At last! It was normal to vilify a traitor and to be able to do so through his son – with an abandoned daughter still in the Soviet Union – would be an offer impossible for the Russians to refuse. So *to* refuse it would be confirmation to the FBI or the CIA that there was something wrong with the defection. He said: 'What do you mean, what he's going to do?'

'He's being taken on as a consultant by the CIA,' disclosed the boy.

The absolute success that Belov was seeking! seized Yuri, at once. And just as quickly he had a balancing thought: wouldn't the CIA set up this sort of approach as the last test before letting Levin in? He said: 'When's it happening?'

'Pretty soon,' said Petr contemptuously. 'The offer was made yesterday.'

Could the boy have been taught to act as well as this, wondered Yuri. He said: 'How long have you planned this?'

'Weeks,' admitted Petr. 'I refused to cooperate at first and then I realized the way to escape was to lull them into thinking I had accepted it. And it worked, didn't it?'

'And they never suspected!'

'Not a clue,' boasted the boy confidently. 'They still think I am at school. Will do, until collection this afternoon. Then the panic will start.'

So he *could* act, thought Yuri. Remembering the letters he knew so well, Yuri said: 'You love your sister very much?'

Instead of answering, Petr said: 'How could he do that! Just run and leave her!'

A madman made him: a madman still in power, thought Yuri. He needed time, a period to seek out the

364

hidden dangers. Yevgennie Levin had to be protected, at all and every cost. Nothing could interfere with achieving the complete and ultimate object of the operation, getting a KBG man into the heart of the CIA. And that hinged upon whatever he did – or did not do – in the next few minutes. He said: 'How have you been treated since the defection? All of you, I mean?'

Petr shrugged and said: 'OK.'

'Just OK?' If there'd been American hostility, it would indicate mistrust.

'Better than that, I suppose,' conceded the youth reluctantly.

'Well treated then?'

'It's a pretty impressive house,' said Petr, in further concession. 'There are guards and helicopters every-where, particularly after the scare.'

'What scare?'

'I don't know how the Americans found out but appar-ently a search was launched by Moscow to find us. One night there was a hell of a flap. You wouldn't believe it!'

I would, thought Yuri: I would. So Kazin *had* somehow leaked the information. He wished he knew what the Americans were going to do with the dossiers: they should have arrived by now. What was he going to do if for some reason the Americans did not react as he expected? Defection was forever. The words thrust themselves into his mind, shocking him. Preposterous. Whatever faced him if he were recalled to Moscow Yuri knew he could never imagine becoming a traitor. His mind moved on, to another remark of the boy's, the idea initially not an idea at all. He said: 'You love your country?'

'Of course I do: why do you think I want to go back?'

'How much?'

There was a by-now familiar shrug. 'You know what it's like: it's not something you can *say*. It's something that's there: something you can *feel*. Always feel.'

It was, agreed Yuri. The Russian characteristic that the West found impossible to comprehend, maybe because it was so difficult verbally to express. The idea was hardening: if it were a trap then he'd be confronting one trap with another. Forcing whichever agency it was to try something else, which by their so doing would provide positive confirmation that Levin was not yet completely secure. He said: 'Do you love your country enough to work for it?'

'Work for it!'

'By doing exactly what I ask you to do?'

'What?'

Petr listened with growing and obvious incredulity and then said: 'That would mean going back to Connecticut!'

'Yes.'

'And never returning to Russia.'

'But becoming a Soviet hero.'

'I don't know if I could do it.'

'No one has suspected you so far.'

Petr shook his head in refusal. 'Natalia,' he said. 'I won't turn away from Natalia, like everyone else.'

Kazin *had* to be destroyed, by what he had done, thought Yuri. He said: 'I promise you – if you do as I ask – that Natalia will be released.'

'*When* she is released,' bargained the boy.

It was an easy concession, agreed Yuri. He'd gained the time and set his trap. 'A deal,' he said. 'Hurry: you've a train to catch.'

39

Because of the CIA's worldwide and detailed use of Yuri's material it was to be several months before a full assessment was finally compiled upon the success of the propaganda coup. But from the first day it was being likened to the brilliant use of Krushchev's secret denunciation of Stalin at the 20th Party Congress in February 1956, which by coincidence was the comparison in that later, complete assessment.

As with the Krushchev speech, the Agency broke the story in the New York *Times* – which Yuri considered ironic, after the arrangement he'd made with Caroline – which ensured its global syndication as well as publication throughout America. NBC rushed out a television documentary which was again shown in every European and English-speaking country, and an author was commissioned through one of the Agency's front publishing companies to write an instant non-fiction book which on publication week entered the bestseller lists of the New York *Times*, the *Washington Post* and the *Los Angeles Times* on the strength of advanced publicity. The book got on to the bestseller lists in ten other countries but achieved its record in the New York *Times* which had made the initial disclosure, remaining in its charts for a total of fifty-six weeks. An independent company made a film from the book, which Warner Brothers distributed, guaranteeing constant embarrassment to the Soviet Union for almost two years.

The KGB's internal investigation in Moscow was conducted in absolute secrecy – as was the actual trial of Panchenko and Kazin – and precise details never leaked out, although the GRU were successful with some planted stories, the majority of which were concocted but all of which were published, keeping the presses and the cameras turning. It was never discovered, for instance, that Kazin's protests of innocence were destroyed by Panchenko's production of the protective tapes he'd made. Or how Panchenko's murder of Agayans was proved by ballistic tests upon the security chief's pistol, which he was carrying at the moment of his arrest.

The executions were carried out on the same day as the verdicts were returned, in Lefortovo prison. Panchenko walked unaided to the post and refused to be hooded, standing upright and gazing defiantly at the firing squad. By then Kazin's mind had gone completely; he had to be carried to the stand but just before the command was given he started to laugh hysterically.

The Crisis Committee were involved from the moment of the arrival at Langley of the translated dossiers, long before their publication in the New York *Times*. That first day Harry Myers rightly judged their propaganda worth: it was he who used the word dynamite in the promotion cable to Drew.

'Who's got whom by the balls now!' demanded Norris when the success became more fully evident.

'And Kapalet's right there, in the centre of things,' said Crookshank. 'If this is his first shot what the hell is there to come in the future?'

'You know what this means!' demanded Myers, sniggering in his excitement. 'OK, I know we've got a long way to go and the worm's still in the apple here some place, but with this material we've drawn even.'

'Better than even,' disputed Norris. 'John Willick's story was a five-minute wonder, forgotten already. And only we know we've got an ongoing problem. We can keep this running for months; for years.'

'Kapalet isn't our only bonus,' reminded the converted Crookshank. 'Yevgennie Levin is our ace in the hole.'

'And he's already settling in,' reported Myers, whose job had been saved by supposed reversal. 'We're going good: real good.'

The New York *Times* exposure was the first indication Yuri had that he might be safe and within twenty-four hours there was a personal message from Vladislav Belov, informing him of the arrest of Kazin and Panchenko. It said, further, that the recall order had been cancelled. With it came the assurance, following Yuri's full report of his encounter with Petr Levin, that Natalia was soon to get her exit visa.

Yuri was determined to celebrate but could not give Caroline any explanation for it, so he said it was because he'd got a salary increase, which she seemed to accept. They went across into Brooklyn to the River Café where she had taken him that first night and then, the nostalgia established, to the same Mexican café. He was conscious of the mood, even before they left the restaurant, and when he made the approach in bed she held him off and said: 'I want to talk, instead.'

'What about?'

'Us,' she said. 'I told you a long time ago that I loved you. Don't you think I've been very patient?'

'Yes,' he agreed.

'So?'

'I think I love you too.'

'What are we going to do about it?'

Did she love him enough to be told the truth? Absurd thought, more absurd than considering defection before he'd known what had happened to Kazin. He said: 'What do you want to do about it?'

'Just because one marriage didn't work doesn't mean I'm not willing to give it another try.'

What sort of conversation was this! He said: 'There are problems.'

'Like the marriage you said didn't exist? These absences are pretty damned odd, you know.'

'I didn't lie: I'm not married.'

'What's the problem, then?'

Could there be a way fully of adopting the William Bell identity? He said: 'Let me try to work something out.'

'How long?'

'Soon,' he promised. 'I'll try to make something work soon.' What? he demanded of himself. What the hell could he do? Did he love Caroline as much as his forgiving father had loved his unfaithful mother? A pointless question, leading nowhere. The letters were still unread, in the safe-deposit box, he remembered suddenly.

40

Yuri ran, literally and from the decision because it was a decision he couldn't make. He told himself the obvious way to end the affair with Caroline was belatedly to agree to Granov's suggestion about closing down the apartment, and just disappear. Then he told himself that Caroline might cause difficulty with the Amsterdam publication, trying to find him, and eventually confronted the fact that he was putting his own barriers in the way of his own problem. That he had, simply and brutally, to say he didn't love her and wanted it over. And couldn't do that because he did love her and didn't want it over. The one situation for which there had been no training and no preparation because it was inconceivable to anyone in Dzerzhinsky Square that a Russian intelligence officer would fall in love with anyone but another Russian, preferably another KGB officer.

He lied about an assignment in South America and the night before he left 53rd Street they had their first real argument. At its height she actually asked him if he wanted to call it quits – giving him his opportunity – and Yuri said no, just a little more time, and she said how much and he said until he returned, just pushing back his self-imposed and impossible deadline.

Yuri hated Riverdale and the claustrophobia of the Soviet compound, refusing to mix or become part of their limited social environment, finding it easy to make comparisons with long-forgotten Kabul.

It was his third evening there, his mind constantly upon Caroline, that he recalled again the unread letters between his parents still in the safe-deposit box in the Second Avenue bank. He went there the following day, early, wanting to give himself enough time and when he explained it would not be a short visit the bank official allocated a study room just off the main, box-lined vault.

Yuri gazed first at the fading photographs, trying for an emotion he had not been able to find in the cramped loft in the Lenin Hills dacha. The soft-featured woman, hair caught high and full on top of her head, *did* look too demure and innocent to have done what she did, cheat and cuckold. Had she loved them both? Or just turned to Kazin in the terror of war, frightened and confused as people were frightened and confused in war, doing things which at any other time would be unthinkable? His father had been a handsome man, reflected Yuri. And before the deforming injury he would have been impressive, too, with his broadness and his height: it would have been easy to be proud of someone like his father. Had his mother felt pride, as well as love? She had loved, Yuri knew: his father had told him during that stumbled, inadequate account. And it was inadequate: still so many unanswered questions.

The last photograph was of the three of them together, at the wedding. Yuri concentrated upon Kazin. My supporter, his father had said. He'd also said he did not know how long the affair had been going on. Not then, surely? Surely she hadn't married one while she was sleeping with the other? Yuri tried to remember his impression when he'd first seen the picture. Proprietorial, he recalled. Kazin appeared to be looking at his mother as if there was already something between them, an understanding. Yuri shook his head in the empty, metalled room, refusing the impression. It was a trick of the camera, a half-caught expression. How could it be anything else?

Now that the personal danger was over – now that Kazin was dead – Yuri felt differently about the imagery of the man. Later, during their confrontation, he had been over-indulged and bloated but that man actually wasn't there in the photo, and it had been wrong to think him so. Heavy, certainly – a hint of how he became – but no more than well built. Still impossible to understand . . .

Yuri stopped the pointless drift, laying the photographs aside to turn to the frail, brittle correspondence, lifting the bundles completely from the box to set them out on the greater space of the table.

Initially he did not attempt to read the contents. Determined upon a chronology, Yuri went through the letters establishing by date that they were consecutive, his mother's to his father, his response to hers. And then he began to read.

It appeared to have been a stilted courtship in the beginning – the strange formality he had recognized in the loft – with some indication that her family had disapproved: there was an early letter, a copy Yuri guessed, of a plea not to his mother but to her family in which his father had stressed his prospects. A secure and rewarding career, the man had promised. And he had written something else: 'I will always honour your daughter.' A pity, thought Yuri, that she had not been able to return that honour.

The change, to Stalingrad, was abrupt and obvious, his father's letters on scraps of paper, the writing scrawled and almost illegible, in pencil. Yuri strained to make sense, suddenly aware of Kazin's name. Our courier, the man had been called. And by his mother, not his father. And then another reference. This time 'Our beloved courier'. Yuri swallowed against the hypocrisy, reading on. There was no description of the horror of the siege, of course, because that would not have been permitted, but his father had hinted at the awfulness. There was a reference to noise above which it was impossible to speak, and that there were no longer in the city any animals, a clue to how they'd stayed alive eating the cats and the dogs and finally the rats. Where, wondered Yuri, had the beloved courier been then?

And then another abrupt change, which Yuri could not immediately understand until he realized it was the period of his father's hospitalization. Still in Stalingrad, at first – the Stalingrad from which he knew Kazin had by now been evacuated – and from the dates a long gap between their writing. In that first letter his father had written 'I am not dead, as you thought', and Yuri wondered if there were an explanation for everything in those seven words. And maybe in the next line: 'I will be ugly.' Yuri blinked against the blur making it difficult for him to focus, which came again when he coordinated his mother's reply, reminiscent of the stiffness of the courtship letters. 'There was an official communication, telling me you had been killed.' And then: 'How are you hurt? What does ugly mean?'

From his father's reply – 'my arm has gone' – Yuri accepted it would have been impossible for his mother to imagine the true extent of the untreated injury: that it would have been a shock when she first saw him.

Which from another letter he saw had been in February 1943, when he'd been airlifted from the relieved city to Moscow: 'I existed in the thought of seeing you again,' his father had written. The jar came to Yuri from a sentence in his mother's reply. 'I will care for you, until you are better . . .' What had 'until' meant? Had she been setting a time limit upon a relationship she had resigned herself to be over, having already established another? He went back to the Stalingrad letters, calculating the gap. A full three months, he saw. Three months when she believed her husband to be dead, with their best friend always there, to comfort her. Could she be criticized for falling in love again? Shouldn't the feeling instead be pity, for the dilemma she faced when the man reappeared from the dead?

Yuri stretched back in the upright chair, trying to relieve his ache of concentration. Yes, he decided, answering his own questions. He'd looked for an answer in the letters and he'd found it. What had happened to his parents was the other sort of destruction that war caused. Except that they had not been destroyed. His mother had made an understandable mistake and when she'd realized it she had returned to his father and lived out her life with him.

There was not much correspondence left. Yuri leaned forward again, reading the letters in sequence, tracing his father's recovery and recuperation against his mother's frequent assurances that she would care for him – 'my duty' was an often-used phrase – not immediately aware

374

until there was a reference to his father's promotion within the intelligence service that the letters now were no longer wartime-dated but afterwards. And then he became aware they marked another separation, this time his father's promotion through what had by then become the KGB. There was a posting to Tbilisi in Georgia, and again in Karaganda in Kazakhskaya.

There was only one letter left, from his mother to his father, and Yuri frowned at it, recognizing from the date another gap between those from his father's travels. And made further curious from its origin, the maternity clinic at Bakovka.

'The pain has gone now,' she had written. 'I don't know for how long but I am to summon them if it gets too bad again, as bad as it was when you were here. I know I said it then but I want to say it once more, because I am frightened.

'I am sorry. I tried and I failed. I am ashamed and I beg your forgiveness, as I have so often begged your forgiveness in the past, always to fail again. We know the reasons: that they will always exist. That I am weak . . .'

Momentarily Yuri looked away, uneasily, forcing himself to go back to the neat, precise script. 'I have always loved you, in my way. I only wish, my darling, that it could have been a different way, a complete way. Like it could have been. But wasn't allowed to be. This has to be the last time I hurt you: could there be any way worse, than how I have hurt you this time?

'He doesn't know the truth. His knowing before you is unimportant. I owe you that, at least. I want this to be final: we've talked and cried too often for there to be any words or tears left although I am crying now. You were always more tolerant of my tears than Victor: always more tolerant about everything.

'The doctor who gave me the injection said he thought it was going to be all right. I want it to be all right – to be easy like I've always wanted everything to be easy – but I am very afraid that it won't be. So very afraid. Weak, in every way.

'I know you promised, when I asked, but I did not

believe you. If anything should happen – the anything we could not talk about – please try. You were so close once and could be again: if I were not between you, as I've always been between you, would there really be any reason to go on as enemies? If that anything of which I am so frightened happens there will have to be a meeting between you, after all. You will have to tell him, if I can't. Ask him to be kind: he can be kind and good, you know. He saved your life when he could have let you die, didn't he? Ask him to protect whoever is inside me, against the truth about me.

'There is more I want to write, and will, but the pain is coming back and so I will stop, until they make it go away . . .'

The letter ended there, unsigned.

There was no blur of emotion, no feeling at all. Yuri felt empty, hollowed out, trying to comprehend it all. It had not ended with the war, as he had imagined. His mother had remained with his father – 'my duty' – but continued the relationship with Kazin. Which would have been easy, with his father's necessary Second Chief Directorate postings, throughout the other republics. The reason, most probably, that she had not accompanied him. *Always more tolerant.* Could it really have been that his father loved his indecisive, weak mother so much that he had been prepared for all these years to tolerate a *ménage à trois* rather than lose her completely? Yuri, so undecided about love himself, found it difficult to believe but it was the only explanation from the letter that lay before him.

His father . . . Yuri abruptly stopped the further reflection, moving to a fuller understanding. The man might have tolerated it, Yuri thought – clearly *had* tolerated it – but he had extracted his own bizarre revenge from them both.

The words and phrases forced themselves into Yuri's mind. *He doesn't know the truth, not yet* was the first. And then the second: *There will have to be a meeting between you.* And perhaps the most telling of all. *You will have to tell him if I can't.* Except that Vasili Dmitrevich Malik had never told anyone that the child born to his lawful wife in the Bakovka maternity unit that June day in 1965 had been the son of Victor Ivanovich Kazin.

And then the final, complete awareness engulfed Yuri. Victor Ivanovich Kazin, who had hated and tried to destroy him, had been his real father. Whom he, in turn, had put before a firing squad in Lefortovo.

Yuri destroyed the letters and the photographs in a demolition brazier on a Bronx reconstruction site, two days later, and from a public call box there telephoned Caroline at her apartment on 53rd Street, talking over her surprise that he was back so soon.

'One question,' he said.

'What?' she demanded.

'How much do you love me?'

'More than I have ever loved anyone: could love anyone, ever again,' she replied simply. When he didn't immediately reply, she said: 'Why?'

'I needed to know,' he said.

'Are you coming home?'

'Yes,' he said. 'I'm coming home.'

Epilogue

Natalia Levin arrived at Kennedy Airport blinking her nervousness, her even more uncertain grandmother beside her. They both gazed around expectantly for her parents and became more disorientated when they were greeted instead by Votrin, the Ukrainian who had liaised the letter exchange with the Americans at the UN. There was special immigration dispensation, through which he accompanied them, and immediately beyond the luggage reclaim he handed them over to David Proctor, who said to Natalia: 'Welcome to America, Miss Levin. Your parents are waiting.'

'Where?' she demanded at once, her English heavily accented.

'Somewhere safe,' said Proctor, in familiar assurance. 'You'll be with them soon.'

The FBI supervisor did not lead them further out but back into the airport complex, where the helicopter waited, its engines already started. 'Quicker this way,' said the man.

The sun hurt Natalia's eyes, so she put on darker sunglasses and squinted behind them, not trying to see whatever it was they were overflying. Beside her the old woman, who had never been in a helicopter before, said: 'I'm frightened.'

'Not long now,' promised Proctor.

It wasn't.

The family, Galina leading, ran from the Connecticut house before the rotor blades settled and had to be restrained from getting too near, too quickly. Levin cried and Galina cried and Natalia cried and the old woman cried, hugging each other and kissing and then hugging more, holding each other at arm's length as if they were unable to believe what they saw.

Petr joined in the embraces, but more controlled, and he didn't cry, either.

Eventually they turned, Natalia encompassed between her mother and father on either side, and started to make their way back inside the house. But Petr hung back.

'Mr Proctor?' said the boy. 'I know I'm too young at the moment; that there is still college. But I've been thinking about the future.'

'What about it?'

'You know how good my grades are?'

'Brilliant.'

'And I've got perfect Russian?'

'Yes.'

'What do you imagine my chances would be of joining the Bureau, when I graduate?'

The bespectacled man smiled. 'Excellent,' he said.

'Would you help me: sponsor me?' asked the boy.

'Consider it done,' said Proctor. He took his spectacles off, to polish them. Petr Levin would be a fantastic recruit to the Bureau: just fantastic.